BLOOD BORN

A NOVEL

KURT BUBNA

Blood Born

Trilogy Christian Publishers

A Wholly Owned Subsidiary of Trinity Broadcasting Network

2442 Michelle Drive

Tustin, CA 92780

For information, address Trilogy Christian Publishing

Rights Department, 2442 Michelle Drive, Tustin, Ca 92780.

For information about special discounts for bulk purchases, please contact Trilogy Christian Publishing.

10 9 8 7 6 5 4 3 2 1

Library of Congress Cataloging-in-Publication Data is available.

ISBN 979-8-89041-742-8

ISBN 979-8-89041-743-5 (ebook)

Dedication

For those who belong to the “fellowship of the fractured,” whose brokenness drew them to the One who gives new life.

Table of Contents

Main Character List in Alphabetical Order

Adalhard: husband to Linza, *faðir* (father) of Gustav, Agi, and their four sisters

Agi: seventh and youngest child of Adalhard and Linza, third son, later renamed Arrius

Amadeus: Roman senator, husband of Claudia, adopted father of Justus and Arrius

Arrius: Agi's Roman name, main character, son of Adalhard and Linza, adopted son of Roman senator Amadeus and his wife, Claudia

Ayla: the old Hebrew slave of Amadeus and Claudia, nanny to Justus and Arrius

Ayla Rose: a young Jewish woman in Jerusalem who becomes the wife of Arrius

Cassius: a centurion in the Italian cohort stationed in Jerusalem

Claudia: wife to Senator Amadeus, adoptive mother to Gustav and Agi (later Justus and Arrius)

Gustav: second son, age five when introduced, adventuresome, talkative, later becomes Justus

Justus: Roman name given to Gustav, sixth child of Adalhard and Linza, big brother and protector of Agi/Arrius

Kaamil: Bedouin boy adopted by Ayla and Arrius

Linza: wife of Adalhard, birth *mothær* (i.e., mother) to Gustav and Agi

Mark: young follower of Yeshua, friend to Arrius

Mary Magdalene: disciple of Yeshua (Jesus), friend of Ayla

Pontius Pilate: the prefect who ruled Judea, including Jerusalem

Quintus: older Roman soldier who trained Justus and Arrius

Saul: persecutor of *The Way* (Christians), later known as Paul the Apostle

Seneca: firstborn child and son of Arrius and Ayla

Tasco: young legionary from Gaul

Tikva: second child and first daughter of Arrius and Ayla

Yeshua (Jesus): rabbi, teacher, Messiah

Death would not come easy for any of them, and the thought of the girls being abused repeatedly by Roman soldiers made Ada determined to find the cave—they had no choice.

In an unwavering voice that shook everyone, Linza yelled above the storm, “Out. Everyone out of this miserable hole and follow your *faðir* closely. Boda, you stay behind your sisters, and no matter what, don’t let go of Gustav. Ready? Let us move!”

The girls still huddled together. They looked miserable, frightened, and weak from the distance they had already traveled. Ada knew the thought of moving in this storm to the Witch’s Cave seemed ludicrous.

Then Linza yelled even louder, “Go! Now!”

Ada scrambled to the top of the ridge and reached out his hand to help them up the now slippery slope. One by one, the girls, Gustav, Boda, and then Linza, crawled slowly on all fours to the top, where the force of the wind and rain now stung their eyes like beer poured on an open wound. Every step forward was a battle. Every moment was more painful than the last.

As they moved up the mountain, Ada could hear his girls crying. He feared that if any one of them stopped, they would never move again. Boda and Linza were less than ten paces behind him, but all he could see were their silhouettes when the lightning momentarily illuminated their drenched and weary bodies.

Adalhard was sure he could find the cave but was uncertain if his wife would survive the ascent. He wondered how she kept moving while in the grip of excruciating labor.

Under his breath, Ada prayed, “Oh Thor, our protector, god of thunder and storms, I beg you to stop this assault on my children.

Please strengthen my wife. Help us, or we perish."

"The cave is just there, at the top of this hill. Keep moving. We cannot rest here. Not now. Not yet," yelled Adalhard as he wiped a mix of water, sweat, and mud from his eyes.

It began to hail; the balls of ice were the size of quail eggs. Fortunately, the thick forest provided some cover, but the trees and the brush, not to mention the steep incline, made every step difficult. It was like trying to swim upstream in the Rhine during flood season.

"*Faðir*, I cannot see, and I cannot feel my fingers," cried Gisela, the youngest daughter. Linza was close enough to give her a stern look and yelled, "Stop complaining about what we cannot change!"

In addition to dragging Gustav along, Boda took his baby sister's bag to carry it for her in an act of uncharacteristic kindness.

"Shove your hands inside your coat for a bit to warm them," said Boda.

But the fact that she was scrambling up the hill on all fours made that impossible.

They were now only an arrow's flight from the cave, but the hail and their utter exhaustion made it seem like the old witch had placed a curse on anyone who tried to find haven in her abysmal cavern.

Moments seemed like days. The closer they got to the cave, the farther it seemed.

Linza, struggling to breathe through her pain, said aloud,

"One more step. One more breath. Just one more." Her growing panic was apparent to the older children, Boda and Odila. But all the children could see that her pain was now regular and beyond description.

Adalhard had briefly moved ahead of his family in search of the cave. They collectively sighed when they saw and heard Adalhard rushing down the hill toward them, screaming, "It is here. We are safe!"

Adalhard took Gustav in his arms, got behind Linza, and pushed her up the hill. She slipped more than once and planted her face in the wet and moldy leaves, but shelter was coming, and that was all that mattered.

When they finally entered the pitch-black cave, the sporadic lightning pouring through the entrance flashed twisted shadows on the walls. The sounds of the children whimpering echoed throughout the cavern. It seemed like demons hid in the darkness, watching and waiting. The musty, stale smells made it unpleasant to breathe deeply.

Linza spoke first with a frightful tone, "This place is bigger than I imagined, and I sense evil lives here."

Adalhard and Boda had been there many times while out on a hunt, but Linza and the girls had only heard about it. Of course, no one could see anything yet, but the echo off the walls indicated that the old witch's cave was enormous.

The girls were still whining and shaking from the damp cold, but Odila said she was finally grateful for a dry place to rest. Gustav, who would typically be wandering off to explore, fell asleep in his sister Ishild's arms.

Adalhard spoke to his son, "Boda, find the hideaway of dry wood we left after our last outing. It should be against the wall about twenty paces from the right side of the cave entrance. We must start a fire as far back in this old boar's hole as possible."

Boda was already looking before his father finished speaking. The fire would provide warmth and much-needed light for the care of Linza.

"It is here, *Faðir*, and dry!"

"Good, Son, good. Thank the gods. Take some of the smaller pieces of wood with a handful of dry leaves, if you can find any, and move along the wall until you must duck down to stand. I will bring my flint to you in a moment."

"Yes, but will the light be seen outside the cave?" he asked, unveiling concern for their safety.

"If we keep the fire small and away from the cave entrance, we should be fine." But everyone heard the concern in Adalhard's voice.

Adalhard quickly grabbed the two flint stones from his bag and found his way to Boda with another small pile of kindling and mostly dry leaves. Strike. Strike. There was a spark on the second strike but no flame. Strike. Strike. Strike.

"Yes, *Faðir*! There was a small flame for a moment; let me give breath to it while you try again."

Together father and son did what they had done a hundred times; they brought life to dead wood that would bring a bit of warmth to them all.

The filthy faces of six children, eyes flooded with tears, looked intently at Linza. They were drenched to the bones, shivering, and hungry.

"The gods made my children strong," Linza said as she forced a smile. "Come closer to me, my children. Are you not comforted by the sweet smell of burning wood and the glow of a small fire?"

However, her momentary smile was banished from her face and matted head as another birth pain hit her hard, so harsh she cried out in pain before she could muffle her scream with her hands.

Odila and Saxa had seen other women give birth. Odila, at fifteen, had helped Linza deliver her younger siblings, and she rushed to her *mothær*'s side.

"What can I do, *Mothær*? We have nothing needed to prepare for a birth. No hot water. No clean cloths. No birthing chair. You *cannot* have this baby here and now!"

"Yes, daughter, here and now is exactly where this baby will be born. I feel like this boy is already pushing his way through me for air."

Gustav, who woke up with Linza's scream, rushed into Linza's arms with wide-open and concerned eyes. But then he looked up into Linza's face and said with a tender smile, "*Mothær*, you said 'baby *boy*.' That means I will not be the baby boy anymore." Gustav quickly sat up, puffed out his chest, and declared, "I will be the best big brother."

Linza spoke with a surreal calmness to her children, "Ishild, you must keep Gustav near, and yet do not let him or Gisela see the birth. They are too young, and this may not end well. Odila and Saxa, you will help me bring our young fighter into this world. Boda, keep the fire going and help your *faðir* as needed. He will keep an eye on us and his sword and bow ready near the mouth of the cave should we have any unwanted guests."

The children nodded, and Boda said, "Yes, *Mothær*, we will be ready."

But they were not ready. Not at all.

Adalhard stepped near her. He was not, by nature, an affectionate man. He was a hunter, a farmer, and a feared tribesman warrior when needed, but tenderness and compassion were strangers to him. However, Linza had a special place in his old crusty heart, a place no other woman ever held.

Her eyes met his. Ada hoped Linza could not see the fear on his face. It was not concern for his life or anxiety about the Romans but fear for her. How would Adalhard survive with seven children and without her help?

Ada bent down to Linza and gently kissed her on the head as he whispered, "You are the jewel in my crown, the smile on my face, and the warmth in my soul. I cannot imagine my life without you. Be strong, woman. Be strong for me and this mucky brood."

Linza pushed him away, looked up at him, and growled, "You have no crown or jewels. And this stank hole is not a good place to give birth, nor is this the right time, but I have no choice. Grab your pathetic little sword and stand watch while I push this brat of yours from my belly."

Linza saw the painful look on Ada's face and managed to say to him between her next deep breaths, "I am sorry, my *friðill*. You have been the love of my life." By the look in her eyes and timbre of her voice, Linza was saying goodbye.

She wiped a tear from her cheek as she pulled her skirt up and moaned to her daughters, “It is time.” After six children, nearly thirty-five years, and far too many eggs and potatoes, Linza was not a tiny woman. Without a birthing chair or harness to help hold her up, Odila and Saxa did their best to steady their mother as she squatted. The girls balanced Linza as she rocked and pushed, rocked and pushed.

Linza placed her filthy wet coat beneath her to receive the child. Odila’s primary role was to help the baby down and then to sever the birth cord with a knife before wrapping the child up.

Odila made eye contact with Saxa as she pointed to a stream of blood now running past their feet and into the fire. The smell of burnt blood began to spread through the cave. Odila kicked some dirt and rocks into the flow, attempting to divert it from the flames that seemed to long for more blood.

Without thinking, Saxa whispered, “This cave is cursed. It demands a blood sacrifice.”

“Be quiet, girls! I will not hear of curses or blood.”

Gustav was doing his best to see what was happening. Despite Ishild’s attempts to keep him away, Gustav was impossible to contain. He looked up at his sister and wondered aloud, “Do babies fight to stay in the belly or fight to come out?” Ishild shook her head and told him to be quiet, but that never worked with Gustav either.

Boda turned his back to his mother and stared at the flame shadows dancing on the cave walls. He muttered to the darkness above him, “Gods, I feel helpless and afraid.”

Adalhard overheard Boda, pointed his finger at this son, and said through clenched teeth, “No tribesman admits to fear. You must stay strong."

Linza took another deep breath. She squeezed Odila and Saxa's arms, and she could see that the girls did their best not to scream from the pain of her grip.

They were all unprepared for what happened next. When the baby was free, Linza fell back against the cave wall. She hit her head hard and then slumped into a pile just as Odila grabbed her newest brother. He was howling, eyes and mouth wide open, and he gasped for air between loud cries.

Gustav also started screaming as his *mothær* collapsed. Blood was everywhere. Boda yelled at Saxa to take the baby so that Odila could cut the cord. Adalhard dropped his sword and rushed to his wife's side.

The noise, confusion, and panic were almost as thick as the smell of smoke and burning blood. Odila had seen no less than a dozen women give birth, and the combined blood from them was less than what her mother was losing. On impulse, Linza's family came to her side.

Linza's skin was cold to the touch, and her color pale. As she struggled to open her eyes, she said with a raspy voice, "Give me the boy. Where is my son?"

Saxa gently placed the baby on Linza's chest, and Linza wiped some of her blood from his eyes and face. Instinctively, the boy turned his head and mouth looking for a breast. Linza let him latch on for a moment as their eyes met for the first and last time. She said to the baby, barely more than a whisper, "This is not your fault. My death is not your doing. I know your path will often take you where you do not want to go, little one, but greatness is in you. I see it."

Linza then looked up at her family. As her heavy eyes scanned the circle, everyone except Ada was in tears. "I am so sorry to leave you. You must care for your *faðir* and this child. I am so sorry...so, so sorry..." Her voice trailed off, and she was gone. Then, and as if a blinding fog had settled in that gloomy place, there was nothing but silence. No more crying. No sound. Nothing but eight people barely breathing and all in shock.

Death was too familiar in their land. Loss was a part of every Germanic tribe member's life. Despite the pain and the broken hearts, they had to move forward. This moment would pass, and for now, they would survive.

Gustav asked a question only a five-year-old would ask in that situation. "*Faðir*, what is his name? What will we call the baby?"

Without hesitation, Adalhard looked up at the cave ceiling as if speaking to the demons hidden in the shadows, "Agi. His name is Agi, for he is blood-born and blood-cursed. Höd, the darkest of our gods, has left me with this...this child...and he may be the end of us all."

CHAPTER 1

Ten Years Later, 1 AD, Rome

The glow from the setting sun reflected off their dull practice swords and made the dust cloud around them seem ghostly. Metal on metal rang throughout the courtyard. Both fighters were covered in sweat and dirt. Several watching legionaries seemed to match each movement of a gladius with their own bodily twitches and groans.

"You must hold your sword higher, boy. Always protect your flank with your shield. Always! And use your height to your advantage." The soldier, a crusty old legionary named Quintus, was relentless. He was hired by Justus's adopted father, Senator Amadeus, to make a soldier out of Arrius's older brother, Justus.

Justus was born to fight, and even when not with Quintus, he trained for hours on his own. Every day except Friday, he went to the home of the retired legionary for training. At sixteen, Justus was strong and much taller than most Roman boys his age. The young man was also known to be as thick-headed as he was tough and bold. The senator and his wife, Claudia, gave him the Roman name of Justus in memory of her grandfather, but Justus hated his name. He was Gustav, son of Adalhard, from the northern tribes of Germania.

His little brother, Arrius, at almost eleven years of age, was not formally allowed to train yet, but he often tagged along with his wooden sword and shield to watch his brother spar with Quintus. Arrius frequently practiced with his toy weapons and was always learning from Justus.

"We will be great legionaries someday, Big Brother. Heroes of Rome!" yelled Arrius at his brother, who was in the thick of a mock battle with Quintus.

Justus knew it was his unavoidable destiny to fight as a Roman, but it often plagued his conscience to think he might have to battle with his people someday. Years before, he relinquished his absolute refusal to become Roman, but he was still a tribesman in his heart. On the other hand, Arrius rarely mentioned home, and he spoke Latin better than Justus ever would.

Quintus barked, "You listen like a wild dog, boy. Keep your shield positioned. And do not look at my sword; watch my eyes. The eyes tell all."

A sharp move by Quintus caught Justus off guard. He barely raised his shield in time to protect his shoulder from another biting sting. While being careful not to discourage Justus, Quintus was an excellent teacher and seasoned veteran who constantly pushed the young fighter.

Justus moved like the wind, quietly and quickly, and he struck fast too.

"Good! Better! Now move to my weak side and strike."

Justus laughed, "There, old man. How did that feel on your backside?"

It was clear to Justus that Quintus never wanted him to hold back, but Justus noticed that his blows to the old soldier were becoming tougher to take and the bruises harder to hide.

"Boy, I will crush you under my foot like the sneaky scorpion you are."

Before Justus knew what hit him, he was on his back, staring up at the ugly, toothless grin of Quintus, with a sword point uncomfortably pressing on his breastplate. With sweat in his eyes and dirt in his mouth, Justus cursed the old legionary who had bettered him once again.

"Talk less. Gloat less. And always expect the unexpected, or your cockiness will cost you the battle and your life."

Typically overconfident, Justus underestimated his opponents, whether Quintus or another young soldier in training.

"You cheated, Quintus. You used a move you have never shown me."

"There is no *cheat* in war, boy. There is nothing fair about a battle or fighting for your life!"

Justus tried to squirm out from under the sword and foot of the old man.

"But—"

"And there is no *but*! Either kill or be killed. I will repeat it *slowly* just in case you still do not understand my Latin. Always…expect…the unexpected."

More than anything, Justus hated to lose, but every loss to Quintus made him stronger, and he knew it.

"I yield, you bad-tempered old bear."

"I doubt it," said Quintus, "but we are done for the day."

Justus wiped his eyes, spit out what dirt he could, and said as he looked up at Quintus, "In all seriousness, Quintus, I am honored to have you as my teacher."

"You should be," Quintus laughed. "But I do what I do for money, not for your honor. I need some good wine tonight."

Justus rose gradually, but as he got to a knee, he reached out and moved like lightning as he stuck his sword behind Quintus's leg and knocked the old man backward over it. Quintus swore as he landed hard on the front of his shield that fell beneath him.

Justus smirked. "Always expect the unexpected, Quintus. Always."

Justus and Arrius had everything they wanted and more than they needed. Life in Rome was difficult at first. The weather too hot. The food too different. And the language, Latin, a challenge. The boys were told to never speak to each other in their native tongue. Of course, they still did so at night while in their beds. Justus encouraged his brother to never forget their language.

As the boys walked home after drilling with Quintus, Justus decided to take a forbidden route. Claudia had told him many times, "Stay off the road marked *Vicus Fanni*. Horrible things happen there." Those intriguing words only made the temptation stronger, and today Justus decided to investigate.

Justus grabbed his brother by the arm and said, "Arrius, we will take a shortcut home today via Vicus Fanni."

Arrius struggled out of his brother's grip. "We are not supposed to use this road. Mother said—"

"I know what she said. But she is not our *true* mother, and we can handle anything together, yes?"

Justus knew that Arrius did not like admitting he was afraid or looking weak to his big brother. He often took advantage of his little brother's desire to be respected and accepted by him.

"Okay, if you say so, Justus."

"I have my sword, I have my shield, and I have you, Little Brother. Any enemy we might face will tremble and run before us!"

"I do not like it when you call me *little* brother. I am almost as big as you."

Justus snorted, "Your mouth is as big as mine, but you have a long way to grow to catch up with me, Agi."

"Arrius. My name is *Arrius*. We will both be punished if the senator ever hears that name."

Justus felt a twinge of compassion for his brother, remembering the cruelty of their adopted father. "Sorry. I know." But his adrenaline flowed at the thought of the adventure ahead, and he was determined to proceed. "Now stay close to me, *Arrius*; let us keep moving."

The street was narrow and dark. The tenements on either side rose high and blocked out most of the sun. Justus realized they would not be home before *prima fax*—the lighting of the first torch. Running down the street center was an open sewer, which was unusual because the Romans built the first underground sewers in the city about 500 years before. Of all the great cities in the world, Rome took pride in its modern ways. An open line of filth meant this road was a poor area and uncared for by the Senate, but still Justus was not dissuaded.

"I feel sick, Justus. The smell on this road makes it hard for me to breathe."

Just then, they both practically tripped over a man lying in the street. He looked dead and smelled horrible but was probably passed out from too much wine. The man's left arm was dangling in the sewage.

"Justus, let us go back. This is wrong. I am afra… The senator will beat us when he finds out."

Justus slapped the back of Arrius's head. "He will not find out if you keep your mouth shut."

Justus's pulse began to race as he wondered if they might get robbed or beaten up by a mob—a mob who hated rich boys of privilege. However, he had grown accustomed to ignoring the voice of warning in his head. He dismissed it now.

"Looking for a little fun, boys? I can give you an hour of bliss like you have never imagined." A woman stood in an open doorway half-dressed and smelling like cheap wine. Her hair was matted, her fingernails long and filthy, and her face covered in some heavy-colored paste.

"Keep moving, Arrius."

Arrius looked at his brother with a mix of fear and confusion on his face. "Does she mean what I think she means? I wonder if we are lost; maybe she can help us get out of here."

Justus shook his head. "Yes, she means *exactly* what you think, but her help might kill us with the pox."

The common prostitutes in Rome were as infected as the rats they lived with. Just before dark the boys arrived home. As they walked up the path, they could smell roasted goat.

"I do not ever want to go there again, Justus. Promise me."

"I promise to knock your teeth out if you ever mention this to anyone."

Justus would never hurt him—at least not badly—but Arrius promised to keep their secret nonetheless.

"Let us go and eat. Adventure makes me hungry."

"Your adventures make me sick," Arrius mumbled under his breath.

"What?"

"Nothing."

"Hurry up, Little Brother. Ayla will have our dinner prepared and waiting."

As an old Hebrew slave, Ayla was as round as she was tall. Her primary household duty was to care for the boys. She fed them, washed them, made sure their garments were clean, and became a surrogate grandmother to them. She also was a good cook, and roasted goat served with fresh-baked bread was her specialty. Justus's stomach rumbled at the thought.

"Where have you two been? What kind of trouble did your brother get you into today, Arrius?"

Justus gave him a look that made it clear what would happen if he spoke the truth.

"Oh, Quintus ran late today. Nothing special happened."

Justus knew that Ayla saw through the lie, but she would not press for the truth. She was a servant, and slaves had no rights.

"I suppose some things are better left unknown and unsaid,

boys. Now go wash your face, hands, and feet—especially your feet! You two smell like you ran through the sewers."

Justus snickered.

Arrius shook his head as the boys walked away to clean up. "That was close. What if she tells the senator? What if—?"

Justus interrupted, "Arrius, cease your wearisome words! Why are you always so afraid? When will you see that every day is an adventure?"

"When will you learn to follow the rules?" demanded Arrius.

"Arrius, remember what our Latin teacher said last week when he quoted Socrates. 'To find yourself, think for yourself.' Maybe it is time you started thinking for yourself."

"You quoting a dead philosopher to justify almost getting us killed does not make me feel better, Justus."

Justus rolled his eyes as he continued to wash his foul feet. "I would rather die living life to the full than live like a dead man."

"And which Roman or Greek philosopher taught you *that* foolishness, Justus?"

Justus hesitated. "Our father, while we were on a hunt for boar many years ago."

Justus had not thought of Adalhard for a long time, and quoting their dead father brought a wave of sadness.

"Do you blame me, Justus?"

"Blame you for what?"

"For our mother's death, our father's death, for—"

"Stop it, Agi. Just stop it. Death comes to all. I blame the gods for our pain, not you."

Justus knew Arrius was fighting to hold back his tears. He never tolerated any show of emotion from his younger brother.

Arrius turned his face away. "No matter what you say, Justus, when I am alone, something evil whispers in my ear, 'All is lost because you are lost. All you love is at risk because you are cursed.'"

Justus had nothing to say. They had been down that road many times. Too many times.

Just then, a crow squawked loudly. They both looked up at the bird sitting on the ledge of the window. Crows were considered as messengers from the gods to their people.

Justus frowned as Arrius spoke soberly, "Brother, the whisper gets louder as time goes by." Arrius added with a quiver in his voice, "What will the gods do with us? What is to become of you and me?"

As the huge black bird watched the boys, it cocked its head to the left before lifting its beak and squawking again.

Were the gods sending a warning?

Chapter 2

Two Years Later, 3 AD, Rome,

Home of Senator Amadeus and Claudia

Ayla, you serve me and our house, and you cannot give in to those boys. I am counting on you to be my eyes and ears and to keep them in control."

"My lady," Ayla pleaded, "Justus is no longer a boy, and he is drawn to trouble like a cat is drawn to mice."

Claudia glared at Ayla. "I do not care. You must find a way. I will not have Justus destroy both of my sons."

"Yes, my lady," said Ayla, even though she knew her efforts would fail.

Arrius, now thirteen, was generally the quieter and wiser of the two boys. But he followed his brother into one altercation after another. Justus was tall and still had more strength and weight than his brother, but Arrius was large for his age as well. The two of them together were undefeatable in any brawl—and brawl they did, often. If a fight didn't come to them, they would create one and then laugh about it for days.

Arrius started his training with Quintus when he turned twelve. However, after watching his brother and Quintus spar for years, Arrius grew quickly in skill and strength.

One day, when the senator asked about Arrius's progress, Quintus replied, "I am surprised at the boy's determination and work ethic—something I often saw in Justus, but Arrius is focused as if he is fighting demons. Occasionally, something unknown and unseen triggers Arrius into a rage. When he explodes, the safest place to be is out of his reach."

One of the few joys for Roman slaves was learning how to discretely listen in on household conversations. Gossip was slave currency in Rome. Ayla would often stand in the shadows and listen to family conversations or the boys' banter.

"I will miss you, Little Brother. We have not been apart even one day for many years."

Arrius grinned. "You will miss my sword defeating yours in training."

Justus laughed that infectious laugh that always made Ayla smile.

"No, I will miss using your backside to sharpen my blade!"

Both brothers laughed just as they heard Ayla's call to breakfast.

"You two had better be out of bed. I have been up all night preparing a last meal for Justus."

"I do not think I like the sound of *last* meal," Arrius said with a sober tone.

Justus puffed out his chest and raised a fist. "No worries, Little Brother. Nothing and no one can destroy me. I am invincible!"

"I *still* do not like it when you call me *little*; I am almost as tall as you and far more handsome."

"But I am still faster." And with that, Justus raced toward breakfast as he yelled, "To the victor go the spoils!"

Ayla watched as Arrius, right on the tail of Justus, used his foot to sweep out the leg of his brother, who collapsed to the floor. Arrius jumped over him and said with a smile, "What does Quintus say? 'Always expect the unexpected.'"

Justus yelled, "You offspring of a wild goat. You had better be behind Ayla's apron before I catch up with you."

Arrius snorted and was gone before his brother had his wits about him.

Ayla caught up with the boys in the kitchen and yelled, "What are you up to now? Sit down!"

"I am here, Ayla, ready for my *last* meal. What have you prepared today for your favorite Roman?"

"I have no favorite Romans. You, of all people, should know that, Justus."

Ayla began to plate their food as her thoughts wandered. She had been stolen from her village by Egyptian traders when she was a young woman. Her small town was off the beaten track but not far from a major trade route along the Mediterranean Sea. The Egyptian nomads were slave traders who frequently took advantage of finding children or young adults alone and vulnerable. Ayla was taken while drawing water from the well near her village in Palestine. Usually, her father or brothers would have heard her screams and rescued her, but they were searching for a lion who was killing sheep, and she was all alone.

Eventually, she was sold into slavery after a long and challenging journey by sea to Rome. Ayla frowned at the memory. She had grown to love and appreciate Claudia, but she was a slave. Nothing more. Nothing less. She shook her head to be free of her reverie and focused her attention again on the boys she had grown to cherish. She understood their pain; they had all been abducted and displaced from their homeland.

"I made you my famous bread, hot from the oven fires, and wheat pancakes with dates and honey."

"And hard-boiled eggs? Where are the eggs?" clamored Justus.

"Yes, and eggs. I will need ten fewer chickens to care for when you leave, Justus!"

"As we eat, tell us one more story, old woman; one more before I leave for Syria."

"Syria. Hmmm. Not far from the promised land and my people."

For many years, and without the senator or his wife's approval, Ayla told the boys many stories of her people—about their heroes and their failures. She told them of a single God whose name could not be spoken but who was so great that He created everything and everyone. Ayla told them of Abraham, Moses, David, and Gideon. Of course, the boys loved the war stories of David best. Arrius appeared to read her mind as he begged, "Tell us the one about David and the giant." "Ugh, you have heard that one a thousand times. You should tell it to me this time."

Arrius, always the best listener and most enthusiastic, did not miss a beat. "David was just a boy, not much older than me. He lived in the hills caring for his father's sheep. He had defeated bears and lions and bandits who had tried to run off with the animals. David did not fear anything or anyone, but his older brothers always picked on him."

Ayla smiled slightly as he glared for a moment at Justus and then continued.

"His brothers were dumb and ugly and—"

"Stick to the story, young man."

"Yes, Ayla."

"His brothers were off to war against a mighty army. Their king, Soul—"

"*Saul,*" corrected Ayla.

"Saul was terrified because the army he faced was brutal, and their king was a giant! For forty days and forty nights, the giant, Goliath, swore at and cursed your people."

"The Hebrews," Justus added.

"And no one knew what to do or how to defeat this army of vicious tribesmen."

"Close enough." Ayla smiled.

"David was sent by his father to bring meat and cheese to his brothers. When he arrived at the camp, he heard the giant, and it brought fire to his bones.

"'How dare this uncircumcised barbarian speak evil of our gods,' David said to his brothers."

"Just one," Ayla corrected.

"One what?" said Justus.

"Just one God. Yahweh is how we say His unspeakable name."

"Oh yeah, just one god."

Arrius continued, "His brothers wanted to beat David up and send him home crying to their father, but David was bold.

"'I will kill this man, cut off his head, and feed his oversized carcass to the birds!' said David. And with five stones and a sling, he defeated Goliath. Took off his enormous head with the giant's own sword and sent the whole enemy army on the run!"

"And what is the lesson of David and Goliath, boys?"

"Always expect the unexpected!" Justus said with a grin.

"And? What else?" asked Ayla.

"Never underestimate the power of the gods," said Arrius.

"Just one. The only one who is your refuge and rescuer in battle."

"If you say so," said Justus with a sneer.

"Ayla?"

"Yes, Arrius."

"Is your god truly mighty? And if He is, why did He need a shepherd boy to defeat Goliath? Why did He not just send a plague or a horrible storm or something from the heavens to help your people?"

Ayla's chest puffed with pride as she listened to the insights and questions of Arrius. Unlike his brother, he was a thinker. Arrius frequently wanted to know the *why* behind the *what* of her stories.

"An excellent question, and one I have pondered at times too. Here's what my people believe: Yahweh chooses one simple and often weak man to work through so that all men will have hope."

"Hope for what?"

"Yahweh often chooses the youngest, the least, and the humble to do a great miracle so that His name alone is praised among men."

Arrius looked out the window with a reflective face as he said, "Because if your god used another giant to defeat a giant, then the *giant* would be praised, not Yahweh."

"You are correct."

Justus, rarely patient with these conversations, spoke up as he stuffed the last piece of bread and cheese into his mouth, "I would still want a giant, not some scrappy baby brother." Then he punched Arrius in the arm.

"I will show you scrappy!"

As Ayla had witnessed so many times before, the boys began to wrestle in the kitchen. Instead of immediately shooing them away, she allowed them this one last time before Justus left.

Ayla knew the bond between Justus and Arrius was intense. She had never seen two boys love and care for one another more than these two.

She wondered to herself, *How will Arrius survive without his brother?*

More than once, to protect his brother, she had seen Justus take a beating from the senator. Amadeus was prone to drunkenness, violence, and outbursts of anger, which were often inappropriately directed at the boys. As near as she could tell, the senator tolerated Justus but had severe issues with Arrius. Why, she did not know.

As the boys knocked over a bowl of fruit and a vase of water, Ayla's patience evaporated, and she yelled, "You boys take the fighting outside before you break something in here!"

"Yes, Ayla," said Arrius as he returned the hit to his brother's arm, and the *battle* began again.

"Out! Both of you, out. Now. What am I to do with you boys? Ignore me once more, and I will pummel you with something worse than the five stones of David."

Ayla always hoped and prayed that somehow, years later, perhaps, her stories would impact the boys for good. Nevertheless, she suspected tragedy and heartbreak lay ahead for them.

CHAPTER 3

Year 3 AD, Rome, Home of Amadeus and Claudia

Justus enlisted as a legionary just a few weeks after his eighteenth birthday. When he was younger, he told everyone he would end up in the Legio 1 Gemanica, the First Germanic Legion led by a ruthless general, Publius Quinctilius Varus. Despite the legion's name, most legionaries were Roman, not former tribesmen.

So everyone was surprised with his commission to serve in Legio X Fretensis, the Roman Tenth Legion in Syria. No Roman loved Syria. Justus was placed in the Cohors 1 Italica Civium Romanorum. This cohort was an Italian auxiliary unit of noncitizens, and auxiliary soldiers generally got the worst jobs and pay. His assignment, however, could still be a path to Roman citizenship.

Years later, General Varus lost three Roman legions to Germanic tribes when they were ambushed in the Battle of the Teutoburg Forest. In that infamous battle, Varus was betrayed by Arminius, a former tribesman of Germania taken captive as a boy just like Justus and Arrius. Arminius, the once Germanic prince, now Roman citizen, and leader of a cavalry unit, led Varus into a trap. The defeat of Varus and the destruction of three legions contributed to Rome's eventual strategic withdrawal from Germania.

Several weeks later, Amadeus was drunk again and on a rampage. The smell of his garlic-tainted sweat mixed with stale wine was almost too much for his wife, Claudia, to bear.

"Amadeus. Stop. Please stop! You are going to kill the boy." Claudia pleaded to no avail. The senator had come home in a foul mood. Claudia inwardly seethed at the perfection Amadeus demanded from their youngest adopted son and the harsh abuse he delivered when Arrius neglected to follow his exact instructions.

"The barbarian brat brought this on himself. He will learn to do as I command or suffer the conse…conseq…*consequences* of his foolish choices."

The older Arrius got, and the drunker Amadeus was, the more he openly defied the senator. Sometimes the offense would go unnoticed, but today, to Claudia's dismay, it did not.

The leather strap began to swing again, striking Arrius from his shoulder blades to his calves. Claudia cringed at the sound. The senator had beaten her boys countless times over the previous nine years. Before Justus left for Syria, he often took the blame and the beatings. Now, however, Amadeus focused his hateful attention on the only son left in his home.

Claudia did what she could over the years to protect Justus and Arrius as much as possible, but she knew they were never truly accepted as sons by Amadeus. The only time he did not beat one or both boys was when he decided to beat a slave. The slaves, however, were smart enough to avoid their master when he returned from a binge.

The senator continued in rage, "And what have you to say for yourself? How long must I put up with you, boy?"

Arrius cried out, "I am sorry. I am sorry. It will never happen again."

It was obvious to Claudia that the senator wasn't looking for answers, only sick, cruel satisfaction.

Claudia heard Ayla yell from the kitchen, "Dinner, Master. Your meal is prepared and hot." Ayla was attempting to distract her master with the only thing he loved more than wine—food. At over five talents in weight, or almost three times the size of Arrius, he had worked up an appetite.

"Thank the gods, boy, that I am exhausted and famished, or I would beat you 'til morning!"

"Enough, Amadeus, let us eat, and then I will give you a bath," said Claudia as seductively as she could under the circumstances.

A bath and its other pleasures were more of what Amadeus loved.

"Fine, you know I do this for his good," he said, pointing at Arrius, draped over a stone bench half-naked.

"It is time, Husband, for food and wine, and then I will tend to *all* your needs."

Claudia had long lost whatever respect or love she had once held for this beast of a man, but she would use whatever means she could to distract him from her son.

After leaving Amadeus to gorge himself, Claudia went to Arrius with a broken voice and tears in her eyes and said, "I despise that man. He has no heart for anyone—not even me any longer."

"I am sorry, Mother."

"You have *nothing* to be sorry for, Arrius. Nothing."

"I bring suffering to every woman in my life."

"Nonsense, you bring me great joy, my son."

"First, my birth mother…then Astra, my father's concubine… now you," said Arrius as he struggled to stand and clothe himself.

"I will not hear of it, Arrius; many women die at childbirth, and your brother told me you were the longing and delight of Astra's heart."

"But—"

"Enough. That is enough. Be still now. Let me tend to your wounds. Ayla said this ointment is something new; it will help you heal."

Claudia believed the balm might mend his back, but she worried far more about what she could not see—the soul of Arrius. A once tender boy became a hardened young man. She knew that Arrius's belief in his curse caused him to retreat deeper and deeper into an emotional abyss of shame.

No one, including Claudia, could foresee the dark days ahead for her beloved son.

Chapter 4

Year 7 AD, the Teen Years, Rome

Quintus screamed at the boy as he spit on the ground to make his point. "Push yourself, Arrius. You must step faster, boy. Move your legs and stay on my weak side *if you can.* You will be a legionary soon enough if you can survive my abuse."

"If I can? Old man, I will crush you like my foot crushes a scorpion!"

Quintus was getting older and slower, but over twenty years as a legionary still gave him an advantage. If nothing else, his mental prowess gave him an edge. At seventeen, Arrius was strong and skilled, but it was clear to Quintus that the young man wrestled with self-doubt that sometimes caused him to hesitate. And in battle, hesitation was costly. Quintus had trained hundreds of men, and not one of them had the determination of Arrius, but something in his head blocked the boy from becoming his best.

"A scorpion, eh? How do you like that sting?" Quintus yelled as he tapped the boy in the thigh with his sword. "I told you: stay to my weak side, or I will strike you down before you know what hit you. Stay still. Die still."

Quintus saw that Arrius was growing angrier by the moment, and he knew how to push Arrius to his limits. Years ago, he decided to use Arrius's fury to try to overcome the doubt he saw in his eyes. Better than anyone, Quintus understood Arrius. He saw his internal struggle, and the legionary recognized the boy's rage could be his friend or foe. Controlled, it would make him fierce; uncontrolled, however, his wrath would make him foolish.

"Yes, use your temper, boy. But it *must* stay controlled. Let it make you vicious in battle. Let that barbarian out, but control it, or it will defeat you before I do."

Arrius cursed.

"There. That's better. Eyes on my *eyes*, not my sword. Your weapon will go where your eyes go."

Arrius shifted quickly to his left and yelled, "Are you trying to defeat me with your ugliness, Quintus? Looking at you has killed many women I hear."

Quintus laughed, but the distraction gave him an opportunity to strike. In a moment's time, Arrius was once again on his back, looking up at the scarred and wrinkled face of his trainer. "How many times must I say it, Arrius?"

"I know. I know! Now get your dung-filled boot off my chest."

"Say it, boy."

Arrius growled through clenched teeth, "Controlled anger is my friend. Uncontrolled emotion is my foe."

Quintus barked, "Yes, and what else?"

Arrius tried to push the dirty boot off his chest. "Always expect the unexpected."

Quintus smiled, showing his missing teeth, and then he scraped his boot off on the breastplate of Arrius.

"That was unnecessary, you old goat farmer."

"Perhaps, but better some dung on your armor than your guts spilling out from a wound."

Despite the harsh banter, Quintus was more than a trainer. He loved Arrius as a son. The old soldier never treated him poorly, and he never inflicted pain for his gain as the senator so often did. During Arrius's years of training, it seemed to Quintus that Arrius took the blows and his words as a gift from the gods.

"Someday, like you, Quintus, I will train men and lead them into great battles for the glory of Rome."

"I am sure you will, Arrius, but not today."

Quintus puffed out his chest and said, "It took me years to become the incredible man I am and hundreds of real battles…battles you are yet to face, boy."

Chapter 5

Year 7 AD, Rome, Home of Senator Amadeus and Claudia

The courtyard was quiet except for the sound of doves calling to each other. The wisp of a gentle wind smelling of jasmine brushed his curly, light brown hair. A slight chill was growing as the sunlight was shrinking.

Arrius rarely had moments of peace, and life without Justus was boring and lonely. If he wasn't training, he wandered the streets of Rome looking for trouble.

Much to the delight of Arrius, Amadeus suffered from gout. The sudden and severe attacks of pain, swelling, and tenderness in his joints made the senator meaner than usual but easier to avoid. He would often drink himself into unconsciousness, which made him far less of a threat to Arrius or any of the slaves in the home. Besides, Arrius now towered over his adopted father. Amadeus once mentioned to Claudia he feared having his throat slit by his embittered barbarian son.

There were rumors that Claudia was having an affair. No one blamed her. Marriage vows were held loosely in Rome, but she made it obvious that she'd lost whatever fondness she had for Amadeus years before. Arrius knew that Claudia hated the senator because of his cruel treatment of her sons and his narcissistic and abrasive treatment of her. She was an easy target for the affections of another man.

Justus had left almost four years earlier to fight for Rome. Occasionally, Arrius would get word from his brother, but he longed to be reunited in person. Within just a matter of months, he would join his brother's legion. It didn't matter to him that Syria was hot and dusty; all he wanted was to see the one he loved more than his own life.

"You are set on leaving us, Arrius?" Claudia asked with a sad tone. "Are you ready to leave our home so soon? The senator could easily find you a post here in Rome." Arrius knew that Claudia loved this once barbarian boy now turned into a fighting Roman man.

"I must go. I was born for battle. Besides, the politics in Rome would kill me faster than any sword."

Arrius could never avoid his destiny. He was born a barbarian and fated to fight. You can take the boy from the wild northlands, but you cannot take the ferociousness out of the boy.

Arrius tried to comfort Claudia, "I suspect the senator's days are numbered. If something or someone doesn't kill him, he will die from too much wine soon enough. But what will happen to you, Mother, when he does die? Will you be okay?"

Claudia smiled. "I will. I have made *other* arrangements for my future."

Arrius knew Rome always cared for the elite—especially if the person was as beautiful as Claudia. He suspected her other arrangements referred to her lover, rumored to be another senator.

She would indeed survive and probably thrive.

Claudia's voice grew soft with concern. "Will you ever return home?"

Arrius assumed she meant Rome. "Rome is now in my blood, and you will always matter to me."

"I am grateful for both of those things, my son, but I meant Germania—your first home. Do you think you'll ever return north?"

Arrius was surprised. In his nearly thirteen years with this woman, she'd never once mentioned his homeland. "I have no one there. I would be seen and treated as a Roman and killed on sight."

"But what of your sister? What was her name?"

Arrius remembered every detail of her face, and he did think of her often.

"Saxa, her name was Saxa."

"Yes, of course, Saxa, a beautiful name. You used to cry out her name in your sleep when you were much younger. Perhaps you could be reunited with her."

"I am Roman, and as a legionary, the Saxa I remember would take my head off with her sword."

"Perhaps, my son, but blood is blood."

Arrius was frustrated. "And *my* blood is cursed; she will remember that too. I am responsible for the death of our mother, father, and everyone she once loved. Revenge is the way of my… *those*…people. There is nothing and no one in Germania for me."

"Arrius, my dear, dear son, how long will you insist upon holding onto a lie? You were just five years old when we saved you from a life of savagery and barbarism. No one, at such a young and innocent age, can be blamed for such losses."

The details of what happened were sometimes obscured by a deep fog in the back recesses of his mind, but Arrius knew he was not *saved* by Amadeus and Claudia. He would never forget the terror of his captivity.

"I am hungry, Mother. Please excuse me. I want to find Ayla and see what she has prepared to satisfy my belly."

Claudia nodded. "Go, let her spoil you as she always does. Sometimes I am jealous of the affection and attention you give to that servant."

Arrius objected, "You mean *slave*, don't you, Mother?"

Arrius could see on her face how Claudia struggled with a tinge of both guilt and irritation at his question.

"She is the senator's servant. You know I have always treated her well. She has never been beaten, never gone hungry, and always has a warm bed to sleep in."

A slave is still a slave, thought Arrius to himself as he turned and walked away without comment to find the food he could smell cooking in the kitchen.

Ayla chuckled, "I thought you would show your face the moment you smelled my cooking. You are as predictable as your brother."

Arrius affectionately wrapped his arms around Ayla and said, "My brother can probably smell your bread in Syria."

"When you leave, be sure to take some fresh bread and dates with you for Justus."

"And start a war with the Syrians over your bread? I think not. They would attack our camp and kill every man to get to this delicacy, Ayla!"

She smiled. Arrius always was the smooth talker who knew just what to say to get another slice of bread with olive oil.

"I will miss you, Arrius, but I will have at least six hours more free time every day when you leave. Cooking for you is like cooking for an army!"

"Ayla?"

"Yes, what do you want from me *now*?"

"I will miss you more than you know."

And with that, her eyes began to water. "My body and my mind are failing. Every morning I wake up aching and tired, asking Yahweh to take me to Sheol so I can rest in paradise. You are the only thing that keeps me alive in this immoral and forsaken land."

"Ah, you will live forever, old woman."

Ayla sighed, "No, I won't, Arrius, not here. I know my days are numbered."

Arrius hated the thought of losing another person he loved. "The gods will take my life long before yours, Ayla."

Ayla stopped what she was doing, looked lovingly at Arrius, and spoke words Arrius would never forget. "Life on this side of eternity is short, my boy, but truthfully, *this* side is not all there is."

Arrius turned away his face and said, "You have no idea what the gods have in store for me, but somehow death follows me like the moon follows the sun."

CHAPTER 6

Year 8 AD, Rome, Home of Senator Amadeus and Claudia

The time passed quickly, too quickly for Claudia. For many years, the center of their universe was this once barbarian boy, now a Roman young man, who would be missed more than he knew or she could imagine.

Arrius would depart with his cohort in less than a week to join the Tenth Legion and his brother in Syria. The Roman general Pompey conquered most of the Middle East decades before. In fact, most of Europe and North Africa, including the Middle East, formed a single political and economic entity. However, the Bedouin tribes of the region resisted the occupation and often made a nuisance of themselves. Additionally, the wind, sand, and heat made the area a challenge for every legionary. The Bedouins would often attack Roman outposts in small groups in the middle of the night. If the tribes ever united under a single leader, they would present a serious challenge.

Claudia was enjoying the sunset, red wine, and some last moments with Arrius as they sat in the airy reception hall.

"I worry about you and your brother. Every legionary faces great danger wherever Rome rules, but why Rome cares about a land full of sand and vipers is a mystery to me."

"Trade routes, Mother, and seaports. The land may be forsaken and barren, but the Roman roads through that region and its deep ports lead to the wealth of Egypt."

Claudia slapped her leg and raised her voice. "Rome has enough gold, and we have lost too many sons in pursuit of power and glory."

Arrius countered, "Never enough gold, Mother, never enough. Besides, Rome is the world, and the world is Rome."

"You truly are a Roman now, my son."

Arrius fidgeted in his seat. "I never know how to respond to statements that affirm my Roman upbringing, Mother. On the one hand, I am proud, but on the other, being deprived of Roman citizenship because I am an adopted son of *questionable* blood makes a part of me outraged."

Claudia knew this was a touchy subject.

As he stared at the cup, Arrius slowly stirred his wine. "Perhaps I will earn my citizenship in battle and in service to the empire. The only path for me is to distinguish myself as a legionary so that I might be awarded the prize of becoming a citizen of Rome by a general."

Claudia sighed and waved her hand. "You are Roman. Regardless of what *anyone* says, Roman first, Roman always."

"Pray to the gods, especially Mars, that I succeed. I must if I am to redeem my life and to break the curse."

Claudia shook her head. "You carry with you your worst enemy."

Arrius looked up at her. "What enemy do you speak of, Mother? I kill my enemies. I don't carry them anywhere."

Claudia, by nature of being a woman and a mother, was intuitive. She saw how Arrius reacted to emotional pain. She knew he could endure physical torment from Justus, brutal training by Quintus, and abuse from Amadeus, but inside—deep within his soul—Arrius was broken. He seemed incapable of letting go of the lie that he was cursed and the cause of evil to those he loved.

"My dearest son, your greatest foe lies within you like dead bones buried in a tomb. The enemy I speak of is the lie you simply cannot or will not be free of."

Arrius stood and threw his glass against a stone wall, surprising Claudia. "I grow weary of your thoughts regarding my past. You will *never* understand what I have known or what burden I carry."

Claudia began to cry. "But I do, Arrius, more than you can imagine. *My* mother died at *my* birth, and I lost two sons before they took their first breath."

She could see that Arrius was stunned even though he'd heard the senator speak of losing a child while he beat Arrius. Amadeus would often say between clenched teeth and severe blows, "You are a pathetic replacement for the son I *should* have had."

Arrius sat back down next to Claudia and rubbed both hands through his hair. "I have never heard anything—not one word—from you about your loss. And no one ever whispered even a rumor to me about your mother dying during *your* birth."

Arrius placed a strong arm around Claudia's shoulder as she sobbed, and her entire body shook. He was speechless as Claudia thought to herself, *My son is years away from knowing how to process his grief, let alone help me with mine.*

Arrius finally whispered, "Why have you never spoken of this,

Mother?"

"The gods brought us together, my son. You brought great healing and wholeness to me. I only wish…I wish there was something I could do to dig this poison out of your mind. I *do* know your pain. I *do* know your loss. But I do *not* know how to change what you believe. And that belief is the heavy stone you carry, a stone that I fear will crush you someday."

Arrius said nothing. What more could he say? And Claudia knew there was nothing she could do to bring the freedom her son so desperately needed.

She sighed and said, "Maybe someday the gods will do what I cannot. Maybe someday you will see how you bring blessing rather than a curse to those you love."

Arrius stiffened and said, "Nothing and no one can change what I am. No man or god."

Hidden out of sight, Ayla watched and listened to their entire conversation. She often eavesdropped on whoever was in the house and whatever was being said.

But Ayla spoke as she stepped out from under the vine-covered portico. "My lady, the meal is prepared. Are you and Arrius dining alone tonight?"

Claudia gathered herself and wiped the tears from her eyes as she replied without looking in Ayla's direction.

"Yes, the senator has other *business* to attend to this evening. We dine alone." Claudia looked up at Arrius. She was aware of his fond affection for Ayla, so she spoke tenderly to her servant, "Ayla."

"Yes, my lady."

"Would you be kind enough to join my son and me for dinner tonight?"

Ayla grabbed a fistful of her apron in one hand as she stepped back a bit and stammered, "Uh…why…um…of course, my lady. I would be honored, but what if the senator—"

Claudia interrupted, "He will not return until late, and I can deal with him if need be."

"As you wish, my lady."

Arrius was beaming with satisfaction. "I will clean up, ladies, and join you shortly."

"Please do sponge bathe before dinner, Arrius, or Ayla and I will seat you at the far end of the table tonight." Both women laughed as the joy of their lives smiled and excused himself.

"I will miss that boy," Ayla said as she watched Arrius depart.

Another tear escaped Claudia's eyes. "*We* will miss him, as I fear we may never see him again."

Chapter 7

Several Months Later, 8 AD, the Early Years in Syria

The march to Syria was miserable for Arrius and his fellow legionaries. The journey took the newest cohort of the Tenth Legion nearly three months to complete as they traversed both sea and desert through Greece and central Asia.

Typically, legion cohorts avoided travel in the winter because inclement weather was too hard on the legionaries and the Roman roads. Nearly five hundred men, plus carts and animals, wreaked havoc on muddy roads. But Legio X Fretensis, the Roman Tenth Legion in Syria, had lost over two hundred legionaries over the last year. Besides dying in battle skirmishes with the locals, a pandemic from a disease previously unknown to the Romans killed many men and left hundreds more weakened. The Bedouin tribes took advantage of the situation and were attacking Roman patrols every day. Publius Sulpicius Quirinius, the Roman governor and legate of the Tenth, was concerned about an organized uprising, which is why he insisted Rome supply him with new recruits as soon as possible.

Arrius was excited to join his brother. The Italian cohort auxiliary unit in Syria that Justus belonged to had distinguished itself in battle, and Justus now served as a centurion overseeing eighty-five men. If things went well and his brother had enough influence,

Arrius would be reassigned to his brother's cohort. Rome often put brothers together, believing a family bond was a powerful motivator in battle.

Arrius arrived in Syria with much of his cohort in misery. Nearly three in ten men suffered from dysentery, and many others were tending their wounds received in a clash along their journey.

Arrius gave his brother a strong embrace when he found him.

Justus stepped back, looked his brother over from head to toe, and said with a serious tone, "Little brother, you look horrible, but you survived a march that would have killed a lesser man."

Arrius waved his concern off. "And you, Justus, look as fat and ugly as ever. Ayla gave me bread to bring to you, but I ate it all a couple of moons ago. I don't think she completely understood the length of my journey."

Justus smiled. "Oh, she understood, but that old Jew wanted me to know she thought of me."

"And she did, Brother, often."

"So how is Claudia?"

"Mother is as good as any woman could be living with that pig, the senator."

"And how did you manage without me to shield you from his wrath these past three years?"

Arrius gave his brother an evil smirk. "Between his much-deserved illness and my much-observed size and strength, he gave up beating me some time ago."

Justus slapped his brother on the arm and added, "If I ever return to Rome, I will slit his throat in the night and bring *my* wrath to him."

"He will be long dead before either of us see Rome again, Justus. But tell me, where did you get that scar?" Referring to a long mark on Justus's right cheek.

"From the crooked sword of some mangy Bedouin. They are wild and bold people. Truth be known, they remind me of our people. They fight like crazed barbarians."

As they walked together to find a tent for Arrius, Justus went on to tell what Arrius suspected was a largely embellished tale of how a small group of twelve Bedouins snuck into their camp early one morning and how all of them met their death by his sword. Arrius later found out the truth from another legionary that it was only two men who crawled into his tent late one night, hoping to kill a Roman centurion. Somehow, they'd gotten past the guards, but in the struggle with Justus, one of them managed to use a small knife to cut his face while attempting to cut his throat.

Arrius was exhausted but excited. "I look forward to fighting alongside you, Brother."

"That time will come, Arrius; it will come soon enough," said Justus soberly. "But killing these Bedouins has come at a great price. Many of my men have died. Too many. These desert dwellers come at night, hiding in the shadows, and they fight without honor because they will not meet us in open battle. Before we can form a shield wall, they come out of nowhere and strike like vipers."

"Let them come! I have killed many vipers in recent months. Rome will prevail."

Justus stopped dead in his tracks, looked at his brother through

Arrius was irritated. "I heard another cohort was attacked last night while on patrol. Five men were killed from Bedouin arrows, and a dozen more wounded. Why does the legate even bother to send men out from the camp after nightfall?"

"Little Brother, we must always protect our outer perimeter to provide a buffer between the camp and the desert scum who would pick at our edges like a man picks on a scab. No real harm could be done to our camp, but patrols are the Roman way."

"Yes, Justus, but the *Roman* way does not protect us from the *barbarian* way, does it? They strike and retreat, strike and retreat, like ghosts on the wind."

"And where, Arrius, is the man who said so many years ago he was longing for a fight?"

Arrius kicked up some sand from the ground. "A fight against an unseen opponent who attacks from shifting sand dunes is *no* fight. It is an ambush. By the time we draw our swords and spears, they have scattered, and we are left to welter in the sand."

"You are not wrong, Arrius, but if you question Quirinius and you are overheard, you will be whipped. So shut your mouth and stop complaining like an old woman. You are starting to sound more and more like our elderly nanny than my warrior brother."

"And you sound like Mother, always worrying about me. I can take care of myself."

Justus shook his head. "After years of fighting desert ghosts, eating too many sand-laden meals, and not having enough wine to drown my frustrations, I *do* worry, Brother. You know all too well how fragile life is in Syria, and we both know our lives are always at risk. Besides, Mother would kill me if I didn't keep you safe.

You were always her favorite."

Arrius feigned resistance, but he knew Justus was right on both accounts. He was the favored son, and Claudia would never forgive his brother should the gods allow his life to be taken by a Bedouin.

Arrius playfully punched his brother in the shoulder. "If you say so, Justus, but I don't plan on dying anytime soon. Mars will protect me. You, however, may *not* be so lucky. The gods think you are ugly and a worthless sack of human flesh."

And with that, Justus took his brother down in the dirt and sand, wrestling him as they had done so many times over the years.

Neither one knew what their remaining years together might bring, but the lifespan of a Roman soldier was short—too short for these brothers.

Ten long, grueling years of misery in Syria had passed. Years of scorching heat in the day and frigid nights. And too many years of seeing fellow legionaries die in frustrating skirmishes with an enemy that seemed to multiply like rodents. No matter how many Bedouins the Romans killed, they flourished.

Two nights earlier, a band of Bedouins attacked and wounded a friend to both brothers.

"Will he survive his wounds, Justus?" asked Arrius.

"I doubt it. The cut is deep, and already it smells of death."

Justus and Arrius had only a few friends in the cohort. Most of the men feared Justus, who had the reputation as a strong but ruthless centurion. Arrius, by default of his connection and because he, too, was seen as more barbarian than Roman, was left alone more often than not.

However, the man dying in his cot was a fellow tribesman from Germania and a trusted friend named Cyrus. The three of them often fought together in what could only be described as a vicious triad. They could sometimes be seen moving and fighting in unison like a desert dust devil—swords and shields laying waste to anyone who had the nerve to attack them.

"Cyrus." Justus nudged his friend. "Cyrus, can you hear me, my friend?"

Cyrus opened his eyes to half-mast but said nothing. Fever, infection, and the loss of too much blood made him incoherent.

"His eyes are empty, Justus. I cannot imagine our life here without him."

Justus placed his hands on his companion's barely moving chest and said quietly, "Tell my mother and father I will see them soon enough." And with that, their friend breathed his last and was gone.

"Death follows me like a lion follows his prey," whispered Arrius. "Everywhere I turn, everyone I care for dies."

Justus stood up and grabbed his brother's arm. "Why do you continue to make everyone's death about you? The death of Cyrus is not on your hands but mine. I led him into battle. I stumbled in the heat of battle allowing a sword to come between us. What is wrong with you, Arrius? Why is it always *your* fault?"

There was nothing Arrius could or would say. Justus shoved his brother aside and left the tent as he yelled at the legionary outside the door, "Get some help and take our brother, Cyrus, to the funeral fires."

"Yes, Centurion," the man said as he saluted and moved quickly to find assistance. Cyrus was one of the largest men in camp, and it might take two or three men to move the body.

Arrius, fighting back tears before leaving his side, said, "I am sorry, Cyrus. I am so sorry. Tell the gods I can no longer carry this.

Many more months passed, and winter came to the desert again. Arrius was stuck in a foul mood most of the time. He'd forgotten the smells of jasmine from their home in Rome. He longed for a glass of fine wine always found at the senator's table rather than the cheap drink provided to the soldiers.

To make matters worse, a recent dispatch from Claudia brought the news of Ayla's death. According to Claudia, she passed quietly and peacefully in her sleep one night. But knowing he would never see her again sent Arrius into a gloomy frame of mind.

One night, as they sat as close to the fire as possible warming their bones, Arrius said, "Do you remember the story Ayla told us of Jeremiah? She called him the mourning prophet—I think. Didn't he walk the streets of Jerusalem naked?"

"Yes, I recall the story, Arrius, but it wasn't Jeremiah. It was Isaiah. He walked the streets naked for three years. Those Hebrews and their customs are stranger than the Bedouins."

Arrius grinned. "Perhaps, in honor of our Jewish nanny, Ayla, we should walk around the camp naked tonight!"

"You first, Little Brother. But do so before the evening meal; otherwise, too many of my men will vomit at the sight of your naked and hairy backside."

"There's the big brother I love. But it's far too cold for a naked walk tonight. Perhaps tomorrow."

For the first time in a long time, Justus momentarily smiled but then sighed heavily as he said, "Tomorrow, we prepare to march. Our tribune fears the tribes are preparing for battle. Our spies and scouts are warning of something different from the Bedouins. Perhaps they have amassed enough men together to fight us in open battle soon."

Arrius shifted on the ground to warm his other side. "Whatever comes, we will face it together."

Justus sat unresponsive as he stared into the fire.

Arrius knew that something in his brother was off. Deep in his mind, a voice told him this might be the last night they would have together.

"Arrius, wake up. It's time to drag your butt out of bed. We march into the desert today."

Arrius rolled over, hungover and irritated. "Why are we marching in the middle of winter, in the middle of the day, to fight an enemy that will not face us in honorable battle?"

"Ours is not to question but to obey, Little Brother. Besides, our spies tell us a large group, perhaps several tribes and clans, have gathered near the caves of Maaloula. The tribune is dispatching the First and Second Cohort to investigate."

Arrius grunted. "With almost one thousand legionaries, no Bedouin will show his face, let alone his sword today."

"Perhaps, Little Brother, but they are getting more unified and organized. Their hate for us is greater than their fight with each other."

"And the feeling is mutual. I hate them. I hate this place. I hate the sand. I hate—"

"Enough!" Justus interrupted. "Do as I say as your centurion if not your brother."

Arrius swung his feet over the edge of his cot, rubbed his eyes, and shook his head. "So it is like that today, huh? This is going to be a long day."

Justus said nothing, turned, and exited the tent briskly.

Arrius prayed to Mars, "God of war, protect and guide us today. Give us the strength to take the blood of our enemies. Let them be as scorpions crushed under our feet."

Something, however, felt empty in his prayers, and that prevailing sense of dread came over him again as he said under his breath, "Today is *not* a good day to die. Death comes to all, but not today."

CHAPTER 9

Year 18 AD, Syria

Nearly a thousand men stood at attention, chilled to the bone and ready to march if for no other reason than to warm themselves. Roman armor was a gift from the gods for every legionary, but until one marched or fought, the metal was so cold that it felt torturous at times.

Roman generals were obsessed with their prebattle speeches. Publius Sulpicius Quirinius was no exception.

"Centurions and legionaries, we have it from multiple sources that the Bedouin tribes are gathered near the canyons and caves south of us," yelled the legate to his men. "You will seek out, engage, and destroy the enemies of Rome this day or the next. The chieftain, Baildan, defies our emperor and calls his people to rebellion. Too many of your brothers have died at his command. Without mercy and with the wrath of the gods supporting us, you will show Baildan and his desert cockroaches what happens to all those who stand in opposition to our gods and our emperor!"

The men let out a response that could be heard for a league. The ground shook as the Romans stomped their feet and beat their shields. "For Rome! For the emperor! For glory!"

Quirinius droned on for quite some time, and at the right moments, his legionaries responded with louder and louder battle cries. Finally, he saluted and gave the *primus pilus*, the highest-ranking and most respected centurion of the First Cohort, the nod to march.

Justus and Arrius were honored to belong to the Second *Centuria* of the First Cohort, which made up the elite troops of the Tenth. Every *centuria* was a group of seventy to eighty or so legionaries led by a centurion, and each was ranked within the cohort. The five centurions of the First Cohort were called *primi ordines*, and Justus held that rank and title of honor.

Standing tall and looking proud, Arrius gave his brother a smile and nod as Justus turned to order his men to march. The look in Justus' eyes was distant and troubled. *What troubles Justus? I wonder*, he thought to himself. *That is not the look of a confident centurion, let alone my brother. Where is the fire in his eyes?*

A significant disadvantage of being in the Second *Centuria* of the Cohort was the dust and sand kicked up by a hundred or so men in the First *Centuria.* Men at the back of the troop would find a march like today unbearable.

Once the march began, Arrius was close enough to converse with his brother. It was more by blood than rank that Arrius was allowed to march alongside his centurion brother, and this proximity made possible occasional conversations between the two.

"Justus, you seem…you seem less than your usual self today. You have barely said a word, and you look like your armor has doubled its weight on your shoulders. Are you ill?"

Justus didn't respond.

"Justus?"

Still no reply. "Centurion?"

"Be quiet. Talking is forbidden while we march."

Justus never scolded him for chatting. The sound of metal on metal and a thousand men's footsteps always covered any short discussions among the troops. They marched on in silence for some time until Arrius spoke again. "Centurion…Justus…Brother, please tell me, what is wrong? Have I offended you?"

"Once again, you make it all about *you*," said Justus without turning around to look at his brother.

"I…I am sorry, *Centurion*. I will keep my—"

At that moment, a storm of a thousand arrows dropped on the cohort. The man to the right of Arrius went down with an arrow through his neck. The skill of these Bedouins with a bow was remarkable.

"Shields! Form up, men, shields to the ready!" yelled Justus.

The legionaries trained every day, and this was what they prepared for. Quickly and with precision, a shield wall before and above the men was created. The noise of many more—thousands more—arrows buzzed through the air.

The cohort was between two massive dunes and leagues still from the caves of Maaloula. No one expected a battle here so soon and in the middle of the day. Even in the winter, the days were hot, and most of the men were dehydrated from marching. They were waiting for the next stop to refill their canteens from the wagons that followed the cohort with supplies.

"Where are they? Why do these cowards hide in the sand sending arrows to no avail?" shouted Arrius to his brother next to him. "Unless they attack, we stand here behind shields but unable to advance or to kill anyone."

Arrius was right. The Roman way was to use their shields as a moving wall to advance against an enemy or to protect them as they struck out with swords and spears against an attack. Standing in the equivalent of a ditch between two dunes presented a tactical disadvantage to the Romans. Moving a shield wall up the side of a dune was difficult, if not impossible, and the Bedouins were still out of sight just over the dune ridge, raining down volley after volley of arrows.

Justus shouted against the noise of men groaning all around him, "Our shields are protecting us, but they grow heavy, and we grow overheated as if we are in an oven. Something must be done, and soon. I will find the *primus pilus* and secure his orders. Stay put, Little Brother."

Suddenly, the arrows stopped. It is incredible how noisy thousands of arrows sound whizzing through the air and clanging on metal shields. Arrius hoped the Bedouins had retreated, recognizing the futility of their offense. Very few of the arrows found a human target. The silence was welcomed, but the men were hot, frustrated, and angry.

Then it came. At first, it sounded like distant drums beating in rhythm. Thumping. More thumping. Louder and louder, it grew. Arrius knew what was happening, and he understood the sound meant something horrible was coming. All the more experienced legionaries knew precisely what the sound was—camels—those miserable, biting, long-legged creatures of the desert.

The first line of camels spilled over the top of the dunes from both sides as a wave spills on the beach. There was an endless line along the ridge, as far as the eye could see. Then a second line and a third, thousands of men riding thousands of camels poured into the shield wall, collapsing it like grass in a windstorm. The sheer bulk of a camel was more than one or even two men could resist with their shields. But camel after camel plummeted into the Roman wall, decimating it in no time at all.

The army was well-trained, however. Without hesitation, once the wall was breached, most dropped their shields and began plunging their swords and spears into both man and beast. The Bedouins had spears as well, and using them from atop their mounts made them almost unreachable.

The veteran legionaries, who had faced this before, shouted, "Cut at the knees! Remove the legs of the beasts. Slice their bellies open if you can."

The blood began to flow at their feet like a river. Human blood mixed with camel blood. Human feces from killed combatants, mixed with the spilled intestines of countless beasts, immediately drew countless flies.

One young legionary screamed, "The gods have cursed us and sent a plague to punish us!"

Most of the legionaries also had to contend with blinding sand in their eyes and mouthfuls of dust, dirt, and sand that choked them, making it hard to breathe. The Bedouin wore a keffiyeh, a headscarf they could pull over their face as needed.

Arrius fought on. Ruthlessly. Mercilessly. Drenched in sweat and blood, he killed beast after beast, man after man.

Like their old trainer, Justus yelled at his brother, "Move your feet. Keep your sword up. Watch their eyes, not their weapons!" But nothing—absolutely nothing—had prepared Arrius for this fight. His feet were buried in blood-soaked sand, and the eyes of his enemy were hidden more than seen. Arrius looked down the ravine they were trapped in, and all he saw were bodies piling up—Roman after Roman lying dead in the hot sands.

As the battle carried on, Arrius lost track of his brother. At one point, when Arrius was back-to-back with the *optio*, he yelled above the din, "What has become of my brother? Have you seen him? How will we survive this day?" The *optio* didn't reply.

As the sun set on the unseen horizon, the sand trap the legionaries found themselves in was quickly becoming black. All was lost.

Then Arrius heard a voice from twenty or so paces on his left, "Little Brother, where are you?" The words were weak but clear. Arrius struck down the Bedouin before him and moved to find his brother. But as Arrius turned to search for him, another Bedouin kicked him in the head from a camel. As he fell into the sand, Arrius was pierced in his side. The instant he landed in a gritty pool of blood, he cried out, "I now join my fathers."

It was black. Arrius tried to move but couldn't. He croaked from a dry mouth full of sand, "I'm dead. Bound now forever in the underworld." Near him, he could hear the painful groans of men, and then, at barely above a whisper, he heard Justus, "Little Brother…Little Brother…Arrius…is that you?"

Arrius tried to move, this time freeing his right arm. "Justus, I am here. Are we dead? Where are you?"

"No, we are not dead, not yet, but the Bedouin have left us here until the morning. They will return with the sunrise to kill the

for any legionary in the Middle East.

Two cohorts from the Tenth Legion in Syria, the Ninth Cohort and the Italian Cohort, were stationed in Jerusalem—nearly a thousand men. The Tenth was under the command of Valerius Gratus, the Roman procurator of the province under Emperor Tiberius. Valerius hated the Jews, as most Romans did, and irritated the religious leaders of Jerusalem by frequently deposing and appointing a new high priest.

The walled city of Jerusalem was probably the cleanest urban area known to man. The Jewish temple to their lonely God was a work of devotion and elegance. The Jews treated the entire city as if it was a sacred shrine. However, to any Roman, Jerusalem was horrible. No erotic statues or monuments attesting to the glory of Rome existed anywhere. And Arrius could not find enough taverns or a single suitable bathhouse either. The entire region smelled like a latrine pit and rotting wet wool when it rained. As far as Arrius was concerned, the only thing the Jews knew how to do well was make wine, and Arrius devoured it like water.

Sadly, Arrius had given up on everything since the death of his brother five years before. He did not care about being a legionary. He was indifferent to battles or glory. And most evident to everyone, he no longer cared about honor. Though Arrius was born in a cave in Germania, he once wore a legionary's uniform with pride. Even though he had been stolen from his homeland and lived his entire life believing he was blood-cursed, he and his older brother were survivors. Gustav, who became known as Justus, his Roman name, had been Arrius's lifeline to reality. Now, with his brother gone, he lost all hope. When Justus died, a part of Arrius died.

As Arrius finally stood to put on his armor, he shook his head, wiped something foul from his chest that smelled like rotting meat or worse, and washed his face with some dirty water. As he rubbed his hands through his dark, oily hair, he moaned, "The gods have sent me to this wretched place as maltreatment for my misdeeds."

Arrius's centurion in Palestine, a large and chestnut-colored man from North Africa, was called Cassius because no one could pronounce his African birthname. The Latin word *Cassius* means *rejoice*, and Cassius was once known for his infectious laughter before being promoted to centurion. However, leadership and Jerusalem robbed him of his joy; he rarely laughed anymore.

Arrius joined his cohort in the fortress courtyard just in time for morning drills. The sun sat low, but the day already felt unbearably hot. Tiny and annoying gnats swarmed in thick clusters, and flies, apparently drawn to the legionaries' rancid smell, buzzed the soldiers incessantly.

"Why do we train and drill, legionaries?" yelled Cassius.

"To become our best for the glory of Rome!" the men replied with gusto.

"And why do we want to do our best?"

"For the glory of our emperor!"

Arrius thought his head would explode as the continuous chanting went on and on. However, after an hour of swinging his *rudis*, a wooden training sword, and losing a bucketful of sweat that reeked like stale beer, his head was finally clearing.

"Arrius!" shouted Cassius. "You have great potential. If only you could keep your head in the fight and your belly from too much wine."

"I would rather keep my head empty and my belly full," muttered Arrius.

"What? What was that, Legionary?"

"Nothing, Centurion…nothing worth repeating."

Having lost many men in a hundred battles over the years, Arrius knew that Cassius understood the agony of loss. He also knew that his centurion was hard on him because he had not given up on him as others had.

"When we are done here, you and I will run a few leagues together. Perhaps running in full armor in this blood-boiling heat will bring you to your senses."

"As you command, Centurion," said Arrius half-heartedly. "As you command."

Arrius longed for death. He muttered to himself, "Perhaps running in this god-awful weather will finally end my suffering and my wretched life."

Arrius came to a breaking point sprinting the steep hills in the blistering sun. The foul air outside the Sheep Gate of Jerusalem's walls made him dry heave and feel lightheaded. He halted to catch his breath.

"Did I tell you to stop, Legionary?"

Arrius bent over with his hands on his knees and could barely breathe as he choked out, "No, Centurion, but…"

"Keep your pathetic excuses to yourself, *Little Brother*."

Arrius was stunned, stood straight, wiped his brow of dust and sweat, and said, "What did you call me? No one, not even you, Centurion, calls me little brother."

Cassius laughed. "You are too pale, too weak, and too skinny to be *my* little brother, Legionary. When you are done throwing up your bowels, we will take one more lap around these ancient walls just because we can."

Arrius sucked in as much air as he could into his lungs and started moving again—more a trot than a run—but moving, nonetheless. Oddly, the memory of his brother, Justus, and his love for him helped him put one foot in front of the other.

Cassius was impressed. "You are a strange one, Arrius. Just when I expect you to quit—or die—you find something deep and carry on. There is greatness in you."

"No, Centurion, there was greatness in my brother and only a curse upon me."

"Curses are for old women and fools to believe in. We make our own destiny. I was taken as a slave from my tribe many years ago, forced into service to Rome, and I felt my life was over. Look at me now, however. No, you are only cursed if you believe in such things, and I do not."

Arrius said nothing. There was nothing to say. He *did* believe in curses; it was his people's way, and there was no doubt in his mind he was damned by the gods forever.

And the fact that Cassius could talk and run at the same time annoyed Arrius.

"Arrius, you must find your path back to the man I know you are inside. Grieving is normal, but unresolved grief is a torturous and slow way to die."

Arrius braced himself for one of Cassius's pithy quotes he had become famous for over the years.

"My people have a saying—"

"Of course they do," wheezed Arrius between breaths.

"What was that?"

"Nothing. Please, I beg you. Tell me what *your* people say." Arrius did not even try to hide his sarcasm.

Without a beat, Cassius spoke, "There are many ways to die, but death by a bottle is a fool's death."

Arrius stopped again and investigated the ebony and glistening face of his commander. Something in him clicked. He *did* want to die, but facing his mother, father, and brother in the underworld as a drunk would bring eternal shame on all of them. The time had come for him to pull it together so he could find his end in battle. Any other death was unacceptable.

"Centurion?"

"Yes?"

"I live with the memories of the deaths I have caused. Cursed or not, *everyone* I have cared for in my life is dead. Death clings to me like stink on a camel."

Cassius smiled and chuckled a bit.

"I am serious, Cassius."

Cassius leaned in toward Arrius and placed a hand on his shoulder. "*Centurion* Cassius to you."

Arrius turned his face away. "Centurion, I wander through every day with a burden I cannot carry, and I dread sleep at night because the dead haunt me."

Cassius spoke fondly to the emotionally wounded soldier, as a father would talk to his son. "We are Roman soldiers, Arrius, and we stand together. No mere mortal can carry the burden you bear alone."

As Arrius's despair deepened, something inside him began to crack. Somehow, he knew he was at a fork in his twisted Roman road. He needed someone to believe in him again, and he wondered if Cassius was that man.

CHAPTER 11

Several Moons Later, 23 AD, Antonia Fortress, Jerusalem

The weeks that followed Arrius's epiphany were almost unbearable. Arrius did not want to die a fool's death; he wanted to die with honor in battle as his brother did.

The first week or so of being sober left him with night sweats and uncontrollable tremors. He spent more time in the barrack latrine and on his bunk than he should. Arrius struggled to get back into full fighting shape too. His love for wine and beer had made him fat and soft—neither an acceptable condition for a legionary. However, a sense of honor he learned as a young Roman soldier drove him. If legionaries were anything, they were proud. Proud of Rome, proud of their legion, and proud of the uniform. But pride can only carry a man so far.

Nonetheless, he had given up drinking and was feeling more himself every day for the most part. But on two different occasions, Arrius got drunk and faced the wrath of Cassius again. As it turns out, Arrius discovered that the centurion's heart was as big as his body and large enough to forgive. He knew Cassius refused to give up on him, and Arrius grew more each day into the man Cassius said he could become.

One night, while sitting at a campfire together under a smoke-filled sky made thick from a thousand cooking fires in Jerusalem,

Arrius asked, "How many lost Roman souls like me have you rescued?"

Cassius looked over at Arrius, shook his head, and said, "Not enough."

"What do you mean not enough?"

"The way of a legionary is a dismal and forsaken path. We are plucked from our family and home to fight hate-filled enemies until we win or die."

Arrius nodded and used a stick to stir the embers in the fire as a dog barked in the distance.

"We are told to do unspeakable things…ruthless things… things that eat at our souls, all for the glory of an emperor who does *not* love us. We are expendable. We are nameless villains, scoundrels, and thugs who use our Roman swords and armor to pillage and rape."

Arrius was surprised by Cassius's candor, and he looked around to see if any other legionaries were within earshot. He shifted his weight on the log to turn and look at Cassius. "But the rule of Rome brings the rule of law to those in need. We bring growth, advancement, and civilization to backward peoples."

Arrius could smell garlic on Cassius's breath when he leaned over to look directly into his eyes. "The Hebrews do not need our law; they have plenty of laws. The Jews built cities and armies long before Rome existed. Yet we tax them beyond measure and steal the best of their oil and wine for an emperor who already has more than he needs. The quest for greater power is a demon named lust!" Cassius then spit into the flames to emphasize his point.

Arrius nervously guffawed. "These are *not* the words I would

CHAPTER 13

Several Weeks Later, 26 AD, the Marketplace in Jerusalem

"Are you following me, Roman? Everywhere I turn, I find you watching me and lurking in the shadows." Ayla was as bold as she was beautiful. She had cornered and confronted Arrius at the narrow entrance to the market.

Arrius tried to sound brusque. "Romans do not *lurk*, woman, and what if I am following you? I am the *optio* of the Italian Cohort of the Tenth Legion!"

"*Optio*? What a strange word."

"It means I am appointed by our centurion, Cassius the Great, as second in command."

It was apparent to Ayla that Arrius was trying to impress her, and she could tell he wasn't nearly as gruff as he pretended.

"Romans are Romans. You all look, sound, and smell the same to me," she said with the hint of a teasing smile.

Ayla had noticed Arrius for months. More than once, she caught him staring at her. In fact, of all the legionary occupiers of her country, this one seemed to be almost everywhere she went. At first, Ayla worried he had nefarious intentions. Her cousin was raped by a legionary several years ago, but he never got punished. In her culture, that act would get a man stoned to death, but the

Romans had their laws and did as they pleased.

There was something different about this Roman, she realized. Ayla began to see him as her personal guard. No one dared mistreat her in the market when he was near. Merchants treated her with more respect and bargained less aggressively, or so it seemed when the legionary was close. As strange as it was to her, she also began to have dreams about Arrius.

One night, the dream was so vivid she thought it was real. She saw Arrius on his knees, weeping. He cried out to Yahweh, the God of all Hebrews, and asked for forgiveness. She heard a voice from heaven speak to this legionary in her dream, "Rise. You are free. Take your place in my kingdom, which surpasses Rome's."

Of course, the thought, let alone the sight, of a broken and humble legionary was beyond bizarre. And the words spoken to Arrius were something she would never have expected to hear from Yahweh to any Roman.

Ayla was so close to him that she hoped he could smell her perfume, a mix of frankincense, opopanax, and myrrh. The scent of warm balsamic and the sweet honey-like fragrance overwhelmed most men.

Arrius stepped back a bit, took a breath, wiped some sweat from his brow, and said, "How I look, sound, and smell to you is no concern to me, woman."

Ayla knew Arrius was still trying to sound harsh and detached, like a typical legionary, but his eyes betrayed him. She enchanted him, and Ayla saw something tender buried deep within him.

"Why do you keep calling me *woman*? I do not like it when you do so. My name is Ayla."

Arrius hesitated as if he was embarrassed or surprised by her chastisement, and he looked down as he whispered, "Your name is Ayla Rose…meaning moonlight."

The moment was awkward for Ayla. The way this legionary said her name felt like a fresh breeze on a smoldering summer day or like honey poured on warm bread. She was shocked and wondered, *He knows more about me than I do about him. What is happening here?*

"My name has nothing to do with moonlight, Roman. In Hebrew, it is a variant of Elijah, one of our greatest prophets. Only the Arabs define my name as moonlight. And what is your name? It seems only fair—"

He interrupted her, "Arrius. My name is Arrius."

Playfully she said, "And should I call you *Optio* Arrius?"

Arrius looked down at his sandals. "You may call me whatever you desire, Ayla."

A strong breeze blew her hair across her face at that moment, and Ayla began to feel uncomfortably vulnerable with this man. So, without a word, she gathered her dress, quickly turned, and bolted away in a small cloud of dust. Something beyond words happened between them, and she was both exhilarated and terrified.

When Ayla was a stone's throw away, she looked back at Arrius and saw his stunned expression but continued on her way nonetheless.

And after she rushed off, Arrius scratched his head, cursed, and said out loud, "By the gods! What did I do wrong?"

A voice behind Arrius startled him. "You have frightened her, Arrius."

Arrius turned to find another fellow legionary leaning against a wall. This was the second time a fellow legionnaire had caught him gawking at Ayla.

"How long have you been there, Marcus? Sneaking around me will get you cut by my gladius."

"Long enough to see how that skinny Hebrew consumes you." Marcus wagged his finger, "And your rusty sword could never scare me."

"We will see, Marcus. But you would be wise to use caution with me, for I am annoyed and looking for a good fight. Stalk me again, surprise me once more, and you will become intimately acquainted with my not-so-rusty-and-very-sharp weapon!"

Marcus raised both hands in surrender. "*Pax* to you, Arrius. I was simply on my way to the tavern outside the wall when I saw you engaged with that Hebrew. I was prepared to come to your assistance if needed," Marcus said with a smirk.

"I know well what the Roman male mind is like, Marcus, so trust me when I say that I will *never* need *your* help."

"We use women, Arrius; they do not use us." Marcus clicked his tongue. "Yet it seems to me that she has you by the nose like a bull taken to slaughter. "

Arrius's neck and forehead veins became more prominent, and his jaw tightened. "Marcus, I will say it one more time and slowly because I know you are dull of mind. She is of no concern to you, and what I do is none of your business."

"Ah, but we are Romans, legionaries, and brothers-in-arms; *your* concerns are *my* concerns. I am duty-bound to protect you." Marcus then nodded his head and lifted his right arm to his chest in a mock salute.

Arrius sighed, looked down the road in the direction Ayla departed, and said, "If you are duty-bound to protect me, then protect my choice to love whom I love."

Marcus shook his head, picked at a scab on his forearm, and cursed when it started to bleed. "Mark my words, brother, this will not end well. How could it?"

Chapter 14

Months Later, 27 AD,

the Road to the Antonia Fortress, Jerusalem

Arrius's brother had died almost nine years before, and he had been reassigned to the Italian Cohort in Judea nearly four years ago. What he once believed was a punishment from the gods, being sent to Jerusalem, was now a great source of joy to him. At the center of his happiness was Ayla Rose.

Arrius's centurion, Cassius, became like a big brother to him. It was clear to Arrius that Cassius still did not approve of Ayla, so it became his mission to help Cassius better understand his past and his love for a Jew.

After drinking one evening, Cassius and Arrius were walking back to the barracks located in the Antonia Fortress. Herod the Great built this citadel in honor of his ally, Roman General Mark Antony, on the northwestern corner of the Temple Mount. It housed over six hundred legionaries in the barracks.

Arrius asked Cassius, "Did you know I was raised by a Roman senator and his wife?"

"No, I did not."

"Their names were Amadeus and Claudia."

Cassius shrugged his shoulders and said with a smile, "Well, that explains two things."

"What?"

"Your love for expensive wine and why you are so soft and spoiled."

Both men laughed.

"I did love the Roman Po Valley wine a bit too much, but those days are behind me now, thanks to you. But as far as being soft—"

At that moment, Arrius tackled Cassius like a Greek wrestler, and the two of them brawled in the dirt until Arrius ended up in a chokehold and surrendered. Cassius was older and not as strong as Arrius, but his experience as a battle-tested warrior always proved to be too much for Arrius.

As they dusted themselves off, Cassius asked, "So I am curious, how is it you became the son of a Roman senator?"

"As you know, I once belonged to one of the fiercest tribes in Germania."

Cassius slapped his friend on the back, smiled, and said, "Of course you did."

"I have a vivid memory of what happened even though I was just a young boy. My brother told me the story many times to remind me of our tribal family origins."

Arrius began to recount the story to Cassius. "Gustav—that was my brother's boyhood name in Germania—and I often left our village to hunt or fish. We were brothers born for adventure. One day, we had wandered farther than usual, and we heard horses coming our way, so we hid in the bushes. I had never seen a Roman, but that was about to change."

"It was part of the Roman cavalry?"

"Yes, a small group of three legionaries moved slowly searching for something."

"Or someone," said Cassius.

"We were afraid but felt secure in our hiding spot. However, either a flash from my brother's ax or our smell—which was strong"—both men chuckled—"gave us away."

"Before we knew it, the legionaries surrounded us and were yelling in their ugly Latin tongue at us. We had no idea what they intended. We had heard stories of women being taken, and Gustav told me once that Romans ate little boys, so we fought them with the fury of a badger. Both of us were kicking, biting, and cursing as a large legionary grabbed my brother, and another man nabbed me by the scruff of my neck. The soldiers threw us on our bellies atop their horses."

Cassius chuckled, "Obviously, they did not eat you, but I might have."

"No, they did not. But my brother continued to give them a fight. The last thing I heard Gustav say before the Roman hit him on the head to shut him up was, 'I will soil you and your filthy animal, and then I will remove chunks from your leg with my teeth!' Apparently, the centurion had learned a bit of our language over his years fighting in the north, and he knew Gustav was cursing him. I think that is why he hit my brother in the back of the head hard and knocked him out."

"Many years later, we were told by our Hebrew nanny that the Roman senator and his wife had traveled north to visit the troops and assess the war, which, as you know, was not unusual. The Roman Senate often sends a representative to spy on the generals. It seems politics and war always go hand in hand. But they also were in search of a child."

"You had a Jew for a nursemaid?" Cassius asked with surprise.

"Yes, as fate and the gods would have it, her name was Ayla, too, but I will tell you her story another time."

"Very well; carry on, Arrius."

"So the senator and his wife had two missions: check on the battle and its commanders and take a trophy child home. They were childless. Adopting a child into a family was rare in Rome. Most of the orphans ended up as beggars and thieves living on the filthy streets. Adopting an impoverished outcast from the streets would be an embarrassment. However, finding—or stealing—a child from an enemy was acceptable. And if the child was young, healthy, and showed potential, he could end up in a respected Roman family."

"So that became your fate," said Cassius.

"Yes, my blue eyes and handsome features apparently made me desirable to the senator's wife. But we found out from Claudia, years later, that the senator thought Gustav was too old, too feisty, and too ugly."

Arrius laughed with a snort and then continued, "Claudia had a soft heart, and she somehow knew I would never survive without my brother, so he was spared, and they took both of us into their home as new sons of Rome."

Cassius nodded and placed a hand on Arrius's shoulder as they continued to walk.

"There is a bit more to this story if you are interested."

"Continue. Please tell me everything, Arrius."

"We were two days' ride from the senator's encampment. As the soldiers set up camp the first night, Gustav, always the fighter, was formulating an escape plan. We hoped the Romans would drink themselves into a deep sleep. My brother told me that the only hope for us would be to run in the middle of the night and hide. Of course, the Romans would look for us. Our escape would necessitate backtracking to a stream we had crossed earlier in the day. To lose the Romans would require walking for hours in cold water filled with slippery rocks. Tracking us would be too easy otherwise.

"Gustav told me, 'Agi, when they sleep, we run!'

"The soldiers had bound our hands behind our backs with leather straps and our feet as well. But my hands were free enough to untie Gustav's hands when we sat back-to-back. It took some time and effort, but we got loose and then ran into the forest. Fortunately, the moon was full enough for us to see our path once we made it to the woods, so we ran fast and hard. We did not stop running for what seemed like hours until we reached the stream."

Cassius whistled and rubbed his large, calloused hands together. "So what happened then?"

"We knew our village was downstream, but we also knew the Romans would realize that as well."

"Whichever direction you chose, the legionaries would split up and pursue you," said Cassius.

"I know that now, but we did not know that then. We figured the Romans would expect us to go downstream toward our home, so we set off in the middle of the stream, moving up the hill with the plan to circle back later.

"The water, snowmelt from high in the mountains, was cold—painfully cold—but we pressed on. I was exhausted and complaining until we heard metal on metal. Roman metal.

"'Cursed Roman dogs,' Gustav whispered as we ducked behind a boulder. Then, from behind us and further upstream, we heard the gruff voice of the centurion speaking in our native tongue, 'You tribal water rats have cost us a day. Did you think you could outrun us? We have tracked others—many others—far smarter than you two.'

"As we turned in horror, no more than forty paces from us, the Roman centurion sat on his horse, gloating. We started to run in the opposite direction, but the two other soldiers came at us from downstream. After looking for us and not seeing any signs, the two legionaries circled back to join their centurion."

"Your escape was a valiant effort for two young boys, Arrius."

The two walked on for a time in silence. As the men passed an oxcart hauling vegetables to market, Arrius spoke quietly. "After being recaptured, we lost all hope of freedom. I will never forget the moment we looked at each other, wondering what would become of us. Gustav said he expected death or slavery, but I had no idea what lay ahead."

"A tragic tale," said Cassius. "No one should be taken forcibly from their family and home."

Arrius looked away in embarrassment. "I have never known more fear or shame than I did that day as I told Gustav, 'I am to blame. Everything evil is always my fault.'"

Cassius slapped the back of Arrius's head and said, "Arrius, as long as I have known you, you always overthink everything and take the blame for things that are not your responsibility. You were a young boy caught in a horrible situation that you could not do anything about. I will never understand—"

"No, you will never understand the curse I live with or the burden I carry. Long before our capture, I was responsible for the death of my mother and father."

Cassius groaned and said, "Well, finish the story if you wish."

"Not now, centurion. Another time."

Arrius wanted to tell Cassius about his surrogate mother, Claudia, and the abuse he suffered from the senator. He wished he could explain about his Hebrew nanny, Ayla, in hopes it would help Cassius understand more about his love for Ayla Rose, but his heart was too heavy with shame to continue.

As they arrived at the barracks, Arrius complained, "It is cold. It is late and past your bedtime, old man." He tried to deflect the piercing black eyes of his mentor and friend.

"Very well. Another time then," said Cassius.

Arrius started to walk away but then turned to Cassius. Fighting back his emotions, he said, "I have never told my story to any man because I have never trusted anyone but my brother."

"And I now have your confidence, Arrius?"

"You do, Cassius. You *absolutely* do." Arrius then came to attention and saluted his centurion out of both respect and admiration.

Cassius returned the salute and then spoke with compassion. "Many men live with lies woven into their souls by loss and tragedy, Arrius. It is evident to me that a dark thread of untruth is buried deep in your heart. You are not cursed, my friend, but what *I* believe pales in comparison to what *you* think, and I wonder what it will take for you to live free."

Arrius nodded and turned again to walk away; he, too, pondered if freedom was even possible.

CHAPTER 15

Many Months Later, 27 AD, Jerusalem

Weeks became months, and Arrius and Ayla met every day at about the same time in the market. On many occasions, they met after supper and took secret walks outside the city walls. What had started as an awkward friendship between two people from radically different worlds grew into love—a forbidden love.

"My baby sister, Miriam, asked about you yesterday. The old gossips from the market talk of us often, I am told."

Ayla and Arrius walked together under a full moon along a trail in the Mount of Olives. The mount was a safe place for them to be alone. Located outside the walled city to the east and on a ridge that ran about a *mille passum* or about a thousand paces, it was quiet and peaceful. This time of year, hundreds of olive trees were in bloom with small white, unscented, yet beautiful blossoms.

"If my sister says something to my father, I fear what he will do."

"Marcus and Cassius have stopped asking me about you. They do not understand me or my love for you."

Ayla stopped, turned to face Arrius, took his other hand in hers, and said, "You *love* me?" The moonlight glowed on her face, and her eyes sparkled as they grew full of tears.

"Of course, I love you. I have *always* loved you. My heart aches when I am not with you and beats as fast as a gazelle when you are near."

Her arms encircled Arrius as she passionately kissed him and then whispered, "What are we to do? I am a Hebrew woman. You are a Roman and a barbarian by birth. Ours is a love beyond reason and forbidden by your law and mine."

Ayla began to cry in his arms as they held each other for a long time.

"Ayla?"

She was afraid to speak, move, or do anything that might rob them of this moment.

"Ayla Rose?"

She stepped back and looked up into his eyes. "Yes, my love."

"I have faced death and countless men in battle. I have suffered immense physical pain and torment. I have lost so much, but I cannot lose you or live without you. You are the candlelight in my darkness. Your touch brings the sunrise to my broken and shadowy soul."

"And you are a gift to me, Arrius, but we risk *everything* to love one another. I will be shunned by my own father and hated by my people. And what will Cassius do?"

"Cassius understands our situation. He, too, once loved a woman. He knows me. He trusts me. Cassius will do whatever he can on our behalf."

They started up the hill again, arms around each other's waist and connected at the hip, saying little until they reached the edge of the olive grove. The wind was warm, and the breeze light with a hint of flowering hyacinth.

"I have prayed for wisdom and direction from Yahweh. Somehow—and this makes no sense to me—but somehow a deep shalom comes over me whenever I pray for you. I know he has great plans for you, Arrius, and I feel Yahweh's *chara*—His overwhelming joy—when we are together."

Arrius and Ayla had spoken many times about her faith and her God.

"Ayla, I am not surprised by your prayers but a bit startled by your belief that somehow your Yahweh could play a role in my life. You know I cannot convert to Judaism. My gods would reject me. Anyway, I cannot bear the thought of circumcision."

Ayla nervously laughed and punched him in the arm. "Speaking of circumcision with a woman is probably inappropriate, but I have no false hopes, Roman. I am not sure our priests would accept you."

Arrius's voice uncharacteristically quivered with emotion. "Can *you* love and accept me as I am?"

Ayla smiled and said, "I already have, Arrius. My love for you comes without conditions. Regarding your lack of faith, Yahweh has a long history of surprising people—even pagans like you. However, we must both weigh the costs. The price of our love might be more than we can imagine."

Arrius looked up toward the stars, sighed, and said, "Does your god curse people?"

"At times in the past He has. Why?"

Arrius had never spoken of his fears to Ayla. "Will your god curse you for loving me? The thought of you being hurt or killed because of me is more than I can bear."

"Who knows the mind and thoughts of Yahweh? But this much I do know: *You* are worth the risks. *We* are worth the risks. To not be with you is an anguish I cannot imagine."

From the top of the mount and through the grove of olive trees, they could see what looked like a thousand glowing candles in the city.

"Ayla?"

"Yes."

"I am yours. Regardless of the cost. Despite what may or may not happen. I am yours forever if you will have me."

At that moment, Ayla did something she had never done before with Arrius—she sang to him. Her enchanting voice poured out of her soul and pierced the night like a million stars as she slowly and continuously circled and danced around Arrius with her right hand never leaving his body.

My beloved is mine, and I am his;
he browses among the lilies.
Until the day breaks
and the shadows flee,
turn, my beloved,
and be like a gazelle
or like a young stag
on the rugged hills.[1]

1 Song of Solomon 2:16–17

Ayla stopped circling directly in front of Arrius, and she gazed up into his eyes—eyes heavy with tears.

"What is it, Arrius? What brings waterworks to your strong Roman eyes?"

Arrius looked to the sky. "The last time a woman sang to me was a thousand leagues away and many summers ago when my oldest sister did so for me as a boy."

Ayla put her head on Arrius's chest and heard his heart beating.

Arrius stroked her hair with his left hand and asked, "What was that beautiful song? The melody and words are not of this world."

Ayla stepped back and looked again into a face far gentler than she'd ever seen on Arrius. "It is a song of my people from the Tanakh—our holy scriptures—a song of love and affection, and it is a vow of my heart to yours."

"Will you have me as your mate, Ayla? I cannot imagine my life without you."

"No priests of my people will bind us, Arrius, and I cannot participate in a pagan marriage ritual. But here and now, my heart and life are yours forever. I *will* have you if you will choose me."

Arrius lifted her off the ground and held her above his head with his strong hands on her hips and waist. She laughed until he lowered her to kiss his lips again. She wrapped her arms around his neck as she drank in his love.

Arrius lowered Ayla to the ground and brushed the hair from her face. His words were filled with emotion. "Here and now, we are bound together forever as husband and wife."

Ayla replied, "You are my *bashert*."

Arrius smiled and cocked his head a bit sideways. "*Bashert*? What does that mean?"

"It means *soulmate* in Hebrew, Arrius, and from this moment on, you are and always will be my *bashert*."

"And you, Ayla Rose, are in Latin what we call an *anima sal-it*—my twin flame—and the mirror of my soul."

She wiped a joyful tear from her cheek and leaned her head against his chest again.

Forbidden or not—accepted by others or not—their love would face whatever storms and challenges might come. But neither could begin to fathom the difficulties looming on the dark horizon.

Chapter 16

One Year Later, 28 AD, Jerusalem, Home of Arrius and Ayla

I saw my sister again as I passed by the temple today. For a moment, she made eye contact with me, but then she quickly looked away. I knew my father would reject me; I had hoped, however, given time, my sisters would not. I practically raised them." Ayla was heartbroken and could not hide her tears from Arrius.

Arrius made a fist and shook his hand in the air. "Your family treats you like a leper. Why must they be so harsh to their own blood?"

As expected, the only wedding ceremony they celebrated was that warm night in the olive grove. Unsanctioned by both their worlds, their union was, nonetheless, a bond that could not be broken.

"I have provided you a good home. I care for you more than my own life. All that I desire is to spend the rest of my life with you as your husband and the father of our children. I cannot help that I was born a barbarian or stolen away by Rome to serve her. *Why* should anyone…*how* could anyone stand against our love?"

"The law is the law, and I knew the repercussions of my choice. My father has disowned me and treats me as a pagan. None of that is a surprise to me, and I have no regrets, Arrius. Do you?

Do you want to run from me? Have I ruined your life?"

Arrius shook his head no as his eyes softened. "I have no regrets, and I will never run *from* you, only *to* you, my love. But it is a mystery to me how any father could reject his child, let alone one as beautiful and loving as you."

"The ways of my people are steeped in tradition, and the Torah is clear regarding such matters."

Arrius complained, "And you still cling to your god as a foolish child clings to a worn-out blanket for security."

"*He* is Yahweh. I am not. *He* is Creator and Lord. I am not. But I know Yahweh has not forsaken me or us."

"Your god is weak and worthless if He cannot care for you better than I do."

Ayla grieved the loss of her family connections, but even more so over the hardened heart of her husband toward her God.

"The ways of Yahweh are mysterious. Who am I to question Him? I pray you will not reject our Heavenly Father simply because my earthly father has rejected me."

Arrius raised his voice. "You are not allowed to worship *your* god with *your* people. You are not allowed to offer Him sacrifices in *your* temple. In fact, you are treated like a prostitute and an outcast by *your* people. Perhaps Mars or Apollo would be better gods for you to serve!"

Ayla paused as she pondered how to best respond to her angry husband. "As Job once said, 'Though Yahweh slay me, I will trust in Him.' Arrius, I cannot turn my back on the Lord. I am what I am because of Him."

The two had been here many times before, but it never ended

in meanness.

Arrius took a deep breath and wiped some sweat from his brow. "You are as stubborn as you are beautiful, Ayla."

With a knowing grin, she quickly countered, "And you are as thick-headed as the walls of Jerusalem. But there is something else I wish to share with you, Arrius."

Arrius said, "I am tired of debate and need to return to my men in the barracks. I must go, Ayla. Can we discuss this later?"

Ayla had a twinkle of delight in her eyes. "As you wish. You did, however, bring it up already."

"And what have I mentioned that merits *that* look?"

"What look?" Ayla teased.

"That look! You know what I speak of, woman. Out with it."

"Well, you did mention something about being the father of our *children*," she said as she patted her belly.

"Are you suggesting I take all this armor off to bed you now? My joy, I told you I truly must go. We can talk about and perhaps work on starting our family when I return this evening."

"Too late for *talk*, Roman."

Arrius stammered, "Wait. Are you? Are we? I thought…I mean…I knew—"

Ayla interrupted, "Yes, I am four moons pregnant. Did you think I was getting fat? What did you expect would be the outcome of making love to me almost every other day?"

Ayla had never seen Arrius blush or at a loss for words. "Before the harvest time, you will be a father. You see, Yahweh has not forsaken us."

Arrius sat, almost collapsed, on a wooden stool, unable to take his eyes off Ayla's belly.

"Well, say something, Arrius. Are you pleased?"

Arrius wasn't smiling and looked overwhelmed to Ayla.

"Arrius, have I disappointed you? We spoke of having children. I thought—"

Arrius interrupted, "No, I am not disappointed. I wanted this for you, for us. I just was not prepared. I am sorry, Ayla. Forgive me."

"Forgive you for causing me to be with child?"

"No, forgive me for not knowing what to say. I have never been a father before. As a young legionary, I was trained to prepare for anything and everything, but I have had no preparation for this moment. I do not know how to express what I am feeling."

"Arrius, you will make a wonderful father."

"But…what…what if?" Arrius turned away from Ayla.

"Arrius, my love, why does it feel like a cold shadow has entered our home? What is going on? You *must* tell me, Arrius. Please."

Arrius bowed his head, looking ashamed to Ayla. Clearly, as a soldier, she knew he believed fear should be ignored, but he could not hide his heart from her.

"What if you do not survive the birth? What if my curse becomes my son's curse?"

Ayla moved to stand in front of Arrius and lifted his head in her hands. Tears were forming in his eyes. "This child is a gift. *You* are a gift, and you are *not* cursed, and neither is your son."

"How can you be so sure? I cannot imagine my life without you. What if—?"

Ayla placed a finger on his lips to silence him. "I know you do not yet believe in Yahweh. I know you have no confidence in Him or His care for us, but I have His promise of protection. I know in my soul that all will be well."

Arrius took her in his arms and buried his head in her breasts as he whispered, "Can I pray to your god? Will He hear me? What sacrifice can I offer Him to break the power of my curse?"

"Yahweh hears all prayers offered to Him in faith, even the prayers of an old Roman like you. You will be like our father Abraham, who had many sons in his old age." She kissed the top of his head.

Arrius exhaled as he placed his hand on her belly and prayed, "May the god of your mother and the gods of my people protect and keep this little one. And may our child never suffer from the blood curse I have carried all my life."

Tears streamed down Ayla's angelic face as she spoke, "Husband, I have never heard you pray to anyone; that you now acknowledge Yahweh gives me great hope."

Arrius looked up into Ayla's deep brown eyes.

She cupped his face in her hands as she tenderly said, "I do not fear death. I do not fear giving birth. But I wonder what it will take for the love of my life to be free from what burdens him with such deep shame."

Arrius turned his face away, and his entire body tensed as he muttered through a clenched jaw, "Nothing and no man can set me free. I am bound to this curse forever."

Chapter 17

Year 28 AD, Jerusalem, the Antonia Fortress

Cassius could tell something was wrong. He had known Arrius long enough and knew him well enough to know he was either angry or frustrated—or both.

"What ails you, Centurion Arrius? I have seen legionaries who lose their best friends in battle look happier than you."

Arrius looked away. "I do not want to talk about it."

"I do not care," chided Cassius.

"Leave it alone, Cassius; I am not in the mood for your witty banter."

"Have you been fighting with that Hebrew woman?"

"Her name is Ayla. I hate it when you say *Hebrew* like it is a disease."

"I mean no disrespect to Ayla, but it will take this old centurion time to think differently about any Jew. You must admit, Arrius, they are a strange and troublesome people."

"No more so than every North African I have met."

Both men chuckled, and it relieved some of the tension in the room.

Cassius got a faraway look in his eyes and said, "I met my first

Hebrew in Alexandria many years ago. He was a merchant my father did business with almost every week."

"And what did your father do?" asked Arrius.

"Besides bed every African woman he could, get drunk every night on beer, and beat me on a regular basis?" This was the first time Cassius told Arrius anything about his father or his childhood.

Arrius said with a smile, "I know *proper* Romans consider beer equivalent to camel urine, but beer is what my father drank, too, and far too much."

Cassius laughed. "Germanic men do love their beer, but I will take the honey wine of my land over that bitter poison any day."

"Poison is poison, I suppose. I know the cost of my past excesses," said Arrius.

Cassius understood and agreed, "Yes, the nectar of the gods is both a gift and a curse. My father was a harsh man when he was sober, but too much beer made him mean."

Cassius grabbed his gladius and a sharpening stone to distract himself from the uncomfortable conversation. Speaking about his father was not something he was accustomed to. In the African culture, talking dishonorably about your elders was not allowed, no matter how vile they were.

"So, tell me, besides beating you, what did your father do, Cassius?"

"He was a spice merchant. My father sometimes traveled great distances to collect bay leaves, cumin, ginger, and cinnamon. His specialty, however, was selling the lesser-known *grains of paradise* he found in West Africa."

"My brother, Justus, once gave me some of those grains to stop my bowels from flowing through, and two weeks later, he applied the same thing in some potion to one of his wounds."

"My father said they could do anything from stopping stomach pains to purging the body of worms. He made most of his income from those grains, and the Jews could not get enough of them."

Cassius continued to rub each edge of his sword blade in long strokes on the stone without making eye contact with Arrius. But he thought to himself, *Arrius now knows why I could not give up on him; we share the curse of angry fathers.*

"Cassius?"

Cassius tried to ignore him. He was not sure how he felt speaking any more about his father.

Arrius leaned in. "Cassius?"

Cassius looked up and set his gladius in his lap. "What? What do you need from me that is more important than the edge of this sword?"

"Nothing. Forgive me, my friend. I did not mean to bring up your past."

Cassius shook his head and said, "If you erase your past, you erase the wisdom of your present. I rarely speak of my father, but I will never forget the lessons I learned despite him."

Arrius sighed. "You asked me what ails me, and I will tell you. I fear that I will become an angry and violent father to my child."

Cassius reached out to touch the shoulder of Arrius. He knew this day and this conversation would eventually come. From the first day of Arrius's love for Ayla Rose, Cassius knew it was only a matter of time before she would be pregnant. "Is Ayla with child?"

"Yes, four moons now, but she only told me this morning. How could she let this happen? The child will be of mixed blood and torn between two worlds. Boy or girl, the baby will be rejected by everyone. The Jews will hate the child because of me, and the Romans will despise the child because of her."

Arrius stood, growled, and slammed his fist into his hand as he began to pace. "I have no time to be a father and far less time to live than she does because I am many years older than her. I may be blind or crippled before the child comes of age! Besides, I barely survive on what little Rome pays me now. And for the love of the god, I am a centurion who could die in my next battle."

Cassius stood directly in front of Arrius, placed both hands on Arrius's burdened shoulders, and looked into the troubled eyes of his dearest friend. "Arrius, your future needs you; your past does not."

"What?" Arrius asked, shaking his head. "What are you saying?"

"Your *future* needs you, but your *past* does not."

"I heard your words, Cassius, but what are you trying to tell me? Sometimes you dribble on like an old woman."

"Arrius, you and I cannot undo what has been done to us. We grew up abused and beaten by men who themselves were probably mistreated by their fathers. Sadly, there is nothing we can do about our past. However, your future as a man, a husband, and a *father* is not like this hard sharpening stone but more like the edge of this weapon—changeable and able to improve if you desire it."

"But what if—"

Cassius grew frustrated and cut him off, "I beg you, Arrius.

Stop being a victim who is enslaved to his past or present circumstances and start envisioning the person I know you can *become*."

Arrius threw up his hands, stepped around Cassius, and began to pace again. "But *can* I be a good father? *Can* I change? *Can* I overcome the curse I have carried my entire life?"

"Of course, you *can*, Arrius, but what remains to be seen is, *will* you? If Rome has taught you and me anything, she has shown us that victims can become victors. Look at us. Stolen. Abused. Enslaved. But you and I rule other fighting men and even an entire city now."

Arrius stopped again and dropped his shoulders. "The cursed live at the mercy of the gods, who are heartless beings that seem to find pleasure in our pain. We are but playthings to the immortals who exist to satisfy either their wrath or their lust. And no god has yet revealed himself to me in a way worthy of my adoration, let alone my trust."

Cassius spoke solemnly, "I pray to my ancestors that someday you will find your path. A godless life is a hopeless life. I know the demons call to you from the shadows and the curse of your father is like a millstone around your neck. But the gods can help mere mortals break the cycle of darkness if we let them do so."

"Perhaps, Cassius, but I fear it is too late for me. Hope abandoned me long ago."

Chapter 18

Several Weeks Later, 28 AD, Jerusalem, the Antonia Fortress

Arrius was troubled and barely looked at Cassius as he sat down on an old wooden chair next to the fire and asked, "How are things at home? Are you doing any better with the idea of fatherhood?"

Arrius fluttered about like a bird trapped in a cage. "Yes. No. I do not know. At times I feel completely overwhelmed, but when I see Ayla's belly growing before my eyes, I get excited."

"Have you felt the baby move yet?"

"No, not yet. I am afraid to even touch Ayla for fear of hurting the baby."

Cassius laughed and said, "You will need to get over that fear, or it will be a very long pregnancy for you."

"Can we please talk about something—*anything*—else?" grumbled Arrius, who felt at the same time irritated and comforted by his friend's intrusion on his thoughts.

Cassius smiled and said, "So tell me more about what happened to you as a boy when your brother and you were abducted by the Romans in Germania."

Arrius knew his friend was trying to distract him. "I will tell you what I remember. Where did I leave off?"

Cassius rubbed his hands together. "You were recaptured and had just arrived at the senator's encampment."

Arrius rubbed his eyes, took off his gladius, and sat back in his chair.

"Upon arrival at the Roman campsite, my brother and I were stripped of our tattered clothes and forced to stand naked before the senator and his wife. We were miserable. It was so cold, there was frost on the ground, and we could see our breath. Of course, we could not understand any Latin at that time, but it was obvious that questions from Claudia, the senator's wife, came faster than the centurion could answer."

"Sounds like the typical Roman woman to me," added Cassius with a chuckle.

Arrius went on. "She wore a white gown that almost glowed in the sunlight. Except for a slight limp when she walked, Claudia was the picture of nobility and beauty. At that time, she was the tallest woman I had ever seen. Like most Mediterranean women, she had a narrow and slightly curved nose, olive complexion, black hair, and deep brown eyes."

"Quite different than what you were used to in Germania, I imagine."

"Yes, she was stunning. Years later, however, we found out that the limp came from being born breech and having her leg broken during birth. The leg healed, but because it was never set correctly, one leg was shorter than the other. Claudia did her best to hide this imperfection, but her attractiveness is what most men and women noticed first about her."

Arrius paused, put another log on the fire, and turned to warm the back of his legs. "Claudia and her husband, who was a much older man, were married when she was sixteen. Ayla, our Jewish nanny, once told us that over the first ten years of her marriage, Claudia had several miscarriages. Of course, the senator wanted a boy. Sons are what matter most to Roman men. And at twenty-six, when we first met her, she was desperate for a child too. Any child. Even a stolen and adopted one would do."

Arrius sat down and continued. "Many years later, we were surprised to find out the senator's slave, Ayla, was with us that fateful day even though I never saw her then. Claudia never traveled without servants, and Ayla was the senator's favorite cook. So she told us one night, in detail, everything that happened."

"Apparently, Claudia was initially concerned about my mental capacity."

"For good reason," Cassius said as he grinned.

"As Ayla told us the story years later, Claudia was asking why I was staring up at the sky and why I was not talking like my brother. Of course, as would be expected, Justus was cursing everyone and making crude comments about the legionaries. Apparently, the centurion assured her I was able to speak and only frightened. He also guaranteed both the senator and Claudia that we were strong and mentally sound."

"He lied again," said Cassius, with more sarcasm than Arrius was willing to tolerate.

"I had no idea that my brother was potentially within moments of being killed. He was too old and too belligerent for the senator. We could see the Romans going back and forth in conversation. Ayla said the legionaries wanted money for both of us even if the senator wanted my brother to be killed."

Cassius spit on the ground. "Typical Romans—all about money and murder. There is no honor in killing a child."

"Ayla told us, however, that from the moment Claudia laid eyes on us, she was drawn to both of us. Strangely, in her heart, I think she knew that killing my brother would have killed me."

"Strange that a Roman senator would listen to anyone, let alone his wife."

"I suppose, but Justus stood right next to me and was my obvious protector. In fact, he never took his hand off my shoulder during the entire experience. My eyes jumped from my brother's face to Claudia's. Back and forth. Back and forth. And every time I looked up at my brother, it was obvious there was an undeniable bond between us. Separating us would have been unbearable for me."

"Ayla would often remind us that Claudia told the senator that she could see something extraordinary in us. She told the senator she believed that we were *both* blessed by the gods."

Cassius rubbed his chin. "It is a mystery to me why, but the gods do seem to show favor to your people."

"Yes, well, thankfully, the senator conceded and kept us both, but he was only going to give Justus a month or so before deciding his long-term fate. The centurion then grabbed both of us by the scruff of the neck and dragged us to what would be our cage until we reached Rome."

"And how long did it take you to reach the city?"

"Far too long, and though Rome is famous for her roads, the first two weeks of the journey south was on anything but a road. The rough and muddy trails were challenging to manage and slow to traverse. Justus and I painfully experienced every bump, and besides being in a cage, we were chained to its side."

Cassius nodded.

"We were like wild animals snared in a hunter's trap," moaned Arrius.

"And every day took us farther and farther from home. At first, we did not understand adoption and assumed we were her slaves. Slavery is something we *did* understand, but we had no idea where they were headed. We only knew the beautiful, tall woman made it a point to bring us extra food every night, and she treated both of us with unexpected kindness."

"Kindness from any aristocrat is always surprising," chimed in Cassius.

"Yes, but for no apparent reason, the senator would frequently haul us out of the cage and beat us with a strap or a green branch. He rarely brought blood and generally applied the strap only to our butts and legs, but the pain was severe, nonetheless. It became clear that his intent was to break us."

"And did he? Were you broken?" asked Cassius.

As he swatted at a bug drawn to the warm fire, Arrius replied, "If by *break* you mean, did I eventually accept my new reality? Yes."

Cassius attempted to whack the same bug that now buzzed his head.

Arrius continued, "Justus, on the other hand, figured out the game and pretended to be compliant but remained defiant. I think Claudia saw right through his bold and strong veneer. I think she knew that he was a hurting boy who needed the love she could provide."

Cassius shifted in his seat. "It seems you grew to love her."

"I did, but for a long time, I was afraid and confused more often than not.

"One warm night, under a sky full of stars, Justus and I spoke quietly to each other. 'Brother?' I whispered.

"Justus was tired and said, 'What now? We need to sleep.'

"'This is all my fault, Brother, and I miss our home, Astra, and our sisters.'

"My brother spoke slowly and clearly, 'I know you miss them, but *nothing* is your fault.'

"'Do you think we will ever return to our people?'

"Justus did not hesitate. 'No, Little Brother, I fear our path has taken us far from all we once knew.'

"I started to cry and asked him, 'It seems we will be well cared for by the tall woman, yes? She does seem to love us, and we have never eaten better.'

"He complained, 'True, but we are still slaves.'

"'I think not, Brother; she treats us as sons.'

"Justus turned his back to me as he spoke through a clenched jaw, 'Yet her old husband treats us as captives.'

"We finally fell asleep. Our bellies were full, and my mind more at peace. I will admit to you that a small glimmer of hope began to grow in my heart."

Cassius put a hand on Arrius's shoulder. "It is a sad but moving story, Arrius. I am once again honored you shared it with me."

"And I am honored to tell it to you. You have earned my respect and my trust. But there is one more thing that happened on our way to Rome."

Cassius leaned in.

"The next morning, before dawn, we were startled by the sound of a wild animal just outside the camp. We assumed it must be a bear."

Cassius remarked, "We have no bears in my country, but I have heard the tales of their ferociousness."

"Yes, Cassius, they are both fierce and fearless.

"My brother, always my protector, whispered to me, 'Agi, stay still.'

"I probably spoke too loudly and said, 'A bear?'

"Justus nodded. 'Yes, and he sounds big.'

"With eyes as big as a millstone, I replied, 'And hungry!'

"Justus got that smile he always had when he was thinking something mischievous, 'Let us hope the gods have sent him to eat our captors.'

"I started to panic a little. 'But are we safe in this cage?'

"'No, we are *not* safe. A bear could rip these wooden bars open without any effort, but if he eats enough Romans, he might leave us be.'

"I nervously giggled just a bit but stopped when Justus gave me a harsh look and said, 'Don't move. Don't talk. No matter what happens. Even if the bear approaches the cage, do nothing. Say nothing.'

"It seemed like the bear rumbled around the campsite forever.

Staying still and barely breathing always seems to slow time."

"I remember a similar experience with a lion when I was a boy, but please carry on."

"Out of the corner of my eye, I saw fire and more movement. Much to our surprise, it was Claudia. She had approached the cage holding a sword in one hand and a torch in the other.

"She motioned for us to stay still. Come to find out later, the soldiers were hunting the bear who was stalking us."

"And did they kill him?"

"Yes. We ate bear meat for days. And in case you are wondering, bear is as tough as leather and more fat and gristle than meat. Still, food is food, especially when you are desperate to fill your belly with anything other than roots and berries."

Both men laughed knowingly.

Arrius looked up to a sky filled with stars and sighed. "From that moment on, that woman—our new mother—became special to me. It amazed me that this strange and beautiful Roman cared enough to put herself between us and danger."

Cassius then spoke words that Arrius never forgot, "You will risk all for someone you love more than your own life."

Arrius had no idea how those words would impact his life and pierce his heart in the not-so-distant future.

Chapter 19

Ten Months Later, 29 AD, Jerusalem, Home of Arrius and Ayla

Ayla looked perturbed to Arrius while she was nursing their son. After his birth and being sleep-deprived, Ayla was often irritable. She wiped a bit of breast milk from her son's cheek and said, "I cannot believe it took Rome so long to promote you to centurion."

Arrius knew why his advancement was slow in coming. Nonetheless, after some convincing, Pilate heeded Cassius's advice and promoted Arrius to the rank of centurion in the Italian Cohort of the Tenth Legion. Arrius also knew being a centurion in Jerusalem came with grave risks. Palestine was always one step away from conflict and disaster.

"You are a gift to me, Ayla, as you always believe in me. But how many times must we have this conversation? My foolish years of drunkenness in Syria after the death of my brother held me back. Besides, I was born a barbarian, and Rome has a long memory."

Ayla almost hissed, "Rome favors the rich and punishes the poor and the broken."

"As all men and all powers do," replied Arrius.

"Not *all*, Arrius, not everyone."

Arrius took a deep breath and clenched his jaw. "*Your* people do the same. The Pharisees and Sadducees are men of privilege. I have not met one among them worthy of their power or position. All power is bought, and all the powerful are corrupt."

"You are wrong, Arrius. I listened to a rabbi yesterday; His name is Yeshua, and He is a good leader. He accused the Sanhedrin of corruption. In fact, He called them vipers."

"And He was not stoned by them?"

"No. They may not like Him, but according to our law, He has done nothing to deserve death."

"Anyone who challenges that group of hypocrites should kiss his wife and family each night as if it were his last. Sounds like this rabbi has grabbed the tail of the snake, and His days are numbered."

Ayla shook her head. "Rome does not allow stoning, and rabbis are not killed by my people."

"Pontius Pilate grows weary of his post, your city, and your people. As the current prefect, he may not command a legion, but our garrison of auxiliary troops is itching for a fight. And frankly, Pilate walks a fine line between Rome and the Sanhedrin. If he fails here—the worst of all military assignments—he will be killed by the emperor. I have seen firsthand how the power game is played between Pilate and your leaders, and that puts *anyone* at great risk—even a rabbi."

"As I said, Yeshua is a good man. His teaching is radical, but He speaks as a prophet, and His words are life-changing. He even heals the sick and blind."

"Ah, just what Jerusalem needs. Another Messiah to the rescue. And what does this rabbi say of Rome?"

Ayla shrugged her shoulders. "Nothing, except that we should pay our taxes."

Arrius laughed, "Now I know this rabbi is destined for death. Telling a Hebrew to pay taxes to Caesar will get Him killed for sure!"

Ayla looked at her husband. "Arrius, His teaching is quite different, but He speaks with unquestioned anointing from Yahweh. I was mesmerized and would still be listening to Him if I did not need to get home in time to prepare a meal."

Arrius rubbed some sweat from his brow. "Here, hand me the boy. I will show my son how to wield a sword while you wield a butcher's knife."

"You will not! Who amuses himself with something so sharp and dangerous as a gladius around an infant? Besides, our son will be a man of peace."

"I beg to differ with you, woman. He has barbarian blood in him. He is the son of Arrius. He is a son of Rome. He will—"

"He will be a man of shalom who learns to rule with his words, *not* with a sword."

Arrius was not sure how to respond to her. Having fought many battles in his life, Arrius knew the cost of being a man of war. Peace, however, was not his way, and he could not imagine a different world for his son.

Over a year earlier, the birth of their firstborn son, Seneca, brought Arrius more peace than he had ever experienced. Thankfully, Seneca's addition to their family was uneventful, and Ayla proved again to be an able and strong woman. Arrius's lifelong fear of being cursed began to fade for the first time in his life.

He looked gently into the eyes and smiling face of his son and said out loud, "How can anyone speak of *pax* in a place like this and in times like these? Who has put such foolish ideas into the head of your mother?"

"Yeshua."

Arrius sat down, dropped his chin to his chest, and sighed. "So a radical teacher who stirs the anger of your rulers and cracks a whip in your temple is a man of peace?"

Ayla squinted her eyes. "And how did you know what He did in the temple?"

"I know *everything* that happens in this city. You are not the first person to tell me stories of this…this rabbi."

"And what stories have you heard?"

"Oh, you mean the story of how He stopped a harlot from getting stoned to death and embarrassed a group of respected men in the process? Or perhaps how He *has* broken your laws by touching the untouchable? Or perhaps how He shamed a rich man who gave much to the temple while praising a widow who gave almost nothing?"

"Yeshua shames no one."

"Should I be worried about this Nazarene? Are you infatuated with Him, Ayla?" Arrius said with a teasing tone trying to lighten the mood in the room.

Ayla looked out the window. "Somehow…in a way I cannot explain and in a way like no other human ever has…Yeshua speaks to something deep within me." She then shook her head and giggled light-heartedly, "You, however, are stuck with me, our son, and this second baby who bruises my ribs from the inside!"

Arrius respected his wife more than she knew, and he valued her opinions, unlike most men did of their wives. "Do you actually think He is the Messiah and the Son of your god?"

"The people are torn. Some say yes. Some say no."

"What do you say, Ayla? What is in *your* heart?"

She spoke slowly and quietly, "My people have prayed for a Messiah for hundreds of years. We have prayed for a deliverer from our enemies. We have longed for Immanuel to come."

"And has He come?"

At that moment, Arrius watched as a swallow darted just outside the window, and a warm breeze blew through his home, carrying the smell of someone cooking food on a fire.

"Yes, my love. Yes, I believe He has come, Arrius. His spirit hovers over this city, and His words are carried on the wind to desperate hearts who long for hope, peace, and love."

Arrius embraced Ayla with their son and her growing belly sandwiched between them until Seneca complained.

"This rabbi of yours speaks of *pax* and doing good to those who persecute you. I hope he can walk the path he proclaims. He has chosen a dangerous way. You feel a beautiful day coming, but I see an evil storm approaching."

Ayla looked up into the kind eyes of her beloved. "Husband, you worry too much. But speaking of storms, have you heard how Yeshua once walked on the Sea of Galilee?"

Arrius smirked. "What do you mean 'walked on the sea'? Is this rabbi a ghost or a man?"

"A man, of course, but a very special man if the stories are true."

Arrius slapped his forehead. "And therein lies the issue."

Ayla scowled, "What *issue*?"

"The issue of truth. Are the stories true? Are His teachings true? Is this rabbi a true or false prophet?"

"And what do you know, Arrius, of false prophets? When did you become a student of Judaism?"

"One does not need to be a student of the ridiculous ways of your people to hear the rumors."

Ayla turned away from Arrius and busied herself with some bread dough she had left on the table. "The ways of Yahweh are true, and it wounds me when you call my faith *ridiculous*."

"Ayla, I am sorry. Sorry I do not understand. Sorry that I have offended you. Sorry I can be such a brute sometimes. But you know that I am a simple man who has no time for fables and myths."

Ayla again drew near to Arrius and said, "Perhaps you should hear the story before you judge it to be foolish."

Arrius wished he had someplace to go or something else to do, but he did not. "Okay, I surrender. Once again, your tongue and wit have overcome my insensitivities."

Arrius sat down on a stool with the baby on his lap. "So tell me this story of the rabbi who wades through water."

Ayla jumped up a bit and giggled like a teenage girl. "He did not wade *through* the water. He walked *on* it!"

"Hmmm. This is a story I must hear."

"Have you heard of Thomas? He is one of the twelve."

"No."

"Well, Thomas is a very logical and no-nonsense sort of man. On several occasions, I have heard him make comments indicating he is not easily fooled."

"I already like him. The world could use more men like him… and me."

"Hush. Let me tell you what Thomas told me. The rabbi had just performed an amazing miracle. He fed over five thousand people with just five barley loaves and two small fish."

"Rome should hire him to feed the legions."

Ayla glared at Arrius. "So, after the miracle, the rabbi sent everyone to their homes and villages. Some talked about making Yeshua king right then and there, but He would not allow them to do so."

"*King* Yeshua, huh?"

"Yes, but it is not His time. Thomas said the rabbi was exhausted—"

Arrius interrupted, "I suppose performing miracles will do that to any man."

"Are you going to listen or not, Arrius?"

"Go on."

"As I said, Yeshua was tired, and as He often did, He withdrew from everyone to be alone with Yahweh—"

"And take a nap."

"Interrupt me again, husband, and you will be sleeping in the barracks with your men tonight."

Arrius sat up straight on his stool.

Ayla pointed her finger at Arrius. "You must understand that Thomas is not someone who would fabricate a story."

"Yes, and I still like him. Maybe he is Germanic by blood."

Ayla rolled her eyes. "Well, Thomas said Yeshua told him and the disciples to take a boat and go to the other side of the lake. They had rowed for hours and were somewhere in the middle of the lake, straining against the oars because a strong wind was against them. Then, just before the sun rose over the hills, they saw something or someone walking *on* the water. Not swimming. Not in another boat. Walking! This person—and they did not know it was the rabbi yet—was about one or two hundred paces from them, and He looked like He was going to keep walking right on by the men. And guess what they thought."

Arrius shrugged his shoulders. "They thought they were all dreaming?"

"No. They thought the rabbi was a *ghost*, and they were terrified."

"I would have pulled my gladius out, but I would not have panicked."

Ayla continued, "Of course, it was Yeshua. Thomas said He called out to them to have courage and to not be afraid. That is so like the rabbi."

"And then what happened?"

"Yeshua climbed into the boat, Arrius."

Arrius pretended to be amazed. "And were His sandals wet?"

Ayla threw her hands into the air. "You are hopeless! I do not know why I bother with you. I do not know or care about His sandals. But there was another miracle that happened. The moment

He entered the boat, the wind died down, and the sea immediately became as glass. Thomas said they were all shocked."

Ayla looked him in the eyes. "So what have you to say now, husband? What is that look on your face?"

Arrius lied, "It is the look of a hungry man. When will the bread be ready?"

Despite his jesting with Ayla, Arrius wondered, *If I were going to make up a story about some Messiah, it would be far more believable than a man walking on water. Who is this man?*

CHAPTER 20

Year 31 AD, Jerusalem, Near the Jaffa Gate

Mary Magdalene and Ayla sat together under the shadow of the largest Sycamore tree in the Holy City, rumored to be nearly three hundred years old. It was midday, hot, and windless. Flies circled several piles of donkey dung. The only movement in the narrow street before them was an occasional woman or slave transporting goods from the market.

Ayla squirmed and wiped the sweat from her brow with the sleeve of her gown. "This weather is unbearable. I have never—"

"Ayla, you didn't come to me to discuss the heat. Let us be honest with each other; something is bothering you, yes?"

"Why do I feel like you can see into my soul, Mary? Yes, I am…confused…and maybe upset by what I heard from Judas yesterday."

"Judas Iscariot?"

"Yes, he told me about the tax collector."

Mary gently laughed. "Which one? They seem to be multiplying like rodents around Yeshua."

Bewildered, Ayla turned her head sideways. "It hardly seems laughable. First, the rabbi invites Matthew into His circle, and now—"

"And now you have heard about Zacchaeus of Jericho?"

"I fear for the rabbi's reputation. He cannot allow—"

"One does not tell Yeshua what He can and cannot do, Ayla, and He has no concern for His reputation with the Sanhedrin."

"I know. Of course. But Judas said—"

"Judas has no place casting doubt on the rabbi's actions. His activities are suspect enough, in my humble opinion. Why Yeshua didn't put Matthew in charge of their treasury is a mystery to all of us. Matthew has experience managing money, and Judas does not."

Ayla exclaimed, "And Matthew, as a tax collector, has experience at cheating and lying to line his own pockets."

"Ayla, Matthew is a changed man and a friend. Please do not speak evil of him."

Ayla slumped her shoulders and sighed, "I am sorry, Mary. Forgive me."

"I do. And speaking of forgiveness, did Judas tell you the whole story of Zacchaeus?"

"No, only that Yeshua allowed another despised traitor to our people to follow Him."

"Judas has a way of leaving out the important details. Let me tell you what happened as we entered Jericho."

Mary took a drink of water from her goatskin and offered some to Ayla. The flies were becoming more of a nuisance in the heat and still air.

"We had traveled from Jerusalem to Jericho on the Way of Blood. That road has many robbers and horrible men. I was relieved we'd made it without incident. As always, the crowds were out by the hundreds—maybe the thousands—to catch a glimpse of the rabbi. We were hungry, thirsty, and tired. Somehow, Yeshua has the energy of ten men, and His pace is always strong and fast. However, and this always consistently amazes me, He has a way of stopping for things or people most of us would not bother with."

Ayla added, "Like blind beggars."

"Precisely. Like those rejected by everyone else."

Ayla nodded in agreement.

"So we were on the edge of the village when the rabbi raised His hand to stop us, and then He looked up into a sycamore tree, one smaller than this one but still large. At first, I just saw a tree, and I thought, *Now what? What is He looking at? A bird, perhaps?*"

Ayla giggled a bit. "Judas said Zacchaeus is not much bigger than a bird."

"Yes, he is a short and stumpy man, but he'd climbed up into the tree, nonetheless. He's also not a young man and absolutely too old to be found in a tree. Apparently, he did so to get above the crowds so he could see Yeshua."

"Quite undignified if you ask me."

"Agreed, Ayla, quite improper, but Yeshua has a way of… of making people do the unexpected. Well, anyhow, finding an old man in a tree was surprising, but what happened next stunned everyone."

"Judas said Zacchaeus invited the rabbi to his home. Unbelievable!"

"No, Judas is mistaken *again*. The rabbi invited Himself to the tax collector's home. I was standing right next to Yeshua when

He said, 'Zacchaeus, come down right now and take Me to your home.'"

"Why does He do that, Mary? What is He thinking?"

"Let me finish, and you will see."

Mary shifted her weight and bent her leg over her knee. "Zacchaeus was so happy that he practically fell out of the tree. All the Jews who'd come to see the rabbi began to complain that Yeshua was going to be the guest of a wretched sinner. Of course, the rabbi didn't care, and neither did Zacchaeus."

Mary took Ayla's hand in hers and looked Ayla in the eyes.

"We went to his home. We ate. We drank wine. And Yeshua did what He always does…He asked Zacchaeus many questions, and He listened to the man…truly listened with compassion. Then, and it is hard to describe, but then without any teaching or correction or confrontation by the rabbi, something happened."

"What? Tell me, Mary. What on earth happened?"

"I watched a nonverbal exchange between Yeshua and Zacchaeus that was not of this earth—it was beyond this world and so incredible."

"I don't understand, Mary."

"Frankly, I don't either, but somehow, in a moment's time, the heart of that old, lying, and cheating tax collector changed. It was as if a fire was lit in his very dark heart."

Ayla's eyes moistened. "I know that feeling…that moment with Him when everything changes."

The ladies shared a moment of reflective silence.

Mary smiled as her eyes widened. "But what happened next

shocked all of us. Zacchaeus stood up from his reclining cot where he was eating. He looked around the room and then gazed intently at the rabbi and said, 'Look, Lord! Here and now, I give half of my possessions to the poor, and if I have cheated anybody of anything, I will pay back four times the amount!'"

"Incredible! Judas did not tell me that part of the story."

Mary's brow furrowed. "Sadly, that man is too quick to judge and too slow to forgive as he has been forgiven."

"It is difficult for me, too, at times, Mary."

Mary stood and raised both her hands toward the sky. "I will never forget the words of the rabbi to Zacchaeus, 'Today salvation has come to this house because this man, too, is a son of Abraham,' as He pointed to a crying Zacchaeus." Then the rabbi scanned the room, making eye contact with all of us as He said, "How long will it take for you to understand that I came to seek and to save the lost?"

Ayla whispered, "The lost like me."

"The lost like *all* of us, Ayla, like every single one of us."

Mary sat back down as a breeze began to blow from the north, finally bringing some relief from the heat and the incessant flies.

"Mary, may I ask you something personal?"

"There is nothing too personal between us. You can always ask me anything."

As two Sadducees approached, Ayla fidgeted and quickly covered her head and face with her shawl. One of them, Aaron, she recognized as a friend of her father, but he passed by without engaging her.

"Are you all right? Did you know those men?"

"Yes, but it doesn't matter. No one from my old life acknowledges me anymore. I am dead to them."

"And it is those people who suffer the loss of a beautiful woman, but I am sad that you must endure their shameful treatment."

"I don't know if I will ever overcome their rejection."

"You will, Ayla. It will take time, but you will as I have."

"I am so sorry, Mary. Of course, you understand."

"So what is it you wanted to ask me?"

"This is personal—"

"Yes, you mentioned that; now speak, or I will take a greenstick off this tree and beat it out of you."

Both ladies laughed.

"Okay…have you…do you…do you have feelings for Yeshua?"

Mary gently shook her head from side to side as she looked off in the distance. "If by *feelings* you mean romantic feelings, the answer is no. Not now."

"Hmmm, and what does 'not now' mean?"

"Ayla, when the rabbi set me free, I was living in the backroom of a tanner's shop in Galilee. I cleaned up the entrails of dead animals for a living. To supplement my meager income, I also sold myself on the streets. But I had nothing. I was nothing. And my life was worth nothing. I wasn't welcome by Jew or Gentile."

Mary stood and leaned against the Sycamore as she wiped tears from her face. "Because of my residence, occupations, and demons, I was unclean and unloved. Like you, my family had disowned me, and my community rejected me. I spent my nights wandering the hills north of Galilee, often cutting myself on my arms and legs, hoping to die."

Mary briefly lifted her gown and sleeves to show Ayla her scars.

"I had no idea, Mary."

"I am no longer ashamed of my past. For me, the more tragic my tale, the more terrific the story of my salvation. Yeshua set me free. And then He welcomed me into His inner circle as a follower. He knew I had no other attachments that would hinder me and my life would be forever changed because of Him."

"As mine is too," added Ayla.

"For a time, as I listened to and watched Yeshua, my heart wondered if I might one day become more to Him…more than a friend and follower. I'm sure I am not the first woman to be attracted to Him even though He isn't that attractive to look at."

Ayla's face turned red as she thought of her attraction and feelings for Arrius.

"One day, as we journeyed the first time to Jerusalem as a group, I was fatigued and had fallen far back of the others. Yeshua noticed me. He told the men and other women to continue as He turned and came to me."

Ayla put a hand over her heart and said, "I love that about Him. He leaves no one behind and will find the struggling lamb."

Mary sat back down and placed her hand on Ayla's knee. "He does. He always does. And when He came to me, He spoke words that set my heart in line with His purpose."

"Oh Mary, what did he say?"

Mary squeezed Ayla's knee just a bit. "He said, 'Mary, I have come to this world for a purpose you cannot yet embrace or fully comprehend. And I must dedicate *every* moment to my Father's work. Do you understand?'

"I knew it was his way of telling me He loved me, but not more or any less than He loved the others or everyone. I knew I could not expect to have Him to myself. His mission matters more than me or my desires. So, yes, I once allowed myself to fantasize about our relationship, but no more."

"And you are okay?"

"Better than okay. Our relationship became what Yahweh wanted from that moment on, and I live with such *chara*…such peace. That being said, why did you ask about the rabbi and me?"

"Well, Judas said—"

Mary put up her hand to silence Ayla. "I think I have heard enough about Judas for now. He sometimes gets under my skin like a pebble in my sandals. Only Yahweh knows what will become of that man."

CHAPTER 21

Year 31 AD, Jerusalem, Home of Arrius and Ayla

Cassius reclined before an empty plate of food in the courtyard of the home of his fellow centurion, Arrius. This was the first time he'd been invited to share a meal with his friend and his dear wife, Ayla. Despite the wildfires near Jerusalem that filled the air with smoke, they dined outside because of the unbearable summer heat. The fires cast an orange glow in the western sky as the sun began to set.

Cassius slapped his belly. "Ayla, if I had known you could cook like this, I would have insisted Arrius build a guest room for me in your home."

Ayla blushed and bowed her head.

"And if I had remembered how much you eat, I would have never invited you to dinner," said Arrius.

"Ah, life is filled with many should haves and could haves, isn't it?" suggested Cassius.

"Please, I beg you, Cassius, please spare my wife your African proverbs. I do not want to subject her to the torture I have lived with all these years."

Ayla leaned over and hit Arrius in the shoulder in fun. "And I will not be subject to your rudeness at my table, husband."

"All is well, Ayla. I am used to his abuse. Your husband is a good man. Thick-headed and stubborn as a mule, but good nonetheless."

"Tell me, Centurion Cassius, what else have you learned about my husband that I would do well to know?"

Arrius stood up and stretched his legs as he patted his belly. "Cassius has nothing to say that you do not already know, Wife." He gave a threatening look to his friend and said, "Do you, Cassius?"

"Except for the choice of your husband, I can see that you are an intelligent woman and in no need of my counsel."

Ayla looked up at Arrius, over at Cassius, and back up at her husband. "Men! You are all the same."

Just then, Seneca crawled onto the legs of Cassius and pinched his black skin.

"I suspect you have never seen a black man, have you, little one?"

Seneca looked at his mother and said something in his toddler gibberish.

Continuing as if the boy could comprehend everything, Cassius said, "The gods made the very first people black as the soil of the earth because we came from the earth and to it we return when our days are done. Black is a symbol of strength and courage to the gods. Black is—"

Arrius interrupted, "Enough, Cassius. My son thinks you are black because you are covered in dirt."

Ayla shook her finder at Arrius. "That is quite enough, Husband."

"But—"

"I mean it, Arrius!"

Cassius laughed so loudly that he startled the boy. "My old friend, she is both beautiful and strong."

Arrius mumbled, "And stubborn."

"What did you say?" said Ayla with a furrowed brow.

"Nothing, Ayla, nothing worth repeating. Can I trouble my beautiful, strong, and wise wife for more wine? Our honored guest's cup is empty."

Ayla shook her head, and before going inside, she growled, "Men."

"I like her, Arrius."

A half-smile spread across Arrius's face. "She is a precious gift to me from the gods. I don't know what I'd do without her."

Cassius sat up and slapped his leg. "So tell me, what does your insightful Hebrew wife think of the Rabbi Yeshua? Does she speak of Him with you?"

"Yes, more than I wish if truth be told. I know that she goes to hear Him teach whenever He is in Jerusalem."

Cassius stroked his chin. "So far, Pilate seems oblivious to this man. However, as His influence with the common people has grown, His hatred by the religious rulers in this land has grown too. I fear this will not end well."

Arrius slapped his hands, startling Seneca again. "That is what I have told my wife. I have warned her to be careful, but she becomes more and more entangled with this rebel rabbi with each passing week."

Ayla entered with a container of wine. “He is *not* a rebel, Arrius, but His teachings are a radical departure from the self-centered old men who bore our people with their foolish dribble.”

Arrius threw his arms up. “See what I mean, Cassius. She is fixated on that man and will not listen to me. Perhaps you can get her to listen to common sense.”

As Ayla filled his glass, Cassius asked, “What about this man intrigues you?”

She stopped pouring and asked, “Will you listen with an open mind? Unlike some Romans I know?” looking at Arrius.

“I will, Ayla. I consider myself a philosopher of sorts, and I welcome new teachings and fresh ideas.”

Arrius grumbled, “I don’t think I can take any more of this in this heat. I’m going to take the boy for a walk. Good luck without me here to protect you, Cassius.” And with that, Arrius picked up Seneca to exit the courtyard.

Ayla stood quickly, grabbed the arm of her husband, and whispered in his ear, “Arrius, it is improper for me to be alone with an unmarried man—”

Arrius looked at Cassius and guffawed. “Consider him a eunuch, Ayla. I do. Besides, I will not be gone too long, but I need to walk.”

“My lady, if you are uncomfortable—”

“No, no, if my husband is fine, I am fine. Very few give me a second thought in this city anyway.”

“Thank you for your kindness and hospitality. I hope I have not offended you. But I would enjoy it if you would tell me more of your teacher.”

"And I would be honored to tell you. What would you like to hear?"

Arrius stomped out of the courtyard talking to himself.

Cassius leaned forward and fixed his eyes on Ayla. "Tell me, what have *you* found to be the rabbi's most challenging words?"

"Oh my, we could be here until sunrise discussing all His most challenging teachings. But I will tell you one of His stories that still resonates in my heart."

"Excellent. I love a good story," said Cassius as he rubbed his large, calloused black hands together.

"Yeshua told us a tale of a moneylender who forgave a great debt. This story, however, starts with a meal."

"Perfect, a story beginning with food." Cassius smiled and sat back.

Ayla continued, "Yeshua was eating at the home of a Pharisee named Simon. Near the end of the meal, and completely uninvited, a woman who was a prostitute entered the room, and she came to the rabbi. Simon, of course, was aghast that this woman of ill repute entered his home and was disgusted by what she did."

Cassius said, "I can imagine."

"No, Cassius, I don't think you can."

Cassius nodded his head.

"So Yeshua was reclining and eating with His disciples. He noticed the woman but didn't say a thing to her at first. But then she knelt at His feet and began to weep. Large tears flowed from her eyes onto His dusty feet. Shamefully, her head was uncovered, and her hair was loose. She shocked everyone even more as she washed Yeshua's feet and dried them with her hair. She had also brought with her an alabaster jar of perfume."

Cassius whistled. "Expensive, no doubt."

"It was. And she poured it *all* out—every single drop—on Yeshua's feet. Even the other disciples were uncomfortable because she kept kissing the rabbi's feet. Have you ever seen such a thing, Cassius?"

"No, and you are right, that is not what I imagined."

Ayla blushed and went on. "Then the rabbi smiled at her. He just smiled the entire time as she offered her unrestrained love to Him. Of course, Simon was beside himself with frustration and anger. He was frustrated with the sinner and angry with Yeshua. So Simon thought to himself, *If the rabbi were the Messiah and a prophet from Yahweh, He would know what kind of woman she is*."

"And did He?"

"Cassius, Yeshua knows all things, including the self-righteous thoughts of Simon. So Yeshua told a story to those gathered."

"This is the story of the moneylender?" asks Cassius.

"Yes. And here is how Yeshua told the tale. This creditor had two debtors. One owed him five hundred denarii, and the other fifty."

Cassius whistled and said, "Five hundred denarii is more than I will make in my entire career as a soldier."

After straightening her apron, Ayla paused for a moment before she continued. "As it turned out, neither lender could repay his debt, but here comes the best part of the story: The moneylender forgave both men. Completely. They were *both* free of their financial burden."

"What is this man's name? I want to borrow from him."

Ayla smiled. "You are missing the point of the story, Cassius. After telling the story to Simon, Yeshua sat up, looked him in the eye, and said, 'Simon, which man will love the moneylender more?' Simon didn't hesitate. The answer was obvious. He said, 'The one with the greater debt forgiven will love him more.'"

"That *is* logical, I suppose," added Cassius.

It was impossible for Ayla to sit still; she was giddy with excitement. "Simon was trapped by his arrogance. Yeshua told Simon he was right, but then He drove His point home with that self-righteous Pharisee. 'Simon, when I entered your home, you didn't provide a washbasin for me to wash my feet. You didn't greet me with the customary kiss of honor. You didn't anoint my head with oil.'"

Cassius slapped the table with his hand. "Even in a Roman home that would be poor treatment."

"And Yeshua continued, 'This woman, whom you consider to be worthless, has washed my feet with her tears. She dried them with her hair, Simon, then kissed my calloused feet nonstop and anointed them with costly oil."

"Simon must have wanted to run and hide at that point," added Cassius.

Ayla's eyes filled with tears. "Here's the best part. Yeshua turned away from Simon and said to the woman, 'Though your sins are many, they are *all* forgiven. You no longer will live under the shadow of guilt and shame.'"

Cassius sat back and said, "What happened next? Please tell me."

Ayla continued, "Yeshua then stood, embraced the woman as

if she were his long-lost sister, looked back at Simon, and said, 'Those who are forgiven much love much. Those who are forgiven little love little.'"

Cassius rubbed both his temples and said slowly, "Simon… loved…little."

"Sad but true, Cassius. Especially when you realize that Yeshua has the authority as the Son of Yahweh to forgive us of our many sins no matter what the size of our debt."

Cassius sat speechless as Arrius returned to the courtyard.

"What is wrong with you, Cassius? Has my wife upset you?"

"No, Arrius, quite to the contrary. She has given me much to consider, for I am a man with a great debt."

It was clear to Ayla what Cassius meant, and she smiled at him.

"My wife does have a way about her, Cassius. If she has offended you in any—"

"Not at all, my friend, not at all."

Arrius looked at Ayla, who was beaming, and then back at his friend and said, "I feel I must warn you, Cassius, the stories she tells of this rabbi may rob you of your sleep."

Cassius stood to leave and rubbed his face. "Or give me the sleep I am robbed of. The stories of this rabbi fascinate and trouble me at the same time. I hope to hear more. However, like you, Arrius, I worry that His story may not end as expected."

Chapter 22

Almost One Year Later, 32 AD,

Jerusalem, Home of Arrius and Ayla

At nearly eight moons pregnant with their second child, Ayla wasn't sleeping well, and she was exhausted. The fact that Seneca insisted on sleeping sideways between them, his head next to his father's chest and his feet in Ayla's face, didn't help.

"Your son kept me awake last night, Centurion."

"And why is he always *my* son when he's in trouble or a problem?"

"Because, like his father, he insists on doing things his way," said Ayla with a teasing but tired smile.

Arrius rolled his eyes. "Oh, and the Jews *never* insist that they are the only righteous ones. And they *never* act like their god is the only god. And they *never*—"

"Point taken, Husband. Please stop."

"So am I the victor in this battle?"

"If you insist," said Ayla as she poked Arrius in the ribs.

Seneca sat on the stone floor playing with a variety of sticks and rocks.

Ayla never liked his mock battles. "So, Husband, who is your son fighting now?"

"I believe it is a fierce conflict between two sticks named Rus and Tus," said Arrius. "Rus is supposed to be me, and Tus is Quintus, the old legionary who trained me as a boy."

"Why does he insist on playing war? You know how I feel about that, Arrius."

"And you know he is the son of a Germanic tribesman and a Roman centurion. He was born to fight and bred for battle."

Ayla folded her arms over her bulging belly. "No, he is not. As I have told you *many* times, he will be a man of shalom who will follow the way of Yeshua. I will not see my son become a man of war."

"Now he is *your* son! For the love of the gods, woman, you must make up your mind. Need I remind you that when I was young, I was told many stories of your people, men like Joshua, Gideon, and your favorite, David, who were all ruthless in battle against their enemies."

Ayla sat down on a stool, sighed, and shook her head as she said, "For every warrior among my people, I can name many who were priests and prophets who led our people in the shalom of Yahweh."

Ayla knew this was an argument she couldn't win. They'd had it time and time again since the birth of Seneca. Arrius began to pace as he always did when they fought. Ayla recognized her husband was proud to have a son and how he envisioned Seneca's eventual glory in battle. But Ayla dreamed of the day when her boy would be seen as a peacemaker who might bridge the gap between her people and Arrius's.

Seneca let out a little boy's roar as Rus defeated Tus with a quick thrust of his gladius.

"See what I mean? You teach him to fight, and he will only learn to kill. I teach him to love—"

"And he will only be killed," spat out Arrius abruptly.

While speaking softly and gesturing toward Seneca, Ayla looked into Arrius's eyes. "My *bashert*, do you remember the promise you made me the day he was born?"

"Yes," murmured Arrius.

"What? I cannot hear you."

"Yes, woman, you remind me often—*too* often."

Ayla, wounded but determined, replied, "You told me you never thought you would have children, let alone a son."

Arrius stooped down to pick up Seneca.

"You told me you wanted a better life for him than the one you had."

Seneca reached out for his mother, still sitting on the stool, but she left him in his father's arms.

"You promised me that you would do *anything* and everything in your power to protect our son from harm."

Arrius rubbed the head of his son.

"You promised, Arrius. You made a solemn vow before your god and Yahweh that day."

Arrius looked away from the piercing gaze of his wife. "I know, Ayla. I know, but I fear a man of peace may be in far more danger in our world than a man who knows how to fight."

"Yeshua says—"

Arrius reacted, startling Seneca. "Do not quote Him to me now, woman. That Galilean is a perfect example of someone who will not live long. Any man who refuses to take up the sword will die by the sword of another."

"No, Arrius, any man who lives by the sword will eventually die by the sword."

Seneca insisted on going to his mother, but Ayla was so large from pregnancy that she could barely find room for him on her lap.

"I know your fears, Arrius. I have heard you talk in your sleep, and I have seen you frightened awake by nightmares."

"I am a tribesman from Germania. I am a Roman. I am a centurion. I fear *nothing* and no man!"

"And yet you do, my dear *bashert*; you do."

Arrius threw his hands up and turned to leave the room.

"Arrius."

He stopped without turning around.

"Arrius. Please look at me."

Arrius's shoulders dropped as he turned around to see his son attached to the breast of Ayla.

"This is peace," as she pointed to her nursing son. "The calm in our son's heart right now is the quietness of soul I pray you will know someday."

"It is not—"

Ayla raised her hand to silence Arrius's voice. "Yes, it is possible. All things are possible. I have seen it, Arrius."

"Seen what?"

"I have seen a day when my warrior husband will beat his sword into a plowshare."

"And did your rabbi put this absurd idea in your head? Mark my words, Ayla—there will never be a time when any true warrior will turn his gladius into the cutting blade of a plow." As Arrius spoke, the veins in his neck began to throb.

At barely more than a whisper, Ayla answered, "It was the prophet Isaiah who spoke of a time when Yahweh would judge between the nations and settle the disputes of many peoples. He said one day men will beat their swords into plowshares and their spears into pruning hooks. And at that time, nation will no longer take up the sword against nation or train for war anymore."

"Your prophet was a bigger fool than your rabbi. *That* day will not ever come to *this* earth. Not now. Not tomorrow. And not as long as Rome rules the world."

Ayla wiped a tear from her cheek. "Rome only rules what Yahweh allows her to rule."

Arrius rubbed the back of his neck. "I have no idea what I am to do with you, Ayla, but apparently, *this* Roman will never rule his wife."

And that all-too-common statement broke the tension between them as they both smiled.

There was a long and timely pause.

"I have, and I always will love *my* Roman."

As he moved to wrap an arm around Ayla's shoulder, Arrius

said, "And I have, and I always will love *my* Hebrew."

With that, Seneca unlatched, and with milk dripping down his cheek, he said, "Love me too."

"Yes, boy, we love you too," said Arrius with fondness. "You are the best of both of us."

"And sometimes the worst," chimed in Ayla as she stroked his long hair. "But yes, you are loved, little one."

Almost on cue, the baby in her womb leaped as an unspoken declaration to Ayla. *And love me too.*

Ayla could see Arrius choking back emotion as he said, "Ayla, what will be the fate of our unborn child? Are we wise to bring another little one into a world so wretched and broken?"

She sat up straight, trying to give more air to her compressed lungs as she thought, *I, too, feel something evil lurking in the shadows. What is to come of my family?*

CHAPTER 23

Early 32 AD, Jerusalem, Home of Arrius and Ayla

"The fever has consumed her; nothing I do seems to cool her body," said the midwife. Arrius had hired an Egyptian to help Ayla with the delivery of their second baby because no family member or Hebrew would assist them with their child's birth.

"And the child? What of our child?" Arrius asked anxiously as spray droplets filled the air between them.

"It is too soon to tell, but I will keep you informed."

Arrius cursed at the sky. He swore vengeance on his gods and Ayla's Yahweh should she or the baby not survive. His greatest fear—the blood curse—subsided after the birth of his son, Seneca. But now, because of Ayla's condition, every deep-rooted terror in his soul resurfaced.

For days, Ayla was ill, unable to hold food or much water. She alternated between the sweats and uncontrollable chills. At times, she was delirious with the fever. According to Ayla, the baby wasn't due for another moon or so, but apparently, this illness thrust her into an early delivery. The fact that the baby was coming early added additional stress to Arrius. Justus once told Arrius that his birth was early too. Arrius always assumed that was why his mother died at childbirth.

The last sight he had of Ayla was earlier in the day. She sat in a birthing chair, a special seat made with handles for the mother to grip during contractions. The midwife sat on a short stool in front of Ayla, encouraging her and ready to catch the baby. His wife's body was covered in sweat, her belly swollen, and her face contorted. Arrius watched many men die on a Roman cross with less pain on their faces.

"Why did I let her convince me to have another child?" Arrius yelled again, this time at the stars now beginning to appear. "What have I done to deserve this? I will not survive without her." Arrius buried his face in his hands and began to weep. Thoughts of how he would end his life started to flood his mind. Insane thoughts and evil imaginations consumed him.

"Centurion?"

Arrius was startled. Until that moment, he believed he was alone in the courtyard of their home. Instinctively, he grabbed the handle of his gladius as he quickly stepped back into the shadows.

"Who enters my home uninvited?" said Arrius.

"Centurion, we have not met, but my name is Mary. I am a friend of Ayla's and have come to help her."

"My wife no longer has any Hebrew friends. Speak the truth, and be gone, or prepare to meet my wrath."

Mary gently replied, "Ayla has *many* friends among the followers of Yeshua."

"Yeshua? The rabbi? What has He to do with *my* Ayla?"

"Hasn't she told you of Him? Didn't you know she, too, is a disciple of the rabbi?"

Arrius went from shock to anger to confusion in a matter of

moments. On many occasions, they had spoken of the rabbi, but Ayla never mentioned becoming a follower.

"My wife follows and has affection for no man but me."

Mary smiled. "It is not like that, Centurion; her love for Yeshua is pure, but I assure you, like many others, she is a student of the teacher."

"Woman, I know enough of your odd religion to know that *women* are not allowed to be students of a rabbi."

"And yet there are many of us who walk in His steps, Centurion, many. Yeshua accepts anyone who comes to Him and holds all women in high regard."

Arrius didn't know what to say. Mary had him at a disadvantage, and she spoke with a confidence he'd not seen in any Hebrew woman besides Ayla.

"Enough of this for now, Centurion. May I call you Arrius?" Without waiting for his response, Mary then stepped around Arrius. "Let me see how I can assist your wife. The rabbi sent me to help."

"And how in the name of the gods does your rabbi know she is in labor?"

"He knows *all* things, Arrius. He knows she is sick with the fever. He knows the baby comes early. Yet, He told me to trust in Him because He knows that all will be well."

Those words, "He knows," were like drops of water on the desert of his mind. The complete look of confidence in Mary's eyes began to calm his racing heart.

"He knows? Who is this man? How can anyone know anything in this cursed world?"

Mary smiled again as she bowed and nodded her head to the centurion. "If Yeshua says all is well…all is well." And then she hurried to the bedchamber.

The crescent moon rose high on the horizon as a gentle breeze blew through the courtyard. Arrius paced like a legionary on guard duty. Besides dogs barking in the distance, the only sounds piercing the darkness were Ayla Rose's cries of pain and the murmurs of the Egyptian midwife.

Seneca began to stir and fuss. He was wrapped in animal skins and sleeping in the corner of the courtyard. Thankfully, he went to sleep without nursing. However, Arrius knew his son would be awake soon.

His pacing abruptly stopped when Ayla let out a shrill followed by painful silence.

Arrius fell to the ground. "Gods take *me*, not her. Take *my* life, not hers. I freely offer myself as a sacrifice to appease your anger against me." Arrius was lying prostrate in the dirt trying not to sob too loudly, convinced his wife and second child were gone.

For the second time that night, Mary startled him as she placed her small hand on his shoulder. "Arrius, would you like to meet your daughter?"

Arrius, still on the ground, rolled over on his back as Mary knelt beside him. "What? Is she…is the child…is Ayla—"

"Yes, all is well just as the rabbi said it would be. It was a difficult birth, but mother and daughter are fine."

Moving like a man twenty years younger, Arrius leaped up and ran to Ayla's side. He stopped abruptly at the door as he saw her nursing the baby.

The midwife was washing her hands in a basin. "She is strong, your wife. She is very strong. And her fever broke within moments of that one arriving." She pointed to Mary.

Ayla seemed okay. Her hair soaked in sweat and matted, but her eyes were bright, and her smile—that smile that captured Arrius—was beaming.

Ayla spoke in a tired whisper, "Where is Seneca? I am sure he wants to meet his sister too. He must be hungry as well. Let me nurse our children, my *bashert*."

Arris was stunned because he was convinced all was lost. Yet, something mysterious, wonderful, and beyond words happened that night.

Once again, Arrius thought to himself, *Who is this rabbi? How can any of this be possible?*

At that moment, Mary walked in with a very unhappy Seneca. "It seems that both your children have strong wills, Centurion." Mary laughed as she lifted Seneca next to Ayla.

The sight of his children—his beautiful and healthy children—drinking life from their mother was etched forever into his memory. Nothing he'd ever seen in his entire life was as beautiful.

"Come here, my love. Come meet your daughter. What shall we call her?"

Arrius sat on the bed next to the three of them, pulling back hair from Ayla's eyes and wiping sweat from her brow.

"I don't know, Ayla. What would you like to name her?"

Ayla's eyes told him she was studying his heart, and he knew she was examining his thoughts.

"Can we call her Tikva? It means *gift of hope* in my language. I know you thought all hope was lost, but she has proved, once again, that Yahweh is good and the restorer of our hope."

Arrius smiled, bent over, and kissed Ayla and then his daughter on the forehead. "Tikva it is, for my hope has returned."

As the Egyptian midwife left the room, Mary began to sing a Hebrew melody as she gently danced with her arms raised.

Arrius was deeply moved. "What does it mean, Ayla?"

"Mary sings a Psalm of our father David."

Lord my God, I called to you for help, and you healed me.

You, Lord, brought me up from the realm of the dead;

you spared me from going down to the pit.

Sing the praises of the Lord, you his faithful people;

praise his holy name.

For his anger lasts only a moment, but his favor lasts a lifetime;

weeping may stay for the night, but rejoicing comes in the morning.[2]

And it was a new morning.

The sun rose and shone through the open window, highlighting the dust and smoke in the air. The smell of the neighbor's breakfast cooking on a nearby fire filled the room. In the distance, several

---

2 Psalm 30:2–5

roosters welcomed the day. It was as if the entire world around them was filled with the shalom of Yahweh.

Arrius stroked the cheek of Tikva with a callused finger, causing her to suck harder, and said, "Perhaps I should meet this rabbi of yours. I cannot deny what has happened here."

Ayla's eyes became heavy with tears of joy. "When you encounter Him, Arrius, everything changes."

Chapter 24

Year 32 AD, Jerusalem, Home of Arrius and Ayla

Ten days later, all was well and relatively back to normal in the home of Ayla and Arrius. There was, however, a tension brewing in the mind of Arrius.

"Ayla?" Arrius called to her from the courtyard.

Ayla had just finished nursing Tikva.

With a bit more force, Arrius called, "Ayla Rose?"

As Ayla stepped outside, she smiled and whispered, "Sorry. I was putting the baby down for a nap and didn't want to disturb her. But you know how I love it when you call me Ayla Rose. What do you need, my *bashert*?"

Arrius returned the smile but quickly changed his demeanor when he said, "Speaking of being disturbed…there is something that has bothered me since Mary was here."

"Hmmm. I cannot imagine Mary doing anything to disturb anyone. She is the kindest and most gracious woman I have ever known."

Arrius motioned for her to sit next to him. "It wasn't anything she *did*; it was something she *said*."

Ayla sat and fidgeted with her hair. "Did she speak to you about Yeshua? I specifically asked her not to press you with her views. I'm sorry—"

"No…well, sort of…but it wasn't what she said about Yeshua, but what she said about *you* as a follower of that rabbi that concerned me."

Ayla stiffened and said, "Yes, I have meant to speak to you for some time, but—"

Arrius interrupted, "I don't need excuses; I need answers."

"And what answers do you seek, Arrius?"

"First, who is this Mary? Where is she from? How did you become friends?"

"She is Mary of Magdala."

Arrius grunted, "I have been to that small Galilean fishing village. I was not impressed."

"And yet, I assure you, Arrius, Mary is very impressive. She is a remarkable and highly intelligent woman."

"Interesting that you use *intelligent* and *woman* in the same sentence. My people have no problem accepting a woman as brilliant, but you Jews treat women more like foolish, ignorant children."

Ayla smiled. "And one of the things I have always loved about you, Arrius, is that you treat me with respect and admire my mind as well as my beauty."

"You told me your father was belittling toward women—"

Ayla raised her hand and cut him short. "Let us not go to the subject of my father now. I know how he treated me, my sisters, and my mother."

Arrius grumbled, "If I were a Hebrew woman, I wouldn't tolerate—"

"I know, but thank Yahweh you are not a Hebrew woman," interrupted Ayla as she giggled. "Though Mary is a very different woman now and an incredible person, her story is full of heartbreak and tragedy."

"How so?"

"She has told many others her story, and I have heard it myself several times. Believe it or not, she was once full of darkness and demons."

Arrius leaned in as Ayla seemed to hesitate.

"In fact, when she first met the rabbi, she had been living—"

"As a harlot?"

"Sadly, yes, at times, but don't judge her too harshly; it was the only way she could survive. Mary was only thirteen when her father removed her from his home. He had taken her to the priests for deliverance but without success. Later, when she became violent and uncontrollable, he put her on a donkey and sent her away from their village with little more than the clothes on her back. Mary was an embarrassment and cause of shame to him. She never speaks poorly of her father, but many of us suspect that he was sexually inappropriate with Mary when she was young."

Arrius instinctively grabbed the handle of his gladius. "If it were up to me, men who prey on children would have their manhood removed."

"We don't know for sure, but no child is born with demons. Someone abused her, and it ruined her."

Arrius released his grip on his sword and said, "And yet, she is…so—"

"I know, Arrius. I know. The rabbi set Mary free from seven demons and then took her in as part of His inner circle. The miracle of her life is a great testimony to Yeshua's power. It is rumored that the money she made—and she did quite well because of her physical beauty—is now used to help support the rabbi and His men."

"And how and when did you meet her?"

Ayla looked up at the massive sycamore tree in their courtyard. "Nearly two years ago."

"You have known Mary that long? Why would you keep this from me?"

"Yes, for some time. I am so sorry, Arrius. But it happened by accident. I was coming home from the market when I crossed paths with her, Yeshua, and His men as they were on their way to the temple. Of course, at that time, I had no idea who any of them were."

"So how did you go from passing her on the road to friends?"

Ayla lowered her head as she brushed away a tear. "She smiled at me. No Jewish woman had smiled at me for some time, but Mary smiled, and it was like she saw right into my soul."

Arrius placed a hand on her leg and gently squeezed her thigh.

"I cannot explain it, Arrius. I am at a loss for words to describe what I felt. But somehow, I knew she was a gift sent to me from Yahweh."

Ayla looked up again to the sky. "My sisters, my family, my friends—they had all forsaken me, but this stranger embraced me with her eyes and her smile."

"What did you do?"

Ayla laughed through her tears. "I set my basket down at the feet of a beggar, turned, and followed them to the temple."

"I am not surprised you gave food to the poor, but I am surprised you followed complete strangers."

Ayla continued, "Then Mary looked back. I was only thirty or forty paces behind them. But when she turned around, she saw me, and then she came to me. I was thrilled and terrified. Part of me wanted to run from her, and part of me wanted to run to her. But I stopped and just stood there."

"And?"

"And when she reached me, she paused for a long moment, looked into my eyes, smiled, and then took me into her arms. Arrius, I was so happy and stunned and afraid. No woman had held me as Mary did since my mother before she died. I burst into a sob so loud that the rabbi and His men stopped."

"And what did they do?"

"Again, I find it hard to describe to you. And honestly, my memory is a bit cloudy as to what happened next. But before I knew it, I was on my knees gently rocking and wailing, Mary was on her knees next to me, Yeshua had His hand on my head, and all the others—both men and the other women who followed the rabbi—were praying for me."

"You broke down in the street? In public?"

"Yes."

"And…what…how—"

"Trust me, Arrius, I was baffled, too, but as Yeshua and His followers lifted their voices and hands in prayer for me, I was forever changed."

Arrius stood and began to pace before her in the late afternoon sun of the courtyard. "Changed? How? I don't understand what you're saying, Ayla."

Ayla took a deep breath. "That was the moment I *knew* He was the one."

"What do you mean *the one*?"

"The Messiah, Arrius, the Promised One to my people. I knew I would give my life to Him whatever the cost."

Seneca was now at Ayla's feet, intensely sucking his thumb.

Arrius abruptly stopped pacing as he hovered over his wife and son. "You are *my* wife. You are the mother of *my* children. You are to serve *me* and not some trouble-making rabbi. How could you do this? And I am angry that you kept your relationship with Mary from me."

"Forgive me, Arrius. I meant you no harm or disrespect. I have wanted to tell you for such a long time, but I was afraid."

Arrius began to pace again as he threw his hands up. "Afraid? Of me? By the gods, woman!"

Ayla began to cry as she sputtered, "No, I feared you would not understand. I worried you would forbid me to follow Yeshua or have any friendship with anyone in His group. And so I prayed to Yahweh that He would prepare your heart and soften it so that you would accept what I have done and who I have become."

"And what have you become, Ayla? What else do you *need* to *become* but who you are to me?"

"You have given me love, acceptance, provision, and a home, Arrius. But Yahweh has renewed my soul and given me new hope for our future through Yeshua."

"*Our* future? What do you speak of, woman? You are talking in circles. There is no sense in this."

"I speak of something wonderful, Arrius, something beyond this world and something yet to be revealed."

Arrius pointed at their home. "I need nothing more than this and no one more than you and my children—"

Ayla looked up at him through eyes heavy with tears. "And yet you do, my love; you do. You need freedom that I know can only come through Yeshua. He can liberate you from the curse you fear and the unbearable burden you carry."

Arrius slammed his fist into the palm of his other hand. "What are you saying? Are you accusing me of being demon-possessed as Mary was?"

"No, but—"

And with that, Arrius was done. He shook his head and moved to the courtyard gate. "I must attend to my men. I will be home late. Don't wait up for me."

As he left, Ayla offered up a tearful prayer to Yahweh. "Please heal my husband. Protect him. Keep him. Lead him to life. No one can reach him but You."

Almost as if on cue, the wind began to move the limbs of their courtyard trees.

She whispered again in prayer, "I trust this is a sign that You are not done moving in the heart of my beloved, Yahweh."

CHAPTER 25

Year 32 AD, Jerusalem, Home of the Widow Abigail

Ayla met with Mary and several of the other female followers as often as possible. Yeshua spent most of His time north, in Galilee. Since Mary often traveled with Him, as did Simon Peter's wife, Ayla had only a few female friends in Jerusalem. She developed a maternal relationship with an elderly follower named Abigail, who'd lost her husband many years ago.

"I enjoy our times together, Ayla. This old woman wishes she could travel with the teacher, but my days of sleeping on the ground are long gone. Besides, I move slower than a pregnant ox."

"Oh, Abigail, you are one of the strongest women I know. I think you can do anything you want to do, but I am glad you are here with me. I still have so many questions about Yeshua. Thank you for being so patient with me."

"Nonsense, my girl. You require no patience from me. Since the passing of my husband, I love the company. And you can help me make some fresh bread as we speak."

"You have no idea how much that means to me," said Ayla.

Abigail looked at Ayla. "Making bread?"

Ayla's eyes moistened. "No, when you call me 'my girl' and

treat me like a daughter. My mother passed when I was young… too young…and her mother long before that. I am honored by your friendship and affection."

Abigail wiped the flour from her hands and reached out her arms for a hug. Ayla melted into her embrace.

"You know I never had a daughter. Three boys. No girls. For years, I was the only woman in our home, and it was challenging."

"How so?"

Abigail giggled. "Well, let us just say the last time I did sleep outdoors was the night I mistakenly put too much curry in a dish of mutton I'd prepared. Within an hour of that meal, which my three boys and Jonah devoured like wild animals, our house was so—how can I put this delicately? So overcome with a wretched odor that I feared my clothes might never be free from the stench! I was forced out for my own safety to spend the night on the roof."

The women laughed until they cried until interrupted by a knock at the door.

"Are you expecting someone? Perhaps I should leave."

"No, no, Mary told me yesterday she would send John Mark to work a bit on my roof. The last rains revealed a few spots needing repair. Please start kneading the dough. I will see if it's him."

Abigail wiped her hands clean again and covered her head as she moved to open the door.

"John Mark. Are you here to sweep me off my feet? Such a handsome young man. How is it you are not yet married?"

Mark blushed a bit and said, "If only I were an older man and worthy of such a strong and beautiful woman as you."

"Strong. Yes. Beautiful. Once. But enough of your flattery, young man. I have holes the size of a millstone in my roof."

"And I have the material and tools to repair them all. Show me where to start."

"You know Ayla, don't you?"

"Yes, good morning, Ayla, and who is that little one strapped on your back?"

"Good morning, Mark. It is good to see you again. This is Tikva, my youngest, and she can sleep through a thunderstorm, so don't worry about making too much noise."

Mark quipped, "As the daughter of a barbarian and Roman centurion, I can only hope I do not wake her and incur the wrath of her gods."

The moment the words spewed from his mouth, he got an angry look from both women.

Ayla's jaw dropped as she pointed a finger at John Mark. "My daughter has only one Lord—Yahweh—and there are no barbarian or Roman gods in my home."

"Uh…of course…I meant no harm…I apologize for any offense, Ayla. As I am sure you are aware, my father was a Roman. He attempted to teach me of his gods, but my mother, Mary, would not have it."

"And neither will I. Though my husband has yet to accept Yahweh, he knows I will never tolerate *any* idols in my home."

Abigail chimed in as she, too, pointed her finger at Mark, "And you think I am strong."

Marked sheepishly nodded and said, "Time for me to make my

way to the roof."

"Yes," scolded Abigail. "It is."

Ayla added, "All is well, brother; I know you meant no harm."

"Harm or not, time is wasting." Abigail waved at the roof stairs. "I will call you down when we have some warm bread…and mutton stew with extra curry for you to eat."

Ayla and Abigail laughed.

Abigail added, "That boy is harmless. Too loose with his tongue at times but harmless."

"I know, Abigail. He does, however, bring me great hope."

Abigail cocked her head and said, "How so?"

"His father was a Roman centurion married to a Jew."

"Ah, I see. And that brings you comfort, Ayla?"

"It does. I pray every day for my children. But at times, I worry that my son, Seneca, will follow in his father's steps. So seeing Mark practicing the faith of his mother and now following Yeshua encourages me."

After some time, Mark called down from the roof, "Abigail, I am famished and in need of fresh bread and water. Have you forgotten me?"

Abigail yelled at the ceiling, "How could I forget you with all the noise and dust you are creating? But come, the bread is warm, and the water is too."

"Abigail, I can go to the well and draw some fresh, cool water," offered Ayla.

Mark flew down the stairs. "Not necessary, ladies. Hot bread and cool water, when consumed together, give me a headache."

Abigail shook her head, "I do not like your use of the word 'consume,' John Mark. I am a poor widow, and this bread must last me for days."

"And it will. Even if I must multiply it as Elijah did for the widow of Zarephath." Mark nearly inhaled the first piece of bread Abigail handed to him.

Ayla rolled her eyes. "So you see yourself as a prophet and miracle worker now?"

Mark wiped his lips. "I am no prophet, and certainly no Elijah, but Yeshua teaches us that someday we will do the miracles He has done…and even greater ones!"

Abigail clicked her tongue and shook her head. "And how can any man—"

"Or woman," added Ayla.

"How can any man or *woman* do anything greater than raise the dead?"

Mark smiled. "I have an answer, but it will cost you just one more piece of the most delicious bread I have ever eaten in my long life."

Abigail smacked Mark's fingers as he reached for a large center piece of the loaf. She handed him the heel and said, "Once again, your flattery will not work on me, and your 'long life' of nearly eighteen years will soon be over if you touch my bread again."

Mark took what was offered and dipped it in olive oil.

"John Mark, I am curious," asked Ayla.

"Yes, apparently I do love bread more than my fingers."

"No, I am serious. Were you there when Yeshua multiplied the bread?"

"Which time?"

Ayla gasped, "Yeshua did so more than once?"

"Yes, but I was only there for the second time."

"If you make him tell us a story, Ayla, he will indeed eat everything."

"Oh please, Abigail, I will bring you more flour tomorrow."

Tikva began to stir.

"Okay, give that fussy child to me. I will take her to the roof to inspect Mark's craftsmanship. Besides, I have heard this story many times."

John Mark licked the oil from his fingers, patted his belly, and said, "Seven loaves. Yeshua used only seven loaves smaller than what I just ate to feed four thousand men."

"And women and children, too, I assume."

"Yes, Ayla, probably ten thousand people were fed that day."

"Tell me all about it and leave nothing out, John Mark."

"As always, the crowds had come to Yeshua, who was in the middle of nowhere. We were leagues from the nearest village. By day three, whatever food the people had brought with them was gone, yet they refused to leave."

Ayla sighed, "The rabbi enthralled them."

"Yes, Ayla, and then Yeshua called us to Him and said, 'I have compassion for these people; they have nothing to eat. However, I don't want to send them away hungry, or they might collapse on the way.'"

Ayla bent over and placed her elbows on her knees. "It is so like Yeshua to think of others."

"Yes, but this created quite a stir among the inner circle of disciples. One of them, Simon the Zealot, I think, was perturbed and pointed out the obvious that there wasn't enough bread in that remote place to feed *us*, let alone thousands of others."

"Mark, you said that Yeshua had multiplied bread before, true?"

"Yes, but I wasn't there."

"Why didn't the disciples just ask Him to do it again?"

Mark threw up his hands. "Who knows?"

Ayla raised both palms to her forehead in frustration at the disciples' unbelief.

"Yeshua, of course, had a plan. I will never forget the look on His face; it was sort of a frustrated smile. Does that make sense?"

Ayla shook her head no.

"Well, He *did* have a plan, and He asked us to see how many loaves of bread we could scrounge up. We found seven. Did I mention how small and stale they were?"

"Yes, but go on."

"The rabbi told us to have the crowd sit. Then, He took those miserable loaves of barley bread—not nearly as good as Abigail's—and He looked up toward the heavens, gave thanks to Yahweh, and started breaking off pieces as He handed them to the disciples. It was incredible. If I hadn't seen it firsthand, I would have never believed it."

"What? Tell me."

"The faster the disciples broke off the bread, the faster it multiplied right in their hands.

"They couldn't give it away quickly enough. And Ayla, it was *warm* bread. Like it had just been removed from the fire. When I saw what was happening, I started laughing and jumping and dancing. It was unbelievable."

Ayla had heard many stories of the miracles performed by the rabbi. For some reason, with the smell of fresh, warm bread still in the room, she felt as if she could see and hear what had happened that day.

"Mark, I have one more question," Ayla said with a sly look.

"Anything."

"Did you eat more than one loaf that day?"

Mark laughed so loud that Abigail rushed to the room.

"What has he done now, Ayla?"

"Nothing. Everything. Something wonderful. John Mark has fed my soul with hope."

Marked turned and looked at Ayla, "And how did a story about bread do that?"

Ayla grabbed Mark and motioned for Abigail to join them in her arms for a hug. With tears streaming down her cheeks, she said, "I often feel so weak, inferior, and lacking so much. But I realize now *all* Yeshua asks from me is the little I have to offer to Him."

Abigail whispered, "Yes, the lesson of the loaves is unmistakable. The rabbi loves to use the least to surprise and delight us."

Ayla squeezed Abigail a bit harder and added, "And I wonder what He has in store for us next."

Chapter 26

Two Weeks Later, 32 AD, Jerusalem

The morning started normal enough. Arrius was up first, always an early riser. After climbing out of bed, Seneca searched for his father. Arrius found great delight in those first moments of the day spent with his son. The sound of multiple pairs of turtle doves echoed off the courtyard walls. Their unique "turr-turr" call and the fact that these doves formed strong pair bonds made Arrius especially fond of this species. In Jerusalem, the birds were a cultural emblem of devoted love. Except for the doves and the occasional cart rolling by his home, the morning was quiet and peaceful.

"Your father is struggling, Seneca." The boy gave Arrius an odd look, having no idea what his father meant. Nonetheless, Arrius found it comforting to express his thoughts and feelings to someone else even if he could not understand.

"I find these quiet mornings filled with confusion, Son. Am I losing my mind? The stories your mother tells me of her rabbi haunt me."

Arrius stood and began to pace on the rough cobblestones. Seneca looked up for a moment but then returned to playing on the ground with his wooden blocks and colored rocks.

"I *do* long for peace. I am so tired, Seneca. Sleep evades me, and shame overcomes me. But I am what I am. No man, no rabbi, no god, and no woman—not even your mother—can change my past or erase who I am or what I have done. No one. Hope is the pursuit of fools."

Ayla was eavesdropping. "Arrius?"

Arrius stopped, turned toward her, and said, more embarrassed than irritated, "How long have you been there? You know it is best not to surprise your husband. I could react and draw my *pugio* without thinking. My dagger is always at his side."

"My *bashert*, you know you can talk to me about anything."

"I know. But—"

Ayla bent over, picked up Seneca, and said, "But you'd rather talk to your son than me."

"No, I…I just don't know how or where to begin. These past two weeks—"

"I know, Arrius. I have seen your—"

"You have seen my *what*? My doubts? My struggles? My pain? My anger? What, wife, have you seen? Your god plagues me!"

"Yahweh can be relentless, but His pursuit of us is the result of His love. Only those who run from Him see His affections as a plague. His love is not for our destruction, Arrius; it is our deliverance."

Arrius stopped pacing and sat on a bench, bent over, and covered his face with his hands. Ayla sat Seneca down and moved to his side.

"My Hebrew nanny—"

"Ayla?"

"Yes. Ayla once told my brother and me of a man who ran from Yahweh and ended up in the belly of a sea serpent."

Ayla placed a gentle hand on Arrius's leg. "His name was Jonah."

Arrius sat up and looked his wife in the face. "I feel an evil monster devours me, and the stench and darkness of this beast consume me."

Ayla took his hand in hers. "My dear love, do you remember what happened to Jonah?"

Arrius turned his head from her and nodded. "When Jonah admitted his foolishness, Yahweh rescued him."

"If the history of my people is anything, it is a testimony to the patience, mercy, and never-ending love of the Lord. He *always* rescues those who cry out to him."

Arrius stood and began to pace again. "But I cannot silence the voices in my head. And what am I to do with the questions I wrestle with?"

"Yeshua says that those who seek the Lord and His truth will always find what they truly need."

Arrius stopped abruptly in front of Ayla as an idea struck him. "Where is your rabbi now? Has He returned to Jerusalem?"

"No, not yet. The rumor is He may not return for some time or until Passover. He is in the north."

Arrius pressed, "Galilee?"

"Yes, that is where He spends most of His time nowadays, in the wilderness south of the sea."

Arrius clapped his hands together and said, "I will find Him. I will go to Him and demand answers. Pilate will gladly send me to investigate and report back to him about what I find in the north."

"No one *demands* anything of the rabbi, Arrius. And sadly, as a Roman, you may not be allowed access to Him by His disciples. They have grown very protective of Yeshua."

"Ayla, it doesn't matter how difficult it might be. I *must* speak to Him directly. So I will clear this with the prefect and leave tomorrow. I can be in Galilee in five days."

"Will you travel alone? It is not safe—"

"I will take a few of my best men with me. All will be well."

Ayla's eyes moistened. "And what do you seek, my love? What do you expect to gain from your conversation with the rabbi?"

"Answers. I cannot rest and will *never* find *pax* without them."

Seneca stood behind his mother, peeked around her side at Arrius, and asked, "Abba mad?"

Arrius beat the palm of his fist against his chest. "No, Son, Abba determined."

Arrius could tell that Pilate was suspicious and unconvinced. He assumed the prefect would be anxious for word from the north—especially word about the growing threat of the rabbi and His followers. The Zealots continued to stir up conflict in Jerusalem, and the road to Jericho seemed overrun with bandits, requiring a constant presence of legionaries.

Arrius stood at attention while Pilate drank from his cup. It was too early in the day for wine, but that never seemed to matter to his commander. "I need you here, Centurion. Herod can deal with whatever is happening in the north. I already have too few men to keep control of far too many Jews. Besides, my sources tell me this radical rabbi will never return to the city. The Sanhedrin will not tolerate Him in their temple again."

Arrius tried to hide his frustration. "Prefect, you are well-informed and wise."

Pilate nodded, took another drink, and wiped his mouth.

"My sources tell me a different story."

Pilate's eyes widened. "And what do *your* sources tell you, Centurion? Have *you* spoken with Caiaphas? Have *you* some insight that somehow escapes *me* and my eyes in this vile place?"

"Of course not, Prefect. But the word among His followers—"

"And how do you have any contact with this man's followers? Have you become a part of His ragtag rabble? Do I need to worry about your allegiance to Rome?"

Arrius took a breath and chose his next words carefully. "I am and always will be Roman. First. Now. Always, Prefect. You have no reason to doubt my allegiance. I am here to protect the empire. Nothing more. Nothing less." Arrius spoke the truth, but not the whole truth.

"So how do you know anything? What reason would you have to be in contact with any of the rabbi's followers?"

Arrius hesitated. Sweat was running down his back and beginning to form on his forehead.

The prefect leaned forward in his chair. "Answer me, or you will face my wrath!"

"My wife—"

Pilate interrupted and sarcastically said, "You mean the Hebrew woman I allow you to live with?"

The centurion was not accustomed to being the brunt of Pilate's temper. Arrius knew that rage answered with rage would not end well. He also knew that Pilate respected strength, so he spoke with respect and confidence—confidence he did not feel.

"Prefect, sir, my *wife* plays to our advantage. Her connections among the Hebrews, including the followers of this rabbi, provide me with strategic insight and valuable information for Rome and you."

Pilate sat back, looked across the room, and waved his hand in dismissal of Arrius. "Fine. Use her, but do not let her use you or me. If you believe a trip to Galilee is of value, then go. But you can take only one legionary with you. I cannot spare more, and you must return by the full moon."

Arrius wasted no time in any further discussion. He saluted, turned, and left Pilate quickly, wondering how a round trip taking eight days on foot could be accomplished in less than seven. But he would find a way. He had to.

The first man Arrius found in the barracks was Tasco, who was sharpening his gladius. He was one of the youngest legionaries in the cohort but eager for advancement. Tasco was a tall and robust legionary from Gaul.

Arrius barked, "Legionary!"

Tasco jumped to attention and saluted. "Yes, Centurion."

"Can you ride a horse?"

"Of course, Centurion, my people—"

"I don't care about your people. Can you ride? Yes or no?"

"Yes, Centurion."

"Then prepare yourself and gather rations for five days. You and I are traveling to Galilee at daybreak."

Tasco had never traveled to Galilee and never anywhere without his *centuria.* "We travel alone, Centurion? Are there not many dangers along the roads to the north?"

"Yes, alone, but we will move quickly. Our horses and our armor will protect us."

Tasco saluted. "As you command, Centurion."

"And Tasco."

"Yes, Centurion."

"You are to tell only the *optio* of this mission. The fewer who know, the fewer the questions."

Arrius then rushed away to tell Ayla the news and prepare for the arduous journey. Whether or not the outcome of this trip would bring the answers he needed was to be determined, but he was desperate for some resolution.

Chapter 27

Year 32 AD, the Road from Jerusalem to Galilee

The early morning winter air was brisk. Tasco and Arrius could see their breath, and Tasco was jumping up and down, trying to warm himself. Typically, his *sarcina*—the marching pack carried by Roman legionaries—would provide some warmth on his back. Traveling by horseback, however, meant traveling with saddlebags and a bedroll. Fortunately, both men added a wool cloak, trousers, and sheepskin boots to their standard uniform. The horses acted anxious to get moving too.

"Did you get something to eat, Legionary? We have a long ride before us."

"Centurion, the sun is not yet on the horizon. Even the barrack cooks are still sleeping. I managed to find some stale bread and heat some old calda over a barely smoldering fire."

"Warm calda is better than cold calda. No one enjoys the Roman concoction of water mixed with spices cold. Fortunately for you, my wife gave me extra dried fish to share with you. I will dig it out later."

"Thank you, Centurion."

Arrius mounted his horse. "These horses are strong, and our time is limited. We will take the mountainous road through Ephraim past Sychar in Samaria, then northeast to Scythopolis.

From there, we have a direct path to Tiberias on the Sea of Galilee."

Tasco added, "Berbers are the pride and joy of Rome, prized above all other horses. I have seen four of these strong-necked beauties pull many chariots to victory."

"Yes, Legionary." Arrius rubbed and patted the neck of his golden-brown horse, "And we will need their strength to take us swiftly to Galilee and back in less than a week."

Tasco whistled signaling his delight as he mounted his animal in a single move, no easy feat without stirrups. "Marching on foot, that timeline would not be possible, Centurion, but with these glorious creatures doing the work, we will have time to spare."

Arrius goaded his horse in the side and said, "We ride!"

After the initial spurt of pent-up energy, the horses settled into a nice cadence. The sun seemed to rise slowly, hidden by the desert mountains that towered on both sides of the men. When sunshine did climb over the hills, the men finally began to warm up a bit.

They rode for hours before Tasco complained, "Centurion, I am sure there is a well in the village ahead. The horses could use some water, and I need to…to relieve myself."

Arrius chuckled. "As do I, young legionary, and I imagine your backside and legs could use a break too."

"It has been some time since I have ridden, Centurion, and in all my years of being on a horse, I have never used a saddle. I fear this four-horned contraption is wearing holes in my—"

"We will dismount soon, very soon."

“Thank you, Centurion.”

“Don’t thank me. I care about the horses more than I do about you. Strong or not, they are not accustomed to bearing a burden as large as you.”

“Yes, Centurion.”

“Tell me, Tasco, where are you from in Gaul?”

“Lugdunum.”

“Ah, I hear that great city has become quite the Roman capital with its own temple to the gods and a large amphitheater.”

“My home shines like a ruby in the emperor’s crown. Without question, it is the most important place in the western half of the empire.”

“It is good to be proud of your home, Tasco. Tell me, how did you become a Roman citizen? Most Gauls must earn or buy their citizenship.”

“My father was the primary engineer on the first aqueduct—the aqueduct of the Monts d’Or—completed a long time ago. It was the first of three aqueducts built to supply water to the city. In honor of his sacrifice and service to Rome, the emperor granted him citizenship.”

“And how is your father today? Is he proud of his legionary son?”

Tasco stopped his horse. When Arrius realized he was alone, he turned back. “What is it, Legionary?”

“My apologies, Centurion. The pain of my past still troubles me.”

“No apologies needed. More than you know, Tasco, I understand. Do you want to speak of it?"

Tasco prodded his horse back into motion. "My father was murdered by rebellious Gauls who hated him for helping Rome."

Arrius moaned, "The empire's success is often her greatest struggle."

"I'm not sure I follow your meaning, Centurion."

Arrius waved his arm across the horizon. "Rome has conquered many lands, tribes, and kingdoms. Yet not all conquered people learn to love her as you and I do."

"Gaul was uncivilized and uncultured before Rome. If Rome were to fall, the whole world would fall. I cannot imagine my life without the empire," said Tasco.

"Hmmm…my Roman roots agree with you, but at times my Germanic blood still longs for freedom."

Tasco did not respond, and he shifted his weight in the saddle. Arrius knew his comment probably made Tasco uncomfortable.

"There." Arrius pointed to a fallen palm tree on the outskirts of a small village. "Let us secure the horses and find some fresh water for all of us. But don't get too comfortable. I still want us to travel seven or eight leagues more today."

Tasco groaned as he slipped off his horse. "At this pace, we will reach Tiberius by nightfall tomorrow."

"Or sooner, Legionary. Sooner if we can."

The sun had long set, and the road—more trail than Roman thoroughfare—became obscured and perilous without a full moon.

After a long day, Arrius decided to stop, and Tasco set up a make-shift camp while Arrius attended to the horses.

"I doubt we are alone in this oasis, and there may be bandits who would love to kill us and steal our horses. I will take the first watch, Tasco. You get some rest. I will wake you for the second watch."

It didn't take Tasco long to settle on his bedroll. He looked exhausted to Arrius.

Tasco spread his cloak over his legs to provide him some warmth. The moon was still low on the horizon, and it seemed a billion stars were within reach.

"Centurion, may I ask you a question?"

"You need to sleep, Legionary. We have another long day ahead of us."

Tasco was on his back and placed both hands under his head. "Just one question."

"Yes?" said Arrius.

"Why did the gods choose Rome?"

"Choose Rome for what?"

Tasco rolled on his side and looked at Arrius. "Why did Jupiter, ruler of the light and sky, choose the Romans to rule the world?"

"As opposed to choosing the Gauls?" Arrius grunted.

"Yes, why not the Britons or the Gauls?"

"Or the people of Germania," added Arrius. "Who knows why the gods do what the gods do? My wife—"

"She is Hebrew, yes?"

Arrius ignored his interruption. “My wife would tell you that her god, Yahweh, chose the Jews, not Romans.”

Tasco hissed, “The Jews are no better than the Bedouins or the barbarians who cannot rule themselves, let alone the world.”

“And yet the Jews existed as a great nation and military power hundreds of years before Rome.”

“Rome will someday rid this land and the entire world of the Jewish plague.” Tasco quickly added, “Your wife being the exception, of course, Centurion.”

Arrius was annoyed. “Go to sleep, Legionary. We can discuss the merits and choices of Jupiter as *Optimus Maximus* tomorrow.”

Tasco turned his back to Arrius and pulled his cloak over his shoulders.

The night was quiet, too quiet for Arrius. He was near the end of his watch when he heard something. He thought it might have been a rodent trying to get into one of their saddlebags. When he moved toward the horses to investigate, one of the Berbers neighed and seemed unsettled.

Arrius placed a gentle hand on the hindquarter of his horse. “Quiet, boy. You need not fear a creature so small compared to you.”

Then, out of the corner of his eye and despite the darkness, Arrius thought he saw something or someone small move. It was larger than a mouse or an animal. He placed a hand on his gladius and drew his sword quietly, allowing it to settle at his side as he rotated the handle in his hand to give him the best grip. Both horses shifted and snorted. Arrius moved to the head of his horse and stood perfectly still. Nothing. No sound. No further stirring. He whispered again to the horses, "Shhhh…all is well. The night casts strange shadows at times." He was about to sheath his weapon when he saw it again. Someone was hiding behind a palm tree next to a low scrub bush.

Arrius spoke loudly and boldly, "I am a Roman centurion. Come out and surrender yourself now, or be prepared to face me in conflict."

Tasco jumped to his feet, wiped his eyes with his left hand, and took his *pugio* in his right hand. "Centurion, are we under attack? What is it? Where are you?"

Arrius was waiting out of sight in the dark.

Arrius yelled, "To your right, Tasco, the intruder moves to your right."

Tasco rotated and took up a fighting stance. "Centurion, I cannot see anything or anyone. "Who is it? How many are upon us?"

Before Arrius answered, someone brushed by the legionary, either a petite man or woman or perhaps a child. Tasco moved to his left and lunged with his knife. He struck nothing but nearly stabbed Arrius, who was in pursuit.

"Legionary, wake up and get your bearings before you wound yourself or me."

"Someone glanced my side. He's moving toward—"

"I see him." Arrius knew the person was trying to escape out of the oasis and into the desert. But once in the sands, Arrius could easily see it was a young child.

Arrius yelled back, "Tasco, in case this is a Bedouin distraction, stay with the horses. I will run down this little thief."

Arrius moved like a lion hunting his prey. The child was quick but not fast enough. When the centurion caught up, he grabbed the child by the back of his cloak and lifted him off the ground. Arrius could tell, even in the darkness, that it was a young boy, maybe five or six years old. The boy was kicking like an angry donkey, flailing his arms, and turning his head, trying to bite Arrius.

"Enough, boy! That is enough. There is nowhere to go, and I will not put you down until you stop."

The boy began to curse Arrius in Aramaic, the Semitic language of Syria. Arrius knew enough of the language from his time there to understand the boy.

In the native tongue of the child, Arrius spoke again. "Stop, or I will eat you!" Of course, he meant to say, "Stop, or I will *hurt* you," but it'd been years since he used Aramaic. The boy stopped kicking and began crying. Arrius threw the boy over his left shoulder like a bag of barley and headed back to the campsite.

Tasco yelled from the oasis, "Centurion, what is happening? Did you catch him?"

"Yes, we are returning. Please don't attempt to strike anyone with your *pugio*."

Tasco cursed and said under his breath, "Then please don't startle me from a dead sleep in the pitch dark again."

Arrius dropped the boy at Tasco's feet.

"So this is the thief who robs me of my sleep," Tasco complained.

Arrius wiped sweat from his brow. "He steals *my* sleep, not yours. I was about to wake you."

Tasco started to visibly shake from both the cold and the adrenaline rush as he turned toward their fire pit. "Centurion, you let the fire die while on watch."

"I wasn't in the mood to look for more dried camel dung, and I was warm enough. You, however, can find some more fuel now and relight the fire to warm the boy."

Tasco grabbed his cloak and said with little enthusiasm, "Yes, Centurion. Give me a moment."

The boy, looking terrified, remained motionless and silent.

Arrius spoke to him again in his broken Aramaic, "What is your name, boy?"

Still lying on the ground, the child turned over and looked up at Arrius.

"Your name? What do they call you?"

The boy whispered through clenched teeth, "Kaamil."

"What? Speak up."

"My name is Kaamil. I am a prince among my people, and my father will remove your head and your man parts when he arrives!"

"Kaamil, is it? I should call you mouse or rabbit or thief. For you are no prince."

Kaamil began to cry again and buried his face in his sandy hands.

Tasco returned quickly, dropped his load of dried dung, wiped his hands on his cloak, and said, "He is a thief. We should slit his throat and rid the world of another boil on the backside of Rome."

The night sky had just begun to glow in the east with the rising sun. Arrius looked down at the boy and said, "If you run again, I will tie your feet with leather straps. There is no place for you to hide and nowhere for you to run. Do you understand me, Kaamil?"

The boy nodded and said something Arrius didn't understand.

Tasco suggested, "We should at least tie him to a tree and leave him for someone else to deal with. Perhaps slavers will find him."

"No, we will take him to Tiberias and find a home for him there. I cannot abandon him to the desert."

"But Centurion—"

"Look at him, Legionary. He probably hasn't eaten in days. We will take him with us and attempt to find him a home. Am I clear?"

Somehow Arrius knew the boy was an orphan and abandoned. In a way, he saw himself in the child and had compassion for him. Arrius stepped directly in front of Tasco and spoke with conviction. "Am. I. Clear. Legionary?"

Tasco looked at the boy and then back at his commander.

"Yes, Centurion. Perfectly clear."

Arrius knew Kaamil didn't understand Latin, but the boy did know who was in charge.

Arrius had the horses fed and watered. He enjoyed caring for these majestic beasts. Tasco covered what remained of their camel-dung fire with sand as Arrius secured his saddlebags to his horse. Kaamil sat huddled next to a tree. His large black eyes remained fixed on Arrius's every move. Whenever Arrius looked the boy's way, the centurion would smile and nod at the child, hoping to win his trust.

A strange mist had settled over the desert floor.

"I do not like this mist, Centurion. I fear it is a bad omen. First, a thief attacks us, and now this."

"Legionaries do not fear anything. The boy did not *attack us*—he was only trying to help himself to some of our food, and this mist is nothing. I have seen this happen many times before in the desert. Before the sun fully rises, the air and ground warm up quickly. As a result, water droplets are suspended low over the desert floor. It will dissipate soon. This is no omen."

"If you say so, Centurion."

"I say so."

Arrius moved toward Kaamil, and the boy cowered. He knelt at eye level and said, "We are traveling north. You will accompany us. Do you understand?"

Kaamil shook his head yes. Arrius then lifted him on top of his horse in front of the saddle.

"The boy will slow us down, Centurion. I worry—"

"I did not ask for, and I do not want to hear your opinion, Legionary."

"My apologies, Centurion—"

"Perhaps it would be best if you stopped talking, Legionary."

Tasco sheepishly said, "At least his distraction allowed me to warm my cold bones at the fire for a bit and to eat breakfast this morning. Thank you for the dried fish. Please tell your wife—"

"My *Jewish* wife—"

"I hope you know I meant no disrespect yesterday. I only—"

"I know what you meant. But perhaps you did not hear what I

said. You Gauls talk too much and listen too little."

Tasco mounted his horse with a little less ease than the day before, obviously hurting in places he didn't know he could be sore. "As I said, please offer your wife my gratitude. Those fish were delicious. What does she season them with?"

"Her secret is curry."

Tasco replied, "Hmmm. Interesting. Different but tasty."

Arrius smiled. "Yes, but perhaps too much curry, as you and your horse may soon discover."

CHAPTER 28

Two Days Later, 32 AD,

the City of Tiberias on the Sea of Galilee

The midafternoon sun was excruciating. There was no wind, and the desert sun perched directly overhead. A rare, bearded vulture circled above them, seemingly in anticipation of a human meal. Despite having to stop more often to allow Kaamil to relieve himself, they'd made good time. Arrius pushed the Berbers to their limits. He had no idea where the rabbi was and wanted to find him as soon as possible.

Arrius spoke more to the boy than Tasco. "Just over that hill is Tiberias. Herod Antipas, son of Herod the Great, named it after our emperor. We will find lodging and food soon."

Tasco interjected, "And the hot springs. I was told the hot springs here are fit for the gods."

"We will not have time to soak, Legionary. Our priority, and the sole reason for this trip, is to find the rabbi. Pilate expects a detailed report upon our return."

Tasco complained, "Centurion, surely a city built around seventeen natural mineral springs and muscles so weary that I can barely move require we have one short visit."

Arrius was irritated. "Food and shelter—that is all we will have time for."

"And what of the boy? You said we would find a home for the little desert rat. It will be embarrassing to ride into the city with a beggar and thief riding on a Roman horse. Can we at least tie him up and make him walk behind us? He should be treated as a slave, not a son."

Arrius ignored him. After hours of reflection, he had other plans for the boy.

"And where do you expect to find information about your rabbi? By the time we reach the city, it will be Sabbath. The Jews will be in their homes eating their special Shabbat meal, or whatever they call it."

Arrius hadn't considered it was Friday, but he wasn't overly concerned. "We will find someone who can help us. Herod Antipas has settled his capital with plenty of Gentiles from rural Galilee. So many, in fact, that my wife tells me the priestly caste refuses to live in Tiberias."

Tasco cursed the Jews under his breath.

Kaamil, on the other hand, seemed to Arrius to grow more and more excited as they drew near the ridge overlooking the sea. He kept pointing and saying something Arrius couldn't understand. Something about sweet food or sweet bread.

All of them sighed when they began their descent into Tiberias. The wind suddenly picked up, and even the horses perked up.

"Hold them, Tasco. Do not let them run. The horses smell water, and they sense we are close. But we need these two for the journey home, and they will injure themselves if we sprint from here."

When they entered the city from the south, it was quiet. The sun was almost below the hills on the western slopes of the Sea of Galilee, or Sea of Tiberias, as the Romans preferred to call it. Most of the shops were closed. However, several bread and meat merchants had yet to close their stalls.

"Tasco, dismount and hand me your reins. Use the coins I gave you earlier and purchase enough bread and dried fish for three days. I will meet you there before the sun fully sets." He pointed to a rock tower a stone's throw east of the market. "The boy and I will find an inn and see to the horses."

"Yes, Centurion. Bread and fish. I will see you soon."

Arrius barked at a man walking away from the market, "You there. Where can we find a stable and lodging?"

"Follow me, Centurion. You are most fortunate; I am the innkeeper of the very best rooms you will find in all of Galilee. My beds are—"

"Yes, yes. Lead us there without delay. We are tired, and I have no patience for your blabbering."

"Of course, Centurion. And what of your slave?" He said as he pointed to the boy.

Arrius sat up straight in the saddle and barked, "He will remain with me—"

"But Centurion, my beds are not…not suitable for…how shall I put it? For flea and lice-ridden Bedouin misfits."

Arrius goaded his horse and then pulled up hard on the reins, startling the old man. "My silver *is* suitable, I take it?"

"Yes, of course, Centurion, but I fear I will have to charge you a higher rate since I will be forced to burn the cot the boy sleeps on. Unless you will make him sleep on the— ”

Arrius was angry but decided it was best not to argue. “Charge what you will, but offend me again, and your life will not be worth as much as this boy’s life.”

The innkeeper bowed. “And I will see that your Berbers receive my best grain. They are fine animals, fine Roman specimens, magnificent indeed.”

Arrius leaned toward the innkeeper and said with a low voice, “I am in need of information too.”

“Yes, Centurion, how may I help you?”

“Have you heard of Rabbi Yeshua? I have been told He is near here.”

“*Everyone* has heard of this man. I have heard His teachings too. He is a very strange rabbi, but He performs great miracles. In fact, not too far from here, He fed thousands of people with less food than that boy would eat for a single meal.”

Arrius slid off his horse and stepped in front of the toothless old man who smelled like he hadn’t bathed in weeks. He asked in rapid fire, “Where is He? Where can I find Him? Is He close? I have urgent Roman business to attend to and need to find Him as soon as possible.”

“Finding Him will not be difficult, but getting to Him will be *impossible* for a Roman centurion. The people want to make Him king. Your presence near the rabbi, especially if you are not protected by a lot of legionaries, will result in great harm to you. Centurion, I myself am loyal to the emperor, but most who follow the teacher are not—”

It looked like Arrius’s face was on fire as he clenched his jaw.

"Just tell me where He is! I can take care of myself, innkeeper."

In response, the old man took a step backward. "If you follow the coastal trail in that direction," he pointed northwest, "before the sun is high, you will stumble into the masses. But Centurion—"

"Enough! I have heard enough. Take us to our room."

After giving them access to their lodgings, the innkeeper asked, "Is there anything else I can do for you tonight? Perhaps you desire female—"

"No. I do *not*. I do, however, need you to do one of two things."

"Anything for you, Centurion."

"Either watch the boy or go to the market tower and find the legionary I travel with."

The innkeeper held out his hand for payment, and Arrius dropped several silver coins in his palm.

As the old man began to walk backward to the door, he bowed low and said, "As you wish, Centurion. As you wish. I will find your companion, sir, and return with him soon."

Arrius shook his head in disgust. "And I will settle up with you before we leave in the morning."

Kaamil was already asleep when Tasco entered their room.

"Arrius—"

"Centurion, to you."

"*Centurion* Arrius, how is it this…this boy has found his way into our room? I expected him to sleep in the stables at best or in someone else's care tonight. We cannot—"

Arrius had just removed his armor and finished washing his face and arms in a bowl of water. He wiped his face with a small towel and turned slowly to Tasco. "I am done hearing your *advice* about this child. Kaamil is with us, and he will remain with us until I say otherwise. Do you understand?"

Tasco was speechless.

"Do. You. Understand?"

Tasco nodded.

"I have decided to take the boy with us back to Jerusalem. I cannot imagine finding a suitable home for him here. I don't know anyone and cannot entrust him to a stranger."

Tasco's eyes widened.

"My wife's people believe caring for widows and orphans is a matter of religious duty for them. Even a homeless and parentless Bedouin boy will not be turned away by the Jews. Of course, they will convert him and circumcise him—the gods help the poor lad—but they will not reject him. He travels with us to Jerusalem."

Arrius sat on the bed, removed his boots, and then lay down next to the boy, who was not as asleep as he pretended.

Arrius whispered, "All is well, Kaamil. I will protect you as if you were my son."

Surprisingly, Kaamil put his head on Arrius's arm to snuggle and whispered in Aramaic, "Goodnight, Roman."

Arrius took a deep breath. "Goodnight, little rabbit. Sleep well. We travel again in the morning to find the one I seek."

Kaamil looked up at the Arrius's face and said as he yawned,

"Who is this rabbi?"

"I hope to find a good answer to that very question, Kaamil. We will see, boy; we will see."

CHAPTER 29

Sunday, Year 32 AD, Tiberias

Morning always came early for Arrius. Tasco, on the other hand, would probably sleep until midday if allowed.

Arrius looked over at Kaamil resting peacefully on his cot and thought, *What am I to do with you when we reach Jerusalem? I feel an attachment that I cannot explain.*

Just outside the open window, a rooster crowed, showing off, no doubt, to a brood of hens. Arrius stepped to the opening and took a deep breath of fresh, cool air rolling in off the water.

"Good morning, Roman."

Arrius turned to see the boy sitting on the edge of the cot, wiping the sleep from his eyes. Kaamil gave Arrius a half-smile.

"Good morning, little rabbit. Instead of *Roman*, you may call me Arrius."

"And you may call me *Kaamil*, not rabbit."

"I know your name, boy, but I think I will call you my little rabbit, nonetheless, because you are both quick and elusive."

Kaamil shook his head and said something Arrius couldn't quite make out. Something about not being quick enough to outrun an old man. Then without asking or explaining, Kaamil stepped to a pot in the corner and relieved himself.

"It is fortunate that you chose the pot and not the legionary's helmet."

Kaamil smiled again and said, "My mistake. Where is his helmet?"

Arrius laughed and then spoke to the boy in Latin. "So, if we are to be together, *Kaamil*, we will have to work on your Latin."

Kaamil looked curious but said nothing.

Tasco rolled over and exclaimed, "Centurion, what does that mean? What do you mean by '*be together*'?"

Arrius ignored his question. "Time for you to crawl out of bed, Legionary. I want to get moving as soon as possible."

Tasco got up, walked to a basin of water, splashed his face, and pressed Arrius for an answer. "Are we not leaving the boy here in Tiberias? You cannot be serious about taking this desert orphan back with us all the way to Jerusalem."

"Asked and answered already, Legionary. He comes with us, and I will not hear any further challenge from you on this matter."

Tasco mumbled something in Gallic, his native tongue.

Arrius pointed a finger at Tasco. "Let me be clear, Legionary. Any more challenges or complaints by you regarding this matter will be met with my horse's whip against your back." As Tasco bowed his head slightly, he said, "I am yours to command."

"Yes, Legionary, you are, and the next few days will go much better for you if you remember that simple fact."

Kaamil said he was hungry, so Arrius directed him to his saddlebags in the corner of the room. "You will find fresh bread there. I will get you some goat's milk before we leave."

Kaamil rushed to the food as if he hadn't eaten in weeks, but he went to Tasco's saddlebags.

"Not those, you thief, the centurion's—"

Out of nowhere, and before Tasco realized what was happening, Arrius hit him hard on the side of the head. "The fresh bread is in your bags, idiot. And all our bread belongs to Rome, which means it belongs to me, and I will distribute *what* I want to whom I wish and *when* I choose to do so."

Tasco rubbed his head as he sat back down on his cot. "I only—"

"Enough. I have had enough from you, Legionary. In fact, I am tired of hearing your complaints and even more tired of your ugly face. I think it is best if you stay here today while the boy and I seek out the rabbi. Try to stay out of trouble while we are gone."

Tasco smiled. "Of course, Centurion. A wise choice, I am sure. Does this mean I am free to visit the bathhouse at the hot springs?"

Arrius rolled his eyes and shook his head. "Do as you wish. However, I want your saddlebag, your saddle, and *my* armor cleaned and polished as well by my return."

Tasco cocked his head. "You will ride without your uniform and armor?"

"Yes, there is no need to stir up any anger among the rabbi's followers or the crowds."

"And when will you return, Centurion?"

"By nightfall or earlier. I suggest you attend to your duties before you attend to your sensual needs."

"Again, a wise leadership decision, Centurion—"

"Just do as I ask and make sure there is bread and fish available still when we return."

Tasco looked at Kaamil and back at Arrius. "Fresh bread and fish. Yes, Centurion."

Kaamil sat on the ground, covered in breadcrumbs. "I go with you, Roman?"

"Yes, you go with me. We leave soon."

After saddling his horse and giving the Berber ample grain and water, Arrius looked at the adorable and expectant black eyes of Kaamil. "Are you ready for an adventure, little rabbit?"

Kaamil gave him a nod and smiled. "I have heard of this man you seek."

Arrius was surprised. "And what have you heard about Him? How does a Bedouin boy in the desert know of this rabbi?"

"All of the desert people have heard of Him. Some say He is a demon. Some say He is a prophet. Many speak of His miracles."

"What miracles?"

Kaamil raised both his hands to the sky. "He makes bread out of rocks and sand."

Arrius laughed, "Of course, *that* miracle matters most to you."

Kaamil looked a bit offended but continued, "And He raises the dead, Roman. He puts breath back in the lungs of ghosts!"

"Yes, Kaamil, I have heard of both of those deeds, but men are given to exaggeration. And with each telling of a story, the tale grows bigger and better. We will see."

"And where are we going? Will it take long?"

"The innkeeper told me the trail to take. We will go north and west until we find large crowds. I have been told it will not be difficult to find this rabbi. Thousands flock to Him."

"Will it not be hot today, Roman?"

"Yes, but traveling along the sea should provide some breeze."

Kaamil gave him a thumbs up and asked, "Can I hold the reigns today?"

Arrius smiled. "*Can* you, or *may* you? The true question is, are you able to do so?"

"I have led thousands of camels—"

Arrius chuckled. "Guiding a camel is different than directing a Berber."

"I can do it, Roman."

"Okay, we will see if a little rabbit can control a mighty Roman beast."

Thankfully, the trail was easy to find and follow. It was apparent to Arrius that many thousands of feet had recently traveled this path. Arrius and Kaamil left before the sun was over the hills that surround the Sea of Tiberias, but now it was directly overhead and scorching.

"Roman, you said the breeze would cool us, but there is no wind today."

Arrius didn't reply. There was nothing to say.

"Will we arrive soon, Roman?"

"Soon enough."

Just then, as they rounded a corner, a vast multitude of people appeared.

Kaamil whistled in amazement. "Have you ever seen a gathering as large as this?"

Of course, Arrius had—in battle—but he didn't want to talk about those experiences now.

"Kaamil, I am going to leave you there with the horse." Arrius pointed to a tree near the water.

Kaamil began to protest.

"Boy, I cannot ride with *this* beast into *that* crowd. What's more, you both need water and rest. I will secure the horse and return soon."

"And what if I take this horse and run? Or what if a thief wants him, kills me, and steals your animal?"

Arrius knew the boy would not escape as long as he was being fed and treated well. "No one will steal a Roman horse this close to a Roman outpost. Besides, I have you to protect him. Are you not a fierce Bedouin?"

Kaamil sat up straight and puffed out his chest. "Yes. I will protect this animal with my life."

Arrius lifted the boy off the horse's neck, and then he dismounted. After letting the Berber drink, he secured him to a low branch of the Sycamore tree.

Kaamil took a deep drink, too, and asked, "Can I play in the water while you are gone?"

"Yes, you may, but stay close and do not go too deep. I am sure most Bedouin boys never learn to swim."

Kaamil shook his head in disagreement and protested, "I have crossed the length and breadth of this great sea many times."

Arrius was not impressed. "Stay close to the shore. And please try to leave a bit of the bread for me to eat upon my return." Arrius then glared at Kaamil to make his point. "Do you understand?"

"Yes, Roman, I do."

Arrius was unconvinced the boy would obey him, but he had no other option. Kaamil's presence would warn any potential thieves that the animal belonged to a centurion. No one would dare bother what they would see as a Roman slave and a Roman's horse.

Arrius had no hope of blending in with this very Hebrew crowd. With his short, cropped hair, beardless face, and height, he stood out like a beggar at a wedding. The hillside leading up from the waterfront held several thousand people. The ones at the front of the crowd sat on the ground. The people on the outside and in the rear stood. The Jews were practically body upon body as people got as close to the rabbi as possible. Yeshua sat in a boat not far from the shoreline. His voice carried well, and no one made a sound as they leaned into His words and listened. Arrius wasn't happy to be seen, but he worked his way down to the water's edge to the east of the rabbi and only an arrow's shot from the teacher.

The rabbi was surprisingly intense.

"Peacemakers are fortunate…for they will be called God's

children."

Arrius already didn't like what he heard.

"When your friends, family, or neighbors insult you, mistreat you, and falsely accuse you because you follow Me, celebrate and be exceedingly glad. My Father will someday reward you in heaven. You are not alone; remember all the prophets who were persecuted before you."

The people groaned in agreement at the mention of their prophets. When they quieted down again, the rabbi went on.

"The law and your religious leaders tell you it is wrong to murder, and anyone who does so will be judged. But I tell you that anyone who hates someone and curses them will be judged. In fact, if you say '*raca*' to your brother or sister, you will be in danger of the fire of hell."

Arrius knew *raca* was a harsh Aramaic term of contempt.

"All of your lives, you have heard it said, 'An eye for an eye and a tooth for a tooth,' but I tell you there is a better way. If anyone strikes you on the right cheek, turn to them the other cheek also. Do not resist an evil person or return violence with violence."

Arrius had heard enough. He turned to walk away, but the next words of Yeshua stopped him in his tracks.

"If a Roman centurion forces you to carry his *sarcina* for a distance, offer to go beyond his demands and carry it a league more."

At this, the crowd began to fidget and complain. A man near Arrius, a Pharisee who was upset, yelled out, "Rabbi, next you will tell us to love our Roman enemies!"

The crowd laughed.

Yeshua didn't miss a beat. "You have heard it said, 'Love those who are good to you and hate your enemy.'"

The people nodded in agreement.

Yeshua directed His eyes toward the man who challenged Him. "But I tell you to love your enemies and pray to Yahweh for those who persecute you."

Arrius felt as if the eyes of the rabbi turned to him next. In fact, it seemed everyone was looking at him.

Yeshua continued, with Arrius feeling the full impact of His piercing gaze, "Our Father causes the sun to rise on the evil and the good and sends rain on the righteous and the unrighteous—even on the tax collectors and your Roman oppressors."

Almost on cue, a dark cloud that had rolled in off the lake opened, and it began to rain. The shower would pass quickly, as squalls do off the sea, so the people covered their heads and stayed put.

At that moment, Arrius was startled by a voice behind him. "And what do you think of His teaching, Roman?"

Arrius turned around to find a young man directly behind him. "Why would you care what I think?" asked Arrius.

"Because of *all* the rabbi's teachings, I, too, struggle at times when He challenges us to love the unlovely…the lepers, evil women, the treacherous tax collectors, and…and the Romans like you."

Always at his side, Arrius placed his hand on his *pugio*.

The man took a step back. "I mean you no harm, Roman. I am only curious as to how you feel about Yeshua's words."

"Who are you, Jew?" Arrius demanded.

"I am Simon, called Simon the Canaanite by my brothers."

Arrius relaxed and removed his hand from his knife. "And what *brothers* do you refer to?"

Simon pointed to the men closest to Yeshua. "Those men. I am one of the chosen twelve."

"And how do you or any of the *chosen* followers of the rabbi imagine a Roman would feel about His preposterous teachings?"

Simon was not intimidated. "As many of us feel. There is no path to shalom with Rome, and love for our greatest enemy will never set us free from her torturous grip."

Arrius knew a Zealot when he saw one. He decided not to make a scene but abruptly pushed past Simon as he left, intentionally forcing the Jew to move.

As Arrius walked back to Kaamil, he cursed himself for thinking the outcome of his trip to the north would produce any answers. *Love your enemy. What nonsense. This rabbi is a fool. He and all His followers will be removed from this dreadful land by either Rome, the Sanhedrin, or both. Their days are numbered.*

The return trip to Jerusalem went slower with Kaamil. Arrius wasn't concerned because his time in Galilee was shorter than he anticipated. Tasco was unusually quiet. Arrius knew he was perturbed by the presence of the boy.

Arrius used the time to begin to teach Kaamil Latin. The child had a sharp mind and learned quickly.

Near Jerusalem, Tasco did ask, "What will you report to Pilate,

Centurion?"

Arrius didn't answer. He had no idea how to describe a mysterious rabbi who taught love for their enemies while at the same time amassing a following of tens of thousands. Yeshua had so many followers that He could easily resist the Roman presence in Jerusalem if He chose to do so. Only time would tell.

Chapter 30

Year 32 AD, Jerusalem

The sun was about to set as Arrius and Kaamil arrived in Jerusalem via the Mount of Olives. Tasco separated from them and made his way to the barracks. The city was quiet. The air was heavy and filled with the smell of dinner cooking on a thousand fires as a cloud of smoke hovered over the city like a blanket.

"Roman, I have never been here. Is it safe?" Kaamil looked over his shoulder up into the eyes of his newest friend and benefactor.

"Safe enough. But you have nothing to worry about. You are with me."

Kaamil sighed and laid his head back against the chest of Arrius. "Will she…will she want me?"

Arrius knew Kaamil was referring to Ayla. They had spoken together of her and his children during their journey. "Ayla is kind and compassionate—far more than I am. She will accept you with open arms, little rabbit."

"But you have children. What if she—"

"You have nothing to fear."

"But she is a Jew, and her people do not…do not like *my* people."

"True, but my wife's people do not like my people either."

Kaamil laughed and said, "No one likes Romans, Roman."

Arrius playfully grabbed and squeezed the knee of Kaamil, making him jump and giggle. "That is also true, but Ayla is a good woman. She follows the one we went to see in Galilee, and He has told His followers to love their enemies."

"Who loves the one who hates you? That is foolish."

"I will not argue with you about that, Kaamil, but if Ayla can love a Roman, she can love anyone, and she will love you."

Kaamil sighed again as he shook his head.

A stray dog darted out of the bushes and ran across the road, startling the horse. "Whoa, boy, all is well." Arrius reached down to pat the neck of his weary horse. "We will be home soon."

Kaamil spoke up, "Do you have many horses at your home?"

Arrius chuckled, "I have no horses at my home. They are kept in the garrison, but it is late, and I am tired. We will secure him in my courtyard for the evening."

"Roman?"

"Yes."

"Can I stay with him?"

"With the Berber? In my courtyard?"

"Uh-huh."

"No, I will give you a cot to sleep on in my home."

"I prefer to sleep where I can see the stars, Roman."

Arrius hadn't thought about how, as a homeless orphan, Kaamil rarely, if ever, slept with a roof over his head. "You slept inside in Tiberias, and you were fine."

"You did not give me a choice."

"Ayla will not allow you to sleep in my courtyard with this Berber. Besides, it will be cold tonight."

"I am used to the cold, Roman."

Arrius let the matter go, knowing Ayla would not hear of it and no one, not even an adorable Bedouin boy, would convince her otherwise.

Arrius knew Ayla would hear the horse on the cobblestones and run out to greet him as they approached the home. Just as Arrius dismounted, she jumped into his arms and wrapped her hands around his neck before he took Kaamil down from the horse.

"I missed you, my *bashert*. And you are home sooner than I expected."

"Yes, sooner than I anticipated—"

"And who is this young man?" She inquired as she looked up at Kaamil.

Arrius lifted him off the horse, and Kaamil hid behind him. "This is Kaamil. I found him—or better put—*he* found me in the desert."

Ayla spoke to him in Aramaic, "Greetings, Kaamil. Welcome to our home."

Kaamil said nothing.

"Is he mute?"

"No, believe me, the boy can talk, but he is afraid—"

"I am afraid of *nothing*, Roman. Tell your wife how brave I am."

Ayla smiled. "Ah, so he does speak. I wonder if he eats too."

Kaamil looked up at Arrius and then back at Ayla. "Yes, I eat. I must have some more of your dried fish."

Arrius added, "Try again, Kaamil. Say, 'Please, dear woman, may I have some of your—'"

"Yes, my apologies, wife of the Roman—"

Ayla giggled, "Ayla. You may call me Ayla, and I have dried fish, fresh fruit, and bread waiting for both of you, Kaamil." Ayla pointed into the house.

Kaamil looked again at Arrius, who nodded his approval and said, "Yes, wash your hands in the basin, and leave me some food to eat."

Kaamil did not need to be told twice as he bounced into the courtyard and the house without hesitation.

Arrius called out and said firmly, "Wash your face and hands first." He then led the Berber into the courtyard and secured him to a post.

Ayla put her hands on her hips. "You know I do not like the mess these beasts make in my courtyard. The last one left a small lake in the middle, and the children will—"

"I will clean up after him long before the children are awake."

Ayla took Arrius by the hand and said, "So, tell me, my husband, are we collecting children from the desert now?"

"He is an orphan, Ayla. He is seven or maybe eight years old and alone. He can barely remember his mother."

"Do you know what happened to her?"

“No, not exactly, but I do know she died in his arms some time ago, and as near as I can tell, he never knew his father.”

Ayla placed her hand over her heart and groaned, “How has he survived?”

“He is smart, quick, and a thief. He was trying to steal food and coins from our packs when we caught him. I could not—”

“Of course, you could not leave him.”

“Can we find him a home among your people?”

“We already have, Arrius. I can see the attachment he has to you and the affection you have for him. We will make our home his home.”

Arrius lifted her off the ground and above his head in a firm embrace. “And this is why I love you, Ayla Rose.”

“Because I let you put a horse in my courtyard and an orphan in my home?”

Arrius squeezed her thighs in his arms. “No, because your heart is as vast as the desert Kaamil came from, and you never cease to surprise me.”

Arrius let her slide down close enough to kiss her passionately on the lips.

“None of that now, Roman; we have a boy watching us.”

Arrius turned to see Kaamil standing in the doorway, gawking at them. He had fish in one hand, bread in the other, and a mouth full of food. “Roman, are you hurting her? Has she disobeyed you?”

Both Arrius and Ayla laughed as Arrius put her down. “No, little rabbit, I am not hurting her, but I might hurt you if you do not leave me some food."

Kaamil shrugged his shoulders, turned, and walked away as he said, "You are not fast enough to catch me again, Roman. You cannot hurt what you cannot capture."

Ayla snickered, "I can see I will have to keep my eye on this boy. I now have two men in my house who will try my patience."

"Yes, Wife, you have no idea. The boy is a handful."

Ayla led Arrius into the house. "So tell me. How was your time in Galilee? Did you see the rabbi? Did you get to speak with Him?"

Arrius hesitated but knew he had to get it off his chest. "Things did not go…did not unfold as I expected. We have much to talk about, but not tonight. I am too tired."

Ayla spoke quietly and with a spark in her eye. "Hmmm. Tomorrow then. I want to hear *everything*, but are you also too tired to make love to me once the boy is asleep?"

Arrius pulled Ayla close for another hug and whispered in her ear, "A Roman is never too tired for love, Wife. Never."

Ayla smiled and blushed.

The boy shook his head as he walked away and said, "Are you sure you don't want me to sleep outside tonight, Roman?"

Arrius moaned, "This one is probably too aware for his age. And I'm afraid he is too street-smart for his own good."

Ayla giggled and said, "Looks like this boy will change things for us."

Chapter 31

Months Later, 33 AD, Jerusalem, Home of Arrius and Ayla

Arrius returned home from an excursion into the desert with his *centuria*. They'd been in pursuit of a band of Bedouins or bandits that had attacked a trade caravan carrying needed military supplies from Syria to Jerusalem. As was often the case, they found no one and none of the taken provisions. He was irritated and tired. The years of marching, training, and fighting were catching up with him. As he lay on his back across the bed, his undertunic was soaked in sweat. The heat was unbearable. A donkey brayed in the street, probably complaining about the weather, her burden, or both.

Ayla entered and pushed Arrius's feet off the bed. "I just washed the bedding, and now you are soiling it with desert grime and enough sweat to attract the fleas of a thousand camels."

Arrius moaned as he sat up next to her. "I'm sorry. Would you have me lay on the ground?"

"I would have you let me remove your clothes and allow me to wash you clean with a basin of water and a towel before you ruined half a day's work."

Arrius groaned again but stood to disrobe as he found a bit of energy at the thought of his wife bathing him.

"I know what you are thinking, my *bashert*, and whatever fond mood I might have been in vanished when I smelled you. The flies are circling you like a pile of dung."

Arrius shrugged his shoulders. "Too little. Too late?"

Ayla smiled. "Too much. Too soon." But then she stood and began to wipe the dirt and stench from her husband's back and arms. "So, Centurion, how was it in the desert?"

Arrius sighed. "I hate the desert. The sands bring nothing but pain to me. Nothing grows there. Nothing lives there." Arrius cursed. "And nothing good ever happens in the dunes."

Ayla laid her head on Arrius's freshly cleaned back and said, "Is your pain caused by your time in Syria with your brother?"

Arrius shook her off his back and moved to the window, where a breeze finally began to move the air. He heard Seneca playing in the courtyard. "Sometimes, I wonder if my son will have to endure the pain of loss as I have. No man should have to watch a brother die."

Ayla sat on the edge of the bed, unsure how to ask a difficult question. "Why is it that you rarely speak of your brother Justus? Are you ashamed of him? Did he die dishonorably?"

Arrius grabbed the windowpane with both hands as he raised his voice. "No, Ayla, quite to the contrary, my brother died a hero of Rome. Justus should have lived, and I should have died in that horrible place. He was good. He was honorable. He was the better brother. At the very least, I should never have left him to be eaten by the vultures." Arrius then hit the window frame with his fist.

"And if you had stayed with him, would he have lived?"

He shook his head as he continued to turn his back to Ayla. "No, but that's *not* the point."

Ayla spoke softly, "And if you had stayed, would *you* be alive today? Would you be my *bashert*—my soulmate? And the father of our children? Would you—"

Arrius turned with a force that startled Ayla. "No. No. And no! I surely would have died, but it would have been an honorable death defending his life with my blood. Every day and every time I put on my uniform and place my centurion's helmet on my head, I think of him. Every time. Every. Single. Time."

As Arrius turned back to the open window, he spit and cursed again. "I hate myself. I hate this curse I live with. And if I live long enough to kill every filthy Bedouin in this wretched desert, it would not be enough to quench the rage in my soul."

At that moment, four-year-old Seneca walked into the room. The tension was thick. He looked at his mother with tears growing in his eyes. "Abba okay, Immi? He hurt?"

The look on his son's face brought Arrius to his knees with his hands held out toward Seneca. "Your father is okay, Son. I am mad at the bad men, not you or your mother."

Seneca ran past his father into his mother's lap. Arrius rose to his feet, more wounded by his son's rejection than offended.

"Seneca, do you remember the stories your father would tell you about his brother?"

Seneca nodded as he began to suck his thumb with his head against Ayla's chest.

"Your father's brother was a very brave man…who…who was taken from your father in a horrible battle."

Seneca sat up, raised both fists in the air, and roared, "Fight bad men in war."

Ayla gently placed her hand on the side of his head and drew Seneca back to her breast. "Yes, your uncle Justus fought bad men in war…bad men in a bad war…and I pray to Yahweh you never fully understand how bad and evil war is."

Arrius snapped, "War is not evil. *Men* are evil. War is necessary to rid the earth of horrible men so that good men and women and their children can live free of fear. Do not fill my son's head with your foolish thoughts of peace, woman."

Ayla began to rock her son as she fought back tears. "And how, Arrius, has war brought you any freedom? How has it set you free from fear and shame?"

Arrius pressed the palms of his hands against his temples. "We have spoken of this. You married a warrior. You know what I do and for whom I do it."

"I married a *man*. A good man. A kind man. A man who would willingly lay his life down for his brother…for us…if need be. Arrius, you are far more than a warrior. And someday you will put down your sword for good. I pray for that day."

Arrius bolted to a small table in the corner of the room where he'd set his gladius, lifted it, and unsheathed the blade in a single move. The sunlight through the window bounced from the blade against the ceiling. "As long as there are evil men, this sword and my wrath will have blood. A man like me cannot choose the path of peace. To hate my enemies is to love my family."

Ayla held Seneca tight, almost too tightly, as she tried to cover his ears and shield his eyes from the hatred on Arrius's face. She bowed her head and spoke slowly and softly. "Arrius, I know you are in pain, my love. And I know your entire life you have been taught to fight for what you want and that the meek are weak and worthless."

Arrius lowered and sheathed his gladius as he took a deep breath.

Ayla continued without flinching, "But I have come to believe that the meek are blessed, for they will inherit the earth. That the merciful are happy, for they are the ones who will be shown mercy. I believe the peacemakers are not fools but the fortunate sons of Yahweh. The Lord longs for shalom on the earth, not war."

"So, Wife, you would have me herd goats or serve tables for a living? It is *this* sword," as he held the weapon in one fist above his head, "that puts food on our table and a roof over our heads."

Ayla stood with Seneca in her arms. "No, Arrius, it is Yahweh who provides all that we need. The Lord is our hope, our provider, and our life. He is all that we need."

Arrius stepped directly in front of Ayla and spoke words he would someday regret, "Where was *your* Yahweh when my mother and father died? Where was your Lord when a godless Bedouin struck down my brother? Where is your God now that your own family and religious community have abandoned you?"

Ayla rushed out of the room weeping, leaving Arrius seething and yelling at the ceiling, "If You are so great and wonderful, Yahweh, why are Your people so miserable and abandoned? If You are a good God, answer me that!"

Arrius collapsed again on the bed, cursing the gods. *There is no pax or shalom for me*, he thought. Within moments, he was asleep.

The sun had set, and the room was dark when Arrius was

startled awake by a voice he did not recognize. *Arrius, I am the shalom…the pax you long for when you are alone. I have heard the cries of your wife, but I have also listened to the cry of your soul.*

Somehow, whether he was dreaming or not, he knew it was the voice of Yahweh. Arrius was glad he was alone and in the dark, for he began to weep as never before. He then whispered in fear and humiliation, "Depart from me, Lord; I am a broken and wretched man." Above and behind him, he heard the voice again, barely above a whisper, *I never abandon the broken, and I have great plans for you.*

Chapter 32

Several Weeks Later, 33 AD, Jerusalem

Cassius entered the barracks to find Arrius sitting alone at a table, rubbing his temples. The flies this time of year were unrelenting. A dozen or so flittered in and around three empty cups.

"What troubles you now, Arrius? It seems you are a man carrying the weight of a camel on your back."

Arrius sighed as he took a swat at a fly. "Where should I start? Bringing the Bedouin boy into our home has created more tension and trouble than I expected. Kaamil is wild and sneaks out of the house at night to wander the streets. Tikva is teething. And the words of that troublemaker, Yeshua, still trouble me."

Cassius offered unsolicited advice. "So you are tired of the Bedouin? Of course, he is wild. What did you expect? Return the boy to his people or at least tie him to his cot at night, rub wine on your daughter's gums, and ignore that rabbi and what some consider as weak teachings."

With more anger this time, Arrius swiped at another fly. "I cannot abandon the boy. I am not weary of him, only fed up with his… his lack of discipline. But the little rabbit thief has stolen a part of my old heart. Regarding my daughter, my wife would kill me if I suggested using wine on Tikva's gums. And if the rabbi's teachings are so *weak*, why do they hit me so hard?"

Cassius shrugged his shoulders and filled one of the empty cups with fresh wine. "If you are going to ignore my advice—"

Arrius chuckled, "I don't recall asking for your advice, and it seems a bit too early to drink wine." Somehow Cassius always had a way of making Arrius smile no matter how dire the situation.

"Arrius, I don't recall you ever *asking* for my wise counsel, but when has that ever stopped me?" Cassius laughed, hit the table hard with the palm of his hand, and after taking another long drink, he said, "The water in this vile place tastes like donkey urine, and I will drink what I will."

Arrius offered a mock salute. "I am grateful for your friendship, Cassius, even when I am *not* so grateful for your advice."

Cassius leaned in as he whispered, "Has Pilate settled down since you gave him your report from Galilee?"

Arrius stood and began to pace as he typically did when stressed. "No. Pilate has not stopped badgering me since I returned. He is concerned the rabbi is on the path to insurrection. Yesterday, he sent a messenger to General Valerius asking for more legionaries."

Cassius scratched his head. "As commander of the Tenth, and because he hates the Jews as much as Pilate, the general might honor Pilate's request—but I doubt it. Currently, Valerius has less than two legions under his command. He's not going to weaken his position in Syria based on rumors in Judea."

Arrius pounded his fist on the table, stirring another group of flies. "Yeshua is annoying, but He is *not* an insurrectionist. I have told Pilate the man is a lamb among lions. My wife assures me the rabbi is harmless, and everything I have seen and heard confirms her belief. Bringing more legionaries to Jerusalem will only aggravate our situation here and solve nothing."

Cassius asked, "Then what bothers you, and why do you still call Him a troublemaker?"

"Cassius, do you know what He says we are to do with our enemies? Have you heard what He tells His followers regarding Rome and our men?"

Cassius took another drink of his wine. "No, but I am sure you intend to tell me."

"This rabbi…this leader of thousands…this…this *man*…He tells His followers to *love* their enemies. He is an utter fool. Yet Yeshua's words are like pebbles in my sandals, and His words echo off my mind like arrows bouncing off a stone wall. His madness does not pierce my soul, but the arrows are relentless."

Cassius prodded, "Are you certain?"

"Certain of what? Speak plainly, Cassius."

"From where I sit and from what I have seen in these past weeks, it does seem as if His words have penetrated something deep inside you."

Arrius sat down. "Ayla agrees with you, and she, too, irritates me when she points that out."

"Your wife is wise."

Arrius grunted. "My wife is a woman who holds onto wishful thinking that somehow I will become a follower as she has."

Cassius laughed. "Okay, maybe she is not as wise as I think."

"The other day, I caught her telling my children and Kaamil

one of the rabbi's ridiculous stories."

Cassius slapped his leg and interjected with sarcasm, "Cut out her tongue!"

"Not at all helpful, Cassius."

Cassius laughed. "Arrius, why are you always so quick to dismiss my advice?"

"Why does a goat eat the flowers and not the weeds? Answer me that riddle, African, and perhaps you can actually offer something that might help me."

Cassius sat back and said, "As you know, I have heard some of this rabbi's teachings. I find His stories neither ridiculous nor subversive. In fact—"

"Oh, for the love of the gods, man. Have you become a follower?"

"No, but there is something different about *this* Jew. I cannot place my finger on it or wrap my mind around it, but He is intriguing. He dresses like a commoner, but He speaks like a king. His words have a ring of authority to them—"

"His words are not intriguing; they are infuriating."

"Arrius," Cassius leaned in again toward his friend, "you worry too much about another Jewish sect that will surely fade in time. And if you try to push your wife away from this rabbi, you will only drive her closer to Him. I know women, and I know Ayla. If you argue with her, you will lose. But if you let it go, she will eventually let Him go."

"I think it is safe to say I know my wife better than any other. She is no fickle fan of this man. Something at her core has changed. So, Cassius, if you are my friend, I need your support.

What can I do to rescue my wife from following a man who would likely turn this city into a riot next week? Ayla tells me He is certain to come to Jerusalem next week for Passover. Pilate will not tolerate an upheaval during this Jewish festival, and the Sanhedrin can no longer afford to let this man challenge their authority."

Cassius stood and straightened his tunic. "We are Romans. This city is ours to command. I suggest you stop worrying so much about your wife and children and turn your full attention to your duties. You married a Hebrew who follows a Hebrew. Accept it for what it is right now. And accept that she will teach your children what she chooses to teach—that is the way of all mothers. However, you and I both know that if the rabbi creates a problem for Rome, we will deal with Him as we must. In the meantime, be the centurion I trained you to be and lead well."

At that moment, Tasco entered the partially illuminated room, saluted, and stood at attention. The morning light peered through the upper windows, highlighting the dust and smoke from dozens of breakfast fires throughout the Antonia Fortress. The young legionary was panting. "Centurion Cassius and Centurion Arrius, our spies have told us of a plot against Pilate. The Zealots intend to ambush him."

Jewish Zealots throughout Judea, and especially in Jerusalem, were a constant source of irritation to Pilate. Of the four sects of Hebrews—the Pharisees, the Sadducees, the Essenes, and the Zealots—the Zealots were the most vocal and violent against Rome.

Arrius looked up. "When? Where? How? And who is leading this ambush?"

"It…the…uh—"

"Spit it out, soldier!" yelled Arrius.

"Centurion, we have yet to gather all the information and know very little—"

Arrius lifted his hand to silence the soldier. "You have interrupted our morning with information that is already well-known to Pilate and us. Every other day there is a report of another insurrectionist's plan to kill the prefect. You are as dumb as you are ugly."

"But Centurion—"

Cassius rubbed his face and spoke calmly, "Tasco, leave us and come back after you have something we can use with details we can act upon."

Tasco looked at Arrius. "Centurion Arrius, I only—"

Arrius stood up and barked, "Are you deaf as well as ignorant? Do *not* bother us again until you know more. Beat it out of your spies if you must, but find out more before you waste any more of our time."

With sweat dripping down his face and eyes open wide, the legionary saluted again, turned, and left the room as quickly as he entered.

"Besides all your other problems, you must have had a bad night's rest, Arrius. You were a bit tough on the young Tasco."

"He irritates me to no end. I am still sorry I took him with me to Galilee. And how do you think I slept? I sleep with all my children and a wife in a bed made for two."

Cassius smiled. "My people have a saying—"

"Seriously? Are you going to give me a proverb rather than a solution? Men my age should live in a home free from the inconvenience of children always underfoot."

“But Arrius, you have told me a thousand times how your little ones are more valuable to you than gold.”

Arrius took a sip of his warm calda and said, “Gold. Not sleep! More valuable than precious metal, but *not* precious sleep.”

Both men finally laughed together, breaking some of the tension in the room.

Arrius moved into a beam of light to inspect and sharpen his gladius. “So, Cassius, what if *this* plot *this* time is a true threat to Pilate?”

“If Tasco returns with a name or names, we will root them out like vermin and send them to their death on a cross.”

Arrius smiled. “By the gods, it has been too long since we have hung some scum.”

Later that day, Tasco found Cassius overseeing a dozen or so men sparring in the fortress courtyard. Arrius was not present.

“I bring good news, Centurion,” he said as he saluted.

“And?”

“The Hebrew swine we use for information swore he didn’t know any of the details of the plan to assault the prefect.”

“So why are you here, and why are you smiling? You are fortunate Centurion Arrius is elsewhere.”

“But I *do* have details *and* a name. We offered him more coins, and when he began to negotiate for more silver, we knew he knew more about the ambush, so we beat him with clubs until he told us everything.”

"Very well, Tasco, what did you find out?"

"The rebels are led by a murderous man named Yeshua Barabbas. We have been watching his movements for some time now, Centurion."

Cassius moved closer and grabbed Tasco's breastplate. "Are you sure? Yeshua Barabbas?"

"Yes, Centurion, Yeshua Barabbas."

"Describe this man to me. What does he look like? How old is he?"

Cassius let go of the legionary and stepped back.

Tasco looked to his left and right before speaking. "He is an older man, fat as a pregnant mule and as ugly as one. He has a scar that runs the length of his cheek and two missing teeth. Rumor has it both marks came in the same fight. Why do you ask, Centurion?"

Cassius's jaw went tight. "I have had some other dealings with this mangy dog; finally getting rid of him will be a pleasure."

"Yes, Centurion, it is my honor to serve—"

"I know. I know. Enough of your bootlicking. Go to the stables. I believe you will find Centurion Arrius there *pruning* Pilate's horses. Tell him I have need of him immediately."

"What did you say he is doing?"

"That is not your concern, Legionary. Just go find Arrius and give him the good news."

Tasco saluted and was beaming as he made his way across the fortress courtyard to the stables.

The heat, smell, and flies in the stable made it Arrius's least favorite place in the fortress. However, he was on a mission of love for Ayla. She would use horsehair he collected to make jewelry that she could sell in the market. Items such as bracelets, necklaces, barrettes, and even earrings made from rare horsehair were popular with some women. The trick was cutting just enough from the prefect's horses to be used but not so much to be noticed. Pilate was a Roman equestrian knight of the Samnite clan of Pontii, hence his name Pontius, and he prided himself on the strength and beauty of his "favorite beasts of Rome," as he liked to call them.

Tasco stepped into the west entrance of the stalls and saw Arrius standing next to a beautiful Berber stallion with the horse's tail in his hand. "Centurion Arrius."

Arrius flinched. "Legionary, you startled me."

"My apologies, Centurion. I was sent with orders from Centurion Cassius, and I bear good news as well."

"Cassius knows not to bother me when I'm in the stables, so this better be good. Out with it. Why must I put up with your pathetic presence twice in one day?"

The legionary hesitated out of fear.

"Speak, or you will feel my manure-stained boot in your backside."

"I…we…we have valuable information now regarding the planned attack against our prefect."

Arrius got within a hand's length of Tasco's face. "I will determine if what you have is valuable or not. What have you discovered from your worthless Hebrew spy?"

Tasco did not make eye contact with Arrius. "We know the

leader's name, Yeshua Barabbas, and we have his current location. He and his men are hiding just outside the city in Bethany. Thirty or so Zealots plan on ambushing Pilate on the road from his residence in Caesarea Maritima to Jerusalem. As you know, he is due to arrive tomorrow. The prefect no doubt left Caesarea three or four days ago and could be within three leagues of Jerusalem by now."

Arrius always sounded and looked harsher with the men than he was in his heart. It was more important to him that his men feared and obeyed him than that they liked him. But he stepped forward again and placed his hand on Tasco's shoulder.

"Well done, Legionary. Well done. *This* information is both valuable and useful."

Tasco's shoulders relaxed.

"Go now to the barracks. Alert the First *Centuria* that we march before sunset. Tell them we move at full pace to Bethany. Instruct *Optio* Domizio to outfit only half the men with short javelins—no more than forty men. I plan on moving as quickly as possible. We will strike this rebel Yeshua Barabbas in his sleep and burn Bethany if we must to destroy him before he has the opportunity to attack Pilate."

Tasco smiled. Battle is what every legionary lives for, so he saluted Arrius and bolted out of the stables to the barracks.

Arrius stuffed what horsehair he could into a small bag as he thought to himself, *I can hardly wait to climb Golgotha and crucify some more worthless Jews.*

He was conflicted whenever he felt scorn for Ayla's people. What's more, he knew she hated the part of his duties that involved what she considered ungodly and barbaric. Nonetheless, Arrius knew a crucifixion was coming, and his pulse raced with anticipation.

CHAPTER 33

Year 33 AD, the Village of Bethany

Bethany was a small village on the southeastern slopes of the Mount of Olives, less than a league outside of the walled city. Entering the town undetected would be impossible for the First *Centuria*. Eighty-plus Roman legionaries never marched with stealth. However, with only one main route into and out of the town, Arrius had a plan to trap Yeshua Barabbas.

The gathered legionaries stood at attention in the Antonia Fortress courtyard. The evening was colder than usual, so only the men holding the twenty or so torches had some warmth. The others were ready to march and get their blood moving. The tower of Antonia, located in the southeast corner, had a small fire burning to warm the two watchmen.

Arrius jumped up on an oxen cart and raised his voice, "Legionaries, you will have the opportunity tonight to rid Rome of some rebel rubbish!"

The men stomped, beat their shields with their spears or swords, and shouted in approval.

"With the Jewish Passover approaching next week and a large infestation of Hebrews flooding this godforsaken city, Pilate anticipates an increase in Zealot activity. You men tonight will be the spear and shield of Rome."

The soldiers replied in unison with a roar, "For Rome and for the emperor!"

Arrius raised his voice. "Less than thirty or so insurrectionists are held up in Bethany—the slums outside of Jerusalem—and we will trap them and rid the earth of their stench before they know what has hit them."

The men were working into a state of rage.

Arrius raised his hand to silence the century and motioned for *Optio* Domizio to join him on the cart. "Here is our plan."

Arrius placed his hand on Domizio's shoulder. "The *optio* will take half of you, the legionaries without spears, through the village, and there will be no show of force as you pass through it. You will seem to observers as a group on your way to Caesarea Maritima. March as quickly as you can until you reach the well just outside Bethany. However, when the full moon is at its zenith, you will turn and quickly reenter, making as much noise as possible.

The men rumbled in approval as the *optio* raised his fist in celebration of their anticipated assault.

"I will lead the men with spears, and we will join the *optio* and his men from the west at the same time. This plan will accomplish two things. First, we will cut off any path of escape for those Jewish dogs."

As the men realized the simple but effective plan, there was more grunting and shield thumping.

"The second thing this will do for us is make our enemies come out of hiding. When they hear the rattle of Roman weapons and the roar of Roman legionaries, they will believe they have no choice but to face us in battle. They will run out of their holes like a badger flees a fire."

The battle cry of the gathered soldiers bouncing off the rock walls of the fortress was deafening.

Arrius raised his hand again. "For Rome and for the emperor!"

And the men reverberated in a frenzy, "For Rome and for the emperor! For Rome and for the emperor! For Rome and for the emperor!"

Optio Domizio turned toward Arrius, smiled, and saluted, "In Bethany, at the moon's zenith, we will join you in victory, my centurion."

As expected, the first half of the century marched through Bethany without a hitch. A few old Hebrew men sat outside their small homes with an animal skin flask of wine and lodged quiet curses at the legionaries, but no one was alarmed. The townsfolk of Bethany were no strangers to this sight, though it was a bit unusual to see only half a century marching after dark. For several days, the rumor was that Pilate was returning to Jerusalem soon, so some assumed this group was joining his protection detail somewhere between Bethany and Caesarea.

Domizio stopped with his men just a stone's throw past the village well. He sent them off the road to hide in a nearby olive grove and told them to get off their feet and rest. Unless they were off duty and drinking, most of the legionaries would typically have been asleep by this late hour. So, rather than have the men stand in attention, he allowed them to sit. The *optio* wanted his men as fresh as possible to run back to the edge of town when the moon was at its peak. Most of the soldiers sat or reclined on their shields, but no one felt like sleeping. The pre-battle rush was exciting. Besides, the air was cold and heavy, which made it too uncomfortable to sit for very long. Domizio could see the breath of the men with him as well as those across the road from him. Thankfully, the time passed quickly.

"*Optio*?"

Tasco found his way to their leader and spoke a bit too loudly.

Domizio spoke without making eye contact, "Yes, Legionary? But keep your voice down."

Tasco whispered, "*Optio*, are we going to attempt to arrest the leader, Yeshua Barabbas?"

"If we can and if he doesn't get killed in the attack. Pilate would love to make an example out of him and hang him naked on a cross."

"I thought—"

Domizio turned and looked Tasco in the face. "Your responsibility is not to *think*, Legionary, but to *fight*. I have watched you for weeks. I know you are seeking glory and favor with Pilate, but a dead soldier is soon forgotten. Do your duty tonight; stay alive and kill whoever chooses to fight. If Barabbas is a coward, he may survive; if not, he will die with his men."

Tasco nodded.

"Now, make your way across this road, find Cyrus, and tell him to gather the men and make ready. The moment approaches."

Tasco weakly saluted and moved to the other side and asked another young legionary, "Where is Cyrus?"

"Over there, behind that clump of burnt trees."

Though the moon was full, Tasco didn't see a large boulder, and he tripped over it as he approached Cyrus.

"Pick up your feet, Legionary! It would be embarrassing to tell your mother that you died when you fell on your own gladius."

Tasco nervously laughed and said, "If I die tonight, tell my mother I was a hero of Rome."

Cyrus shook his head. "You young bucks are always in search of heroism. Trust me; I will tell your mother you were so afraid that you soiled your sandals. But what is it? Why are you falling at my feet?"

"The *optio* says you are to get the men up and to make ready. We fight."

Within moments, the *optio* stood in the center of the road and called his men to arms. "Form up, men. Wipe the dust from your backsides and ready your swords. On my command, we march double-time and with as much noise as possible to the village. We join our brothers in battle."

The men quickly moved into place and pulled their swords.

"Ready? Now!" shouted Domizio.

And forty-plus men let out a cry that shook the ground and startled a hundred roosting birds.

Hearing the battle cry of the men with Domizio was his cue, and Arrius and forty men with spears rushed Bethany from the opposite direction. Screams of terror from women and the cries of children filled the air.

As expected, the Zealots, throwing on their robes and wiping sleep from their eyes, grabbed what weapons they could and met the Romans in the streets. The legionaries had been given strict instructions not to burn the village, so they'd left their torches just outside of town. Someone, however, knocked over a lamp in the skirmish, setting a house ablaze.

Though passionate and committed, the Zealots were untrained and no match for the legionaries. The smell of blood and the burning house was intoxicating to the Romans. They attacked the rebels with unrestrained fervor.

The legionaries with spears formed a line eight men wide and pressed a group of insurrectionists backward, trapping the rebels against a stone wall. The Romans easily pierced those who stood their ground because they were without shields; the Judean short swords provided no protection. The soldiers stabbed in the back Jews who tried to retreat by climbing over the stone wall. Legionaries were trained to throw their spears as javelins.

Only thirty paces away, Tasco and five other legionaries formed a shield wall. These rebels had never faced a hedge of Roman shields. Foolishly they kicked at the Romans or struck them with their swords, attempting to create a crack, but each time one of them stepped forward, a gladius struck like a viper from behind the wall and killed or mortally wounded the person.

Arrius was in a sword fight with a young Zealot who looked barely old enough to shave. The sounds of metal against metal rang throughout the small village. Arrius was impressed with the boy's strength and determination, but Arrius was exceptionally skilled with a gladius. Hundreds of hours with his mentor and trainer, Quintus, prepared him for battle. He knew to keep his eyes on his opponent's eyes and to keep his feet on the ground. He slid his sandals on the surface of the uneven cobblestones, always remaining in a slightly knees-bent position of perfect balance. In no time at all, he ended the life of the untrained Hebrew teenager.

In fact, twenty or so Jews died quickly. Several others were mortally wounded. Five men, when they saw all was lost, attempted to run. Arrius, however, had anticipated some would try to escape toward the desert, so he'd instructed three of his legionaries to wait in the shadows to apprehend anyone who ran.

Two of the Zealots were struck down immediately, so the other three dropped their swords and fell to their knees in surrender. Once bound, they were brought to the centurion.

As the legionaries showed no mercy and killed the wounded Hebrews, Arrius asked the largest man, who had a scar on his cheek and two missing teeth, "Who are you? What is your name, Jew?"

The man swore, spit at Arrius, and said through clenched teeth, "I am Yeshua Barabbas, protector of Yahweh's holy temple, guardian of Jerusalem, and enemy of Rome."

Arrius smiled as he took the handle end of his bloodied gladius and struck the man hard in the forehead. Barabbas fell backward as a dead man.

Chapter 34

Year 33 AD, Jerusalem

The stories of Yeshua continued to fill Jerusalem, and Pilate placed his legionaries on high alert. Like a storm brewing on the horizon, evil's presence felt tangible to Arrius.

Arrius was annoyed with Ayla. "This rabbi of yours will get Himself and all of you killed. My men tell me He is in Bethany and plans on coming to Jerusalem for Passover."

"Arrius, you know that all good Jews come to Jerusalem for our holy days. It is Yeshua's right and His religious duty to do so."

"Your leaders hate Him, and I promise you, this will not end well."

"You are worried about nothing, Arrius. The people love Yeshua, and some talk of crowning Him our king."

"Then He will certainly die. Pilate already has one Hebrew king to deal with, and He will not tolerate another—especially if Yeshua stirs up trouble."

"Great men are not afraid of great trouble, but Yeshua teaches His followers to love and to turn the other cheek. He consistently tells us to treat even Romans with respect and kindness."

Arrius smacked his fist into his hand. "He is a fool! Turning the other cheek only means both cheeks get bruised."

"Why are you so harsh concerning Him? The rabbi is a good man who does good things and only wants good for all men—even you."

Arrius was torn. The reports his men gave him about Yeshua were disturbing, but Ayla held fond affection in her heart for this rabbi. Rome, however, was intolerant of anyone who challenged the peace or profit of the empire.

Arrius sighed and rubbed the back of his neck. "I don't argue for or against His *goodness*, Ayla, but I have seen many good men killed by wicked men. Goodness is no shield against evil or against a Roman sword or cross. I worry what will become of your rabbi, and I also fear what will happen to your friends."

Ayla put her hand on the armored chest of her husband and said, "You too are good, Arrius. Your heart is good, and there is goodness in you that I have always seen. I also know Yahweh will protect us no matter what may come."

Arrius tensed. "There is nothing virtuous in me except the love that I have for you and my children."

Ayla shook her head as her eyes began to tear. "Yahweh knows all, and He sees what I see and more. Time and time again, the Lord has shown me that He has great plans for you, plans for good and not evil."

Two days later, on Sunday, the day after Shabbat, Ayla gathered her basket as she prepared to go to the market. "I could use your help with Seneca today. I need to purchase some meat and vegetables, and your son is too much to handle anymore when my hands are full of food. He gets his curiosity and energy from you!"

Arrius smiled. "Why don't we all go together? It's a beautiful day, and I need to stretch my legs."

"Stretch your old bones, you mean. But shopping is for women, and your presence will make everyone nervous," Ayla said as she playfully poked him in the ribs.

Arrius stood, yawned, and rubbed his eyes. "Fine, but I will walk with you until we reach the market. Perhaps I will take Seneca on an adventure while you shop."

"He will love the time with you. How soon can we go?"

"I am a Roman centurion, and I am always ready."

Ayla giggled and said, "Then get your Roman centurion sandals on, and let us leave now. I prefer to beat the heat and the crowds."

The road from their home to the market circled up a hill and was busier than usual. Large crowds had begun to arrive for Passover. As many as a million people would converge on the city for the greatest holy day of all.

"Have I told you the story of Passover and why it matters so much to my people?"

"Yes, you have told me *many* times."

Ignoring him, Ayla continued, "After four hundred years of bondage and slavery, the Lord sent His servant Moses to set the captives free from the tyranny of Egypt."

"Is this where you compare Romans and Caesar to those Africans?"

Ayla smiled and pressed on, "Where was I? Ah, yes, to set His people free. And Yahweh used ten plagues to break the back of the evil Pharaoh. First, turning water to blood, then the plagues of frogs, lice, flies, killing the livestock, boils, hail, locusts, darkness, and finally killing the firstborn children. These signs were given to show the whole world that Yahweh is the Lord."

"Your Yahweh is harsher than any of my gods."

"No, Arrius, your so-called gods inflict cruelty without reason, but Yahweh did so to protect and save His people."

"And the blood curse?" asked Arrius.

Ayla glared at him. "The blood was *not* a curse. Can I go on?"

Arrius rolled his eyes and sighed, "Can I stop you?"

"Before the final plague, Moses commanded the people to mark above their doors with lamb's blood so that the angel of death would *pass over* our people. So we celebrate Passover to remind us that the blood of a lamb protects—and still protects—the Lord's people from harm. The Paschal lamb is sacrificed to remind us of the Lord's redemption and protection."

"And how does the death, sacrifice, and blood of an innocent lamb bring good to your people?"

"As Yeshua teaches, without the shedding of blood, there can be no forgiveness for sin."

"And I thought I was fixated on blood and curses. You Jews and your teachers disturb me."

As Arrius and Ayla reached the hill's summit, they could see and hear a large crowd on the road to the Temple Mount. Thousands, maybe tens of thousands, were yelling and waving palm branches in the air.

Arrius grabbed Ayla by the arm and abruptly stopped there. "We will go no farther. Here, take the boy and the baby. Return home *immediately*. A riot like this will cause Pilate to send his troops to keep the peace."

"But can you hear what they are saying? They are crying out, 'Hosanna'!"

Ayla jumped up and down. "And look, my *bashert*, that is Yeshua they are praising!"

Arrius wiped sweat from his brow and almost growled, "Ayla, I will discuss this no further. Go home now."

Ayla knew not to argue with him when he had that look and took that tone.

"As you say, Centurion, but this is a wonderful moment you are robbing from me. Look, the Messiah, our King, comes to the Holy City riding on a colt!"

Before she finished speaking, Arrius rushed off to the barracks to rally his men.

Arrius slammed open the barracks door. "To arms, legionaries! To arms! Trouble brews on the road to the Temple Mount." He wasted no time in gathering his cohort. Seventy-eight men stood ready to march in a matter of moments. His men lived for battle. Every day they trained for the opportunity to display the power and glory of Rome. The sun was high and the heat oppressive in full armor, but his men were itching for a fight. They hated Jerusalem and the Jews.

However, at that moment, a messenger arrived from Pilate with a simple and straightforward order for the troops.

"You are to stand down. No interference will be presented to this mob of Jews. Unless they begin to riot, you are to stay ready but stand down. In fact, stay out of sight so as not to incite or irritate the people."

Arrius read it and shook his head. He had very little respect for his prefect. Pilate was often indecisive and weak. He seemed more interested in avoiding conflict than exercising Roman influence and law.

"Tell the *optio* we hold," barked Arrius at the nearest legionary.

"Certainly, Centurion," said the man, saluting and heading toward the second in command.

"Turning to a young legionary and a veteran standing near him, he said, "You two leave your shields and spears, swords only, and come with me. We will discreetly make our way to the temple to keep an eye on this crowd and their rabbi."

"Yes, Centurion."

They headed for the temple, but as they moved through the crowd, Arrius cursed and grumbled, "This way is taking too long. We will circle around and take the Zion Bridge."

His men looked at him with wide eyes as one of them adjusted his helmet chin strap. This access to the temple was reserved for the upper class of Jerusalem and nobility. The three of them would be very conspicuous and not welcomed. Not at all.

Sensing his men's hesitation, he said, "We need to get into the temple compound quickly. We have no choice."

Neither man replied.

As they turned the corner, the temple edifice literally shined in the midday sun. The sheer mass and opulence of the building was stunning. It was one of the largest buildings in Jerusalem, standing a hundred cubits high and another hundred cubits wide. The walls exceeded the height of twenty-five men. With polished white marble overlaid by pure gold, the Jews often remarked that if you looked at the temple in the daylight, it would blind you.

"Despite how I feel about these annoying Hebrews, their temple truly is a wonder of all wonders," said the younger legionary.

"Careful, boy, the centurion's woman is a Jew."

Arrius ignored them both. He'd heard it all before. Many times.

Just as they entered the Court of the Gentiles, known to the Romans as Herod's colonnade and marketplace, Arrius stopped abruptly and instinctively reached for his gladius. Yeshua was turning over the tables of the moneychangers, driving out the dove merchants, and yelling at the top of His lungs, "My house shall be called a house of prayer, but you make it a den of robbers!"

"Stay behind me, men, but stay close."

Arrius prepared himself to intervene should the temple's leaders or the people react. It would probably mean death for him and his men. The Jews would not stand for Roman interference in temple affairs. They had their own troops to handle such situations. Surprisingly, however, no one opposed Yeshua. He seemed like a madman to Arrius, a person who was bent on creating mayhem and chaos.

But then, as soon as it began, it stopped. Except for a few money changers scrambling to collect their coins off the ground, no one moved, and it was so quiet you could hear doves cooing.

The first to move or speak was a blind man who called out in the direction of Yeshua, "Rabbi, can I come to You?"

Yeshua looked across the stone courtyard, and everything in His countenance changed when He saw the man. "I am here. Come to Me."

The man immediately came out of the crowd with another person who led him by the hand directly to Yeshua.

The rabbi asked the beggar, "What do you want from Me, My friend?"

"Rabbi, I want to see."

"And so you shall, Abdiel Ben-Ammi."

The beggar began to weep. "Rabbi, You know my name?"

"My Abba knows all His children."

The blind man fell to his knees and looked up to a face he could not see. "It is enough that Yahweh remembers me and knows my name. Bless You, rabbi."

Arrius watched and listened in amazement. He felt his heart beating rapidly behind his breastplate.

Yeshua looked up to the sky and smiled, "Yes, Abdiel, Yahweh knows you, and He can heal you—and *all* the infirmities of His people—if they but turn to the Lord."

Yeshua then placed both His hands on Abdiel's eyes and said only one word, "Open."

It was as if time stood still. Even the doves stopped their cooing, and it seemed that no one dared take a breath as they watched in awe.

Abdiel then stood and shouted, "I see! Hosanna! My eyes are

open! Truly blessed is he who comes in the name of the Lord! I can see!"

In a collective gasp of amazement, most of the crowd in the courtyard exploded into shouts of praise. Caiaphas, the high priest, and his cronies, however, watched with eyes full of hate.

Arrius looked at the two legionaries with him. "What is this magic? How is this possible?"

His men stood speechless.

Arrius then felt a gentle hand on the back of his arm.

"My *bashert*, did I not tell you this rabbi is the Messiah? He is the Son of David and the hope of Israel."

Arrius turned and whispered in frustration, "Why are you here? I sent you home."

"How could I not be here? He calls to me, Arrius. I hear His voice on the wind, and He calls my name."

Arrius was filled with terror and frustration when he took hold of his wife's shoulders and said, "I hear His voice, too, but His words and actions will bring Him death. Look at your priests. They boil with rage. What will become of your rabbi now? What will become of you?"

Chapter 35

Four Days Later, 33 AD, Passover Week, Jerusalem

Ayla found a way every day to go and listen to the rabbi. She knew Arrius was upset with her, but it didn't matter. She had to be with Yeshua. The whole city was abuzz with His presence and teachings.

Arrius stood in the bedroom chamber doorway with his hands on his hips. "Ayla, I noticed you have yet to repair my *pteruges*."

Ayla frowned as she admitted, "I know I have fallen behind in some of my duties as a wife this week."

Arrius nodded knowingly.

Ayla whined, "But you know how I struggle to restore those ridiculous leather loin coverings."

Arrius replied with a teasing smile, "So you want me to walk around Jerusalem naked?"

"Only here and only with me, Arrius. But I will never understand why Roman soldiers wear a skirt."

Arrius raised a hand, and Ayla knew he was about to ask her what mattered most to him. "Did you go to the temple again yesterday?"

"Yes, Arrius, I did."

"Why do you insist upon putting yourself at risk? You are a

mother, the wife of a Roman centurion, and unwelcomed in the temple by your own people."

"I am free to enter the Court of the Gentiles."

Arrius ran his hands through his thick hair and snapped. "Free to enter, but still at risk."

"I love that you worry about me, Arrius, but I am among friends when I am near the rabbi; He would not let anything happen to His followers."

"He carries no sword. He has no army. He is hated by your leaders and continues to poke at them like a child who likes to irritate a wounded dog," said Arrius.

"He would never poke any dog, wounded or not," replied Ayla with a smile.

"You know what I mean, woman, and He *does* poke and poke and poke, relentlessly accusing the Sanhedrin of corruption and hypocrisy."

"But the people love Him, Arrius."

"Perhaps, but the wrong people *hate* Him. People with power. People who can get your rabbi crucified. Pilate still has his auxiliary on high alert because of that man."

Ayla shook her head. "Pilate would never allow a good and innocent man to be crucified."

"Ayla, sometimes I wonder if you are blind or I. To protect his power and standing with your leaders, Pilate would crucify his own mother!"

Ayla shook her head and sighed, "I trust Yahweh as our children trust us. Besides, Yeshua frequently tells us to have the faith and trust of a little child."

Arrius pointed his finger at Ayla. "So your mind is set then. You refuse to trust *me*?"

"Arrius, I have entrusted my *whole* life and future into your care. I have been scorned by my family and shamed by my people for loving you. But until your eyes are open, you will not and cannot understand my commitment to Yeshua."

Arrius raised his fists to the sky and yelled, "Cupid and Venus, my love for this woman is like a spear in my side. She will get us both killed."

Ayla said in jest, "My *bashert*, why do you have to yell so loud? Are your gods deaf?"

Arrius and Ayla both laughed. This was a typical pattern in their relationship. Argue. Fight. Yell. Laugh. Their love for each other was stronger than their struggles.

After a few moments, Arrius spoke with a sternness in his tone, "If you go to the temple today, I am going with you. This is *not* up for discussion or debate. And we will stand in the shadows and as close to an exit as possible. Your protection is what matters most to me."

"I welcome you to go with me," she replied softly. "I will ask our neighbor to watch the children."

Ayla knew Arrius was surprised that she did not resist his attendance with her to the temple.

"What are you up to now, Wife? Why do you want your intimidating Roman centurion husband with you today?"

Ayla looked down at the dirt. "I want you to hear Him again."

Arrius shook his head as he nervously rubbed his hands. "If I am with you, of course I will *hear* Him."

"No, Arrius, I want your *heart* to hear Him. He alone has the words of life."

"You are both curious and wonderful to me, Ayla. A strange and wonderful woman who perplexes, provokes, and prods me like no other. But I will listen to your rabbi if it makes you happy."

"We will see, Arrius."

After entering through the Golden Gate, they weaved their way through the narrow and overcrowded streets of the city. Extra market booths were everywhere. The sounds of laughing children, women haggling over prices, and merchants hawking their wares filled Jerusalem.

Arrius was not the only Roman present. Pilate had every legionary available and strategically positioned throughout the walled city. The men were told to be seen but not easily provoked. Pilate wanted the Jews to know any foolishness or acts of rebellion by the Zealots would be met quickly and forcefully.

"Your men are surprisingly well-behaved today, Arrius."

"They are not all my men, but my cohort is out in full force today too. Pilate is on edge far more than usual. Rumor has it his mystic wife has him in an uproar over dreams of doom and gloom."

Ayla spoke at a whisper, "She is a dark creature. I hear rumors too. Rumors of pagan blood sacrifices and orgies. She is evil and hated by my people."

"There are no orgies," Arrius said with a laugh. "Herod and your religious leaders would not tolerate that in their *Holy* City. But we centurions keep our distance from her, nonetheless. Sometimes we wonder if she has too much power and influence over Pilate."

"Shhhh…listen, can you hear Him? The rabbi is already teaching."

"Do not shush me like a child, woman—especially in public."

"My apologies, Arrius, I meant no disrespect. My excitement got the better of me."

It seemed like thousands were squeezed into the compound. People stood without any personal space and without making a sound. Except for an occasional pigeon's wing flapping and the distant sound of men praying, the only sounds heard were the clear and penetrating words of the teacher.

A younger man stepped closer to the rabbi and said in a loud voice for all to hear him, "Rabbi, which commandment is the most important of all?"

Yeshua took a deep breath, looked at the man with compassion in His eyes, and said, "The most important is, 'Hear, O Israel: The Lord our God, the Lord is one. And you shall love the Lord your God with all your heart and with all your soul and with all your mind and with all your strength.' The second is this: 'you shall love your neighbor as yourself.' There is no other commandment greater than these."[3]

The man seemed stunned and was momentarily silenced by Yeshua's response. He said to the rabbi, "You are right, teacher.

---

3 Mark 12:29–31

You have truly said that the Lord is one, and there is no other besides Him. And to love Him with all the heart and with all the understanding and with all the strength and to love one's neighbor as oneself is much more than all burnt offerings and sacrifices."[4]

Yeshua's face lit up. He moved directly in front of the young man and placed a hand on his shoulder. As Yeshua looked straight into his eyes, the rabbi spoke with great tenderness, "You are so close, brother; you are not far from the kingdom of God."

The crowd collectively sighed and wondered out loud to each other, *"Who is this man who speaks of the kingdom of God as if it is His realm?"*

The Jewish leaders grabbed the hem of their long and flowing robes, turned, and stomped away. None of them dared to ask Yeshua any more questions.

Arrius scratched his head. "He speaks of a kingdom as if He is a king, Ayla."

"Because He is, Arrius. He is."

Arrius mumbled, "By the gods, who does this man think He is?"

Ayla took Arrius by the hand. "Yeshua knows who He is, my *bashert*, and soon I think the whole of Judea will know as well."

Arrius released her hand and said as he turned to leave, "*If* He survives the week, and I doubt He will."

---

4 Mark 12:32–33

Chapter 36

Year 33 AD, Jerusalem

After hearing the rabbi, Arrius and Ayla walked home without saying a word to each other. Ayla knew that Yeshua's words were difficult for Arrius to hear. Yeshua spoke of the destruction of the temple and about the end of all time. He also told stories of fig trees and vineyards and love for your enemies. Arrius's jaw tightened, and he appeared irritated the more Yeshua spoke. Ayla could see the veins in her husband's neck pulsing.

Ayla wiped tears from her eyes as she walked several paces behind the man she loved. *Too much too soon,* she thought to herself. *My husband believes the words of the rabbi to be somewhere between suicidal and seditious.*

Just before they turned the corner to their home, she spoke, "Arrius?"

He acted as if he didn't hear her.

"Arrius, can we talk about what happened? Can I give you, perhaps, more insight into what I believe Yeshua means by His teachings?"

"It doesn't matter. I don't have to understand the man to realize where this is all headed." Arrius stopped, turned to his wife, and pointed his finger at her. "We are two days from your Passover feast. Two days from all of this being over," he vented as he aggressively waved his hands in the air. "I pray to the gods your rabbi returns to the north and that you never see Him again."

Ayla's eyes began to fill with tears again. "How can you say such a hurtful and hateful thing? We return home to a daughter that lives because of Him."

"Because of Mary, not your rabbi, Wife."

"Arrius, *Yeshua* sent Mary. *He* sent her to help. *He* told her all would be well, and it was. She whispered His words into my ears and brought hope as I was struggling and fearing death. My precious *bashert*, Yeshua is life. His very words are life."

Arrius rubbed the growing tension in his neck and sighed, "If words judge a man, then *all* of His words must be weighed. Any man who publicly speaks of the destruction of the temple either is insane, a fool, or he has a death wish."

"Arrius, I cannot pretend that I understand everything Yeshua speaks of, but I believe the *temple* He referred to is His body. Of late, He often speaks of His death and His rising to life. I think the rabbi speaks of His eventual resurrection at the end of time."

"Oh, He will die," grumbled Arrius. "And His *temple* will be destroyed. But that will be the end of it. Mark my words. His body will rot in the pit with the many others Rome has crucified."

"Your words are cold and calloused, Arrius. I do not like this very Roman part of you."

"Then you explain to me how a dead man ever breathes again. Dead is dead. Have you seen a man after we have crucified him? Have you watched the blood and color flow out of a body? I have killed hundreds. I know death. There is no life *after* death—not on this planet and not at the end of time—only the underworld and darkness await us."

"My people—"

Arrius interrupted her, "*I am* your people now. Your father's people are rebellious and fanatics who resist the inevitable. Rome rules the world. Your people are gullible and search for a Messiah to set them free. How many other messiahs have come and gone? How many others have told your people what they wanted to hear only to serve their desire for money and power?"

Ayla bowed her head as tears now streamed down her face and neck.

"Ayla, I am sorry to hurt you, but you must wake up from this fool's dream that you insist is reality—it's not."

Ayla knew he struggled with a wide range of emotions regarding Yeshua, so she tried to be patient with him. "Arrius, Yahweh has given me new hope about the man you will become. I don't know how, when, or where it will happen, but something…something wonderful is coming. I just know it."

Ayla spoke softly, "I know you speak out of fear for the children and me, but I would gladly sacrifice my life for the kingdom of heaven as you would sacrifice yours now for Rome. I do not fear death. I do not fear my future or yours."

Arrius tenderly took her in his arms, and then he stepped back and looked Ayla in her tear-filled eyes. "If you die, I die. I do not fear death, Ayla Rose, but I *do* fear life without you. Can we talk more later?"

"Of course, Arrius. I have so much more I want to explain to you about the rabbi's teachings."

The courtyard fire was crackling and emitting random sparks. The moon was full on the horizon, and a breeze played with the treetops. Ayla and Arrius sat on a wooden bench together as she nursed Tikva.

"I love that sound," said Arrius.

"What sound?"

"The sound of my children drawing life from your breasts."

"Are you still jealous of them?" she said as she raised a single eyebrow.

Arrius laughed, "A bit. Just a bit. Does that make me a bad father?"

Ayla leaned into his broad shoulder as he placed his robe around her back. "No, just a normal man."

"Tell me more of this rabbi of yours. What other strange teachings has He used this week to captivate my wife?"

"Are you serious? Do you truly want to hear more?"

"Woman, you know I say what I mean, and I mean what I say. So, yes, tell me more."

Ayla smiled. "Have I told you the story Yeshua tells of a father and two sons?"

"No. Does it have a happy ending, or will I hate this father as I hated my Roman father?"

"It does, but it has a surprise ending too."

"Okay, tell me," said Arrius.

"A man, another good man like you, had two sons. He raised them with a firm hand but a loving heart. The oldest son was a hard worker. Reliable. Faithful to his father. The youngest son was always difficult and far more challenging—"

Arrius interrupted, "Ah, I see, the exact opposite of my older brother and me!"

"This is not about you," chided Ayla, "Let me finish."

Ayla took a breath and continued, "The youngest son did the unthinkable. He came to his father and asked for his share of the family inheritance. No son was entitled to his inheritance until the death of his father. Essentially, this rebellious younger son said, 'You are taking too long to die, old man. I want what is mine now!' The father was, of course, hurt by his son's insensitive actions. The oldest son was angry. He thought of selling his brother into slavery."

Arrius was surprised. "Really? Slavery? That is horrible. What brother would sell his brother into slavery?"

"Well, the rabbi may not have added that part, but His story made me think of a true story about our forefather, Joseph, and his brothers. But that is another story for another time."

"Go on, Ayla. What happened?"

"The youngest son took his share of his father's estate, a large sum of money, and he traveled to Rome to waste it on women and drink."

Arrius laughed, "So this youngest son *is* the smartest son?"

Ayla was not amused. "No, he's not, and that is not funny."

"I'm sorry; carry on."

"After many moons, the youngest son ran out of money. In fact, he was penniless and starving—"

"And then he died. Yes? I thought you said this story had a happy ending."

"Oh, for the love of all things holy, will you hush and stop interrupting me, please? Let me tell you."

Ayla shifted Tikva to nurse the other side as she continued.

"So the youngest son ended up as an indentured servant to a farmer who raised pigs. Can you believe it? His job was to feed the pigs. One day, it struck him: *These unholy swine are eating better than I am! If I am to be a slave, I might as well be at home with my family.* So he decided to return to his father—"

Arrius scratched his head and asked, "How did he afford the passage home?"

"I don't know. That's not important."

"Okay, Ayla, but you know how I am bothered by inconsistent details."

Ayla sighed and continued, "What the youngest son didn't know is that every evening his father sat on the hillside just above their home looking for his son's return. Are you listening, Centurion? Every day the father longed for the return of his wayward son."

Arrius slapped his knee and interrupted again. "Another foolhardy Jew!"

Ayla punched him in the leg as she continued.

"One evening, just as the sun began to set on the horizon, the father saw a man coming up the road. At first, the father thought this man was a beggar, perhaps a leper. He was dirty and dressed in rags. The father said out loud to himself, 'There is no way this is my son.' But then, the father recognized the cloak, dirty and torn as it was, as the last gift he gave his boy on the last birthday they celebrated together."

"I would have sent the dogs after that boy and run him off."

Ayla didn't miss a beat. "Not *this* father. He got up and ran down the hill to his long-lost son. The son had prepared a speech of contrition he would offer to the father, begging not for forgiveness but a job."

Arrius groaned, "Was it a long speech? You know how I tire when Pilate gives long speeches."

Ayla, however, was unable to speak. Tears of joy ran freely down her cheeks.

"I am horrible. Forgive me, Ayla. I will stop interrupting you."

After a long pause and a deep breath, Ayla said, "Do you want to know what the father said to his son?"

Arrius turned and looked Ayla in the face. "Yes, please tell me."

"Here is what the rabbi taught us. Through his tears, the son said, 'Father, I have sinned against heaven and against you. I am no longer worthy of being called your son.'" Ayla sat up excitedly. "But you will never believe what the father did. He called his servants and told them to get his son a new cloak, a new family ring, and new shoes. He told his servants to kill the fattest calf and to prepare a feast to celebrate. For the father said, 'This son was dead and is alive again; he was lost and is found.'"

"And did they celebrate?"

"Yes, for days!"

"And what of the older brother?" Arrius thought of Justus.

"I am sad to say, Arrius, that it didn't go well for him. He was angry at the mercy, grace, and forgiveness offered by his father."

"I would be too," grunted Arrius.

"But you miss the moral of this fable, Arrius."

"And what is the lesson to be learned here, Wife?"

"Yeshua teaches us that our Father, Yahweh, is good and not angry with us, though we have *all* wandered far from Him. None of us deserves forgiveness, Arrius, not one. But Yeshua tells us again and again that Yahweh is loving and looking for us—His lost sons and daughters—and He is ready to redeem, restore, and renew our lives."

Ayla could tell that Arrius was more moved by this parable than he let on. All Arrius knew of a father was wrath and rage.

Arrius looked into Ayla's eyes. "Thank you for sharing this story with me. Never had it entered into my heart and mind that *any* father or god could be good and loving. Truth is, this story unsettles me, Ayla. I have only known anger. My first father hated me, blamed me for my mother's death, and he bound me with a blood curse. My second father was jealous of my brother and me because of the love Claudia had for us."

Ayla leaned into her husband's chest, with the baby now sound asleep in her arms. "My heart aches for you, Arrius."

"Ayla…I fear the anger in me will drive my children from me someday."

"Arrius, the love of Yahweh and Yeshua can heal your soul."

Arrius squeezed her with his right arm as he quickly wiped tears from his face with his left. “I pray to the gods I can become the man you and my children deserve. Perhaps someday.”

Ayla looked up at her heart-weary husband, put her index finger on his lips, and said, “Not *perhaps*. Not *maybe*. But *someday* in the not-too-distant future, my love.”

CHAPTER 37

Friday Morning, 33 AD, Passover Week, Jerusalem

There was a loud pounding on the door. Arrius and Ayla were sound asleep. Later that morning, Ayla had plans to finish preparations for the Passover Shabbat to begin at sunset.

"Arrius! Who is it? What is happening this early in the morning?"

Arrius wrapped a robe around his body, grabbed his gladius, and moved toward the door. "I don't know. Probably nothing. Stay put."

Kaamil woke up on his cot, and the younger children began to stir. Ayla always insisted her babies sleep with them.

"But—"

"Stay here and keep quiet, woman. Let me see."

Ayla knew that Arrius was always grumpy in the mornings, but being roused from sleep so early made him even grumpier.

"I only—"

Arrius turned his back to Ayla and left her before she could finish. He rubbed his eyes, brushed the hair off his face, cleared his throat, and shouted through the closed door.

"Who knocks on a centurion's door long before the moon sets?

This had better be an emergency!"

"Centurion, Pilate summons you. There is a disturbance you must attend to immediately, sir."

Arrius opened the door to find two legionaries standing at attention with a torch and full battle armor.

"What is so important that it couldn't wait until daylight?"

"I don't know, Centurion, but Pilate requires you *immediately*."

"Give me a moment to dress and stop looking so terrified; I never beat anyone before I have had my breakfast."

"Yes, Centurion," the men said in unison as they saluted.

Arrius slammed the door in their faces and murmured as he went to his bedchamber, "What in the name of Mars is going on now?"

"Who is it? What is happening, Arrius?"

Both younger children were now wide awake.

"I don't know. Some sort of disturbance, and Pilate has summoned me."

Ayla was worried. "Now? At this hour? The whole city is asleep. What could be so urgent? Will you be in danger?"

"How am I to know? You ask too many questions too early," Arrius said abruptly.

"I was only concerned for your—"

"I know," Arrius tried to be a bit more tender in his reply, "but I have no answers, only an order to appear in Pilate's court as soon as possible."

Ayla forced Seneca to roll over to his belly and began to pat his back while the baby was fussing to be fed.

Arrius splashed some water on his face as he grumbled and then began to dress. “I will be fine.”

Ayla sat up in bed startling the children. “Whenever you tell me you will be *fine*, it usually means anything but *fine*.”

“Don’t worry. It is probably something to do with that Arabian wolf, Barabbas. We have had him locked up for days now waiting for his crucifixion, and his comrades are stirring up trouble. I will personally nail that man to his cross and enjoy every moment of it.”

“Arrius, please don’t talk like that in front of the children.”

“I am sorry, Ayla. It’s just too early, and it’s been a long week. Don’t worry. I’m sure I’ll be home before sunrise.”

Ayla, still deeply concerned, said, “Arrius?”

Arrius stopped dressing and looked at her. “Yes?”

“Please be especially careful today. I had a dream two nights ago that a violent squall would fall on us before Passover. It was an omen and a sign from Yahweh, I think.”

“It’s nothing. Just another overreaction by the prefect. Save me some eggs, and don’t let Kaamil eat everything. Like I said, I’ll be home before sunrise.”

Fully dressed in his armor, shield, and sword in hand, Arrius stepped out into the brisk cold morning.

“Lead on, Legionary. Let us go to Pontius.”

“Should we stop by the barracks, Centurion, and gather more men?”

”No, not until I know what is happening.”

"And what do you think is happening, Centurion?"

"I think this wretched city will be the death of me yet. Another Passover. Another million wretched Jews to watch and control. Another night without a warm bed and my children. But I have no idea what is happening. Something in me, however, fears it has to do with that rabbi."

"Which one?" said the youngest legionary.

Arrius cursed and spat on the ground. "The only one who is causing trouble. Yeshua has stirred the Jewish leaders into a feeding frenzy. I have seen wild dogs better behaved than these pompous *religious* men."

The men said nothing more to each other. But something evil and ominous was in the twilight air. Something horrific was happening.

Pilate's primary residence was in Caesarea along the coast. He only traveled to Jerusalem when there was trouble in Jerusalem or during major Jewish feasts. Pontius Pilate was the fifth Roman governor of Judaea under Emperor Tiberius, and like most Romans, he hated Judaea, especially the Holy City.

Arrius and his men entered Pilate's inner court, the praetorium, located within the Antonia Fortress, and found the prefect pacing and screaming at a slave for more wine.

When Pilate saw Arrius, he screeched, "Where have you been? I have been up all night haggling with these Jews!"

"My apologies, Prefect. I was unaware of any turmoil requiring my immediate attention."

"Unaware of any conflict! Have you not been paying attention, Centurion? The Sanhedrin has petitioned me all week to intervene in their ridiculous power struggle."

Pilate continued to complain to Arrius. "The *rabbi* is accused of sedition and refusing to pay Caesar's taxes. My spies tell me just the opposite, but the man is from Galilee, so I sent him to Herod. He can do with him as he pleases. I will not be sucked into their idiotic charade."

Arrius spoke cautiously, "I fear Herod will not solve your problem, sir. He does not have the political prowess to stand against the high priest."

"*My* problem? Centurion, let me be clear. If Herod returns that fool, this will be *your* problem. The Sanhedrin swims upstream against the people. There will be a riot in the streets the day before Passover if this situation does not end well."

"Yes, Prefect. *My* problem. I live to serve you and Rome. How can I help?"

Pilate continued to pace back and forth. "My wife complicates this whole ordeal."

"How so, Prefect?"

"Procula distracts me with her dreams and warnings and bad omens from the gods. I should have left her in Caesarea. She thinks that because she is the granddaughter of Emperor Augustus, she has power over me. Over me! What am I to do with that woman?"

Arrius stood at attention. Though the early morning air was cool, sweat was dripping down his back. The warning from Ayla was echoing through his mind. "What dreams, sir?" Arrius asked cautiously.

Eventually, Pilate collapsed in his chair and sighed loudly. "Never mind. It doesn't matter. None of this matters if Herod will simply take this burden off my back and rule like the king he *thinks* he is."

Before Pilate finished speaking, he heard a commotion from outside the praetorium in the courtyard. "Oh, the gods. Herod is a coward! He has sent this rabbi back to me."

Just then, a legionary stepped into the room and walked up to Arrius to whisper in his ear.

Pilate stood and shrieked, "Out with it, Legionary! The centurion is not my nursemaid. What did that son of a swine, Herod, decide? I knew he would send that worthless rabbi and those spineless Judeans back to me. They are all cowards. Drag them in here immediately."

The legionary's wide eyes darted between Pilate and Arrius.

Arrius interjected, "As you know, the Sanhedrin, in fear of defilement before Passover, cannot enter this room. They humbly request your presence in the courtyard."

Pilate threw his wine cup at the legionary and swore, "*They* fear defilement! Those Jewish dogs stain the air that I breathe. *They* defile the streets that I control. *They* defile everything, everywhere. Curse them!"

And with that, Pilate wrapped his red knee-length tunic tighter around his body and stomped to the entrance. "With me, Centurion. Stand close and look formidable."

Arrius had never seen Pilate so distraught. "Yes, Prefect."

The chief priest, Caiaphas, bowed and said with an irritatingly nasal whine, "Honorable Prefect, we return with news from Herod."

"Do not pretend to honor me. I sent this man away to *your* king, Herod. I am tired, hungry, and extremely wary of your games."

Yeshua was wearing an expensive robe. A mocking gift from Herod, no doubt. Arrius was not shocked but saddened to see a beaten and bloody Yeshua who stood before him. The chief priests and their allies, the teachers of the law, vigorously accused Yeshua of everything from sedition to blasphemy.

Pilate was screaming again, "You brought this rabbi to me falsely accusing Him of breaking *your* laws, not Rome's. You have accused Him of inciting the Jews to rebellion, but I see right through your scheme! You are jealous of His favor with the people. However, I have thoroughly interrogated Him and have found no basis for your charges against Him. Even Herod sent Him back because He has done nothing deserving of death. But to satisfy your bloodthirst and need for justice, I will have Him flogged and set Him free."

Pilate turned, walked away briskly, and left Annas and Caiaphas looking as if they were ready to burst into flames with anger. The prefect went back inside the palace and summoned the rabbi.

As Yeshua entered the room, His hands bound with leather, the rabbi moved slowly, but His head was not dropped in defeat or despair. His left eye was swollen shut, and blood was dripping from His mouth. There was an open wound above His left ear matted with dirt and hair. Pilate had seen many men beaten, but none this bloodied who could still walk, let alone stand. The purple robe, drenched in blood and sweat, was beginning to cling to the rabbi's body.

Pilate slumped in his chair, drinking another cup of wine. For several moments, Pilate simply glared at Yeshua until he finally spoke, "You bewitch me, rabbi. How could one man merit such fear and hate from your leaders? They accuse you of much."

Pilate stood up, stepped toward Yeshua, and almost whispered as he said, "Are you the king of the Jews?"

Yeshua looked into Pilate's eyes and said, "Is this what you believe or what you have heard from others?"

Pilate stepped back and laughed, a bit too loudly and unconvincingly, "Am I a Jew? What do I care of these things? You have been betrayed by your countrymen, not by Rome or me."

Yeshua took a deep breath and said, "My kingdom is not of this world. If it were, My followers would fight to protect Me and resist the so-called religious leaders. Yes, I am a king, but My kingdom is not of this world."

Pilate turned ashen as he stumbled back to his seat. Before he could stop the words from tumbling out of his mouth, he said, "So you *are* a king."

Arrius could hardly believe the scene before him. He thought to himself, *What is happening? Who is this man?*

With surprising strength and clarity, the rabbi spoke again, "The reason I came into this world is to testify to the truth. Everyone on the side of truth listens to Me."

Pilate shook his head and said through clenched teeth, "And what is truth, Jew?"

Pontius Pilate stood, looked again at Yeshua for what seemed like an eternity to Arrius, and then he went outside to the chief priests with Yeshua in tow. By now, daylight was peeking over the Temple Mount, and a large crowd gathered in the courtyard.

Pilate demanded Barabbas be brought to him immediately. He then spoke loudly for all to hear, "As I have said, I find no basis for any charge against this man"—pointing to the bloodied rabbi—"He certainly has done nothing that merits death. 'Nonetheless, it is the custom for me to release to you one prisoner at the time of Passover. Do you want me to release "the king of the Jews"?'"[5]

One of the chief priests, as if on cue, yelled, "No, not Him! Give us Yeshua Barabbas."

Arrius was so stunned that he grabbed his gladius by instinct. There was no way the prefect and governor of Judaea would release a man known to be a murderer and insurrectionist. The capture and imprisonment of Barabbas happened on his watch. Of all men, *this* man deserved to die on a Roman cross. But then the whole crowd began to chime in, "Release Barabbas! Release Barabbas! Release Barabbas to us!"

Pilate raised his hands and quieted the mob. Arrius knew the prefect was desperate to set Yeshua free. He was certain that Procula's warnings rattled Pilate's soul.

"This man," pointing to the rabbi, "is innocent. He has done nothing! What crime has He committed? I have found no grounds for the death penalty."

And the louder Pilate yelled, the more the crowd screamed, "Release Yeshua Barabbas! Crucify Yeshua Bar-Joseph. Crucify Him!"

5 John 18:39

Pilate was sweating profusely, and he said a third time as he gestured to Yeshua, "I will punish Him and then release Him." But the masses would not hear of it. The more Pilate objected, the more the people insisted. "Crucify Him!"

Pilate then ordered a basin of water to be brought to him, where he washed his hands and declared, "I am innocent of this man's blood; this act is upon you, not me."

And the people answered, "His blood is on us and on our children."

Arrius could not help but think of *his* blood curse, and he thought to himself, *These Jews have no idea what they are doing; they bring a blood curse on themselves and their children without hesitation. Fools.*

Pilate turned to Arrius, "Centurion."

"Yes, Prefect."

"Have this man flogged and see to it that He is crucified today, and release Yeshua Barabbas now."

For a second, Arrius stood motionless and in shock.

"Do you hear me? Get him," pointing to Yeshua Barabbas, "out of my sight!"

Arrius saluted and proceeded to untie the hands of Barabbas.

The criminal spoke condescendingly to Arrius, "We *will* meet again, Centurion, and the next time you will not be so lucky."

Without thinking, Arrius hit Barabbas in the gut and grabbed the hair on the back of his head, jerking his face up. "Yes, Barabbas, we will meet again, and when we do, you will die at my hand and without mercy."

The legionaries with Arrius, Tasco being one of them, immediately grabbed Yeshua. They dragged him aside, twisted some thorns from a nearby bush together, and placed it on his head like a crown. They took the purple robe Herod had used and rewrapped it around the rejected rabbi. The soldiers repeatedly hit Him in the face and mocked Him as they said, “Hail, King of the Jews!”

It was several hours before noon, or about the third hour on the day of preparation for the Passover.

Arrius stood speechless as he watched the crowd disperse. He had seen Roman cruelty, and he’d participated in Roman brutality. But as Barabbas laughed and rejoined his crew of Zealots, Arrius looked up into the cloudless sky and uttered in agony as he shook his fist toward the heavens. “Gods of Rome, gods of my father, God of my wife, how can you let this happen? How am I to explain this to Ayla?” A black vulture, an uncommon bird of prey in Judea, called to its mate high in the Judean sky. The early morning sun lit up the temple as if it was just another day in Jerusalem—but it wasn’t. Yeshua’s life would end soon.

CHAPTER 38

Year 33 AD, Golgotha, Jerusalem

After more beatings and abuse, Arrius finally intervened and told his men to take Yeshua to Golgotha to be crucified. They didn't waste any time securing a Roman *patibulum*—the crossbeam—from a pile always found just outside the praetorium. The legionaries, out of sadistic spite, intentionally found the heaviest one. This part of the Roman cross was a significant burden to bear for anyone, but to carry such a load after a flogging and a severe beating was extremely difficult.

Yeshua stumbled three times along the brick road that led up the hill to what the Jews called the Place of the Skull. Each time, He slipped in His sweat and blood. Some of Yeshua's hair had been pulled from the roots, and the blood was running from His back down His legs. The flies were already feasting on His open wounds.

The third time He fell to His knees, an African man came and knelt next to Yeshua. Simon, a merchant from Cyrene, was in Jerusalem for the Passover. He and his sons, Alexander and Rufus, came to Jerusalem to capitalize on the annual Jewish celebration's business opportunities.

Simon spoke with tenderness, "I am so sorry, rabbi. My sons and I have listened to Your teachings. This is no way to treat a good man."

Arrius yelled at Simon, "You there! What is your name?"

"Simon, Centurion."

Arrius saw Simon's act of kindness as a chance to help the rabbi—even in a small way. "So you are fond of this man?"

"I am, Centurion. I have found His teachings to be both challenging and comforting."

"Are you a Jew?"

"No, Centurion."

"Then this man's blood will not make you unclean for Passover."

"No, Centurion."

"Good, you will take the *patibulum* and carry it for this…this rabbi. We have wasted enough time."

"It is my honor to help—"

Arrius cut him off, "I don't care about your honor, African. Take it from His shoulders, and let us be done with this."

As he took the crossbar off Yeshua, Simon looked into His bloody face and said, "Rabbi, my heart is heavy for You. I will gladly carry this burden for You."

Arrius was shocked at what he saw and heard next.

Yeshua smiled at Simon, revealing a missing tooth, a deep cut in His tongue, and a mouth full of blood, as He said, "Simon, your act of compassion will never be forgotten."

Arrius thought to himself, *How is it possible for Yeshua to demonstrate kindness on the worst day of His life*?

"Rabbi, I care not about being remembered, only that You know how sorry I am for You." Every word was an effort for Yeshua. "Simon, in the future, your people will suffer much and carry many unrighteous burdens before I return, but you and this act of love for Me will always be remembered."

Simon bowed his head and wept at the teacher's words. "Forgive us, rabbi. Please forgive us."

Yeshua's eyes seemed to smile even though His mouth could not. "All is as it should be, Simon. This was written about long before this day."

Simon walked several paces behind Yeshua, who moved with unnatural resolve now toward Golgotha. Some in the crowd spit on the rabbi. Others cursed Him. A few threw rocks that landed hard on Yeshua's broken and bleeding head and back.

A growing number of followers, however, made their way to the road. Every one of Yeshua's followers, men, women, young and old, wailed uncontrollably. With every step taken up the hill, Arrius's heart grew heavier and heavier.

Then Arrius saw her. Ayla, too, was on her knees weeping. The centurion made his way to her side, roughly grabbed her by the arms, and lifted her to her feet. "Ayla, what are you doing here? This crowd could turn and riot in a heartbeat. You must go home."

"I cannot, and I will not. How can *you* lead Yeshua to His death? How can *you* be any part of this?" And with that, she collapsed to her knees again and let out another loud cry. There was nothing Arrius could say. He didn't have a choice. It was his duty to obey; he had led many men to their death up that very hill.

Then someone, undoubtedly another female follower of the

rabbi, offered Him a drink of water as she tried to wipe the blood from His face.

"Ayla, I cannot deal with you now. I cannot be distracted from my responsibilities. I beg you. Go home. Attend to our children and leave here before things get out of control."

Arrius knew getting her to listen was a hopeless task. Ayla wrapped her arms around his feet in what he saw as a futile attempt to stop him. He shook her off and headed for the woman who'd stopped the rabbi.

"You there. Woman. That's enough. Back away. Leave Him be, or you will be wiping *your* face with that cloth!" Many of the women following the crowd were sobbing.

Yeshua turned to them and said, "Daughters of Jerusalem, do not weep for me; weep for yourselves and for your children."[6]

In addition to being angry with Ayla, Arrius was livid at the poor woman who offered kindness to the rabbi and dumbfounded by Yeshua's words. *How can He still be thinking of others and worried about the children of these foolish women?*

Arrius, Tasco, several other legionaries, Simon, and Yeshua slowly made their way up the hill until they reached the summit.

Arrius barked, "Tasco, take the *patibulum* from the African."

Arrius pointed at another legionary, "You, take this man," referring to Yeshua, "strip Him and get Him nailed to a cross immediately. I want this to be over with as soon as possible."

The legionaries knew their jobs, and they wasted no time. The Romans were experts at inhumane torture and crucifixions. The goal was always the same—apply the maximum amount of pain on

6 Luke 23:28

the criminal with minimum effort from the legionaries. One soldier would secure the crossbar to the vertical part of the cross called the stipe. Two legionaries then stretched out Yeshua's arms, while two more simultaneously placed a large nail in the center of both wrists. As they struck the nails with large hammers, Yeshua let out an ear-piercing scream. Each additional pound of the hammer made the rabbi shriek in agony.

With every blow and every excruciating cry from Yeshua, Arrius cringed. He had overseen the execution of many men, but this time and with this man, he was sick to his stomach.

At a distance, there was a group of women huddled together crying. Arrius recognized Mary, the woman who assisted in his daughter's birth, and much to his dismay, Ayla was among them.

"Why is my wife so stubborn? Why would she subject herself to this horrific scene and horrible injustice?" he said out loud to himself as he paced back and forth in front of the crosses. Arrius was beside himself. He never imagined Ayla seeing this part of his duty as a centurion.

As the legionaries cast lots for the rabbi's clothes, they started to argue with each other. As Tasco threw the dice, Arrius stepped into the middle of their argument and kicked him in the side without warning. The force of his kick sent Tasco to the ground in pain.

"Centurion! What have I done?" said the stunned Tasco.

Arrius grunted something unintelligible as he stepped away and began to pace again. To this point, he'd intentionally not made eye contact with Yeshua. Arrius couldn't bring himself to look at the rabbi's barely recognizable face. When he finally did look up, their eyes met for a moment, and Arrius could see the weight of a billion souls in Yeshua's eyes. Arrius also saw the darkness in his own heart.

The centurion shook his head in frustration. "Why would Pilate put *that* sign above his head?" On it were written the words, "THIS IS YESHUA. THE KING OF THE JEWS." Of course, the Sanhedrin members, present to gloat in their victory, complained to Arrius, "Pilate offends us with that sign. Take it down, Centurion."

Arrius ground his teeth and said, "What is written is written! If Pilate wouldn't listen to you, why should I?"

The two insurrectionists, partners with Barabbas in his rebellion but not pardoned by Pilate, hung on crosses to the right and left of Yeshua. One of the men added his insults and curses against Yeshua. To the centurion's amazement, Yeshua remained silent when He was attacked and only looked like He was overwhelmed with sadness rather than anger.

The criminal cursing Yeshua goaded him and said, "Aren't You the Messiah? If You are, then save Yourself and save us."

The other criminal, watching all that was happening and knowing Barabbas should be on the center cross, not Yeshua, finally yelled at his friend, "Don't you fear God? We are being punished justly; you and I are getting what we deserve. But this man… this rabbi has done nothing wrong."

Yeshua looked at the man, and once again His eyes smiled despite His pain.

The criminal then said, "Rabbi, I beg You to remember me when You come into Your kingdom."

Yeshua struggled to take a deep breath as He said, "Trust Me, today, this very day, you will be with Me in paradise."

Arrius was stunned by the exchange.

Yeshua was quickly bleeding out. Arrius was surprised He hadn't died from the scourging He took from the *flagrum*, the lead-tipped whip the legionaries used to beat him.

Only about three hours had passed, but Arrius knew Yeshua would not survive much longer. Strangely, a darkness fell over the city. There was no storm, but it was as if the sun refused to shine.

A small band of several women, including Mary Magdalene, approached the cross. A young man was with them as well. Ayla stood near but at a reasonable distance. The legionaries yelled at the group to step back, but Arrius immediately stepped in and told his men to leave them alone.

Arrius felt as if he were listening in on a private conversation. Yeshua spoke to the oldest lady and the young man, "Woman, here is your son. John, here is your mother."

When Arrius realized the older woman was the rabbi's mother, many memories flooded back to him of Astra, his father's concubine, and Claudia—the only two women he'd ever known as mothers. Arrius turned away so his men couldn't see his face as tears began to stream down his cheeks.

Arrius moaned, "Yeshua's mother. Here. Now. Oh gods, how could you let this happen? For the first time in my life, I am ashamed to be a Roman."

The strange darkness continued to swallow up the light of day as Yeshua gasped, "I am thirsty." Arrius ordered his men to offer Yeshua some vinegar soaked on a sponge. With cracked and bloodied lips, He received the drink.

Yeshua cried out in a loud and surprisingly strong voice at about the sixth hour, "Eloi, Eloi, *lema sabachthani*?"

The legionaries said to Arrius, "Who is He praying to? What does the Hebrew pray?" Arrius knew enough Aramaic to understand the meaning. "He prays to His God, 'Why have You forsaken Me?'"

The men shrugged their shoulders and said nothing. Arrius felt as if his heart was being ripped from his chest. He looked up again into the face of the rabbi and heard Him say, "It is finished." And Yeshua took His last breath.

Immediately, as if synced to Yeshua's final moment, an earthquake shook the ground and all of Jerusalem. The legionaries, superstitious by nature, cried out, "Darkness and now this! The gods are angry! This man's blood will be upon us!"

Ayla found her way to her husband's side amidst all the confusion. By now, Arrius had collapsed to his knees and was openly sobbing. It was as if a long-buried stream of suffering and tears welled up within him. Ayla knelt before her Savior and her Messiah—now dead—and next to her husband—now broken—as Arrius exclaimed through his tears, "Surely, this man was the Son of God!"

"Yes, my *bashert*, Yeshua is the Passover Lamb sacrificed here and now, once and for all."

Arrius turned to look at Ayla, the love of his life. *How is it possible that she seems both sorrowful and yet at peace?* he thought. He had watched her change under the instruction of Yeshua. He'd listened to her recount the rabbi's many teachings. And he'd seen enough men die to know this man was far more than just a man.

With a cracked and hoarse voice, he said, "What am I to do now, Ayla? How can your god ever forgive me for this? How can *you* forgive me?" as he pointed to the bloody corpse of Yeshua.

She wrapped her arms around her rocking and sobbing husband without speaking.

Because it was the day of preparation for Passover, the Jewish leaders did not want the bodies left on crosses during the Sabbath. They demanded that Pilate break the legs to expedite their deaths. So Pilate sent word for Arrius to do so.

A legionary approached Arrius. "Centurion, we are commanded to finish this immediately. Pilate demands we break the legs."

Arrius looked up at the man and nodded, "Deal with him and the other," pointing to the men to the right and left of Yeshua. "The rabbi is dead already; there is no need to break Him, but to satisfy Pilate and these dreadful Hebrews, pierce Yeshua's side with your spear."

Ayla looked at her husband through swollen eyes and a tear-stained face. "Must we, Arrius?"

"He is gone, Ayla; He will feel no pain. I promise."

Tasco was standing nearby. He took his spear—and with far too much force—he shoved the blade into the rabbi's heart.

As Tasco pierced Yeshua's side, an unexpected burst of blood and water ruptured out. Arrius and Ayla were close, too close, and to their surprise some of Yeshua's blood splattered on them.

Arrius fell back, shocked and sickened. Ayla, however, remained on her knees as she turned to her husband and said with a supernatural calmness, "Today, my love, you are *blood born* again. The first time resulted in death; this time into eternal life. This blood was shed for your sins…for my sins…and for *all* sins."

Arrius finally stood, but slowly, like a man knocked down by a severe blow. He took Ayla into his arms and held her tighter and closer than ever before. His entire body shook again as he sobbed and whispered into her ear, "Blood born. Born again. How is this possible? And yet, it is. I cannot explain it, Ayla, but I feel even the burden of my curse is gone."

Arrius then offered to Yahweh his first heartfelt prayer of surrender, "God of my wife and Father of this man, forgive me for my part in His death. I vow before heaven and earth to no longer serve Rome but You, Yahweh, and You alone."

Ayla heard every word of his prayer, but more importantly, she knew that Yahweh was fulfilling His promise to her. She knew, despite his years of agony and self-hatred, her husband was destined for greatness in the kingdom of God. This gruesome moment of death and despair ushered in a new life for the man she loved.

"Yeshua will live *in* us and *through* us now," she sighed.

Arrius and Ayla walked home heartbroken. There were no words to express the depth of their grief. When they entered their house, Ayla took Tikva from her friend and neighbor's arms while Arrius fell exhausted and face down on the ground next to his son.

At first, Seneca thought his father wanted to play with him, but when he saw the tears of Arrius, he became afraid and began to cry.

Arrius composed himself, looked into the fearful eyes of his son, and said, "It's okay, Son. It's okay. Your father did a bad thing today, but somehow—"

Ayla spoke up, "Rome. *Rome* is evil, Arrius, and you are not

Rome…not anymore."

Of course, Seneca had no idea what his father and mother's words meant, but something was different in his father's eyes, which calmed his fears.

Little did Arrius or Ayla know how much things were about to change.

CHAPTER 39

The Day after Yeshua's Crucifixion, 33 AD, Jerusalem

Early the next morning, on the Sabbath, Arrius was startled by a loud pounding on the door as an urgent voice yelled, "Centurion, Pilate demands you join him."

Arrius hadn't slept all night, and he couldn't bring himself to eat breakfast. He opened his door to find a legionary who saluted him.

Ayla entered the room and said with concern, "What is it, my *bashert*?"

The legionary ignored her and said to Arrius, "Pilate is in a foul mood, Centurion. We *must* leave now."

"You will wait for me outside, and I will join you when I am ready, Legionary."

"Yes, Centurion," said the young man as he saluted again and stepped back. Arrius closed the door in his face.

"Now what, Arrius? The sun has barely risen, and Pilate summons you again. For what reason now? It is still the Sabbath."

As Arrius put on his uniform and laced his boots, he shook his head in dread. "I have no idea, Ayla. Perhaps there is an uprising by Yeshua's followers."

"Not possible, Arrius. All I saw on His disciples' faces was fear, not boldness. Besides, the rabbi taught us to turn the other cheek. We will not take up swords against Rome. Not now. Not ever."

Arrius sighed, "As soon as I can do so, I will retire my commission. My required twenty-five years of service to the emperor are almost completed. Pilate will have no choice but to let me go. But for now, I still must report to him as summoned."

"Be careful, Arrius. There is deep spiritual power still hovering over the city. I feel it, and I fear it."

Arrius grabbed his sword and helmet and kissed Ayla on the top of her head, assuring her. "I will be fine. Aren't you the one telling me that Yahweh will always protect me?"

Ayla smiled.

Without another word, Arrius opened the door and joined the impatient legionary.

Pilate was indeed in a mood. "Where have you been? I called for you hours ago." Pilate exaggerated, as usual, but Arrius had no energy or desire to defend himself.

"My apologies, Prefect. I came as soon as I could."

"Stop with your excuses, Centurion. I am ready to flog the next man who irritates me. My wife hasn't let me rest since the crucifixion of that rabbi, and now the chief priests and Pharisees are demanding—how dare they—*demanding* that I seal the tomb where the rabbi rots and place a Roman guard outside of it."

"For what purpose, Prefect?"

"Precisely! For what purpose? These idiots are afraid the followers of Yeshua will try to steal the body. I curse the day I entered this godforsaken city. Who would steal a corpse? Who would have the nerve to touch the mangled and bloodied flesh of that man?"

Arrius stood silent and still.

Pilate continued, "To make matters worse, these stupid and superstitious Judeans tell me the rabbi prophesied He would rise up from the grave on the third day. How ridiculous." Pilate mockingly forced a laugh. "No man comes off a Roman cross alive, and no human has the power to resurrect himself from the grave."

Arrius again felt the weight of his part in the crucifixion.

"Well, Centurion, say something. What am I to do now?"

"On your orders, Prefect, I will seal the tomb and place my best men on guard. I will see to it that no one disturbs the tomb of the rabbi."

Pilate shouted, "See to it. Immediately! I cannot…I *will not* let this dead man or His radical followers continue to rob me of my peace."

Arrius saluted Pilate and left quickly to find his men in the barracks. On his way, he decided it was best to place sixteen legionaries—two *contubernium*—at the tomb.

Lucious and Rufus, both decani or leaders over a *contubernium*, were told by Arrius, "You two grab your men, your gear, and enough food for three days. You are on special duty by the orders of Pilate."

Lucious and Rufus looked at each other with a knowing expression. Special duty meant guard duty, and that meant facing both boredom and difficulty. Roman guards operated under strict rules. Each man was responsible for six square feet of space, and they could not sit down or lean on each other while on duty. The schedule required eight men on and eight men off duty for four hours at a time. If any one man fell asleep while on duty, the entire *contubernium* would be beaten and possibly executed.

"Yes, Centurion. We will gather our men and report to you quickly."

"As soon as possible, men. Your lives depend on following Pilate's orders."

Both men saluted and hurried off to gather their men, weapons, and supplies.

The large stone, fitted in a channel with a slight decline, made it easier to roll it downhill and into place. The design, however, also made it very difficult to open the tomb once closed. The wealthier Jerusalemites used this method to discourage grave robbers from entering.

With gravity against them, it took three legionaries to move the stone into the open position so that Arrius could confirm the body was present. Once the stone was rolled back in place, Arrius sealed the opening himself. Made from common clay, the Roman seal was embossed with the Roman imperial mark and attached to the tombstone with a leather strap. The seal was the sign of authentication that the grave was occupied and not to be disturbed. Anyone found breaking it would do so under penalty of death.

Arrius was still physically and emotionally exhausted. There was no longer any joy or satisfaction in his duties. All he wanted to do was go home to his wife and children.

"Lucious. Rufus. Keep your men alert. Expect the unexpected. Stay sharp. Pilate will not tolerate any failure to fulfill your duty. Do you understand?"

"Yes, Centurion."

All the men knew the consequences of letting anyone near the tomb. They would rather die with their swords in hand fighting off intruders than face the wrath of Arrius or Pilate.

Ayla was busying herself around the house, but the Sabbath requirements regarding work were clear and strict. Thankfully, the younger children were asleep, and Kaamil was playing with a bug of some sort in the courtyard.

Ayla said out loud, "What is Pilate up to now? That man is evil. He will forever pay for what he did to Yeshua." She sat at the window, staring at the sky as she began to pray. "Yahweh, before today, I would have said that the day my father disowned me was the worst day of my life. But yesterday now surpasses the agony of that experience."

Ayla began to weep. "Yahweh, why did You abandon Your Son? Why have You left us without hope? What are we to do now?" Her whole body began to shake as she trembled in tears and cried out, "Yeshua said we should pray, 'Your kingdom come; Your will be done…' How can *this* be Your will, Yahweh? My heart is so broken."

The baby began to cry in hunger, and her milk let down as she picked her up from their bed, "Hush now, Tikva. Oh, how I wish someone would hold and comfort me—but your mother is here. Always here for you, my sweet child."

At that moment, in the early morning light of that room, Ayla then heard a voice, a sound like the wind or rushing water; it was other-worldly, "Daughter of Israel, all is not lost. Do not be afraid. Yeshua's death is not the end of the story."

Her tears flowed freely again as she looked into the adoring eyes of her baby. "Yahweh *is* here. Always near, my sweet Tikva," she whispered as her tears dripped onto the face of her daughter. "But how is Yeshua's death not the end of His story?"

CHAPTER 40

Resurrection Day, 33 AD, Home of Arrius and Ayla

Sunday, the first day of the week, was typically busy for everyone. After the Sabbath, the markets would open and be full of merchants and customers. Arrius usually rose early, long before the sun. Today, however, he remained in bed. He'd slept restlessly. A recurring dream startled him awake in the middle of the night.

Ayla knew Arrius had a bad night because he'd tossed and turned so much. She was surprised he was still next to her. "What is wrong, Arrius?"

"Nothing."

Ayla snuggled closer to him. "Nothing as in there is *nothing* wrong, or nothing as in I have *nothing* to say?"

Arrius groaned, "You know me well, Ayla Rose, perhaps too well."

"I know you still carry the burden of what happened. I also know you had no choice. Pilate and the Sanhedrin are to blame, not you."

Arrius rolled over and turned his back to Ayla. "I still wrestle with the shame of my sin against an innocent man."

Ayla could tell that no words would comfort Arrius, but she

held him closely.

Arrius sighed, "I had a dream. The *same* dream multiple times last night."

Ayla giggled a bit, trying to lighten the mood. "It's official."

Arrius turned to face her. "What's official?"

"You are an old man now. The prophet Joel said young men would see visions and old—*very old*—men would dream dreams."

Arrius grunted and turned away from Ayla again.

"I am only teasing you."

"Sorry, Ayla, I'm not in the mood."

"Well…then…tell me about the dream."

Arrius spoke softly, "It was strange and probably nothing."

"Please tell me everything, Arrius. I want to hear it."

"I was in my homeland, but I was a man, not a child, and snow was falling—"

Ayla interrupted him, "Did you know I have never seen snow?"

Arrius continued, "I was cold, alone, and walking through a dim forest. It was quiet, Ayla, so quiet. There wasn't a sound except for the noise my feet made as I struggled through the deep snow. From time to time, I would turn and look back at my trail. I was shocked to see that everywhere I stepped was drenched in blood, but the blood was not mine. I had no idea whose blood it was. The more I walked, the more exhausted I became, but what kept me moving forward was a light I could see ahead of me at the edge of the forest."

Ayla asked, "What kind of light? Firelight? Sunlight?"

Arrius sat up in bed and rubbed the sleep from his eyes. “At first, I couldn’t tell, but the light drew me closer, like a moth to a torchlight. And the closer I got to the light, the warmer I felt. It was so strange.”

“So the light was good?”

“That’s what I thought, but when I finally stepped into the light, it was blinding and painful. I felt like the light passed right through me. I felt naked and completely exposed. But I kept moving…kept walking into the light…and the longer I walked, the purer I felt. It was as if the light was cleansing my soul.”

Ayla shot up in bed and said, “I know what your dream means, Arrius. I see it clearly. Once, before your encounter with Yeshua on His cross, you were buried in darkness. The blood in your steps represents the many you killed in battle serving Rome. You have always felt alone, surrounded by the silence of your shame and the blood curse you have unjustly endured.”

Ayla was bouncing a bit on the bed as she spoke rapidly. “And my *bashert*, the light is the light of Yeshua. He taught us that He was the light of the world. He drew you into His presence …Yahweh’s light…which was difficult and painful for you to accept because you felt unworthy. But David wrote in the psalms, ‘[Yahweh] turns my darkness into light.’”[7]

Arrius turned to Ayla, and his voice shook. “What am I to do? What does Yahweh want from me now?”

Ayla’s eyes smiled. “Keep walking, Arrius; keep in the light. No matter how painful the journey.”

Arrius lay there pondering Ayla’s words and her interpretation

---

7 Psalm 18:28

of his dream.

Both were startled by a loud knock at the door.

"This is getting old!" said Arrius as he got out of bed.

"Centurion? Are you home? There's been an…an incident."

Arrius opened the door to find Rufus standing there, a terrified look on his face.

"What is it now, Rufus? Why are you here and not at the tomb? I gave you and your men strict orders—"

Rufus interrupted, "Centurion, we…uh…I…uh…the body…."

Arrius stepped into the face of his terrified soldier and grabbed the man's breastplate. "Speak, Legionary! What happened?"

Rufus tried to step back from his centurion, but Arrius would not let him go.

"I don't know. Something happened that I cannot explain. It was early, long before the first watch. Lucious and his men were sound asleep, but I promise you, Centurion, my men were wide awake. Then there was a loud noise, a violent earthquake, and a white light that came out of nowhere. There was a large…man…demon…I cannot be sure who or what he was, but he was massive, larger than any human I have ever seen. His clothes were on fire, or so it seemed, but there was no flame. The light, I swear by the gods, Centurion—the light was blinding. This…this creature…held a large sword in his hand. It all happened so quickly. We had no time to react, but the men couldn't move even if they wanted to. Then, out of the corner of my eye, I saw another being, as massive as the first, maybe bigger! And he was rolling away the stone."

"By himself? Impossible. It would take three strong legionaries or more to roll it out of place."

"Precisely. Impossible. But I assure you my words are true."

Arrius was angry. "And the body? What of the body?"

"When we came to—"

"What do you mean *came to*?"

"Every one of us must have passed out, Centurion. I have no idea how long we were unconscious, but we were as dead men. I woke up face down in the dirt."

"Were the beings still there?"

"No. And the body was gone. They must have taken the body. Demons stealing the dead!"

Arrius pushed the legionary back and beat his fist into his open hand. "Whom have you told this to? Does Pilate know? Where are the men?"

Rufus looked down, and his voice quivered. "No one but you knows. Pilate, as of yet, has no idea. The men ran back to the barracks in fear for their lives."

Arrius stepped forward and poked his index finger into Rufus's breastplate. "They should be afraid. Pilate will have us flogged and then executed for this failure. We are doomed, Legionary. Pilate will kill all of us, me included."

The legionary, of course, was well aware of the punishment that awaited them all. Failure, for whatever reason, was inexcusable in the Roman army.

Arrius gave Rufus instructions, "Run, quickly, back to the barracks. Gather the men and have them meet me just outside the Dung Gate. We will then regroup in the Kidron Valley and come up with a reasonable story. Tell the men to speak of this to no one."

"Yes, Centurion," said Rufus as he saluted and turned away.

Ayla had heard everything. She was standing just inside the door, listening. "Arrius, what are you going to do?"

Arrius replied curtly, "I don't know. I need to think. I must come up with a plan, or this will be my last day alive."

"I am a bit worried, Arrius; honestly, the unexpected death of Yeshua challenged my trust in Yahweh."

Ayla placed a gentle hand on his chest. "But Arrius, I cannot believe that Yahweh has brought you this far only to abandon you now."

Arrius looked away from Ayla in shame. "Or perhaps Yahweh is punishing me and Rome for murdering His Son."

Ayla stated calmly, "I have a shalom about this; all will be well. We must trust in the Lord no matter what has happened or what might happen."

"The Lord I trust. Pilate, I do not."

The composure of Ayla brought Arrius a measure of *pax* in what should have been the worst moment of his career as a soldier.

"I don't know how you do it, Wife, but your words ring true in my soul. I will figure something out."

"Arrius?"

"What?"

Ayla spoke rapidly, "Yeshua told us He would come back to life on the *third* day! What if it is true? What if He is risen?"

"I know the rabbi was special, but how is that possible? No man lives again, especially after a Roman cross."

Ayla grabbed both arms of Arrius as the words bubbled out of her mouth and soul. "The voice, Arrius, the voice of the angel told me, 'All is not lost.' He told me the rabbi's death was not the end of His story."

"It may not be the end of *His* story, but it could be the end of mine. Ayla, I need to go. We will speak of this later…assuming I survive the day."

The men, all sixteen of them, waited in the shadow of the city's walls just outside the gate. It was still early, and the Dung Gate was relatively quiet. However, tensions were high, and the men had been bickering and arguing with each other over who was at fault.

"Centurion, we are all here as ordered," said Lucious as he saluted.

"Let us move. Quickly!" ordered Arrius.

The men formed a double line, led by Rufus and Lucious, as they followed Arrius down into the valley. Arrius knew they had very little time to come up with a story and execute a plan to save their lives. After a brief time, Arrius stopped in an olive grove that shielded them from view.

Arrius spoke to his men with more confidence than he truly had. "I have given this some thought. Our only hope is to fool Pilate. We will take turns punching one another in the face. I will go first, and I'm going to beat you two within an inch of your lives," pointing at the two decani. "I want all of your uniforms bloodied and dirtied as if we were in a fierce battle."

It didn't take the men long to figure out the plan. Rather than explain the unexplainable to Pilate and be killed for their failure, they would fabricate a story of how a large party—perhaps a hundred men—attacked and overran them in the night.

The men nodded as Arrius made the plan clear. “Once we are done with our mock battle, you will return immediately to the tomb. I will speak with the chief priests, tell them what really happened, and *suggest* our cover story.”

“Tell them the truth?” objected Rufus.

“Yes, you fool, the truth. I need them to support us before Pilate and beg him to show mercy to us. They will not want any rumors spreading of anything supernatural happening to their enemy, Yeshua. Those fools will gladly promote our story of Yeshua’s followers stealing His body because the alternative will be their undoing.”

One of the legionaries spoke up, “If they want this kept secret, I say we demand a bribe from them. Make them pay for our silence.”

All the men grunted in approval.

Arrius raised his hand to silence the legionaries. “Right now, I will settle for *living* as a poor man, but if the opportunity presents itself, I will take whatever they are willing to offer.”

The chief priests were in an uproar. Their greatest fear had come to reality. Whether it was a demon, as some suspected, or the Romans failed and the body was truly stolen, this could lead to their downfall.

Joseph Ben-Caiaphas quickly offered his verbal and financial support to Arrius as they stood in the courtyard. “We will stand with you before Pilate. We will praise you and the efforts of your men and insist he not take your lives."

Arrius was disgusted but said, "Thank you, Caiaphas; we are grateful for your support."

Caiaphas interjected, "I imagine, however, that Pilate will still flog the men. But will your men stay the course and stick to the story?"

Arrius was firm in his reply, "Their lives depend on it."

Caiaphas bemoaned, "All our lives depend on it. The people will rise up and demand the Sanhedrin be stoned if this false Messiah somehow magically reappears."

Arrius was adamant. "He was—and I am certain—still *is* quite dead, Caiaphas. Remember I was there."

"Yes, but we all heard Him claim He would come back to life on the third day." The Jewish leaders all moaned with concern.

Arrius was surprised by the candor of the chief priest and the worry in his eyes. He waited for the room to settle. "I, too, heard of His claims. Worst case, His body has been carried off to the underworld. Best case, His followers have taken it and buried it elsewhere. Either way, no one comes back to life after a Roman crucifixion. No one."

"See to it, then, Centurion. We will never speak of this *arrangement* again."

Arrius left the courtyard in a hurry to get back to the tomb and his men.

Arrius returned to his men, who waited at the empty tomb. "It is done. We have the support of that mangy goat, Caiaphas. We will go now to Pilate and tell him our story."

Arrius, however, knew this affair was far from over. A lot was riding on his ability to tell a lie to Pilate and the questionable support of the Jewish leaders they all hated.

"And what if we fail?" murmured Lucious.

Arrius glared at Lucious. "To fail here is a death sentence. We will *not* and *cannot* lose control of this…this situation. Pull yourselves together."

"Yes, Centurion!" the men said in unison as they saluted. They all knew that failure was not an option if they were to survive. Whether Pilate would believe the lie was yet to be seen.

CHAPTER 41

Year 33 AD, Home of Arrius and Ayla

Arrius returned home exhausted. Fortunately, Pilate accepted their report. As planned, the chief priests intervened, and Pilate seemed satisfied—for now. Arrius was surprised that he'd received no orders to flog his men. Perhaps Pilate knew something else was happening, or he was too tired and distracted to care. Time would tell.

"Praise the Lord! I have been so worried about you, Arrius," Ayla exclaimed as she ran to embrace him.

Arrius explained to Ayla the events of his morning and how close he and his men came to being put to death. "For now, it seems Pilate is satisfied with our fabricated story."

Ayla looked distracted to Arrius. "What are you thinking, Ayla?"

"Oh…uh…I knew Yahweh would not allow you to die. But Arrius…I don't know how to explain it…but something unbelievable has happened."

Arrius took off his armor and then sat down on the edge of the bed to remove his sandals. "Yes, Wife, *something* has happened, and my heart has not stopped racing since the knock on our door this morning. My mind is consumed by a thousand thoughts. How am I to process the experience of my men at the empty tomb?

What manner of evil would manifest itself and terrify sixteen Roman legionaries? Who would steal a dead body? If I did not know it, I would think I am trapped in a horrible nightmare—"

Ayla interrupted, "Arrius, I don't know how to tell you what I have learned while you were gone. The entire time you were speaking I have been trying to come up with just the right words to explain the unexplainable."

Arrius took off his boots and sat back, unsure how to interpret his wife's demeanor. Ayla surprised him when she clapped her hands and jumped up and down like an excited child. "I have something to tell you, my amazing *bashert*. It is wonderful news, but this news will *not* calm your racing heart!"

Arrius looked up at Ayla, perplexed. "How can you be happy and smiling at a moment like this? Has the whole world gone mad? And now my wife—"

Ayla almost shouted as she butt in again, "The whole world *is* about to change in ways you and I could never have imagined, Arrius!"

Arrius grew irritated.

But Ayla now spoke with greater passion, "He is alive! Arrius, He lives!"

Arrius bent over and covered his face with his hands in exasperation. "Who lives, Ayla? What are you speaking about? Speak plainly to me."

Ayla raised both hands in the air and almost sang the words, "Yeshua lives. He is risen!"

Arrius slowly looked up at the joy-filled face of his wife as he wondered, *How can she believe such a preposterous thing? Who has bewitched my wife?*

Ayla then began recounting her morning experience. She spoke so fast that Arrius could hardly take it all in.

"The more I thought about what was going on, the more upset I became after you left. I was afraid I would lose both my rabbi and my husband in a matter of days. I prayed. I wept. I tried to eat but couldn't. The children sensed my emotions, and they started to get upset too. Even Kaamil was worried about me. I decided I needed to talk with someone, *anyone* who would understand. So I left the kids with Naomi and ran to find Mary. Oh, Arrius, the looks I got while running down the street with my head uncovered. I didn't even think about what I must have looked like. People probably thought I was a prostitute running for my life."

Arrius shook his head, not sure whether he should be upset or amazed by his wife.

"Nevertheless, I went to two different places where I thought I would find Mary. Everywhere I went, I heard the same thing, 'I don't know where she's off to, but you *must* find her; she has amazing news!' 'What news?' I asked. And people would just smile and tell me, 'Go, find her, and quickly.' Finally, someone directed me to Mark's home. You know, the young man I introduced you to from Alexandria. The disciples spend most of their time at his home when they are in Jerusalem. They shared their last meal with Yeshua in his upper room. I should have looked there first, but I went to the closest spots—"

"Ayla, please slow down. Take a breath, woman. I can hardly track with you. I am so tired. But yes, I remember Mark; his father was a Roman and married to a Jew, right?"

"Yes, yes, but that doesn't matter right now. Let me finish. I haven't gotten to the best part of the story yet!"

Arrius sighed and impatiently said, "Continue, but please get to the end quickly. I need to relieve myself, and I'm hungry. I haven't eaten anything all day."

"I will feed you in a bit. Please be still and listen!"

Arrius knew there was no stopping Ayla when she was like this.

"So I finally found Mary, and yes, she was at Mark's house with several other women. All the women were laughing and crying and singing and dancing. Dancing! Honestly, I got angry. How could they be dancing now? I thought to myself, *What's wrong with these ladies?* Then Mary saw me and ran to me. She practically knocked me over. She was holding me—squeezing me, actually—and forcing me to dance too. I yelled, a bit too loud, I suspect, 'Mary, what is going on?' She stopped, looked me in the eye, and said the three most beautiful words I have ever heard, 'He is risen!'"

Arrius didn't know what to say as he watched his wife pace back and forth in their small bedroom.

"Of course, the other three most wonderful words are, 'I love you,' and when you say that to me, I always blush, but can you imagine it, Arrius—He is risen!"

Arrius was on the edge of their bed, but when Ayla said Yeshua was alive, he bolted up and grabbed her by the shoulders to stop her from jumping up and down. "That is *not* possible. I saw Him die. *We* saw Him die! His body was beaten beyond recognition. His blood was drained, and His body was stone cold."

Arrius began to pace like he always did when he was thinking. "But my men—"

Ayla jumped up and down again. "Yes, your men. They must know it to be true. Mary said she and several other women left while it was still dark and came to the tomb just after sunrise. She said the soldiers were fleeing like they were being chased by demons just as they arrived. The women had gone there to finish what Joseph and Nicodemus started—the anointing of Yeshua's body."

Stunned, Arrius sat back down.

"Oh, Arrius, the stone was rolled away, and since Mary was the youngest and fastest of the ladies, she decided to immediately run back to find Peter and John. The women were concerned that the Romans had moved the body of Yeshua to some unknown and secret location."

"Ayla, I would never do such a thing."

"I know. I know. But there is more. Mary found Peter and John and told them the tomb was open and the rabbi's body gone. They told Mary to stay put while they ran to the tomb to see for themselves. I suppose Peter was concerned they might run into trouble and didn't want Mary to be in any danger. He can be very protective of the women who follow Yeshua."

"And? What did they find?"

"I don't know all that happened to them, Arrius. I am sure they will tell us. But a bit later, the other women arrived back at Mark's home, and they told the other disciples what they saw. They explained how, after Mary left, they were greeted by what must have been angels. They were terrified, but the angels said to them, 'Why do you look for the living among the dead? He is not here; He is risen! Remember when He told you that on the third day, He would rise from the dead.' Then, of course, the women remembered Yeshua's words. But as they ran back to Mark's house, they said to each other, 'Who will believe us? We are only women, and the men will not trust our account of what we have seen.'"

Arrius agreed and added, "I'm not sure I believe them."

Ayla ignored him and continued, "Before the women arrived at Mark's home, the ladies decided to say nothing, but when they arrived, they couldn't contain themselves and blurted out everything. As expected, the disciples didn't believe anything they said. They believed my friends were just being emotional and overcome with grief. Men! Mary told me at that point she couldn't take it anymore, and so she decided to run back to the tomb for a second time to see for herself."

Ayla paused, and her eyes moistened. "Mary said she was standing outside the empty tomb crying, but then she bent over to look into the grave for herself. When she did, she saw two angels in white seated where Yeshua's body had been, one at the head and the other at the foot. The angels asked Mary, 'Woman, why are you crying?' She was still terrified but now a bit agitated—I can see her just like that, can't you?"

Arrius said, "I am not sure how to answer that question. I don't know Mary that well."

"Oh, I can *definitely* imagine it, but anyway, Mary said to the angels, 'The Romans have taken my Lord away, and I don't know where they put Him.' The angels didn't respond to her, and still in shock, she slowly backed away from the tomb entrance. Mary said that as she turned to leave the tomb, Yeshua was standing right in front of her, but she didn't recognize Him at first. Mary thought He was the gardener."

"Wait, I am confused; how could Mary, of *all* people, not

recognize the rabbi?"

Ayla threw her hands up. "I don't know. Maybe the rising sun in her face obstructed her vision. Maybe Yeshua's face was covered with a prayer shawl. Maybe she couldn't see clearly because of all her sobbing. Maybe Yeshua didn't want her to recognize Him. He is funny that way. Whatever the reason, the *man* asked the same thing the angels asked, 'Why are you crying?' Mary answered Him, 'Sir, if you have carried Him away, I beg you, tell me where you have put Him.'"

"I suppose it is reasonable to think the gardener would know," added Arrius.

"Arrius, Yeshua interrupted her question and simply said, 'Mary,' and the moment she heard Him call her name, she knew it was the teacher!"

Arrius was speechless.

Ayla added, "Of course, Mary told me she rushed back to the disciples to say to them she had seen Yeshua alive."

Arrius stood and wrapped his strong arms around his wife as he finally relaxed his clenched jaw. Ayla stepped back and looked up into his blue eyes as Arrius said, "What does this all mean, Ayla? What are we to do now?"

CHAPTER 42

The Six Weeks between the Resurrection and Pentecost, 33 AD, Jerusalem

Ten of the inner circle of Jesus's disciples had encountered the risen rabbi the third day after His crucifixion. All but one, Thomas, were present where they were hiding for fear of their lives behind closed and locked doors. That Sunday evening, however, Yeshua appeared to His disciples out of nowhere. The men were terrified and thought He was a ghost. Not surprisingly, the rabbi gently scolded them for doubting Mary's report. He challenged them to look at His nail-scarred hands and feet and told His disciples to touch Him. "A ghost doesn't have flesh and blood," He said. Even still, they were unconvinced until Yeshua asked them for some food, and He ate it in their presence.

At first, the disciples didn't know what to say. Most of them huddled in the partial darkness of that room, illuminated by only a single candle. John spoke first and asked with a broken voice, "Rabbi, how is this possible? I watched You die."

Then Yeshua opened their minds so they could understand what was written about Him and His resurrection in the law of Moses, the prophets, and the Psalms. Of course, the disciples were thrilled but still struggled to accept the man seated before them. Then, as mysteriously as He appeared, He disappeared.

Matthew stood and looked around the room. In order to see the faces of the other disciples, he had to squint because of his poor eyesight. "No one is going to believe us. I saw what I saw, and I can hardly believe it." There was a collective grunt of agreement among the men.

A bit later that night, Thomas returned. Under a cloak of darkness, he'd gone to check on his mother, who was ill. When the others told Thomas what had happened, he thought they were all crazy. "Grief has made you mad," he insisted. "I will not and *cannot* accept any of this unless I see it for myself."

A week later, all eleven of the disciples were in the house, including Thomas. For the most part, they'd remained secluded because they were still afraid the Sanhedrin would come after them next. The disciples argued quite a lot that week about why the rabbi told them to remain in Jerusalem. Yeshua told them not to go until they received what He called "the promise and power from on high." They knew the promise probably referred to the Holy Spirit, but what precisely the promise of *power* meant was debated among them for days.

The men were eating behind locked doors in the upper room. James, the brother of John, choked on his broiled fish when Yeshua suddenly appeared to them again. Simon, the Zealot, had found a sword somewhere during the week, and he jumped up and pulled it on the rabbi before he recognized who it was. Yeshua simply stood there smiling as He said, "Shalom be with you."

Thomas had stood and was backing up against a wall. He kept rubbing his eyes and mumbling about how impossible it was.

“Thomas,” said Yeshua.

Thomas stopped moving and held his breath as Yeshua moved toward him with nothing but compassion in His eyes. Thomas stared at the floor, unable to look at the Rabbi.

“Thomas, put your finger here.” Yeshua held out His hands to Thomas, but Thomas didn’t move a muscle. Then Yeshua opened His outer garment to reveal His scar where the Roman spear had pierced Him. “Don’t be frozen in terror and shame, My friend. Reach out your hand and put it into My side.” At that, Yeshua took the right hand of Thomas and made him touch His side. “Thomas, you must stop doubting; it is time for you to believe.”

Thomas fell to his knees and began to weep as he looked up into the loving eyes of the rabbi and said, “My Lord and my God!”

Yeshua placed a hand on the head of Thomas and whispered, “Now you see, and you believe; blessed are those who have not seen and yet believe.”

Then, Yeshua stepped back, looked each of His disciples in the eye, smiled again, and vanished as quickly as He had appeared.

After the rabbi left, Thomas sat on the floor and continued to bury his face in his hands and cry. Peter, who usually would have taken the lead in this situation, remained uncharacteristically subdued. The other men knelt beside Thomas and began to rock as they prayed to Yahweh. The rocking in prayer for a Hebrew resembles the flickering of a flame lit in their hearts by the Lord.

After a while, John began to sing a psalm of David, and the men all joined in.

Where can I go from your Spirit?

Where can I flee from your presence?
If I go up to the heavens, you are there;
if I make my bed in the depths, you are there.
If I rise on the wings of the dawn,
if I settle on the far side of the sea,
even there your hand will guide me,
your right hand will hold me fast.
If I say, "Surely the darkness will hide me
and the light become night around me,*"*
even the darkness will not be dark to you;
the night will shine like the day,
for darkness is as light to you.[8]

After singing together, the men returned to prayer for hours, humbled and amazed at how Yahweh turned their darkness into light.

Most of the men didn't sleep that night. However, the debate that had consumed most of their conversations the week before was over. Now, and with a growing sense of hope, they waited for the promise.

Peter was the only one who acted more and more melancholy. During the day, he often withdrew to the roof to be alone. On several occasions, his brother Andrew would follow him and attempt

8 Psalm 139:7–12

to get Peter to open up, but he refused.

Mark checked every day to see what he could do to support the men. His mother, Mary, Ayla, and Mary Magdalene faithfully prepared two meals a day and served the men in the upper room of Mark's home where they were staying.

The weeks passed, and some of the disciples were growing restless. After nearly forty days, Philip asked, "When is this *promise* coming? We have hardly left this home for weeks now. Perhaps we misunderstood the rabbi. Why wouldn't He want us to return to Galilee? Surely we can wait there as well as here."

James, the son of Alphaeus, also wondered out loud, "As we watched Yeshua ascend to the heavens, He told us to 'go into all the world.' Maybe we are waiting for something or someone we will find *as we go*."

John was firm. "No, the rabbi was clear. We are to remain in Jerusalem, and we must be patient and have faith, brothers."

"What do you think, Peter?" asked Andrew.

Peter sighed. He was tired of being asked for his opinions. "I know nothing. Why do you all look to me for answers? But we might as well stay until the Feast of Weeks is over tomorrow. It might be safer for us to travel with the crowds leaving the city as they depart after the festival."

Andrew spoke up, looking directly at his older brother, "No, Peter, I agree with John. The rabbi was clear, and I will not leave until the fulfilled time."

Peter stood up, threw his hands up in the air, and said, "And what does that mean, Andrew, *until the fulfilled time*?"

In a calm voice, Andrew replied, "We will know when we will

know, brother. Yeshua promised *never* to leave or forsake us, so I trust Him to guide us. Do you, Peter?"

Peter mumbled something no one understood as he left the room. The memories of his abandonment of Yeshua during his trial continued to haunt him.

Alone on the roof, Peter gazed up into the star-filled night as he wept and prayed. The more he prayed, the better he felt. After a good night's sleep, a sense of expectation was growing in him again.

It was early in the morning, and Andrew, James, and John were standing by a fire warming themselves.

Peter entered the courtyard and moved to the fire. "Andrew."

Andrew turned to face Peter. "Yes."

Peter knew he wounded his brother and loved him deeply. "I apologize for my attitude last night. I…I am weary, Andrew, and… and frustrated with myself—not you."

Andrew smiled and embraced Peter. "No apologies are necessary. We have all been forgiven of much. How could I hold anything against you?" And with that, Andrew stepped back and punched his brother in the chest.

"Ouch! That is going to bruise," said Peter in jest.

"And how can *Simon the Rock* bruise so easily?"

"Do not call me that. I am not a rock, Andrew, and I fear my soul is bruised beyond repair. But let us gather the others and go to the roof for our morning prayers."

"Gladly," said John. "Today is Shavuot—the Feast of Weeks. Let us celebrate that Yahweh gave us the Torah as we became a nation committed to serving the Lord."

James asked with cynicism in his tone, "And are we a nation still committed to Yahweh? How is that possible when the people rejected and crucified His one and only Son?"

"Point well taken," agreed John. "But we must pray nonetheless."

The disciples, along with several women, including Ayla, who'd prepared the disciples' breakfast that day, as well as Mark, Mary, the mother of Yeshua, and the rabbi's brothers, all gathered to pray. From the roof of Mark's large home, located in the city's central area and not far from the temple, they lifted their voices together in unison to the Lord.

The presence of the Lord was thick and tangible as a cloud among them. Men and women were rocking in prayer, the voices growing louder and louder as they lifted their hands toward the heavens.

There was an unearthly sound above and around them. Everyone immediately stopped praying and looked at each other in amazement. The wind was calm that day, but there was a sound like the blowing of an intense and violent storm. The noise seemed to come from the sky, but it filled the roof and the whole house. Oddly, despite the sound, the air remained still.

Suddenly, something like tongues of fire came to rest on each of their heads. A fire without smoke and flames that did not burn descended on everyone gathered.

Peter then stood and began to shout in a language the others did not understand. In fact, one by one, all of those gathered for prayer stood and danced with their hands lifted as they each spoke in a language unknown to them. Without a doubt, this experience was the promise Yeshua had given to them, and they were all filled with the Holy Spirit.

Because of the Shavuot Festival, many God-fearing Jews from every nation on earth were in the Holy City. When they heard the sound and praises to Yahweh in their native language coming from the roof, the people were amazed and perplexed. Cries of "What is this? What does it mean?" filled the streets around Mark's home. A few hecklers began to mock them and accused the disciples of being drunk.

Peter then raised his voice and addressed the people gathered below. "My brothers and sisters, we are not drunk. What you are witnessing is what the prophet Joel predicted. 'In the last days…, I will pour out my Spirit on all people.'"[9]

Peter continued and quoted, verbatim, an entire passage from the scroll of Joel. His voice and words pierced the hearts of his countrymen as he declared, "Listen to me! Let all of Israel be assured of this: Yahweh has appointed Yeshua, whom you crucified, as both Lord and Messiah."

When the Jews heard this, they cried out, "What must we do?"

Peter spoke with a greater boldness than he'd ever exhibited. "Turn from your sins. Turn from your stubbornness. Turn to the Lord, every one of you, be baptized in the name of Yeshua Hamashiach, God's Messiah, and you will be forgiven. Then you, too, will receive the gift of the Holy Spirit."

With many other words, Peter pleaded with those present, and about three thousand men and women were baptized later that very day. With great joy, thousands were added in a single day to the

9 Acts 2:17

numbers of those who followed the rabbi and their Savior, Yeshua.

Among those listening was a contrite centurion. A man who'd lived his entire life trying to deafen the voices of guilt and shame. A broken man who was born under the burden of a curse he did not fully understand. A soldier who'd taken the breath of many now received the breath of life from the Holy Spirit.

Arrius was one of the first to be baptized that day as Ayla looked on in tears. The resurrection of Yeshua radically changed Arrius's heart, and soon, it would completely change his life. Both joy and agony were coming sooner than Ayla or Arrius could imagine.

CHAPTER 43

Year 33 AD, Antonia Fortress, Jerusalem

Despite the large number of Jews who now claimed Rabbi Yeshua as their Lord and Messiah, the city was at peace. Even though Pilate decided not to intervene if these followers behaved, he kept his legionaries on high alert.

The rumors of Yeshua's resurrection grew despite the best efforts of the chief priests. The harder the Sanhedrin attempted to silence the stories of the rabbi's resurrection and His many appearances, the more the story spread. One report said over five hundred people saw Yeshua at one time. None of this mattered to Pilate as long as things remained relatively calm in Jerusalem. However, what concerned him was a rumor that one of his centurions now offered his allegiance to this Jew rather than to Rome.

The courtyard of the praetorium had several extra fires burning that night because the weather had turned cold. Pilate was drunk. He'd been drinking most of the day to numb his frustration with his wife. She refused to travel with him from their residence on the coast at Caesarea Maritima. After the crucifixion of the rabbi, Procula said she would not enter Jerusalem again. The palace, located in the upper city, was safe and comfortable, but the memories of all that happened with Yeshua bothered Pilate, too, more than he was willing to admit.

One of the praetorium guards entered, saluted Pilate, and said, "Prefect, Legionary Tasco says he bears urgent news for your ears only. He requests an audience—"

"Yes. Yes. Send him in. I am too old and too tired for all of this. Have him enter now before I retire for the evening."

The guard motioned for Tasco to step forward, and the legionary moved out of the shadows toward Pilate. Tasco stepped up to the prefect, removed his helmet, saluted, and said, "Greetings, most magnificent Prefect—"

"Get on with it, Legionary. I am not in the mood for any pomp and circumstance. What *urgent* news do you offer?"

Tasco swallowed hard as he stood tall and motionless. "It concerns the centurion, Arrius. I have discussed this matter personally with him, and he does not deny it."

"Deny *what*?" asked Pilate as he took a sip of his wine and glared at the nervous legionary over the brim of his cup.

"Centurion Arrius has become…is…the centurion has—"

"Out with it, soldier, before I take my horsewhip to your back." Pilate grabbed the whip sitting by him that he often used as a tool of terror.

Tasco blurted out in a cascade of words, "*Centurion Arrius now follows the Jew*, Yeshua."

Pilate slammed his cup down, stood, slapped his whip in his hand, and then moved within a breath's distance of Tasco. "And how does one follow a *dead* man?"

Tasco stumbled over his words and mumbled something about Arrius forsaking the gods to serve the Hebrew God.

Pilate moved directly behind Tasco as he continued to strike the whip in his hand and said, "He is married to a Jew, yes?"

"Yes, Prefect."

"And he has Jewish children, yes?"

"Yes, Prefect."

"In fact, he has a Bedouin child he calls his son, doesn't he?"

"Yes, Prefect."

"And has the centurion abandoned his post or his men?"

Tasco took a deep breath as sweat began to form on his forehead.

"Well? Has he?" shouted Pilate.

"Abandoned? No, Prefect, he has not—"

"Then why should you or I care about what god he worships? My own wife says she now reveres this god of the Hebrews!"

The young man quickly replied as he looked to the left and right in an attempt to see Pilate, who was still lurking behind him. "Prefect, he claims that the rabbi, Yeshua, is his sovereign Lord and king."

Pilate cursed as he walked back to his chair. "Now, *that* is a concern. And he told you this directly?"

Tasco fidgeted and said, "Yes, Prefect. Directly and without remorse."

Loyalty to any king or ruler but the emperor was forbidden. However, Pilate despised treacherous disloyalty within the chain of command. He knew the value of a snitch, but there was a code among legionaries that would not tolerate Tasco's actions against his commander.

Pilate called two of his praetorium guards over. "Take this… this Gaul…this pathetic legionary out of my sight and flog him with thirty-nine lashes."

Tasco practically fell over in shock. His selfish ambitions finally caught up with him.

Pilate looked directly at Tasco. "Your urgent news is of value; your life is not. Any man who betrays his centurion will pay for his foolishness. If you survive the whip, I never want to see or hear from you again."

The guards then dragged a terrified Tasco away. A look of horror marked his face.

Cassius knocked gently on Arrius's door. It was early, and the sun had not yet risen over the city. "Arrius, are you awake?"

Arrius opened the door. "I am now. What brings you to my home at this early hour?"

"May I come in?"

Ayla was standing behind her husband as she elbowed him aside and said, "Yes, of course, Cassius, you are always welcome in our home. Let me prepare a meal."

"I am afraid you may not have much of an appetite when I tell you why I am here."

Arrius motioned for Cassius to sit at the table, where he and

Ayla joined him.

"Arrius, Pilate knows."

Arrius rubbed the sleep from his eyes with one hand and rubbed his head with the other. "I assume you are referring to my newfound faith."

Cassius reached across the table and placed his hand on Arrius's forearm. "Yes, Tasco betrayed you, and he was almost flogged to death last night by Pilate."

Arrius needed no explanation for Pilate's actions. He knew the code, and he knew Pilate. "Tasco and I have been at odds for a long time, but—"

"He deserved what he got," said Cassius.

"Perhaps, but I planned to speak directly with Pilate *today*. I am resigning my commission, Cassius, because I can no longer serve both Rome and Yahweh."

Cassius sighed. "I have seen this coming for months. I knew this day was inevitable."

Arrius stood and walked to the window, where the light began to shine through the opening. Beams of sunlight created streaks through the dust in the room. "Tasco is a fool. If he had only spoken to me first—"

"He is a fool," agreed Cassius. "And the barrack surgeon predicts he will not survive the week."

Ayla gasped and covered her mouth with her hand. "No man deserves to be beaten to death. I will ask one of the disciples if they are willing to visit and lay hands on him to pray for his healing."

Cassius shook his head. "I do not understand you or the way

of Yeshua's followers. This man deserves to die, and he should be hated for his betrayal, not prayed for."

Arrius spoke out of the open window as if he were praying. "I, too, deserve to die. I should be hated for what I did to Yeshua. But the rabbi's words are etched into my soul forever, 'Father, forgive them, for they do not know what they are doing.'"[10]

Arrius turned to face his friend. "I am as a child who cannot speak, and I cannot crawl, let alone walk. But I am committed to growing and becoming more and more like Yeshua. His way and His words are the air that I breathe."

Ayla beamed with joy.

Cassius stood and saluted Arrius. "It would be my honor to accompany you when you have your audience with Pilate. You have served Rome for longer than most, and he cannot refuse your request for an honorable discharge."

Arrius smiled and bowed his head in respect. "And I would be honored to have you at my side one last time, my brother and dearest friend."

The two men hugged each other as Cassius whispered in Arrius's ear, "I will make the arrangements for you to see Pilate today."

Arrius and Ayla spent a great deal of that day praying, and there was no fear in Arrius's heart. After over twenty-five years of service, Pilate could not refuse his request to retire. The prefect would risk the ire of his legionaries if he struck out in anger at one of his most respected centurions. But if Pilate was anything, he was irrational and unpredictable.

10 Luke 23:34

When Arrius and Cassius entered the courtyard, Pilate turned sideways and away from the centurions. Arrius could tell that Pilate pretended to ignore them as he looked over some parchments. He was certain that the prefect knew he was there to resign his commission, and he also knew that Pilate enjoyed making men sweat. Arrius would not speak until spoken to.

The sun was at its highest, and the day turned out warmer than anyone expected. Legionaries could be heard training outside. Roman soldiers practiced with wooden swords and wooden shields significantly heavier than the weapons used in actual battle. So the clashing of wood on wood and the grunting of the men were loud.

Arrius remained at attention even though a fly pestered him without relief. Cassius smiled at his friend's discomfort.

"You find something humorous, Centurion Cassius?"

"No, my apologies, Prefect. I mean no disrespect."

Pilate could see the fly, too, and remarked, "Isn't it fascinating how something so small can annoy us so much?"

The men did not miss his insinuation and replied in unison, "Yes, Prefect."

"And how, centurions, are you going to annoy me? Why are you here?"

Arrius cleared his throat and spoke confidently, perhaps too confidently. "Prefect, it has been my great honor to serve the emperor and Rome—"

"But?"

"But I am here asking to be discharged and released from my duties. I have served—"

“You don’t need to remind me of your service, Centurion. I may be a hard man, but I am not unaware of what you have done for Rome or for me. You have done your duty and served me well, Arrius. Very well. However, this is a crossing-the-Rubicon moment for you. Once you cross that river, there is no turning back.”

Arrius was surprised by Pilate’s unexpected kindness.

“Yes, I know what this means, but thank you, Prefect. Your words—”

“My words are the law in this godforsaken land, and I release you from your commission effective immediately.”

“I am humbled and honored, Prefect.”

“Do you intend on returning to Rome?” Pilate asked.

“No, Jerusalem is now my home, Prefect.”

Pilate stood and faced Arrius. “You are entitled to a parcel of land or silver. Unfortunately, I have no lands to offer you here in Judea. So I will see to it that you receive the equivalent in money. Does that work for you, Arrius?”

Arrius stood tall, saluted one last time, and said, “As you will, Prefect.”

Pilate dismissed the men and returned to his work.

Once outside, Cassius slapped his friend on the back and said, “If I didn’t know better, I would say the gods smiled on you today, my old friend.”

Arrius pointed heavenward. “Only one God matters to me now, and yes, Cassius, I feel His pleasure at this moment as I never have before. Yahweh is good, and His plans for me are more than I deserve.”

Cassius diverted to the barracks while Arrius decided to do something he would never have imagined. He walked up the hill to Golgotha for the first time not to crucify anyone but to pray. Something in him was driven to return to where he first began his journey as a follower.

As he reached the summit of that place where the blood of many stained the dirt, he prayed out loud, "Yahweh, my life is Yours. Once again, I surrender my past, my present, and my future to You. I return to this dreadful place where I took the life of Your Son to remember how His death and His blood set me free from a curse I could not bear. I owe Yeshua everything." In the distance, a golden eagle soared high in a sky peppered with massive thunderheads. At that very moment, a strong gust of wind blew over Golgotha—the place of the skull. Arrius was sure he heard the voice of Yeshua in the wind, "Stay the course, My son. No matter what may come, stay the course." To which Arrius replied as tears streamed down his face, "I will, my Lord and my God. By Your *charis* and strength, I will."

But he couldn't help but wonder what Yeshua meant by the words, "No matter what may come…"

CHAPTER 44

Many Months Later, 34 AD, Jerusalem

The months following the celebration of Pentecost and the explosion of the church in Jerusalem were both magnificent and difficult. Thankfully, for the followers of Yeshua, it was an important season of spiritual growth despite the turmoil.

Followers of *The Way*, as the disciples of Yeshua were now known, grew in numbers by the thousands in Jerusalem. With the growing community of believers, however, came intense persecution from the chief priests. The tip of the spear for the Sanhedrin was a man known as Saul of Tarsus.

Arrius was like a dry sponge as he absorbed as much of the teachings of Yeshua as possible. His formal education in Latin and the fact that he was fluent in several other languages made him invaluable to the twelve. Furthermore, because of his leadership skills, Peter appointed Arrius as a deacon to serve the church in Jerusalem.

Ayla spoke to her husband with pride, "Arrius, from the day you retired your commission as a soldier until now, I am continually amazed by the man, husband, and father you have become."

"Thank you, my love. Sometimes when I look at my own reflection, I barely recognize the man staring back at me. And I'm *not* referring to my silver and receding hair."

Ayla, never happier, smiled and said, "Why is it men grow more handsome with age?"

Arrius returned her smile. "You have never been more beautiful to me. And I am happy that the change you see in me is a good thing."

"Yes, my *bashert*, the life of Yeshua in and through you is evidence of our Lord's goodness."

"I will forever be indebted to Mark. He understood my Roman upbringing and helped me to see the greater truths about Yeshua. He has become a little brother to me, and I always wanted a little brother."

"And he *is* your brother in every way because of Yeshua. I am blessed by Yahweh's profound work in your heart, Arrius."

Arrius raised his right hand to the heavens and said, "If the Lord can change me, He can change *anyone*."

Ayla was aware, however, that something was bothering her husband. "Can you tell me what is concerning you? You woke up early again today."

"I don't know how to completely describe it. As a deacon, I have many important responsibilities. I am honored that my service to our people puts me at the center of everything happening in the Holy City."

Ayla beamed. "I truly am so very proud of you."

"But the followers continue to grow and expand faster than anyone—including Peter—ever thought possible, and with great growth comes greater challenges. We are still wrestling with how to best care for all the widows."

Ayla chimed in, "I thought you said the conflict between the

Hellenistic Jews—our Greek friends among us who converted to Judaism—and the Hebraic Jews was resolved."

"Things are much better but far from resolved. Followers of Yeshua or not, humans are still humans."

Ayla nodded in agreement.

Arrius let out a deep sigh. "And sadly, the number of widows is growing because of that evil man, Saul." Arrius shook his head and took a deep breath. "I still mourn the loss of Stephen. I have never known a better or gentler man than him. As a Hellenized Jew and fellow deacon, we worked so well together, and he was the only one his people fully trusted."

Ayla slapped her palm on the table. "I am ashamed of the Sanhedrin; at times they make me want to renounce my Jewish heritage. How could they allow Saul to operate unchecked? How can they justify and support his actions? It is inexcusable."

Arrius smiled and said, "Hmmm, I wish you would have considered renouncing the Jewish part of your faith before I was circumcised."

"Oh hush, how can a Roman soldier—"

"*Former* Roman soldier," interrupted Arrius.

"How could a *former* Roman brute like you still be complaining about such a small sacrifice?"

"Don't get me started, woman, and there was nothing small about my sacrifice. I would rather take an arrow in my leg than the ruthless and sharp knife of that merciless rabbi."

They both laughed together. It was good to smile and relax a bit. They both knew the lives of all Yeshua's followers in Jerusalem were at risk as long as Saul was free to hunt them down.

On a cold winter night, Ayla was at home with her children while Arrius gathered with a large group of followers outside the city in an ancient olive grove.

Peter spoke fearlessly to the believers sitting under a clear sky filled with countless stars. "On the night the Lord was betrayed, Yeshua spoke of these troubling times. He told us—though we did not understand it at first—of the trouble He would face on the cross. And He warned us often that we would be persecuted for our beliefs as well. None of what is happening to us should be a surprise. Our Lord taught us that in this world we would have trouble but to take heart because He overcame the world."

The crowd of many hundreds nodded and moaned together in acknowledgment of his words.

Peter raised his hands, and the group quieted down. "We have lost too many brothers and sisters at the hands of Saul. As you know, with the authority and blessing of the chief priests, that man is relentless in his attacks against us."

A young widow who had lost her husband at the hand of Saul cried out in despair.

"You know me, brothers and sisters; it is not in my nature to turn the other cheek. It is not easy for me to watch so many suffer at the hands of that monster. But Yeshua told us to pray for—and even to bless—those who mistreat us."

Someone spoke up from the back, "Have we no recourse then? Can we appeal to the Sanhedrin? Surely, a Jew killing Jews is appalling to them."

The crowd applauded in approval.

James, the brother of Yeshua, stood and raised his hand, "I have spoken to the council. I presented our case. And as you know, since the removal of Joseph and Nicodemus from their body, we have no outspoken supporters among the leaders—"

Mark, from the front of the crowd and known for being a bit impulsive, interrupted James, "And what of Rome? Surely, Pilate cannot support such unjust action."

James shook his head and continued, "Pilate continues to wash his hands of any guilt. He took no responsibility for the crucifixion of Yeshua, and he takes none for the brutal actions of Saul either."

Like a cold, wet fog, a heaviness settled over the believers as fear began to weave its tentacles around the people's hearts. But at that very moment, an elderly man—some say it was Bartimaeus, the one healed of blindness by Yeshua—began to lift his strong and weathered voice in song.

"The Lord is my light and my salvation."

And on cue a few voices echoed, "Whom shall I fear?"

"The Lord is the stronghold of my life."

The other voices grew stronger. "Of whom shall I be afraid?"

The old man sang with more conviction and clarity, "When the wicked advance against me to devour me."

The entire congregation replied, "It is my enemies and my foes who will stumble and fall!"[11]

Then the old man almost shouted as his voice cracked with emotion, "I remain confident of this: I will see the goodness of the

---

11 Psalm 27:1–2

Lord in the land of the living!"

And all together, they wept, raised their hands, and sang with the sweetness of angels, "Wait for the Lord; be strong and take heart and wait for the Lord."[12]

Peter, James, John, and the other leaders simultaneously fell to their knees and lifted their hands in prayer to Yahweh as they rocked continuously back and forth. In fact, the entire congregation fell to their knees and lifted their hands and voices in prayer. As on the day of Pentecost, some said they saw tongues of fire descending again upon many. Whatever was seen or unseen, a fresh breeze of the Holy Spirit swept with power through that outside gathering.

Mark walked with Arrius most of the way home that night. The stars themselves seemed to be singing praise to Yahweh. Though there was a brisk wind from the north, Arrius's heart and soul were warmed by a wave of shalom in his soul as he prayed out loud, "Yahweh, Your Son continues to heal this broken man. I have not forgotten my sin or the curse I once lived under, but the weight of it all is gone, and I am so grateful. I would *never* have imagined a moment—even one—where I would know such *pax*, true *pax*."

Mark was moved by the prayer of his friend but spoke earnestly to Arrius. "I feel led to remind you, Arrius, that Yahweh's shalom does not mean the absence of trouble. Shalom is the promise of the Lord's presence despite our struggle."

Arrius nodded but had no idea how prophetic those words were to him. Trouble was on the not-too-distant horizon.

12 Psalm 27:13–14

Chapter 45

One Year Later, 35 AD, the Village of Bethany

The home of Mary, Martha, and Lazarus was larger than most but modest. Their village of Bethany on the south-eastern slope of the Mount of Olives was a common stopping place for the disciples.

The sun had set, and after a time of prayer, the disciples were enjoying a delicious meal prepared by Martha. After supper, Lazarus turned to look directly at Peter. "What are we to do about Saul? He was here yesterday and went from home to home searching for followers."

Peter sighed. "And did he come to your home, my friend?"

Martha spoke up, "Not yet."

Peter continued, "Did he arrest anyone in Bethany?"

Martha spoke again, with her hands on her hips, "Not yesterday."

Lazarus gave his sister a stern look and raised his hand to silence her. "Peter, what my sister is saying far too abruptly is that it is only a matter of time before Saul begins to take followers here in Bethany off to prison. We are willing to suffer for our Lord. I assure you, having died once, I will never fear death again. However, is there a point where it would be wise to hide or perhaps relocate to Galilee?"

In reaction to Lazarus's question, the men filled the room with their opinions as they argued among themselves.

James, the half-brother of Yeshua, stood up and raised his hand to quiet everyone. "As you know"—he looked toward Mary and Martha, who stood just inside the doorway—"my brother had fond affection for you and this household."

Tears began to form on Mary's cheeks, and Martha humbly bowed her head.

James went on, "And whether you three should stay in Bethany or not, I trust the Holy Spirit to guide you. As Yeshua chose His path, you must choose yours. I will, however, encourage you with this truth: there is nothing wrong with hiding. David once hid in a cave from his enemy, another man named Saul."

All the men nodded and verbalized their approval of what James said as he reclined again at the table.

Peter stood and addressed them next. "I agree with James, and I am certain he will agree with me that though it might be wise to hide—or even run at times—we must never succumb to fear."

James stroked his beard and nodded in agreement.

Peter spoke with passion, "Yes, David hid, but our greatest king wrote hundreds of years ago that even when we walk through the darkest valley, we should do so in trust of Yahweh. We must not fear evil because the Lord is with us."

The room erupted in agreement.

At that moment, and to the surprise of everyone, Arrius entered the room unannounced. "My apologies, brothers and sisters, for the interruption."

Peter spoke, "No apologies necessary, deacon Arrius. You are always welcome at our table."

Arrius placed his hand over his heart. "I am both grateful and humbled to serve."

Matthew motioned to a spot next to him at the table. "Please recline with us and eat. But why have you traveled from the city at this late hour, Arrius? What troubles you?"

Arrius remained standing. "I come with disturbing news and a warning, brothers."

The room grew so silent you could hear the crickets outside the windows.

"Tell us, brother," said one of the others.

"One of the temple guards, who is a secret follower of Yeshua, informed me just hours ago that Saul intends to return to Bethany early tomorrow. He has written permission from the Sanhedrin to arrest Lazarus, Mary, and Martha."

The room collectively inhaled with shock.

"The guard said there was a great deal of argument among the leaders because they fear that apprehending people so well-known and loved would create more trouble than it is worth. But Saul argued it was time to make an example of those who were closest to Yeshua."

Arrius took a deep breath and then said soberly, "I fear the twelve might be next."

James stood and spoke again, "Just before you arrived, we were discussing this genuine possibility and what should be done."

"And what did you decide?" asked Arrius.

The room grew quiet again.

"So far, we have only agreed that whatever we do, it must not be done out of fear but faith," said Peter.

Arrius bowed his head and said, "Brothers, the Lord would not want us to be afraid."

Andrew, who typically let his brother do most of the talking, spoke up. "I propose we first lift our voices in prayer. Yahweh is not surprised by this news. He knows all, and He sees all. And now, more than ever, we need to cry out to Him."

Without hesitation, the room broke out in collective prayer.

Almost an hour later, those gathered got up from their knees and dusted the gritty earth off their garments.

Peter spoke first. "Arrius, thank you for traveling to bring us the news of Saul." In a stern voice, he then addressed the other disciples in the room, "Rather than leave in the morning to begin the long journey to Bethsaida, I propose we go *now*. The moon is full, and there will be ample light to find our way. The farther we can get from Bethany, the better."

There was a unanimous nod of approval among the disciples.

Looking at Lazarus, Peter said in earnest, "Brother, I feel led to encourage you and your sisters to go with us to Galilee. When things settle down in Jerusalem—"

Arrius interrupted, "*If* things settle down."

Everyone groaned in agreement as several pounded their fists on the table.

Peter raised his hand again to silence the room. "*If* things revert to normal soon, you and your sisters can return, but there is no point in adding your names to the list of martyrs."

Lazarus looked toward his sisters, and Martha shook her head as she said, "Brother, this is our home. Saul may burn it to the ground if we leave. Our friends are here—"

Mary placed a gentle hand on Martha's shoulder. "Yeshua is not done with us yet, sister, and we can always make a new home. But for as long as we can, we must tell others of our Lord. Like Lazarus, I do not fear death, but I believe in my heart that our life on this side of eternity is not yet over. We should go with Peter."

Martha and Mary hugged and cried together for a moment before Martha wiped her eyes and spoke, "Then we go. I will start packing immediately."

Peter clapped his hands together to get everyone's attention and began giving instructions to the men. Fortunately, they had learned from the rabbi to travel light, so packing up and setting out wouldn't take too long.

James pulled Arrius aside and asked him, "What of you and your family, deacon Arrius? Is it time for you to leave Jerusalem?"

Arrius didn't hesitate. "I cannot abandon my duties to the church in Jerusalem. There are thousands who need care and comfort. Besides, my wife would never leave. Even though her family has forsaken her, she will never leave them. Ayla continues to pray for their hearts to change toward her and toward Yeshua."

James smiled and said, "I, too, cannot leave Jerusalem or the church either. I will return with you and let Yahweh determine my fate."

Arrius, out of habit, wanted to salute James but instead clasped James's forearm in respect. "Your older brother would be very proud of you, James. The church in the city needs your leadership now more than ever before."

Peter agreed with Arrius and said, "As soon as possible, I, too, will return to Jerusalem after taking our friends north to Galilee. I hope to return within a matter of weeks."

James embraced Peter and said, "We will be together again soon, my friend."

The disciples, along with Mary, Martha, and Lazarus, were on the road in no time at all. Several dogs barked at them as they departed Bethany. A few neighbors looked out their windows, wondering about all the commotion so late at night. Clouds were pushing in quickly, and the moonlight was partially obscured, so the group moved slowly but still made good time moving north.

Because Arrius and James were tired, they waited until just before dawn to depart for Jerusalem. They blended in with the dozens of people making their way down the Mount of Olives to market. As the men entered the Golden Gate, James said to Arrius, "I must find Mary Magdalene and tell her what has happened. She needs to hear it directly from me, or she will worry too much about the others."

Arrius agreed. "I was surprised she wasn't traveling with Peter and the others to Galilee."

"Sadly, Mary has no living relatives. However, she recently told me how bonded she is to your family, Arrius. I think she sees herself as a surrogate aunt to your children."

Arrius nodded his head and grinned. "Her value to Ayla is immeasurable, and it seems that Mary is the only one who can get through to Kaamil. That boy is out of control—"

James interrupted with laughter. "All boys his age seem out of control to their parents at times, but Mary does have a special way with the wild at heart."

Arrius stopped and looked directly at James. "She is a great gift to us, James, to all of us. But I am deeply concerned for her well-being. Besides you, I am certain there is no one else Saul would love to imprison more than her."

James reached up, hugged the taller Arrius, and told him, "The days ahead might be filled with struggle, but whatever comes, we will face it together."

Arrius replied, "And Yeshua is *always* with us."

The two separated in peace, but it was a calm that would not last long for Arrius.

CHAPTER 46

Year 35 AD, the Home of Arrius and Ayla

The persecution of the followers of *The Way* continued to increase. It seemed that the greater the suffering of Yeshua's disciples, the more they grew in numbers and the stronger they became in spirit.

Nonetheless, Saul was ruthless and ran freely in Jerusalem and the surrounding areas. He encouraged violent action by his Jewish brothers against Yeshua's followers. Pilate offered no resistance to Saul's brutality either. Jews killing Jews mattered little to Rome if relative order was maintained and taxes were paid.

Ayla had sent word through a friend to ask Mary to join her as soon as possible. She wrote a short note to Mary that only said, "In pain. Can you come?"

Mary rushed to Ayla's home, and when she arrived, she asked, "Ayla, what happened? Are you okay?"

"I'm okay. I will be fine. I guess today's rejection and treatment in the market are *normal for all of us now. But how can a Jew treat another Jew with such contempt?*"

Mary offered a gentle hug as she said, "You have it twice as bad as the rest of us. Hated by many for your marriage to a Roman and now hated by more for following Yeshua."

Ayla lingered in Mary's embrace a bit more before letting her go. As she wiped away the tears from her cheeks, Ayla said, "I am so grateful for your friendship, Mary. I don't know how I would have survived without you."

"Yeshua is your strength, my sister, but you, Arrius, and the children are constantly in my prayers."

"Do you think things in Jerusalem will *ever* improve for us, Mary?"

"Probably not, especially with Saul on the loose. Yet, I pray for him too."

"Mary, you are so much wiser and so much more like Yeshua than me. My anger against Saul overwhelms me at times. So many of our friends"—Ayla began to cry again—"so many of our brothers and sisters have felt his whip and his wrath."

Mary added, "And his stones. I know it isn't natural to have love in my heart for him. I will never forget what he did to Stephen, and my heart is still broken. I also know what Saul would enjoy doing to me as a witness of the resurrection. But Yeshua rescued me, and so I cannot—*I will not*—stop telling everyone about His empty tomb and about the new life He offers to everyone. Sadly, I fear Saul is as demon-stricken as I once was. He doesn't see it now, but he is the arm and instrument of Satan. Nevertheless, if Yeshua can heal me…if He can set me free…if He can forgive me…then no one—not even *that* man—is beyond hope."

Ayla bowed her head. "Mary, I need my heart to change. I need your faith. Far too often, I fear for my husband and my children. I fear for Abigail…and I fear for you too. I don't know what I would do without you."

Ayla's eyes were fixed on the ground, feeling embarrassed and a bit of shame. Mary took Ayla's face in her hands, lifted her head, and looked into her tear-filled eyes as she said, "We must pray."

Ayla let out a nervous laugh and said, "Oh, Mary, you are a gift to me from the Lord. Yes, let us pray."

Mary and Ayla covered their heads with their shawls, and Mary began, "Abba, first, we thank You again for sending Your Son to rescue us. I miss Him so much. We all miss Him. But the presence of the Holy Spirit truly brings the comfort we long for in these sad days. You have wrapped Your heart around our hearts. You have lifted our spirits. You have, somehow, brought us abundant joy in this season, even amid crushing pain. Thank You from the depths of my soul. Yahweh, You know how I have fasted and prayed for Saul of Tarsus. As Yeshua prayed for the Roman soldiers and the Jews who crucified him, 'Forgive them, for they know not what they do,'[13] we too pray for Saul. Forgive him, Yahweh, for he doesn't know what he is doing."

Mary suddenly stopped praying. Her shawl fell off her head as she looked up and said to Ayla, "I see a vision of Saul. He is tumbling…falling…he is terrified. Oh my, Ayla, I see a great light covering him. No! It is Yeshua—*the* light; He is hovering above Saul. Saul cannot even lift his head because it is so blinding. But I see something else happening, Ayla. Somehow truth is pouring into Saul's mind. Yeshua is filling Saul's soul like water fills a bucket dropped deep into a well. As the rabbi once prophesied, 'The light

---

13 Luke 23:34

shines in the darkness, and the darkness has not overcome it.'"[14]

Mary began to weep and laugh at the same time. "Ayla, I see Saul turning from the darkness and hatred and from his anger against Yeshua to faith in Him. All is not lost. *Saul* is not lost forever. The Lord has a great plan for his life!"

Ayla didn't know how to respond. No one, let alone her, would ever imagine Saul as a believer.

Mary covered her head again and wrapped her overgarment tight around her waist. "I must go at once and tell Peter what the Lord has shown me. This news will bring shalom to our leaders."

Ayla spoke reflectively, "I know Yahweh often speaks before He acts. I never thought Saul would see the error of his ways, but you must go quickly and find Peter. I will continue to pray."

For over an hour, Ayla did pray. She prayed for Saul with hope. For the first time in a very long time, she felt her anger and fear being replaced with a settled calmness. "I do not pretend to know or understand all Your ways, Yahweh. I cannot know the when or how of Your plans, but I, too, believe no man is beyond Your reach. No man is hopeless when he encounters Your Son, the light of the world and the light of my life. Amen."

Arrius came home not too long after her prayers had ended. The children were sound asleep, so Ayla had the opportunity to share with him about her visit with Mary, Mary's vision, and her prayer time for Saul.

Arrius admitted to her, "I often wrestle with skepticism fla-

14 John 1:5

vored by a bit of cynicism. I will believe it when I see it, but I am grateful for your *pax*, my wife."

Ayla smiled and took the hand of her husband and best friend. "It will be interesting to see what Yahweh does, but I do wonder what He is planning."

CHAPTER 47

Late 35 AD, Jerusalem

Saul's hatred grew, and he seemed more determined than ever to crush *The Way*. He had been given more letters of authority from the chief priests to pursue the followers of Yeshua throughout Judea. Ironically, Saul's persecution had driven many from the Holy City to other parts of the empire. As they scattered throughout the Roman world, they told others the story of Yeshua.

Arrius was frustrated. "Rumor has it Saul will be leaving Jerusalem soon to fan the flames of rage against us in Damascus and elsewhere. It seems Mary's vision—if it was a vision from the Lord—is long in coming."

"We must hold on to hope, Arrius. Yahweh is greater than any man and every fear."

"Yes, I know, Ayla, but sometimes my old heart and former Roman ways seem to get the best of me. More than once, I think I have felt as Peter did that night in the garden before the crucifixion. I have been told he turned to the sword in fear rather than to Yahweh in faith."

Ayla radiated. "You continue to amaze me with your spiritual growth. I feel you have surpassed me."

"Thank you, my love. I am moving forward slowly, I think, but forward is good, true?"

"Yes," exclaimed Ayla.

Arrius's countenance quickly changed when he noticed Kaamil was not home. "And where is my Bedouin son?"

Ayla shook her head. "Do not be angry with him, but he ran out of the house earlier, frustrated that I gave him some chores to do before bed."

"What are we to do with him, Ayla? We have given him a home and food. We have brought him into our family and treated him as a son, but three years have passed, and he still runs the streets like a wild animal."

Ayla clasped her hands in front of her mouth, carefully weighing what to say. "Yahweh blesses those who bless the orphans, my husband. I know it has not been easy—"

"Not easy?" Arrius grunted. "Wife, it would be easier to live with a wild donkey."

"Arrius, Kaamil lived for years alone and uncared for. Even an unbroken donkey takes time to train. He simply needs more time, my love. Yes, he is untamed and unruly, but I know a man who was once very much the same, and yet he has changed."

Arrius grinned and said, "Ayla, sometimes you frustrate me more than that boy."

Ayla smirked. "So it seems *frustration* is an effective tool in the hands of Yahweh, who is molding you into the image of His Son."

The hour had grown late, too late for a knock at their door. Arrius opened the door to find young Mark smiling and out of breath. "James and the other leaders of the church in Jerusalem are gathering to discuss Saul and whether we should send messengers to Damascus to warn the believers. They are requesting all the deacons to come and join them immediately."

Ayla sighed, "Arrius, it is so late. Surely—"

Arrius spoke before she could finish, "Ayla, I have duties. My place and responsibilities require I attend. I will not be long."

"Hmmm, the last time you said that at this hour, I didn't see you until sunrise."

Arrius gave her a look, gathered his cloak, and said, "I'll be home long before breakfast, Wife. You worry too much. Besides, tomorrow is the Day of Preparation, and no one will want to stay late. I'm sure the decision to send someone on ahead of Saul or not will not take too long."

"Ah, but you forget how my people love to debate."

Arrius laughed as he stepped to the door. "No, I am married to one of *your people* who loves to debate."

Before he knew what was happening, Ayla grabbed him by the shirt, pulled him close, gave him a passionate kiss, and then whispered, "See to it that you are not gone too long, my joy and *bashert*."

Arrius smiled. "Have I told you today how much I love you, Ayla Rose? I will see you soon." Then he darted out the door.

Ayla decided to begin her preparations for Sabbath early because it was always easier to do so without the children underfoot. Besides, she thought to herself, *If Arrius does come home sooner than later, I might surprise him. I know how to relieve his tension.*

She heard a dog barking in the distance. Then another dog just down the street yelped as if someone had kicked the animal. Curious, she looked out the eastern window of their home.

"What in heaven's name is this crowd up to?" she said out loud. Then it dawned on her; they were headed straight down the road to her home.

"Oh Yahweh, these men are headed for us!" The torches revealed about a dozen angry faces.

One of the men said, "There, look, someone has spotted us through the window."

Another young man shouted, "It is her! She has seen us. We need to surround the house quickly, or she will escape."

Ayla watched through a crack in her front door as three of the men broke into a run and ran to the opposite side of the house.

A brutish man with several teeth missing and a nasty scar yelled through her bolted window, "Woman, we know you are in there, and we know you are alone. Your scum of a husband was seen inside the walls. Come out and bring your Roman piglets with you. It is time for you to feel the wrath of Yahweh."

Ayla quickly surveyed the situation. *If I go out there, they will stone me. If I don't, they will eventually break in. Maybe Arrius has been warned and is on his way.*

"Roman harlot, it will do you no good to hide. We, the true sons of Abraham, will drag you from your home and deal with you." Another man next to him slapped him on the back and yelled, "Yes, and my friend has a surprise for you, you Roman lover."

All the men laughed.

Ayla was beside herself. She knew it was Barabbas who spoke, and he'd sworn vengeance against Arrius and his blood.

Then a commanding voice from the back of the crowd yelled out, "We should barricade her door and burn her and her house of sin to the ground. Let Yahweh's fire purify her. If she is holy, like Shadrach, Meshach, and Abednego, she will survive the flames. If not, she will perish in her sin."

Ayla had heard Saul rant against the followers in the temple, so she recognized the voice as Saul's.

Without hesitation, several men began to gather whatever they could find to block Ayla's door, and then someone threw his torch on the roof. Then another, and another. Within moments, the entire roof was ablaze.

Ayla knelt by her bed where both of her children were sleeping, but Seneca began to stir and cough. He opened his eyes, looked at his mother, and said, "Mommy, what wrong? Why is it smokey? My throat hurts."

Ayla tried to smile as she whispered, "All is well, my son; all is well. Remember mommy's friend, Yeshua?"

Seneca coughed again and nodded as his eyes turned in terror to the blaze surrounding them.

"Yeshua is waiting for us, and we will be with Him soon…very soon…in a perfect place forever."

"What about Abba? Will he join us?"

Ayla grabbed Seneca and held him to her breast as she silently wept—not in fear but in sorrow for Arrius. She knew his pain would be traumatic and almost too much to bear. "Yes, little one, Abba will join us in the blink of an eye someday."

Ayla was rocking Seneca as he continued to cough against her.

She prayed for Arrius, "Yahweh, how will my husband survive without me—without us? He has suffered so much loss."

The tears continued to flow, not only for her suffering or the death of her children happening before her very eyes but for her best friend and the love of her life. Ayla was grateful Tikva never woke and never knew what was happening. The smoke snuffed the life from her body first.

As Ayla choked and cried, she prayed again, "Yahweh, as Your Son once prayed…now I pray…forgive these men. I do not hold their trespasses against them…and I pray for Saul too, Lord. May Mary's vision be fulfilled. May Your kingdom come, and Your will be done…in Him and through Him…to the surprise and joy of many. I beg You to hold my husband tightly. He will try to run from You and seek revenge on Saul. Hold him…help him…for he belongs to You."

She was barely able to speak now through the dense smoke and coughing. The fire was everywhere, and debris was falling from the ceiling as she prayed one final thing, "My children and I…into Your hands…Yeshua…we will see You soon."

And just moments later, Ayla was in the strong yet tender arms of her Savior.

As if stung by a scorpion, Arrius suddenly bolted up from his seat in the assembly and said out loud, "Something is wrong. Terribly wrong, brothers. I sense it in my spirit. I beg your forgiveness, but I must return home immediately."

Peter, who had returned to Jerusalem just weeks before, waved him to the door. "Go, Arrius; we will pray Yeshua's shalom upon you and yours."

Arrius stepped outside and started at a slow pace, but he was at a full sprint with Mark at his side before long. Panic and rage were welling up in him in a way he hadn't felt for a very long time.

Before he saw it, he smelled it. The odor of fire burning wood and flesh. Since he had torched many villages as a centurion, the stench was unmistakable to him. As he turned the corner and saw the leaping flames, he knew what had happened. He knew Ayla and his children were gone. He also knew this was the handiwork of Saul.

Except for Kaamil, who was not home, all was lost. Arrius's family was a casualty of a war where he'd never picked up the sword, but that was about to change.

Standing in the shadows of the fire, he recognized his old enemy, Yeshua Barabbas. Every ugly, violent, and hate-filled cell in his body began to boil. Arrius instinctively reached for his gladius that hadn't hung at his side for many moons. He then bolted for Barabbas but was tackled face down into the dirt by Mark.

"Arrius, he is armed, and he will kill you too! You cannot fight him. Not here. Not now."

Arrius rolled over to his back with Mark still holding him down as he screamed at the top of his lungs, "Yahweh, why have You abandoned me once again to my cursed fate? No God can overcome my blood curse. Not even You!"

Mark knelt beside his friend and said nothing. There were no words.

Then Mark heard the angry voice of his dearest friend say

through clenched teeth, “Barabbas will die at my hand, and Saul, too, will pay. I know this is his doing. These Jews will suffer. They have yet to see the full measure of my wrath and vengeance. I will kill them all!”

Chapter 48

Six Months Later, 35 AD,

a Tavern Outside the City Walls of Jerusalem

Arrius was lost in his grief; a shadowy season of his soul consumed him. In no time at all, he returned to his old ways of anger, brawling, and binge drinking. He was bent on revenge against Barabbas and his new mortal enemy, Saul.

"We need to go," said Mark for the twentieth time. "Mary Magdalene and Kaamil hope to see you tomorrow. Let me take you to my home, brother."

"Leave me be! And I am not your *brother*. Not anymore. Your god has abandoned me, so I have abandoned Him. I curse the day I chose to follow Yeshua."

"You are in pain—"

Arrius interrupted, "You have *no idea* what I feel. You have no idea who I truly am. Leave now, or you will see a side of me once buried in a tomb as your rabbi was, but now very much alive again."

Mark sat silently next to his friend for a long time before speaking. "I cannot leave you, Arrius. My mother faithfully taught the Scriptures, and I remember the words of Solomon, 'A friend loves at all times, and a brother is born for a time of adversity.'"[15]

Arrius said nothing, and the two men sat in the tavern for another hour or so. Arrius drinking while Mark was inaudibly praying.

Through slurred speech, Arrius finally spoke, "I will find him. I know Syria. I once served Rome in that godforsaken land. Damascus is only a five-day journey from here and less if I can buy or steal a horse. A man like Saul will be easy to locate and easier to kill."

Mark asked, "In all your years as a legionary and centurion, did killing ever bring you comfort, my friend? Did taking the life of Yeshua Barabbas bring you *shalom*?"

Within days of Ayla's death, Arrius located Barabbas in his favorite hiding place in Bethany. Arrius had slit his throat and brutally disemboweled the man.

Arrius spat on the ground and yelled at Mark, "Yes! I found great pleasure in taking the life of that depraved villain, but your God's shalom is *not* what I seek. Vengeance is all I need, and I will have it. I. Will. Have. It. Before I take my last breath, I will watch the life flow from the one who stole my life. Saul is a dead man."

Mark placed his hand on Arrius's shoulder, but Arrius quickly shrugged it off. "You need sleep and food; please let me take you to my home. Besides, you are in no condition to travel. Come with me just for the night. I beg you, Arrius—let us go now before the city gates are closed."

Arrius rose, stumbled a bit, and said, "Just for the night. Only tonight. I leave for Syria in the morning."

---

15 Proverbs 17:17

"Okay, my friend, just for tonight. Mary will prepare some food for your travel when we see her in the morning."

"I don't want to see *her* or the boy. Mary will only—"

"I know you don't want to see Mary, but she was Ayla's friend, and she hasn't slept well since that night. Mary feels responsible for what happened. She wonders if Saul was looking for her and if *she* was his intended victim."

Arrius gave Mark a stunned look. "Saul was looking for Mary?"

"We don't know for sure—we may *never* know, but Mary had left your home just before Saul and his thugs showed up. As the first witness to the resurrection, Mary is hated by the Jewish leaders."

Arrius leaned on Mark to steady himself. "Mary must know I will avenge the loss of her friend, and I will remove any threat to her."

Mark whispered, "Mary prays for Saul. Yeshua taught us to—"

Arrius interrupted with fire in his eyes, "Do not speak to me again of *that* rabbi. I don't care what He taught! Yeshua's words are like a shard in my foot and hot coals in my hands. They bring me nothing but pain."

Arrius continued to lean heavily on Mark as they walked up the steep road to the walled city. The night was crisp and clear, with the moon rising on the horizon. Mark began to whistle a tune. He was known for his uncanny ability to almost sing with his whistle. The song was low and soft and in a minor key that somehow pierced the darkness.

Arrius groaned, "What melody do you whistle, Mark?"

"It is nothing."

Arrius was in no mood to put up with Mark's timidity. "Tell me."

"Are you sure you want to know? I fear the wrath of that gladius at your side."

Arrius stopped, and from only a hand's length away, he looked his friend in the face. His breath soaked with beer. "Tell me, or you will feel the impact of my boot on your backside!" Arrius wasn't serious; he could never harm Mark.

Mark's voice quivered. "It is a song of David found in the Psalms."

Arrius looked away. "And?"

"And David sang a psalm to the tune '*The Death of a Son*'; it was something he wrote after the death of his son Absalom."

At first, Arrius didn't say anything as he began to stumble up the hill again, but after several moments, he asked, "David suffered loss?"

Mark spoke solemnly, "Yes, great loss."

Arrius sighed. "And he was a man of the sword."

"Yes, Arrius, our greatest warrior king."

"Sing me this psalm."

Mark looked at Arrius. "Are you sure?"

Arrius nodded.

As Mark began to sing, his voice was like an angel.

The Lord is a refuge for the oppressed,

a stronghold in times of trouble.

Those who know your name trust in you,

for you, Lord, have never forsaken those who seek you.

Sing the praises of the Lord, enthroned in Zion;

proclaim among the nations what he has done.

For he who avenges blood remembers;

he does not ignore the cries of the afflicted.[16]

Arrius began to sweat and fidget with his coat. "Enough. I have heard enough. Yahweh will not need to avenge *my* loss. I will."

The words, however, did strike a deep chord in Arrius's soul: *the Lord does not ignore the cries of the afflicted.*

Arrius and Mark walked on in silence.

The following day, and far too early for Arrius, he heard Mary singing at the fire, preparing breakfast. Mark had sent word to Mary that Arrius was at his home. She came early with Kaamil to help prepare a morning meal. Not long after Arrius arrived the night before, he'd passed out and fallen asleep on a mat in the corner of the guest room.

"Breakfast will be ready soon. Time to drag yourself out of bed." Mary sounded far too happy and was far too loud for a hungover Arrius.

Arris rolled over, covered his head with the blanket, and re-

16 Psalm 9:9–12

sponded, "Is that fried pig I smell?"

Mary yelled back from the courtyard, "Anything but *that* for you, Centurion."

Knowing she would not let him be, Arrius sat up on his cot and wiped his eyes. He was startled to find Kaamil sitting across the room with his back against the wall.

Arrius shook his head as he sniffed loudly to clear his congested sinuses. "What are you staring at, boy?"

At first, Kaamil said nothing and glared at Arrius.

Arrius stood to wash his face at a basin of water found in the corner of the room. Without looking at Kaamil, he said, "You know it is best that you are with Mary now. She is a good woman, kind, and she has no children. She will care for you as well as…"

Kaamil's eyes were filled with tears as Arrius turned to him.

Arrius swallowed hard. "As Ayla…as your mother would have wanted—"

Suddenly, Kaamil stood up. "I have no mother. I am cursed! Everyone I love dies."

The boy had no idea how devastating those words were to Arrius.

Arrius sighed deeply and sat back down. "Did you know I was an orphan?"

Kaamil wiped the snot from his nose on his sleeve and the tears off his cheeks. "Mother told me."

Arrius motioned for Kaamil to come and sit next to him. "Did you know that I, too, am cursed and that I lose those I love?"

Kaamil looked up into the eyes of Arrius. "No, Roman, I did

not know that part of your life. Why? Why do the gods hate us so?"

Arrius buried his face in his hands. "I do not know, boy. I truly do not know."

Mary called out again, "Breakfast is ready."

At that moment, Mark entered the guest room and said, "You know she will not relent."

Arrius complained, "Leave us be, Mark. The sun has barely cracked through the window."

Mark smirked. "And will that stop Mary? When she calls, she calls, and you must go to her or endure her nagging."

Arrius stood and chuckled a bit as he said, "Though I do not fear any man or any god, part of me does fear *that* woman." Arrius brushed his hair out of his face, wiped the tears from his eyes, and swatted at an annoying fly before reaching his hand out to Kaamil. "Come. Let us eat, boy."

Mary was still sitting by the fire when they made their way outside.

Arrius pointed a finger at Mary as he said, "Why do you call me *centurion*? I no longer fight for Rome."

"Then why do I see the sun reflecting off your Roman sword?"

Arrius didn't answer as he walked away to find another basin of water to wash his hands.

Mary shook her head and said, "Hurry back; your fried *eggs* are almost done."

Later, as they sat at a well-worn wooden table eating, Mark, Kaamil, Mary Magdalene, Mark's mother, and Arrius ate without any conversation.

Finally, Arrius broke the tension. "Mark, thank you for opening your home to me…to us. I do not deserve your kindness."

"No one *deserves* kindness this early in the morning," Mark said with a smile.

Arrius nodded in agreement and said, "I will be leaving today for Syria."

Mary Magdalene's sun-wrinkled face looked at Arrius with such caring eyes that he had to turn away as she said, "Perhaps you should see Peter before you go."

"I have nothing to say *to* him and need nothing *from* him."

Mary put her clasped hands to her lips and said tenderly, "He loves you, Arrius. You matter to him. You matter to *all* of us."

Arrius pushed himself away from the table, stood, and said through clenched teeth, "Nothing and no one matters now. I will gather my things and leave immediately."

Mark spoke with a quirky smile on his face as Arrius turned to walk away. "Then I travel with you, Arrius. You will get lost without me!"

Kaamil immediately chimed in, "And me too."

Without turning around, Arrius raised his hand to silence them and said, "No, neither of you will join me, and I am already lost. I go alone."

Mark ignored Arrius as he jumped up from the table, kissed his mother on the cheek, and said to both women, "His tongue is as sharp as his blade, but he will not turn me away, and I cannot abandon him now. He has gone off course in his anger, but I know Yeshua wants me to go with my friend."

His mother said, "Are you sure? Will you be safe?"

"Yes, Mother, I am certain. All will be well."

Kaamil started to rise from the table, but Mary put a gentle hand on his shoulder. "Kaamil, you are only nine years old, and Arrius is too angry right now. You cannot go with him. Not now. Not on this trip. Do you understand?"

Kaamil turned to Mary. "Will he return soon? Will I ever see him again?"

Mary smiled. "Yes, Kaamil, someday you will. The Lord showed me last night in a dream that Yahweh is not done with your father yet."

Arrius moved quickly out of the city before Mark had time to gather what he would need for a long trip. Arrius hoped Mark would not pursue him, but before the sun was directly overhead, the young man joined him on the road.

"Brother Arrius, did you miss me?"

Arrius scowled and cursed under his breath as he barked, "I told you to stay home! I will not allow you to—"

"And I told *you* I was coming." Mark patted his old friend on the shoulder. "And I will not allow you to escape me."

Arrius shook his head. "You are as stubborn as you are ugly."

Mark laughed and said, "My mother would disagree, but you

are stuck with me, nonetheless."

Arrius cursed again, shook his head, and said, "We will see. It is a long road to Damascus."

CHAPTER 49

35 AD, the Road to Damascus, North of Jerusalem

Damascus was over forty leagues from Jerusalem. It would take Arrius and Mark at least eight or nine days to walk the distance, even at a good pace. The desert sun was brutal. Mark had the advantage of youth, but Arrius was used to walking long distances without stopping.

For the better part of two days, they walked together in relative silence. Mark knew his friend was hurting and quietly prayed for Arrius as they traveled. Besides, the weather was too hot for him to talk, and his throat was so dry that he could not even whistle.

On the third day, Mark attempted to engage Arrius in a conversation. "This scorching sun and your intense pace will kill me. If I die here, please bury my body deep in the sand and tell my mother I love her."

"Mark, you are as soft and weak as a woman."

"A stubborn, old woman, I suppose?"

Arris chuckled a bit. "Yes. As I have said. Stubborn. Ugly. Weak. That pretty much sums you up."

Mark had blisters and sores where he didn't think he could get blisters and sores.

Arrius shrugged his shoulders. "I told you to stay home."

Mark picked up his pace a bit. "And I told you, you would have to kill me to stop me."

"Looks like the desert of Syria will do that job for me."

Mark was not amused. By nature, he was a complainer, and Peter often challenged him to have a better attitude. Mark knew he had lived a relatively affluent and sheltered life. Trials and struggles were not common to him until he became a follower of Yeshua. Yet, Mark spoke with confidence, "Though [Yahweh] slay me, yet I will trust in Him."[17]

"What?"

"Nothing. Just something Job once said—"

"I grow weary of your constant quotes from your useless scriptures."

Mark didn't miss a beat. "Perhaps I should quote the Roman philosopher, Lucretius, to you. My father loved to quote him at the most inopportune times. Lucretius once taught, 'The first beginnings of things cannot be distinguished by the eye.' What did he mean by that? I wonder."

Arrius didn't bite.

Arrius's silence never hindered Mark. "Maybe he meant that Yahweh works in the hearts of men before we can see the fruit of His workings."

Arrius grunted a short reply, "Lucretius was Roman, and he did not believe in *your* god."

"Ah, Arrius, but *all* truths begin and end with Yahweh. You say you are now mistrustful of His words. But I say you resist Him because you still feel His love for you, and it shakes you to your core.

17 Job 13:15

I know you, brother."

"You do *not* know me—the real me."

Mark had heard the stories of Arrius before his encounter with Yeshua at the cross. But he stopped in his tracks and grabbed the arm of Arrius, forcing him to stop as well. "I know who you *truly* are, my friend. And I know that it is impossible to deny the One who gave His life for both you and me."

Mark knew that if they were not friends, Arrius would have used his enormous fists to shut him up. He was also convinced Arrius could not resist his unconditional love for long.

"What am I to do with you, Mark? You not only march like an old woman, but you ramble on and on as one too."

Mark just smiled as they walked on.

Mark knew that Arrius was hoping to go farther, but after some passionate debate, Arrius conceded to stop and said, "We will set up camp here. I will gather some dried dung to use for a fire. You stay here and stay alert; there are thieves on this road."

Mark collapsed in the sand. "And what have we worth stealing?"

"Nothing, but they don't know that, and they'd kill you just for your fancy cloak."

Mark was nervous. "Then why don't we gather some dung for the fire together?"

"Because I need some peace and quiet. Stay put. I will not be gone long."

Mark stood and brushed off the sand. “Fine, but if they *do* kill me, my mother will kill you!”

Arrius dropped his pack and handed his gladius to Mark. “Here, keep this with you just in case.”

Mark turned the sword in his hand, still complaining. “Just in case a band of marauding, murdering misfits decide to attack me while you are gone gathering camel and donkey dung.”

Arrius shook his head at Mark and slipped away into the darkness.

The silence of the desert night was unnerving for Mark. He missed the sights, smells, and sounds of the city.

He spoke partly to himself and partly to the heavens as he babbled on. “What am I doing? This man…this…this Roman… this…this…*hater* is impossible. He will not listen to me. He will not listen to Yeshua. He absolutely will not listen to Yahweh. He’s hopeless. Why didn’t I stay home? Why do I always have to be so reckless and impetuous?”

A large mouse-eared bat suddenly swopped close to his head, making Mark jump as he unsheathed the gladius. “Now I am being attacked! Any second a lion is sure to appear and maul me to pieces.”

Mark began to use the sword to dig a hole in the sand for cover.

“This will not end well. I will never understand Arrius. How could he leave me here alone to die?”

Chapter 50

Year 35 AD, the Syrian Desert

The night wind was warm and blowing from the south. Arrius hated the desert, but he loved the desert sky. He always felt awestruck when he was alone under a billion stars.

Much to his frustration, images of Ayla and the children bombarded his thoughts. The rabbi's teachings also flooded his mind like a river in flood season. The undeserved love of Mark and Mary Magdalene—people who'd seen him at his worst—seemed to be invading his heart like a Roman legion invading a fortress. He had wandered off into the desert to be alone, but then he felt something or *someone* present with him.

At that very moment, movement in the sky caught his eye, and he looked east to see a group of shooting stars. He counted seven falling stars. Far more than he'd ever seen at one time. In the Roman culture, meteor showers were considered a sign from the gods. They meant that something good or bad had happened or was about to happen.

The presence he had felt was now overwhelming. Arrius let go of his collection of camel fuel and stared into the night sky as he whispered his first prayer in a long time, "Yahweh, is this a sign from You?"

Several moments passed. Nothing. No response from the heavens. Nothing but the wind blowing across the sand.

Irritated with himself, Arrius shook his head and began walking to the top of a dune as he said out loud, “What am I doing? What kind of fool speaks to the heavens? There is no god. There is no—”

And then he heard it—a gentle yet unmistakable voice riding on the southern wind.

“Arrius.”

“Who goes there?” shouted Arrius.

He heard it again but louder, “Arrius.”

He instinctively reached for his gladius but realized he’d left it with Mark for his comfort.

“Arrius. Will you open your heart to Me again?”

Arrius was beside himself with a strange mix of both curiosity and terror.

“Arrius. It is Me. Yeshua. *I am* here.”

In a moment’s time, he felt every cell in his body come alive. Despite the warm night, his skin had goosebumps. He could no longer stand, and he fell as a dead man with his face in the sand.

“Arrius, I know your pain. I feel your sorrow turned to anger. I ache with you.”

Arrius began to sob. “Leave me. I am a dark and broken man. I am not worthy—”

“No man is worthy apart from Me and My work in his life, but to leave you would be to deny Myself, for I am in you, and you are in Me.”

His whole body was shaking now. Arrius felt as if his heart would explode.

"I…I have denied You. I have failed You. Ayla would be so disappointed in me."

"Ayla, Seneca, and Tikva are with Me now in paradise. They only suffered briefly, but if you stay on this course of vengeance, you will suffer for many years to come."

That gentle warning pushed him to the limits, and his anger got the best of him. "Saul is responsible for the deaths of my wife and children! He is an evil man who deserves no mercy."

Between his sobbing, he moaned in anguish, "But I, too, am responsible. I should have been there for them. I will never forgive myself."

"Arrius, fear not. I was there with them in the flames; they were never alone. *Never*."

Arrius rolled from his belly to his back as he screamed at the heavens, "But what of *that* man? What of Saul? He must suffer for what he has done."

"Saul is mine now. He follows Me, and the awareness of what he has done weighs heavy on his heart, as your grief weighs heavy on yours. He will suffer *for* Me but not *from* Me. The path I have for him will not be an easy one, but he will be my voice to many."

Arrius beat the sand with both of his fists. "He cannot be forgiven! You cannot let him live!"

Softly, almost at a whisper, the voice on the wind said as it dissipated, "Are his sins greater than *yours*? Yet I have forgiven you and set you free." That statement hit him like a spear to his chest and pierced his soul.

Yeshua was gone, and the rage in him began to dissipate as the words reverberated over and over in his mind: *Are Saul's sins greater than yours?*

Arrius sat up and then moved to his knees. As he looked up and opened his palms to the heavens above him, he prayed with humility. "Yes, my sins are as countless as these stars. My failures are more numerous than the sand of this desert. I know that I am free from Your wrath, Yahweh, so I have no choice but to free Saul from mine."

Arrius had no idea how long he lay there looking at the stars before he fell asleep. He had not slept well for such a long time, but no man has ever rested better in the arms of Yahweh than he did that night in the Syrian desert.

The sun was peeking above the horizon. Mark was prodding Arrius in the arm with his foot as he said, "Wake up, Arrius! Where have you been? You left me alone the entire night with no fire, no food, and only this sword to comfort me. I was being attacked by wild animals and had to sleep in a hole. And now I find you sound asleep and looking like you have wrestled with the lion who was stocking me. What kind of friend leaves his friend alone in a place like this?"

Arrius stood, and while dusting off the sand that covered his body, he said to Mark, "We must hurry and find our *brother* Saul."

Mark stuttered and stumbled over his words. "Who? What? Brother? Saul? Saul of Tarsus? What happened to you? What in heaven's name are you talking about?"

Arrius looked at him with a smile as he grabbed Mark's shoulders. "Yes, Saul of Tarsus! Yeshua told me last night that he is now a follower—our brother."

"Yeshua was here? Last night? I fear the desert sun has cooked your brain, Arrius."

"No, my young friend, I am well. Better than I deserve. But the Son of Yahweh has changed everything, and He has changed *me…again.*"

Arrius did not know how to explain what had happened, but there was no doubt it was something of a miracle. Little did he know then that it was the second miracle on that very road in less than a week. Saul of Tarsus was no longer an enemy to fear but a brother to embrace.

As they left the dune to find the road north again, Mark kept saying it over and over again in awe, "*Saul, a believer? A brother? What is Yahweh up to? What adventure awaits us now?*"

CHAPTER 51

Year 35 AD, Damascus, Syria

Mark and Arrius were greeted cautiously by Judah, the homeowner who lived on Straight Street, where Saul was staying. Judah was a devout Jew and a leader in the synagogue of Damascus. He welcomed the injured Saul into his home because he was a Pharisee, and by law Jews were to open their homes to traveling brothers. However, Saul's non-stop rambling about the rabbi Yeshua—who he claimed died and came back to life—was met with skepticism.

"Judah, thank you for allowing us into your home at this late hour." Mark knew their host was uncomfortable with Arrius, a Gentile, and that they'd probably woken him up.

Judah replied, "I was told to expect visitors by Ananias. Apparently, Saul has been having visions of important visitors. In fact, Saul insists that Yahweh showed him Ananias in a revelation."

Mark spoke, "Interesting. I do know that Yahweh's ways are often mysterious."

Judah looked intently at Arrius. "You look like a Roman, but you travel with a Jew."

Arrius bowed his head and spoke slowly, "Yes, but I am circumcised and a follower of Yeshua."

Judah shrugged his shoulders as if not to care and said, "Follow me. Saul is in our guest room in the back." He led Arrius and Mark through a narrow hallway to a door covered by a dull curtain.

"Saul, you have guests—*again*. Are they free to enter?"

Saul had been praying, but he enthusiastically said, "Yes, yes, thank you, Judah. Please show my guests in."

Judah pulled the curtain back and gestured for the men to enter. The doorway was small. Arrius had to duck so as not to hit his head. Mark, a much shorter and smaller man, followed closely. The room was quite dark and lit only by a single candle.

Saul remained seated on his bed. "Thank you, Judah."

Judah mumbled something and turned to leave.

"Welcome, brothers, please sit." He pointed to an old wooden bench. Saul was having difficulty seeing; his eyes were obviously damaged.

Arrius sat and took a deep breath. "Do you know who I am?" asked Arrius, sounding a bit more threatening than he meant.

Saul said, "I do not recognize your voice, and I cannot fully see your face, brother. Please tell me who you and your friend are."

"My companion is Mark, and my name is Arrius, former centurion of Rome turned follower of Yeshua."

Saul gasped for air and then hung his head as he said with sorrow in his voice, "I do know you." As he began to cry, Saul spoke softly, "And I am responsible for the death of your wife and children."

The atmosphere in the room was thick with sorrow. Saul, Mark, and Arrius sat in the candle's soft glow for what seemed like a long time.

Saul spoke again and solemnly, “Have you come to take my life? An eye for an eye? A life for a life?”

Arrius stood and began to pace as he spoke. “In truth, six days ago when I left Jerusalem, I had one purpose—to kill you. For months now, my entire world has been full of hatred and rage. When I wasn’t drunk or passed out from drinking, I imagined this moment many times. In my mind, I played out a thousand painful ways I would end your life, but—”

Saul looked visibly distressed, so Mark interrupted, “Fear not, Saul, we are here without weapons and without malice.”

Arrius felt horrible and stopped pacing. “Yes, I should have started with the end of the story. Forgive me, brother. I mean you *no* harm. Yeshua visited me in the desert on our way here, and He told me of your conversion.”

Saul reacted with surprise. “On the road to here? On the road to Damascus, you met Him?”

“Yes,” replied Arrius. “The road to Damascus.”

Saul relaxed a bit and said, “Then we have that in common. I, too, met Yeshua on that very road, and the light of His presence completely blinded me for three days until Ananias prayed for me.”

Mark almost bounced off the stool as he said, “We heard your story. When we arrived in Damascus earlier today, our first stop was the Synagogue. We met Ananias there, who told us all about it and where to find you. He seems like a good man.”

Arrius sat again, not wanting to appear agitated. “My wife, Ayla…” Arrius took a deep breath to stuff his tears. “On the night Ayla died, my wife’s friend Mary had a vision of your encounter with Yeshua. No one believed Mary. It seemed—"

Saul interjected, "Preposterous?"

Arrius laughed. "More than preposterous! Saul, it seemed unbelievable that our greatest enemy would someday become a follower of Yeshua."

Saul asked, "You speak of Mary Magdalene?"

Arrius nodded. "Mary, she meant the world to Ayla, and she has been so very kind to me."

"I am certain this will bring you no comfort, but I must confess to you that I had hoped, on that dreadful night, to find your wife and Mary together. Sadly, I intended to kill both in your home. I was told by one of my sources that they were together while you were out."

"We had suspected Mary was your target," said Mark.

Saul fell to his knees before the men, bowed his head, and said, "Arrius, I would gladly exchange my life for the lives of your wife and children if I could."

Arrius placed his hand on Saul's shoulder. "So would I, Saul—so would I. But they are forever wrapped in the shalom of Yeshua."

Saul looked up at Arrius. "Ananias has returned every day to teach me more about Yeshua. Though my eyes are slow to heal, it is as if my mind and heart's eyes are open and clear for the first time in my life. I had studied the Scriptures for decades. I was a student of the great teacher of the law, Gamaliel. Ironically, I think my teacher has hidden affection for Yeshua and His followers. But now I see how Yeshua is our Messiah, and having met Him alive and well on the same road you met Him, I now know He is the risen Lord."

Saul sat back up on the edge of his bed, lifted his hands toward the ceiling, and prayed, "Forgive me, Yahweh. A thousand times a thousand, I pray, please forgive me, Yeshua, *my* Messiah and *my* Risen King."

Arrius felt as if they were in a dream. This man, the encounter, and this experience were surreal and beyond anything he would or could ever have imagined.

Only Yeshua can change a man like Saul, thought Arrius.

Mark spoke up, "I feel I need to leave the two of you alone for a bit. I think the Holy Spirit has something for you. Thank you for allowing us to meet you at such a late hour, Saul. My friend Arrius is not known for his patience, and neither of us would have slept much tonight until we had this meeting. Excuse me for now. Perhaps we will meet again tomorrow."

Saul extended his hand in Mark's direction, and he took it in a warm embrace. "Until tomorrow," said Saul.

After Mark's departure, an awkward silence filled the room. Mark was always good at making people feel comfortable, but without him, Arrius felt uneasy.

Saul broke the silence, "Arrius?"

"Yes, brother."

Tears started to flow down Saul's face again. "Can you forgive me?"

"My wife, who was far better than me and far wiser, once told me a story of Yeshua's that I have never forgotten."

Saul wiped the tears from his face. "Please share it with me."

"Apparently, Simon Peter once asked the teacher, 'Lord, how

many times must I forgive my brother who sins against me? Up to seven times?'"

Saul added, "Yes, seven is the number of perfection with my people."

"But Yeshua answered, 'Not seven times but seventy-seven times.'"

Saul whistled with amazement and said, "*Impossible* for any Jew."

Arrius and Saul chuckled over that truth.

"Impossible for *any* man," added Arrius. "But Yeshua then told a story of a king who wanted to settle his affairs with his servants. Amazingly, the king forgave the debt of a man who owed him ten thousand bags of gold. Who would forgive such a large debt but a merciful and loving king?"

Saul nodded in agreement.

"A few days later, however, this same servant became harsh and demanding of a fellow servant who only owed him a hundred silver coins. He grabbed his friend and began to choke him. His friend said, 'Please be patient with me; I will pay you back soon.'"

Saul smiled. "I think I see where this is going, Arrius."

"Yes, the first servant, the one forgiven of so much, had no mercy and had the man thrown into debtors' prison. But when the other servants saw what this ungrateful man did, they were enraged and reported what they saw to the king."

Saul asked, "And what did this king do?"

"He was so upset and disappointed that he said to the man, 'I forgave and completely canceled everything you owed me. You should have shown mercy to others as I showed mercy to you.'"

Saul stroked the end of his beard. "I imagine things did not end well with this man. Kings can be harsh when they feel slighted. I believe I can see the moral of Yeshua's story. But what did He mean to teach us by this tale?"

"The rabbi taught His followers to forgive as they have been forgiven…to release others from their personal wrath and judgment."

Once again, the air was thick with emotion as Arrius said softly and with great reverence, "Saul, only Yahweh knows the depth of my sin and the heights of His mercy toward me. If I have been forgiven of so much—*and I have*—how could I not forgive you?"

Saul fell to his knees again before Arrius, nearly knocking over the lampstand this time as he bowed to the ground before him, sobbing.

Without hesitation, Arrius took a knee next to Saul, put a hand on his back, and prayed as the Lord had taught His disciples, "Yahweh, Father in heaven, Your name is above all names. Your kingdom has come and is coming more and more each day. Your works and purposes are being accomplished here through the broken and humble, like my new brother, Saul, and me. Thank You for meeting our every need, but most of all, thank You for meeting our desperate need to be forgiven of *all* our debts—our sins are legion—too many to count."

Arrius could barely speak through his sobs as he continued, "As You, Yeshua, forgave me, I now forgive this man—my new brother—for all he has done against me, my Ayla Rose, and my sweet children. I release him from the debt he owes just as You have set me free time and time again. Bless him, Yahweh, and use him to the surprise and delight of many others. Amen."

Arrius was then stunned by this thought: *Through blood, I was born and cursed. Through blood—the blood, Yeshua—I became free and born again. And now, forever, Saul and I are blood-born brothers because of the One who sacrificed His blood for us.*

Both men, kneeling in the dirt of that small room, embraced each other as brothers bound *not* by a curse of foul blood but by the cleansing blood of the Lamb.

Saul couldn't help but wonder, *Can I trust a Roman who has surrendered everything to follow a Jewish rabbi?* Only time would tell.

CHAPTER 52

Late 35 AD, Damascus

The next day, and for many days to come, Saul, Mark, and Arrius met together. Saul's eyes were damaged, and his heart was broken over all the harm he'd caused to so many, but Mark and Arrius marveled at his intellect. Saul's insight into the Scripture regarding the prophecies of the Messiah and how they were all fulfilled in Yeshua was stunning.

Saul had Mark and Arrius recount as many of the stories and teachings of the rabbi as they could. In fact, Saul asked Mark to assist him by writing down as much about Yeshua as he could remember, and Mark was honored to help.

One morning, after they'd eaten breakfast together, Saul leaned in and placed his hand on the knee of Arrius. "Tell me the story of the lost lamb again. The one where Yeshua taught about leaving the ninety-nine."

Mark laughed with joy. "That is one of my favorites, Saul."

Saul rocked back and forth with excitement. "Yes, Arrius, please tell me the story one more time."

Arrius sat back and did his best to recall all the details of one of

Ayla's most-loved stories.

"As was often the case, tax collectors—"

"Like Matthew," interjected Mark.

"Like Matthew and many other traitors to your people, including women with bad reputations and all sorts of sinners, all of them gathered close to Yeshua to hear Him teach."

Mark spoke up again, "The rabbi never turned anyone away."

"Not even Romans," continued Arrius. "But the leaders of Israel constantly complained about the many outcasts drawn to Yeshua."

Saul sighed and shook his head. "My people can be so blind and so stubborn, and I was one of those hard-hearted men."

Arrius went on. "Yeshua sat down and told a simple yet powerful story. He knew the Sanhedrin and teachers of the law would be offended, but that never stopped Him. The rabbi said, 'Imagine one of you has a hundred sheep, but as you are securing your flock in the fold, counting each and every one, you notice that one of them is missing and lost. What would you do?'"

Mark sat up straight and said, "The rabbi loved to let that question linger as He looked directly at the most senior Pharisee in the crowd."

Arrius smiled. "Yes, He would wait until they squirmed, and then He would answer His own question."

Saul clasped his hands. "Yes, yes, tell me again how Yeshua put the self-righteous in their place."

"The rabbi gave the *obvious* answer. Any good shepherd would leave the ninety-nine who are safe and secure to retrace his steps in the hope of finding the one."

Saul spoke quietly, "And when he finds the lost lamb, he doesn't beat the foolhardy sheep, but with joy, the shepherd places him on his shoulders and takes him home."

Arrius looked down at the ground and said solemnly, "I was that foolish, stubborn, and lost sheep who thought I knew better."

Tears began to stream down the face of Saul. "As the prophet Isaiah wrote, 'We all are sheep who have gone astray, each of us to our own way rather than the way of Yahweh.'"

Saul placed both his hands over his face as he started to weep and said, "And the Lord put on our Savior the iniquity of us all… our sin on the sinless one."

All the men silently sat as they reflected on the prophet's words fulfilled in Yeshua.

A gentle and cool breeze began to blow through the house. Saul covered his head with his tallit, the prayer shawl used by men, and said, "And tell me once more, what did that shepherd do when he returned home, Arrius?"

Arrius cleared his throat. "He called his friends and neighbors together for a party. He said, 'Come rejoice with me; I have found my lost sheep.'"

Mark finished with the moral of Yeshua's teaching. "The rabbi taught us that in the same way, there is more rejoicing in heaven over one sinner who repents than over ninety-nine righteous persons who do not need to repent."

Saul sat moved by the simple yet straightforward truth of this parable. "The Pharisees and the Sadducees, we *think* we are so righteous. We act as if we matter most to Yahweh. But the Lord came for the broken and the lost." Saul shook his head. "Why did I not see this years ago?"

Arrius stood to look out the open window. "Ayla was a collector of lost lambs. She accepted me, of course, but many times over the months after the death and resurrection of Yeshua, she would bring a wounded soul into our home for dinner. I heard my wife tell that story a dozen times or more. Without her…" Arrius began to pace slowly. "Without her, I would be dead and trapped in my sin and the darkness that consumed me."

Saul began to weep again. "Arrius, I am the chiefest of sinners. I am so—"

Arrius didn't let him finish, and he knelt in front of Saul. "My amazing wife would not have you carry the burden of your sin any more than she would want me to carry mine. Ayla did not just speak of grace, Saul—she lived it, and it is the *charis* and goodness of Yahweh that has brought us here."

Saul looked into Arrius's eyes and then to the face of Mark. "I am beginning to understand that it is the grace of the Lord that saved me, not my righteousness, which was never worth more than a filthy rag. And Arrius, your forgiveness and kindness to me is a gift I will never forget. I do not deserve your love, brothers, but I am forever changed because of Yeshua in you."

Mark was a gifted writer, and he did his best to record all that he could about Yeshua on the scrolls Saul provided. Then, with Saul's encouragement, Mark copied everything he'd written on a second set of parchments to keep a written record for himself and others.

Mark was excited. “When I see Peter again, I will ask him to help me fill in the blanks and record more details.”

“Speaking of Peter,” said Saul. “How will I ever convince him that I am no longer his enemy?”

Mark spoke confidently, “I will take you to him myself. When Peter and the others see what we see and hear what we have heard, they will welcome you with open arms. And if they do not listen to me, I will enlist the help of a friend named Barnabas. You will like him, Saul. I think you two have a lot in common. I know Peter will listen to Barnabas because he is deeply respected and has the ear of the twelve.”

Saul raised his hands in a questioning gesture. “We will see, young Mark. We will see.”

CHAPTER 53

Several Weeks Later, 35 AD, Damascus

It has been said, "Life is like a river, ever flowing and always changing." Much change came into all their lives due to Saul's conversion and his new relationship with Arrius and Mark. The men spent many days and most of their time together in Damascus with Saul. Arrius took note that Saul began to take a keen interest in Mark and loved him like the son he never had.

Saul continued to pour through the Scriptures, finding prophecy after prophecy confirming Yeshua was the long-sought-after Messiah. Many times, he told his new friends how surprised he was that he had never seen the truth about Yeshua before. Saul's ability to absorb the teachings of Yeshua amazed the followers in Damascus. In no time at all, Saul was teaching in the local synagogue the words of the One he now called *Yeshua, the Messiah.*

In the cool of one evening, Arrius, Mark, and Saul were walking along the Abana River. A crescent moon was rising on the horizon. Mark spoke first, "The Jews here hate you almost as much as Arrius once did, Saul."

Saul responded, "Yes, I fear I may come on too strong at times, but the Scriptures are so plain and clear. Our fellow Jews exhaust me. More and more, I feel the Holy Spirit leading me to share my faith with the Gentiles."

Mark gasped, "Oh, and that will help? The Jews will not tolerate a good Jew like you spending too much time with unclean heathens."

"Unclean, pagan heathens like Arrius once was?" joked Saul.

Arrius decided it was time to give Saul some bad news. "I still have a few Roman friends in this city, and they have alerted me to a conspiracy among the Jews to kill you, Saul."

Saul began to argue that the Jews would never murder a Pharisee. However, Mark and Arrius were adamant that they should return to Jerusalem soon, and they would not take no for an answer.

"If you think it is best, brothers, then I will submit to your wisdom and return to Jerusalem before the next full moon. But I don't feel strong enough for the journey yet, and I need some time to conclude my studies here before I depart."

Arrius looked at Mark and back at Saul. "No more than ten days then, but we must be on guard at all times and be prepared to depart quickly."

Saul raised his hands to the heavens. "Yahweh will protect us, brothers. I have no fear."

At that moment, they all noticed a hawk diving into the river for its dinner. Arrius patted Saul on the back and said, "Like that bird of prey, I have no fear either, but I also know your people are not above murder. I have seen the outcome of their anger firsthand."

The next few days were tense for Arrius. Every quick movement on the streets or in the market of Damascus made him react. He was sleeping fitfully, too, aware that any unusual noise might signal danger.

Several days later, Arrius and Mark sat together at the guest house they'd secured. The home was built next to the city wall. It had what the Jews called a casemate wall, or a double wall that separated the fortified city wall from the inner back wall of the home. This design provided a potential measure of added safety for Arrius, Mark, and Saul because there was only one way into their dwelling that might require fortification if they were attacked.

The sun had set, and Saul was sound asleep on his cot and snoring loudly. He was not an old man, but his encounter with Yeshua on the road to Damascus had taken its toll on him physically and emotionally. Saul also spent many long hours each day studying and teaching in the synagogue.

Arrius was up late and sitting with Mark, who was attending to a bug bite he'd received the night before.

Arrius broke the silence. "The Jews are keeping a close watch on the city gates, and they are looking for any opportunity to kill Saul. These vile men are determined not to let him escape."

"Or us," replied Mark.

"I am aware," answered Arrius.

"Arrius, I think every moment spent in this city is—"

Arrius raised his hand, signaling Mark to be quiet.

"What? What is it? I don't hear anything."

Arrius stood and moved to the front door. "I don't hear anything either; I *smell* something—fire."

Mark chuckled a bit. "This pagan city is full of horrible smells because the sewer runs down the streets in open trenches. These people are disgusting."

Arrius held up his hand again and gave Mark a stern look.

Mark continued, "I still don't—"

Suddenly there was a loud pounding on the door. A man yelled in Hebrew, "Saul! Saul of Tarsus! Open the door. We have *business* with you that cannot wait until morning."

Arrius moved quickly to block the door with a wooden table that he turned on its side. From the conversations and sounds the group made, Arrius could tell that at least a dozen men stood on the other side. "Mark, go wake Saul. Tell him we must leave immediately."

"How will we leave? These men are not going to let us just walk away."

"Wake Saul. Now! We will go to the roof."

"The roof? What good—"

"Mark, just do what I say."

Saul had heard all the commotion and was already in the room, wide awake. "What is it?"

"Arrius wants us to move to the roof."

Arrius was moving whatever else he could to block the door. "Yes, get to the roof, and I will join you in a moment. I have secured a rope to a roof beam, and we will escape through the opening in the wall."

Saul shook his head. "Arrius, you and Mark must run, but I am in no shape to climb down a rope. I might as well jump to my death."

Arrius turned and pointed to the roof ladder. “Saul, I know. Please move to the roof now. I have a large basket there with the rope. Mark and I will let you down in the basket.”

Saul shrugged his shoulders, trying to add a bit of levity, and said, “I guess this is one of those times when it pays to be small in stature.”

The Jews continued to yell at the men inside, and they argued with each other. They knew a former centurion would not go quietly, and the door was now immovable. Arrius half-expected what happened next; the door caught on fire. He let a curse slip but grabbed his outer garment and scrambled up the ladder after Saul and Mark.

“They plan on burning us alive,” exclaimed Mark.

“We will be long gone before they know what we have done. The Jews will not be able to enter until the fire dies down, and we will be far from here before that happens.”

Arrius tied the basket securely to the rope and placed it on the ledge. “Carefully, Saul, climb in, and we will send you down to freedom.”

Saul—always the optimist—said, “Ah, like Moses, my life will be saved through a basket.”

After Saul was in the basket, Arrius gave it a gentle push to the outside of the wall. Arrius and Mark struggled a bit to let Saul down slowly. He wasn’t a tall man, but he weighed more than either man expected.

“This Pharisee needs to fast a bit more,” groaned Mark.

Once Saul was on the ground, he held the rope at the bottom, and Arrius sent Mark down next. Surprisingly, Arrius heard noise from inside the house. The men had pushed through the burning door once the fire incinerated the latch and before the entire room was ablaze. Apparently not content to let Saul burn, the Jews were determined to capture and kill him with their own hands.

Arrius practically leaped out of the wall opening as he swung out with both hands on the rope. However, before he reached the ground, he saw a man over the top of the wall looking down on him. Suddenly, the cord went limp as someone with a sword cut the rope free. Arrius fell and landed hard, stunned for a moment, but nothing was broken.

"Are you okay, Arrius?" asked Saul as he bent over the breathless Roman.

"Yes, I think so. But we must move—"

At that moment, several rocks began to assail them from above.

Mark yelled up at the top of the wall, "Of course, you brought stones with you. You should be ashamed."

Arrius jumped up a bit too quickly and felt dizzy for a moment just as another rock landed next to him. "Move. Let us go! Once we are away from this wall, we will have hours before the city gates are open. These idiots cut the only hope they had of pursuing us."

Arrius, Mark, and Saul moved as quickly as possible, trying to distance themselves from the city. Wisely, Saul suggested they travel north for a day or two, anticipating the Jews would assume they would go south toward Jerusalem. Though there were risks, they also decided to travel at night and hide as best as possible during the daylight hours.

After two days, they were certain no one was pursuing them, and so it was safe to take the southern Roman road through the Golan Heights to Jerusalem. Before they turned south, they rested under a desert date tree. Mark prepared some bread and small fish for the men to eat.

Saul stood and looked out to the horizon as he often did when deep in thought. "Arrius?"

"Yes, Saul."

Saul spoke soberly, "I do not think you should return with us to the Holy City."

Arrius was dumbfounded. "Why not? I need to make things right with Mary and Kaamil—"

Saul turned and looked directly at Arrius. "I had a dream, perhaps a vision, about you last night."

Arrius had learned to take dreams and visions seriously, especially with Saul. "Tell me everything."

"It was unusual—"

Mark interrupted, "And that surprises us how? This is Arrius you are speaking of."

Arrius gave Mark a look and a friendly punch in the shoulder. "Quiet, Mark. Let the man speak."

Saul continued, "As I said, it was unusual, and you were dressed in animal skins. In fact, to help you stay warm against the wind and snow, you were covered in what looked like the fur of a bear. Your beard was long, much longer than it is now, and you spoke in a tongue I did not recognize. Yet, as you spoke, I saw the

Holy Spirit fall like fire on many men, women, and children who were dressed as you were. These people were struck by your heart, by your words, and by the power of the Holy Spirit as many miracles happened through you."

Arrius instantly knew the interpretation of Saul's dream. "Saul, I believe I know the meaning of your vision."

Arrius looked north. "I must leave to my first homeland. I believe the Lord is showing me that my sister, Saxa, lives. We have not seen each other for a very long time, but she will know me, and I will know her."

Mark reacted. "Will they not see you as a Roman traitor and kill you? I have heard stories of these barbarians. They are ruthless."

"I am blood to her, and she is blood to me. They may eventually kill me, but they will listen first to my story, and what a story I will tell. Besides, several years ago, I remember something my old friend Cassius once told me, 'A man will risk all for someone he loves more than his own life,' and I love my sister and my people."

Saul looked up into the eyes of Arrius. "This is your destiny, Arrius: to bring the light of Yeshua to a people trapped in darkness. Truth be known, I envy you, for I, too, have a growing desire to bring the good news to the Gentiles in distant lands."

Mark could see the turmoil on his friend's face as Saul spoke. "I will explain everything to Mary and Kaamil. Mary will raise the boy in the ways of Yeshua, and we will all await your return, my friend."

Arrius took a deep breath and fought back his tears. "One of my wife's favorite characters from the Scriptures was Esther, and I feel like that queen Ayla Rose was so fond of."

"How so?" asked Mark.

"I see now that I was born for such a time as this."

Mark smiled. "Who would have thought a former pagan from Germania, a Roman, and a centurion would ever compare himself to a Jewish woman?"

At that moment, Saul drew near to Arrius and embraced him as he began to sob on his chest once again. "Arrius, the mention of your dear wife takes me back to that horrible moment when I—"

Arrius released Saul from his grasp and pushed him back to arm's length as he held Saul by his shoulders. Saul's eyes were oozing both pus from his injuries and tears from his broken heart.

"Saul, we will not speak of it again."

Saul could hardly talk as he tried to take a deep breath. "But I will never forget the pain I caused you. My eyes are failing me, but the image of that night is forever etched into my mind. I cannot—"

Arrius took Saul back into his arms as he whispered, "Saul, my friend, neither of us will ever forget that dreadful night, but both of us are now free from the curse we once lived under and from the burden of our many sins. Yeshua makes *all* things new."

Maps

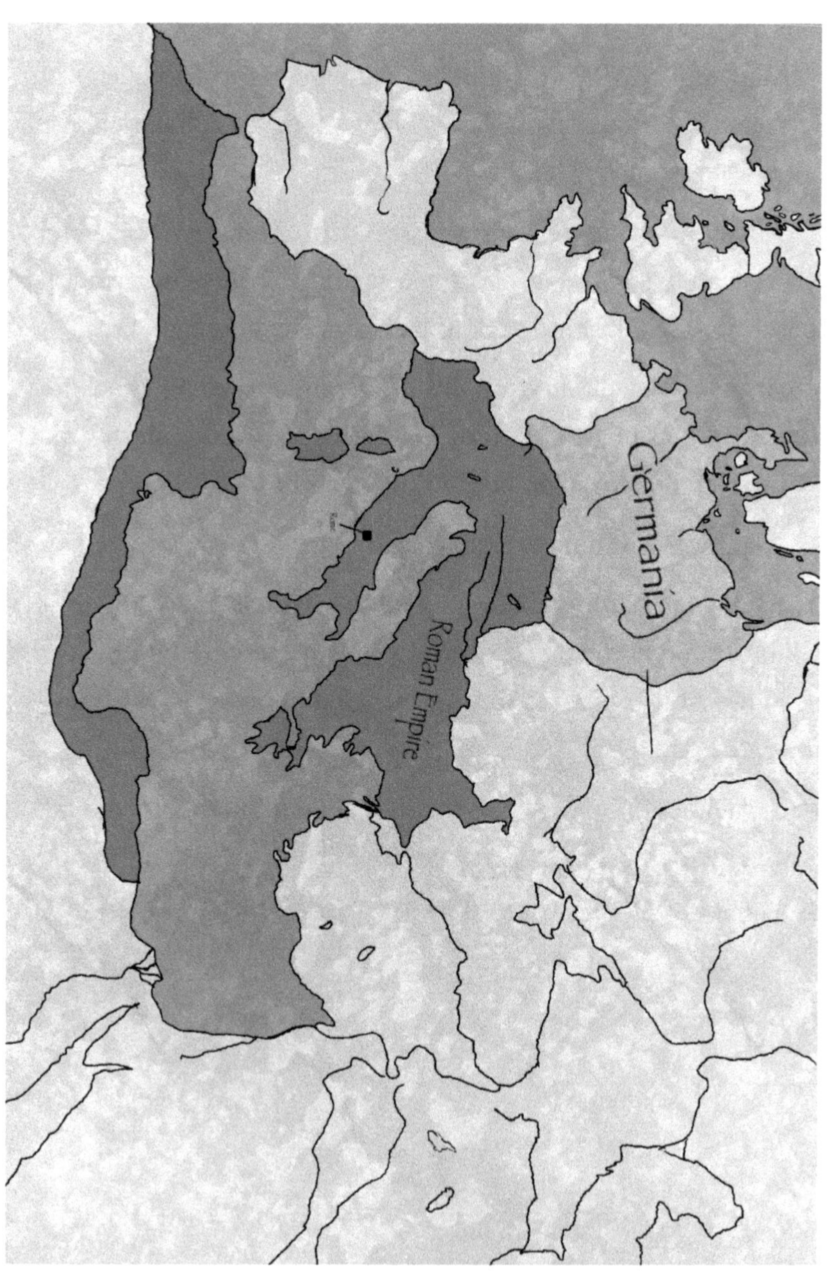

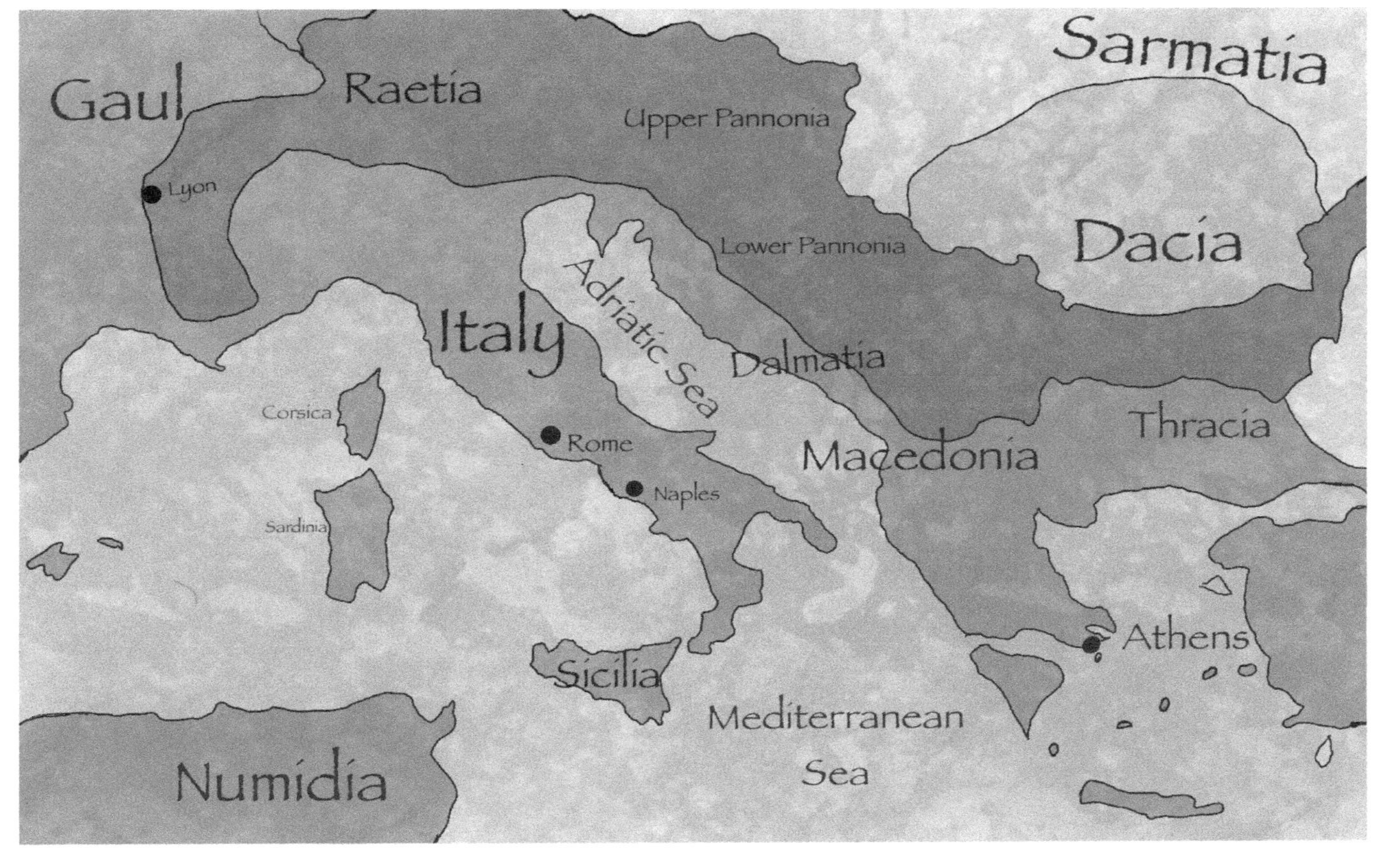
Gaul
Raetia
Upper Pannonia
Sarmatia
Lyon
Dacia
Lower Pannonia
Italy
Adriatic Sea
Dalmatia
Corsica
Rome
Thracia
Macedonia
Naples
Sardinia
Athens
Sicilia
Mediterranean
Sea
Numidia

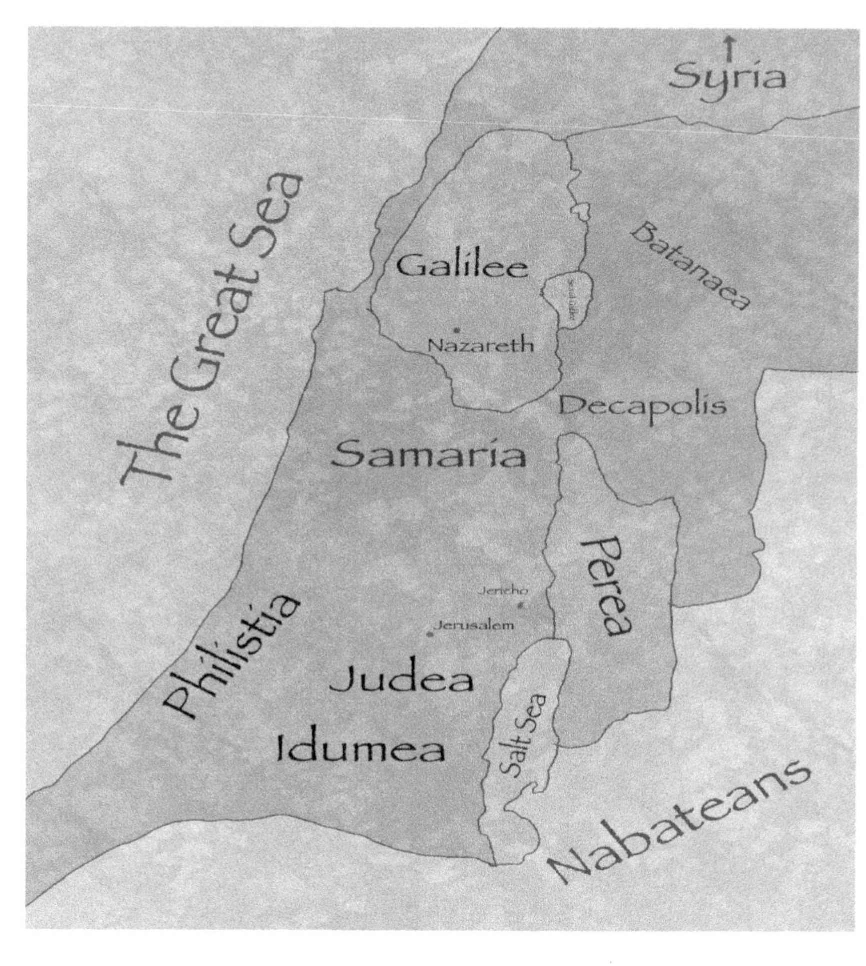

Syria
The Great Sea
Galilee
Batanaea
Nazareth
Decapolis
Samaria
Perea
Jericho
Jerusalem
Philistia
Judea
Idumea
Salt Sea
Nabateans

About the Author

Kurt W. Bubna is the author of seven other books and a regular contributor to several nationwide blogs and periodicals.

Blood Born is his debut novel; the sequel, *Blood Bound*, is coming soon. The next book chronicles the adventures of Arrius's return to Germania in search of his long-lost sister.

Married with four children, six stepchildren, ten grandchildren, and one great-grandson, Bubna lives in Bend, Oregon. Besides his love for writing, his hobbies are paddleboarding, hiking in Central Oregon, and landscape photography.

For more information:

www.KurtBubna.com

Milton Keynes UK
Ingram Content Group UK Ltd.
UKHW021924110424
440929UK00015B/489

9 798890 417428